THE KRY CHRONICLES
BOOK I

S. R. ARRKEWEY

ISBN: 978-1-7379860-0-3
Library of Congress Control Number: 2024917371

This novel is entirely a work of fiction. The names, characters and incidents portrayed in it are the work of the author's imagination. Any resemblance to actual persons, living or dead, events or localities is entirely coincidental.

Cover/typography/illustration by Brandon Dorman
Cover/typography by Candice Broersma
Map created by Casey Gerber
Page design and typesetting by Paul Baillie-Lane

To all those who dream of their own worlds.

CONTENTS

INTRODUCTION   1

PROLOGUE   3

CHAPTER ONE: THE TIME OF THE NOT-SO-CHOSEN ONES   9

CHAPTER TWO: SETH   22

CHAPTER THREE: LOOKING   30

CHAPTER FOUR: WHAT MAKES EVIL, EVIL   36

CHAPTER FIVE: PROPHESIER   40

CHAPTER SIX: KITTY   46

CHAPTER SEVEN: LESSONS   64

CHAPTER EIGHT: A TALK WITH FRIENDS   83

CHAPTER NINE: THE COMING OF SETH   93

CHAPTER TEN: NOT ME!   115

CHAPTER ELEVEN: THE PRICE OF BEING THE CHOSEN ONE   122

CHAPTER TWELVE: WILL YOU BE THE NEXT OF THE CHOSEN   125

CHAPTER THIRTEEN: GATHERING TEAM SETH   139

CHAPTER FOURTEEN: ATTACKED   152

CHAPTER FIFTEEN: FINDING SETH   169

Chapter sixteen: A Water Snake Thing and the

Wrath of Seth   175

Chapter seventeen: A Long Journey   184

Chapter eighteen: The Disputed Lands   193

Chapter nineteen: Up-Closes and Terrifying   205

Chapter twenty: Kry Me a River   215

Chapter twenty-one: The King of Kondoma and

the Chosen One   234

Chapter twenty-two: To Die a Hero or to

Live a Traitor   244

Chapter twenty-three: A Town Forgotten   256

Chapter twenty-four: The Mirror of Night   265

Chapter twenty-five: Truth   273

Chapter twenty-six: Betrayed   280

Chapter twenty-seven: Planning an Escape   284

Chapter twenty-eight: Loral's Story   290

Chapter twenty-nine: Korson Talks with Seth   299

Chapter thirty: To be Invisible   303

Chapter thirty-one: Fighting the King of Kondoma   310

Chapter thirty-two: Death of a King   319

Epilogue   327

THE FROZEN LANDS

REMTAYA

KRYDOM

THE SHIYLEN MOUNTAINS

SEER
VILLAGE

THE FOREST
OF
CONCHING

VENNIRE   ANTI

SELSEN

THE GORGE
OF MIB

THE WHITE HILLS

RUINS OF SHAM ROOK

TERINA

The River Shin

THE LOST MOUNTAIN

CITY
OF
OF LIGHT
NIGHT

KONDOMA

N

The Great World Ocean

Key

★ CAPITAL
● CITY
⚘ VILLAGE
— ROAD
▨ DESTROYED

INTRODUCTION

Terinta, born out of the Great One's wisdom. Look upon the two continents of Terina and Celesta. From the vast sand sea of Celesta to the massive towers of Light and Night on Terina. Divided by the Great World Ocean these two continents hold many wonders and mysteries. From the illusive Cilven wolves to the all-powerful Kry.

Our story begins with the four stages of the planet. The first stage began with small life forms with the beginnings of DNA. This life flourished in the early oceans of the planet and was given a name. The name was Envilea-Anti which meant first life. This first life continued to grow and evolve into a new, more complex life. As time progressed, plants began to grow and find their way upward, reaching the surface.

When the second stage of the planet began, its entire surface was dominated by plants. The flora soon began to grow more complex a great tree was created, the first of its kind. This tree was named Ty-Anti, the greatest that would ever sprout. Life seemed to spring forth from the tree and all plants flourished on it and from it. The being that created the planet, known only as The Great One, blessed the tree and gave it happiness and health. Soon other life came to the surface and the third stage of the planet began.

Four species came forth in the third stage. Two eggs fell from the sky, giving life to the generation of the Dragon. Emerging from the water came the Conchingda. Springing forth from the earth and volcanoes came the Phoenix. Descending from space and the light of the stars came a race believed to be all-powerful, the Kry. These four species were thought to be the wisest of any other races and they ruled the world for millions of years.

Unlike the three other races, the Kry were not created for this world alone. Their origins were shrouded in mystery long ago. Despite their secrets, the Kry were charged with protecting the planet and overseeing its development.

Other species began to emerge and the fourth stage of the world began. A key race came to be, one that would bring both great joy and great devastation to the planet. Known as humans, these creatures were blessed as the Great One's children. The Great One had a purpose for this world, and humans would play a vital role. However, the Kry were charged with watching the Great One's creation, and as the old maxim goes, may the Kry be kind.

PROLOGUE

The wind blew cold and hard against the trees as the clouds moved across the sky like prowling sharks. Evening had just barely begun, and the last remnants of the sun were over-shadowed by the thick, dark clouds. A house on the edge of the forest sat silently in a grassy clearing. Torias hurried to the window and looked out into the frigid night air. His hair was long and matted. He didn't have time to bother with washing; he had more important matters to deal with.

"Is it time?" he asked, his eyes darting nervously over the icy, dark landscape.

"Yes," an unkind, raspy voice whispered in the darkness. "Do you remember what you have to do?"

"I believe so," Torias said worriedly. He watched the still, silent land for any sign of movement. He had heard some townsfolk talking behind his back the last time he was in the village. They could have been planning to come and creep up on him tonight. He couldn't take any chances with sabotage. After tonight everything was going to change; life was going to improve.

"Remember you must chant the words properly and the knife must glow before you are finished with the spell," the hissing voice reminded Torias as it echoed within and around him. At first it had seemed so pleasant to have the voice in his head. All the time, night and day, it would tell him things that filled him with happiness and excitement. Now it hurt as it spoke within him, but what the voice promised far outweighed any discomfort he felt.

"Very well," Torias said with a hint of trembling in his voice. He turned from the window and ran across the small, dark room. He swiftly pulled open a wooden drawer; inside was a silver-colored dagger with inscriptions surrounding the blade. Torias picked it up and studied the writing for a moment. It was power that he was holding in his trembling hands, very few could even hold the blade let alone use it as he intended. He carefully, yet hurriedly, put the knife inside his robe before turning to peer into the darkness that filled his house. Two red eyes glinted in the corner, scrutinizing him deeply like an animal prepared to pounce.

"I must be going," he said hurriedly to the red eyes staring back at him.

"Be swift," the dark, raspy voice demanded. "You must not think for a second, only do the spell and be done with it."

"And what you promised?" the man asked. "Will you give it to me? Will I be rich?"

"Yes," the voice screeched. "You will receive your just reward."

"Good." Torias's eyes gleamed in anticipation of what would be rightfully his. "I'll return soon."

He rushed to the door that led outside, opening it with great force. Torias looked up to the sky to see dark vapors slowly spinning around. Already the night was changing in advance of the approaching storm. This storm had formed for a purpose; something was coming and he was going to help it. He shut the door and began to run across the open plain which separated his lifeless cottage from the edge of the woods.

I can do this, Torias thought to himself. *I will do it for myself and for my family. Now they will realize that I'm not a failure. They will see.*

He reached the edge of the woods. His black hood ruffled in the wind. He closed his eyes and breathed in deeply.

"I'm going to do this," Torias said, with a smile.

Torias entered the forest keeping to his toes as he moved deeper inside; the tops of the towering trees swayed their thick trunks keeping most of the trees still. Even with the growing wind, the only sound was that of their ruffling leaves. Torias moved gracefully through the trees, as silently as he could. Most of the creatures who could threaten his plan were seeking shelter from the oncoming storm, huddled in holes, perched on tops of trees, or lurking in the underbrush. This was no ordinary weather; it held more meaning than the creatures of the forest could detect. The wind howled through the trees, bringing with it rain and thunder as lightning blazed through the sky. Suddenly, Torias heard what sounded like women talking frantically. He stopped and listened intently.

"I can't believe it's time," said a voice from the darkness.

Torias recognized the woman's voice. It belonged to the daughter of the orphan keeper in the village.

"Well, it is, but you must be silent my dear! We don't want to excite any of the animals," another woman hushed. Torias's mouth curved into a slight grin. *I knew she would be around*, he thought. The orphan keeper was good friends with his target.

"Are you alright?" the first woman asked.

"Yes," the expectant mother answered weakly, with a deep sadness, "I just wish..." The frail voice gave way to a groan of deep pain. The other women started to soothe and speak comforting words to her.

Torias crept closer to the women, making sure to stay as quiet as possible. He could make out six figures walking together. Four of them were carrying a stretcher that another woman was lying on.

"There you are," Torias said quietly to himself.

"So what exactly did the personage say?" one of the women asked.

"All she would say was that he was going to be very special," the woman with child who was on the stretcher explained weakly.

"We are almost there," someone exclaimed.

"Hurry! We haven't much time," the orphan keeper urged.

Torias walked as swiftly and silently as he could. He was almost upon them. He could see candlelight and torches.

"There's the cave," the woman whispered, pointing.

"Good," The orphan keeper said. "We'll be safe there."

Torias looked over the torchlight and noticed a large cavern before him. *Just like he said there would be!* he thought excitedly.

As the group of women entered the cave, Torias followed in pursuit. As he approached, he could hear moaning and groaning.

"It's almost here!" said someone excitedly. Suddenly there was a great scream.

"You can do it!" another woman said. "We are all here for you."

Torias inhaled once more and pulled out the knife. He closed his eyes and exhaled. *It's time*, he thought. Torias sprang into the light, chanting a spell which thrust the woman closest to him against the cave wall. The woman fell limp to the ground without a sound. Hearing the commotion, the other women spun around and looked at Torias with a gasp.

"What are you doing here!?" the orphan keeper demanded, fear and anger in her eyes.

"I'm here to fulfill my destiny," Torias yelled. He lifted the knife and began to chant the spell that he had practiced for so long.

"Tria, help!" a eager mother lying on the cave floor begged, her legs raised and her stomach swollen with child.

The orphan keeper turned and looked sadly at the soon-to-be mother. "I'm sorry, but you'll have to do this alone," she sighed. Tria turned and held up both her hands, staring angrily at the man. The two other women began to hurry over to the pregnant mother.

"Don't move!" Torias shouted as he stopped chanting and looked at Isna and Vish who he knew to be friends of his target. Vish and Isna stood apart, concerned looks on their faces. Torias started chanting again. "Lock dornok." Tria chanted. A blue light shot from her hands toward Torias, who stopped chanting to deflect it.

"You can't stop me Tria, you are too weak!" he shouted.

"I am stronger than you think Torias!" Tria shouted. "Ignis flow!" she recited.

Suddenly fire sprang forth from the cave, surrounding Torias. He screamed at the top of his lungs. "Ignis diffuse!" As quickly as it appeared, the fire fanned away from Torias and spread to two more women. The women screamed, Tria chanted another spell and the fire was extinguished. "Super lumina!" she chanted loudly. Suddenly the rest of the women were surrounded in a blue light and then vanished from sight.

"So it is just you and me," Torias said smiling. "Why haven't you transported your friend that I am going to dispose of?" he taunted. "Oh, that's right; you can't transport pregnant women!" Torias laughed.

Tria screamed another spell, but Torias was ready. With one word, thousands of rocks fell upon Tria. She screamed and then was silent.

"Farewell," smirked Torias, laughing. He turned to the pregnant woman who was still on the ground. She looked at him in terror as he lifted the knife and began to chant the spell once more.

"Please," she begged. "Why are you doing this?"

"Because I need to," Torias replied. "Rag sly rag sly…" He chanted. Again the knife began to glow blue as he approached her.

"No!" she screamed. "You will not touch my son!" Torias raised the knife and plunged it downward.

The terrified mother writhed and held up her arms as the blade pierced her chest. She stared at Torias in agony and disbelief.

"Oh," Torias smiled darkly as he looked into her pain-ridden eyes, "your child was never the target." Torias knelt above the woman, holding firmly to the knife as the woman struggled to keep her eyes open.

"I…. am …. Ssssorry. Sss…" She panted before closing her eyes.

A sudden explosion of blue light pushed Torias away and knocked him against the wall. The whole cavern was illuminated as if the sun was shining from every corner. Torias gaped in terror as a black-haired woman clothed in brilliant white robes peered down upon the lifeless form of the mother. A small, helpless infant appeared crying beside her. The woman gazed upon Torias with sad, yet incensed, eyes.

"What you have done here today will be your curse." she said angrily. "You will never be able to find peace for what has happened here."

"No matter," Torias said, spitting on the floor of the cave. "I've done what I have come to do. Now I will have my inheritance and will be praised by my family." Although Torias smiled, deep down he was trembling in fear of the glorious being.

"The kingdom of your family will never be yours. Instead, you will die a poor, old, crazy man. And you will be forever haunted because of this day," the illuminated woman prophesied.

"No!" Torias screamed. "He promised me that I would become King. He promised me that I would inherit the riches that my family had to offer."

"The thing you trusted has lied," the robed woman stated bluntly. Torias forced himself up and ran as quickly as he could out of the cave. The white-robed being looked down upon the child and smiled kindly yet sadly. "Goodbye Seth, we will meet again." The being looked upon the lifeless woman, bowing her head before vanishing. The cavern was plunged into darkness once more except for a bright light that radiated from the body of Seth's mother. A name appeared in the air, formed by the light. It slowly rose and vanished, leaving the child alone in the cave crying.

CHAPTER ONE

THE TIME OF THE
NOT-SO-CHOSEN ONES

14 years later

"The seventh Chosen One is dead, they just keep dying."

"What?!" Soven yelled. He walked around the changing divider, dressed in his Chief Judge uniform while his servant held his robes, ready for him to put them on.

"The Chosen One is dead," the servant repeated.

Soven walked over to a mirror to inspect his clothes.

"When did this happen?" he asked as he slipped the dark robe over his body. "The Chosen One left our city only a week ago. It takes about three weeks to get to the city of Kondoma. He couldn't have died so fast."

"Well, it looks like he got there sooner than we thought and was killed," the servant answered. "I was ordered to summon you to the council chambers for an emergency meeting."

Soven nodded, understanding the urgency. "He wasn't killed the way the others were, was he?" he inquired nervously.

"I'm afraid so," the servant responded sorrowfully.

Soven eyed his servant while shaking his head in disgust. "Of all the ways the evil King could kill the Chosen Ones, he had to choose that way."

The servant pulled slightly on Soven's robes to make sure they fit properly.

"You know what the saddest part of this is?" Soven asked. The servant did not answer. Soven looked at himself in the mirror for a while. "Parkens?!" he shouted suddenly, startling the servant.

"Yes, sir?" the servant Parkens asked shakily.

"My question was not rhetorical," Soven said with impatience.

"What is the sad thing, sir?" Parkens asked with disinterest.

"The sad thing is that I don't care about the Chosen Ones anymore. They come, they go, and they die. What is the point?"

"My cousin thinks that we are all here because of an accident and that life is meaningless," Parkens answered.

Soven stared at Parkens with a look of annoyance for a second. "That question was rhetorical," Soven stated.

"My apologies sir," Parkens said meekly.

"The last Chosen One was 25. When I was 25, I was courting a very attractive senator," Soven said grinning.

"I'm 20," Parkens said.

"Really? Well that *is* a good age to start courting. Have you found anyone yet?" Soven asked with interest.

"I thought I was courting Kitty, but she doesn't think of me that way," Parkens said, dejected.

Soven shrugged. "Kitty had the perfect man, but let him go."

"Well, thank you, sir." Parkens said happily. "That means a lot coming from you."

Soven looked at Parkens for a second. "Oh," he smiled. "I didn't mean you."

"Who did you mean sir?" The hurt in his voice was palpable.

"Orin," Soven stated. The servant stood there contemplating this revelation.

"The King and the counsel are waiting for you," Parkens said hurriedly, trying to change the subject.

"Right," Soven said as he hurried out the door. He walked down the long, luxurious passages of the castle. His footsteps echoed across the long empty hall, almost becoming hypnotic. "I hope this is the last one," he mused aloud to himself. "Please, PLEASE! Make this the last one," he begged. "Oh, Great One, please let the council vote not to select another Chosen One." He dragged his feet, only to be stopped by the sound of his name.

Soven looked at the person approaching him. "Evan," Soven smiled. "How are you?" he asked.

The prophesier looked very prestigious in his long blue robes. He was nineteen but looked eighteen and about five foot nine inches tall. "Are you going to the council?" Soven asked.

"Yes," Evan answered. "The chief prophesier wants me there." Evan looked at Soven with a questioning eye. "Do you think they will vote for another Chosen One?" Evan asked.

Soven sighed softly. "I think so," he answered, looking down at the floor.

"Great," Evan said, sarcastically. "I should think that the council would listen to the prophesiers and realize that the time of the Chosen Ones ended centuries ago." he stated in frustration as if he had been telling people the same thing for a long time.

"Well, you cannot blame the council for it all," Soven explained. "They speak for the people it's been fourteen years and they are tired of it, the people want the war to end, so the only thing that they can think of is to get a Chosen One to defeat the evil king."

Evan rolled his eyes and nodded. "The people are smarter than that," he insisted as they both commenced walking down the hallway to the council chambers.

"No matter, the people will likely still want another Chosen One," Soven said with a hint of annoyance in his voice. "But that will not stop me from hoping otherwise." He smiled at Evan as they reached the larger counsel doors.

"I will see you inside," Evan said as he walked away.

"Good luck." Soven disappeared behind a corner and studied at the large, luxurious doors for a while. He wondered how many times he had walked through them without even noticing how beautiful they looked. *Someone worked very hard to make these doors and put their life into them. Then when they were installed, people admired them for a time until eventually they were forgotten.* Soven was startled from his thoughts when he heard loud voices emanating from the chamber.

He sighed, closed his eyes, and opened the big, magnificently decorated doors. He was at once surrounded by the din of people talking frantically throughout the room. He looked from one side of the Council chamber to the other, scanning the face of each council member. Most of them seemed extremely irritated, while others looked as if they were about to fall asleep.

"Silence!" Soven shouted at the top of his lungs. He grabbed a large gavel and slammed three times on his desk. The chamber swiftly grew silent and each senator dispersed to their seat. There were two groups in the center of the Council chamber. One group was clothed in red robes and each member had a shaved head. Soven knew them to be the priests of Remtaya. The other group was clothed in blue, and some wore gloves on their hands. They were the prophesiers of Remtaya. Evan stood with that group. Most of the people in the prophesiers were of the chosen race or had blue gloved hands. While all the priests didn't have gloved hands. Soven remembered that not to long ago no one from the chosen race could be a priest or hold any religious office. It was a racist belief the priests and many people held about the chosen race that had only been recently rectified.

"I am the chief judge," Soven stated. "Please bring in the King and Queen so that they may preside and see the people." He quoted.

"All rise for King Leo and Queen Julia!" A guard called out to the senators. Everyone rose from their seats, causing a low yet resounding drone to sweep over the chamber. Soven watched as the doors opened and the King and Queen walked in gracefully. The King had his right hand up as the Queen rested the palm of her hand on his. The King looked to be 50 years old. He was rather lean for a King and small, but what he lacked in size and weight he made up for in wisdom. The Queen was around the same age but was plumper than her husband by a small measure, both rulers were considered to be some of the greatest monarchs of the Kingdom of Remtaya in a century.

The King and Queen took their seats calmly and the Queen gave a kind, royal wave of her hand, as was customary to show that she and her husband were ready for the business of the day. Soven and the rest of the Senate stood and watched intently as the King and Queen began to give their opening remarks.

"I, the King of Remtaya, have come to hear the words of the Senate, who hear the words of the people." the King stated.

"I, the Queen, do understand the Senate who understand the people." The Queen quoted.

"All be seated," the same guard said. The senators sat, the same drone echoing through the chamber again. Soven nodded at the King and queen, they nodded back with approval.

"Bring forth the Chosen One," Soven commanded. The doors that led to the center of the chamber opened and four guards carrying a wooden coffin entered the room followed by an old, white-haired man and a crying young woman. The four people placed the coffin in the middle of the room and left. For a moment the room was almost completely silent. The only sound was the erratic sobbing of the young woman. Then one of the priest's walked out to the middle of the room.

"Chief Judge," he began, "I would think that the Senate ought to look inside to view the horror which has taken place."

A sudden storm of muttering spread across the chamber as the one-hundred senators spoke quietly to one another.

"We already know what is inside," Soven said, not really wanting to see what was in the box.

"I think it would be prudent to do so," the priest said. Soven looked at the King, hoping he would say no. The King looked across the massive chamber, then nodded in approval. Soven closed his eyes and then said yes. Three guards came to the coffin and pried it open. There was a gasp across the hall as the assembly looked inside the box. The body of a 25-year-old man lay inside with only one thing missing, his head.

"Do you see the horror?" the robed man asked in a loud, theatrical voice. "Do you see what our enemy does to those we send to save us? Look upon the headless form of the Chosen One and cry, for this is the seventh time this has happened," the robed man cried out. "I declare that the next Chosen One be given an entire army so that when they reach the Kingdom of Kondoma they may be finally victorious in their quest."

Soven rolled his eyes in annoyance. "You have no say here. You are charged with the religious aspects of our people, nothing more, nothing less, or have you forgotten that you are a priest?" Soven's words dripped with sarcasm. "Now, may we put the lid back on the coffin?" he asked with impatience, not wanting to see more.

"I assure you that I have not forgotten my place," the priest said defiantly. "I am merely stating what we believe the Senate should do."

"The Senate hasn't even decided if we should ask for another Chosen One." Soven clarified.

The priest smiled darkly, bowed, and stepped back with his group.

"Before we hear what the Senate will decide, what should be our next course of action?" the King asked all who were present. "Perhaps we need to hear the story of how the Chosen One died." The King looked at Soven who reluctantly approved.

All they are going to do is embellish the story to us so the Chosen One looks like a hero, Soven thought to himself.

The old, white-bearded man walked up to the coffin and looked down sadly. Then he looked up at all of the council members.

"The Chosen One," the old man began, "was a great person who only cared for the common man and whose only purpose in life was to try to save us from the monstrosity that is the evil king."

Soven sighed and put his hand on his head. *Oh, please!* he thought in exasperation. He knew how the Chosen One behaved before he embarked on his quest, and caring was not in the now-dead man's thoughts.

The old man's story continued. He spoke of how they found an easier route to the kingdom and was about to begin telling how the evil King dispatched the Chosen One.

"The Chosen One fought bravely and he had brought the King to his knees when suddenly, without warning, the evil King transformed into a terrible bloodthirsty monster. The Chosen One bravely fought, but not even he could stop it." The man began to sway as the story reached its climax. "The Chosen One raised his sword and thrust it into the monster's heart, but nothing happened, for the monster was not alive. It was evil magic that was the monster's life source. Thus, without anything to do, the Chosen One charged us to leave before the monster could capture us. And then, with a single swipe of the monster's enormous claws, the Chosen One died." The man fell to his knees and he and the woman began to weep uncontrollably.

The room was still as Soven and the rest of the senate looked down upon the now-sobbing man and woman. Soven, whose mouth was slightly askew as he considered the man's outlandish tale, looked around the chamber at his fellow senators. Most had the same expression on their faces. "Well," Soven stated, "that was a very fascinating and truly unbelievable story." He paused before continuing. "Yet, can you explain to us how the evil king/monster was not alive, but yet dark and powerful magic made it alive?" he asked.

The man looked at the woman who had miraculously stopped her incessant crying and was now looking at one of the guards at the doors of the chamber fluttering her eyes at him. She then looked at the man who was attempting to get her help.

Soven, shocked at what he was seeing, shook his head in annoyance. "Why did you both go with the Chosen One?" he asked bluntly. "In fact, who are you people? I do not remember you two at the farewell reception."

The man looked at Soven with a sheepish smile. "I was traveling to Remtaya with my granddaughter for our act," he said, gesturing toward the woman. "We are performers." The man ended with a dramatic bow.

"Then where are the rest of the people that went with the Chosen One?" Soven asked, looking around for anyone that could tell him what was going on.

"He said they were slowing him down, so he killed them," the woman said with a very high-pitched voice.

"So, are you saying that the Chosen One killed the people who had originally accompanied him because they were slowing him down, and then settled with you?" Soven asked in disbelief. Both the old man and the woman nodded.

"Why?" Soven asked with frustration.

"He fancied me," the woman said, batting her eyes.

Soven sighed and rubbed his eyes with exhaustion and impatience. "Just tell me what really happened," he demanded.

The man looked at Soven in shock. "What do you mean?" the man asked.

"There have been seven Chosen Ones killed by the evil King, and each had their own, little fantastic story of how they died and who the evil King really is. Remember? Last time it was said that the evil King was really a vampire who sucked the Chosen One's blood and then beheaded him, a completely inaccurate and racist view of vampires, mind you," Soven recounted wholeheartedly. "The only correlation between the death of each Chosen One and their fantastic and unbelievable stories is that they were all beheaded. So why don't you stop trying to immortalize the Chosen One's failure and tell us what really happened," Soven demanded.

The man glanced at the woman who appeared extremely distraught. He stared everyone in the eyes. "What I said was the truth," he stated.

"You're at fault," Soven clarified. "Think carefully, as we have heard what you said and will investigate further. The liars who have come before you have been sent to jail," Soven warned.

The man's eyes widened and he began to falter. "Well...if I must... I will tell you what really happened," the man said in a very distressed voice.

"Good," Soven said, calmer now. "We will simply remember your glowing account of the Chosen One, not that it's bad of course, you just shouldn't have wasted our time," he explained.

The man bowed slowly. "We went to the castle to kill the King and were about to do so when the King advanced toward the Chosen One and began to duel him. The duel lasted only a few minutes and then the evil King ("the vile of the world," The man said under his breath) chopped off the Chosen One's head. He then let us go with the body."

Suddenly, the woman began to cry uncontrollably.

"Be silent," Soven demanded. "We know that this is an act. If you have nothing to say here, then leave," Soven told the woman. The woman's weeping ceased and she gazed up at the man, smiled, and walked away.

The man stared at the Council. "Good day," he said quickly and then they both exited the chamber.

Soven sighed loudly. He waited until the man had disappeared before looking down at the guards at the great hall's central entryways. "Is their story credible?" he asked.

One of the guards looked up at Soven and walked forward. "They were reported to have joined the Chosen One a few days before the other group members were killed."

"And what of his late companions?" the Queen asked, with worry in her voice. "Did he truly kill them?"

The guard nodded and looked over at the Queen. "He reported it himself before he trans luminated with the two magicians."

One of the senators stood and looked toward the guard and his fellow politicians. "What reason did he have to outrightly murder his companions? His actions are criminal and go against the laws of our country. He may have paid the ultimate price, but is it appropriate for us to memorialize him as a fallen hero?"

The hall erupted into chaos as nearly every senator rose and began to argue either for or against their fellow's proposal.

"He is a fallen hero!" one of the senators shouted in rage.

"They said the others were slowing him down!" another shouted in passion.

Soven arose from his seat and pounded his gavel on the desk. "Quiet!" he shouted with powerful authority. "Senator Burk's remarks are valid. The question remains, should he be honored at all?" Soven asked loudly, making sure everyone heard him.

Suddenly the head priest stood and looked at the rest of the hall. "My lords, I do not condone what our fallen brother has done, but I do wonder what the people of Remtaya will think if their deceased hero is villainized during these trying times."

Soven studied the rest of the senate as the King stood and addressed the assembly. "This is an issue for another time, my friends. The actions of Vicel Rask are questionable, but his time is at hand. We must focus on more pressing concerns."

Soven nodded to the King in full agreement. "Now that we have heard the true story, I ask what the Senate wishes to do next." The Senate chamber began to grow in noise.

"Silence!" Soven cried out.

One of the senators stood up. "I call that we select a new Chosen One."

Many of the other senators in the room began to cheer and applaud in approval.

Another senator rose. "I call for deliberation before we select a new Chosen One. We must determine why none of the others have succeeded. I suggest we ask the prophesiers to tell us," the senator emphasized.

Finally, Soven thought. "Agreed. We will ask the prophesiers," he stated and motioned toward a man in the hall. "Please, chief prophesier, tell us more."

The chief prophesier arose from his seat and looked around. "Senators," he began, his voice old and crackly as it seemed to hold the weight of a thousand ages on it, "as I have told you for many years, the time of the Chosen Ones is over." The chief prophesier paused for emphasis. "The last Chosen One died three thousand years ago, and it was said no others would ever be born again. The search for the Chosen One is a lost cause for there will be no more. But do not despair. No other Chosen Ones will come for us because we have the power to change our own fate. We do not need a Chosen One to save us. We can save ourselves. We have been given the power through this age to do such things as this," the chief prophesier proclaimed.

One of the priests stood up in the room. "Blasphemy! Complete and total blasphemy!" he snarled, looking at the chief prophesier with disgust. "Have we all forgotten the first Chosen One? The one who will save the believers and the righteous at the end of this world?" the priest fumed, anger in his eyes.

"Not at all," the chief prophesier stated. "The first Chosen One will come again. I believe we all know that. But are you stating that this is the end of our world? That fire will rain from the sky and that all iniquity will be purged?" the prophesier asked.

The priest looked at the prophesier with angry eyes. "No," he admitted, "the prophecies of that time have not yet come to pass. But if the first Chosen One is called the first and last, is not this last Chosen One, the *very last* Chosen One?" the priest asked.

"It is true," the prophesier continued, "that the first Chosen One is termed the first and the last, but he has already come and gone. He will not return until the end. I am speaking of prophesiers proclaiming no other Chosen Ones. The Chosen Ones are no longer prophesied by us, and no other Chosen One will come until the end," the chief prophesier promised.

One of the senators arose. "No matter, I move that we call for a new Chosen One. The people will wish it."

"I assure you that we cannot prophesy another Chosen One. We have tried and we've seen some kill the evil king. But what I and my fellow prophesiers do is foresee future possibilities. The term prophesier is a little misleading. We do gaze into prophecy orbs to see the future, but sometimes they are inaccurate. You cannot expect them to prophesy something that is not there, can you?" the chief prophesier asked.

"Agreed," Soven answered. "We must leave it in your hands and no longer rely on this fantasy."

Suddenly, dozens of senators arose from their seats. "No!" they all cried. "We must have another Chosen One. You must call one to save us."

"Very well!" Soven yelled over the din reluctantly. "We must vote. Those who wish for a new Chosen One, raise your right hand."

Many hands rose at once.

"And for those who do not wish for a new Chosen One?" Soven asked hopefully.

Only a few, along with Soven, raised their hands.

Soven slowly closed his eyes. "Very well," he said. "Chief prophesier, you are called by the Council to seek out a new Chosen One immediately," Soven commanded.

"Understood," the chief prophesier said quickly and then sat back down.

"As we have no further business to speak of, I call this Council closed," Soven said, slamming his gavel on his desk.

"All rise for the King and Queen," Soven said somberly.

The King arose. "I have heard the Council and will do as they say," he stated.

"I have understood what the Council wishes and will do it," the Queen answered.

The King and Queen both retired from the chamber and soon all other members followed. Soven sat for a while looking around, wondering what else could be done. Then, with nothing else to think of, he arose and left the chamber.

I hope we know what we are doing, Soven thought as the doors closed behind him.

CHAPTER TWO

SETH

Seth ran out of the library, clutching his books tightly to his chest. He glanced back at the boys chasing him, with wicked grins on their faces. They shouted his name as he jumped away from some people walking toward him. The books he held seemed to help him concentrate on getting away from the bullies. He hurried away from the boys, hopping from stair to stair on the library steps.

"Come back here!" one of the boys shouted behind him.

Seth turned as he reached the end of the stairs and looked back at the group of older boys. "Can't we figure this out?" he asked a little too quietly. He doubted they heard him because they continued getting closer. He quickly moved away from them and ran into the crowd, his head already beginning to hurt, his heart pounding hard. Thoughts of the others around him dominated his mind as he quickly moved onto the busy streets. He clenched his teeth together and tried not to pay attention to his thoughts.

Seth was fatigued. His legs and his side ached, he was drenched in sweat and out of breath. Seth hated the sensation of sweat clinging to his body, just like he didn't like being sunburned. He slowed and looked behind him, hoping he lost the bullies in the crowd. He smoothed his dirty blond hair back with his gloved hands and walked to a nearby alleyway. The orphanage was close, but he needed to rest. He didn't like to run, that was for stupid people who didn't understand how their minds worked. Hurrying over to the alley, Seth looked at one of the books he checked out before Zimpher and his gang spotted him. He smiled at the title.

"*Particle Ethiristics*," he said to himself with joy in his voice. Suddenly something slammed forcefully into his back. Seth tried to stop himself, but it was too late. He landed on the dirty ground, only to find Zimpher standing over him, a dark grin on his face.

"Did you think you could get away from us, princess?" the teen asked with a dark grin. "You've never been good at escaping," he mocked. "The way you run, and of course your voice, not to mention how you behave." Zimpher moved closer to Seth, who sat up from the ground looking at him with fear in his blue eyes. "What happened to you when you were born?" he asked Seth with a sneer. The boys behind Zimpher laughed at his jeering. "You sound like a girl, princess." Seth looked away from him and down at the ground. He didn't know why that hurt him. He liked girls; they were nicer and better than boys, it was just the way it felt when they teased his high voice. "Oh look," Zimpher said with a laugh, "Princess Seth is sad, poor little princess."

"Zimpher," Seth squeaked shyly, mostly whispering, "why risk getting caught by law enforcement again?" He felt very nervous. Although they rarely attacked and Remtaya was usually a bully-free place for him, he wasn't certain this time.

Zimpher laughed and moved even closer to him, smiling with a wicked grin. "The grown-ups can't save you forever," he warned.

Seth gulped and started to panic as thoughts from Zimpher's mind flooded his own. Visions of Zimpher pinning him against the nearby wall flashed through Seth's mind. He winced at another picture of the bullies kicking him while he lay curled up on the ground. Zimpher always had an unkind mind, and Seth was getting all of it. Despite Zimpher's wish to physically harm him, Seth had a technique that almost always worked. "Help!" Seth yelled, fear overtaking him. Suddenly his head was wracked with pain and the sound of growling echoed in the alleyway. Zimpher's eyes moved beyond Seth whose headache was getting worse. Seth held his hands against his forehead and moved away from Zimpher and his gang. He moaned a little and stood against the wall, closing his eyes as another growl sounded through the alleyway.

"How did you get here?" Seth asked, with fear in his voice. The sound of barking came further down the backstreet. Seth's headache began to subside. He looked down the alley to see a large, black shepherd dog, with white bared teeth, running toward him. Behind the menacing dog was a small creature with big, pointed ears and round, black eyes. The adorable being trotted behind the dog on its small four paws. "Let's get out of here," Zimpher said quickly before he and the others ran out of the alley.

Seth turned to see the shepherd moving toward him. As it got closer, he reached out to the dog and patted him on the head. "Thanks, Shadow," he said gratefully.

"You're welcome," the black dog said in a gruff voice. His mouth moving as he spoke. He licked Seth's arm as the smaller creature crept over to him and snuggled up to Seth's waist.

"What about me?" the little animal asked in a squeaky voice.

Seth smiled and picked him up with one arm, holding the books with his other gloved hand. "Thank you, too, Biz," he said to him.

"Were they mocking you because you're of the Chosen race?" Shadow asked Seth, looking up at him.

"That and other stuff," Seth explained simply. "I don't really get it. Some of Zimpher buddies have gloved hands and he doesn't pick on them."

"Are you gonna report them?" Biz asked.

Seth nodded, looking at the crowd nearby. "Let's get home first," he said to them. They walked out of the alley and back into the crowd. With

Shadow walking quickly next to him, Seth weaved his way through the crowd of people over to a three-story building surrounded by a white picket fence. To Seth's left sat a wooden sign near the fence which read: "Mr. & Mrs. Thomson's House for Orphans." Seth unlatched the gate and walked onto the property. He and his friends passed through the building's front door to find Mrs. Thomson standing in the kitchen, sweeping the floor.

"Hello," Seth said to her as he walked in.

The kind old woman turned and smiled at Seth. "Back already?" she asked.

"Zimpher chased me out again," Seth admitted, putting Biz on the floor. He and Shadow both went running over to the staircase that led to another floor.

Mrs. Thomson frowned and shook her head. "That boy used to be so nice. Did he hurt you?" she asked, walking closer to Seth while looking him over.

"He pushed me down," Seth admitted, "and…" He stopped, realizing he never told the Thomsons about his ability to read minds. They were nice people, but they were also very apprehensive of any of the children using magic. "I think he wanted to actually hurt me, physically," Seth reworded.

Mrs. Thomson looked at Seth with concern and then nodded slowly. "I'll contact his family and inform them of the incident," she assured him.

Seth nodded and smiled. "Thanks. I'd better go let Biz and Shadow into my room," he said, hurrying over to stairs nearby.

"How did they get out of your room?" he heard Mrs. Thomson ask as he moved up the stairs to the second floor of the building. A long, wide hallway stretched in both directions as he got to the top of the stairs. The orphanage, like many buildings in Remtaya, was enchanted to be bigger on the inside than the outside, supposedly to address population growth. He moved through the girls' section of the building before turning to another set of stairs to his right. Before he could start up, he heard a door close and someone call out his name. Seth winced at the sound of his name being spoken from someone else's mouth. He turned to find Tasha, one of the girls in this section, walking toward him.

"Are you okay?" she asked, bluntly.

"Um, yes?" Seth said, unsure of what she was talking about.

"I saw Zimpher and his thugs corner you in the alleyway," she confessed. "You were out of my sight for the most part, but I saw some of what happened."

Seth nodded slowly. He liked Tasha, she was kind and understanding of how mean Zimpher was. He wasn't the only orphan bullied by the older kids of the city.

"I'm fine," Seth said shyly. "I told Mrs. Thomson what happened."

"Good," Tasha said nodding. "I told Tom what I saw, so he might be going to deal with Zimpher and his gang later today."

Seth flashed a worried smile. "I hope not," he stated. "Zimpher is older and stronger than Tom."

Tasha shrugged. "I doubt anything will happen."

Seth nodded, but didn't know how to continue the conversation. A deep, awkward silence fell over them, causing Seth to panic a little. He remembered what his friends told him about ending a conversation, a smile almost reached his lips when he remembered Shadow's suggestion. *Why not end it by sniffing their behinds?* Seth resisted smiling by looking at the floor and trying to think of something else.

"Well," Tasha said, clapping her hands together, "it's been nice talking to you."

Seth looked up at her with a nervous smile, "Oh, ni-nice talking to you, too," he said, before hurrying up the stairs. Seth quickly reached the top of the landing. Turning to his right, he saw Biz and Shadow standing by his door, being petted by some other boys. One of them was gently stroking Biz as he held him on his lap. Another playfully rubbed Shadow's head.

One of the boys looked up at Seth and smiled slightly. "Hey, Seth. Are you okay?" he asked, as Seth got closer.

Seth opened his mouth, but shut it again, feeling he was too far away to say anything. As he got closer to them, he practiced what he was going to say to them. "I'm fine, Tom," he finally said out loud as he neared them. Tom and the others around him looked at Seth with interest in their eyes.

"Did you beat up Zimpher?" one of them asked, with a roguish smile.

"Seth beat someone?" Tom smiled, looking at the boy and then back at Seth. "You're way too passive," he said to him directly.

Seth smiled coyly and shrugged. "I don't believe in violence," he said quietly. He walked up to his door and turned the knob, letting Biz and Shadow into his room. The boys got up and moved closer to Tom, who was looking at Seth with a knowing smile.

"You know, I can show you how to fight," Tom offered, nodding slowly as if he was trying to convey something.

Seth turned and looked at him nervously. "Fight?" he asked timidly, looking into his room, "I don't know."

"Just because you're part of the Chosen race, and haven't hit puberty yet, doesn't mean you have to get bullied for it," Tom explained.

"I'll think about it," Seth said, walking further into his room.

"Okay," Tom said, shrugging. "See ya." He waved as he and the others headed downstairs.

"'Bye," Seth said, before closing the door and sighing. He looked at Biz and Shadow who both looked at him with inquisitive stares. "What?" he said to both of them, before walking over to a chair near his bed. "You know I don't like any kind of violence." he expressed. "Plus, Tom and his friends get picked on just as much as I do. Even more, since they're outside more than me."

Shadow gave a slight turn of his head showing he was still confused about his action. "Remtaya is the safest city in the world," Seth told them, feeling a little cornered. "I mean, no one is killed or dies of disease here because of the spell that rests over the city. Zimpher and his gang shouldn't even exist here, because there is no reason." He peered down at Biz who gave a slight snort. "Well, I'm right, aren't I?" he asked both of them.

"Feed us," Biz squeaked, sounding annoyed.

Seth looked at his window and the sunlight pouring out of it. "Oh, it is that time," he said, getting up. He walked over to a cabinet on the wall of his room. "The usual?" he asked Biz and Shadow. "Two bowls of dog food and two bowls of water please," he commanded. The cabinet twinkled like wind chimes in a soft breeze. Seth opened it to find just what he asked for; two bowls of dog food and water, each one the correct size. He placed the bowls on the floor, letting his friends come to the food when they were ready.

He moved back to the cabinet and thought about what he wanted. "Three slices of bacon, some scrambled eggs and a glass of juice please," he asked politely. The cabinet chimed once more, and Seth opened it to find what he had ordered. He walked back to his bed and began to eat while looking out the window. As he ate, he thought of the spell that had given Remtaya so much. He began to feel thankful for how fortunate he was to live in such an amazing city. "One would think people wouldn't want to fight at all in such a wonderful place," Seth thought out loud.

Shadow finished eating his food, giving a shake and a slight snort before hopping up on Seth's bed and resting next to him. "Not everyone thinks as you do," Shadow said to him in his low, gruff voice. "The city has been under this spell since before the Kry wars," he expressed. "No one alive remembers how the city was before that wizard saved it all those years ago."

"I know," Seth said, nodding, before taking a drink of his juice.

Suddenly, a bell began to ring, sending its loud bongs throughout the whole city. Seth stood up and hurried to his window, pulling open the curtains to see what was going on. He unlocked the windows and pushed them open to poke his head outside. The morning air was still chilly over the large city. Seth looked out at the massive wall that encircled the town as the bell rang out. Everyone on the street below him stopped what they were doing and looked around as the sound continued. The dinging eventually stopped and all fell silent.

"Citizens of Remtaya!" a voice suddenly echoed loudly. It was the Queen's kind and peaceful, yet strong and steadfast voice. "I bring you sad news on this bright day." Seth looked around a little more as she continued to talk. "Vicel Rask, the seventh Chosen One of the new age, has been killed." Seth heard people below him gasp and some of them began to cry. He looked down at the crowd with mixed feelings about this news. It was horribly sad, mostly because it was all in vain. "But," the Queen's voice boomed calmly, "my husband and I have counseled with the senate, and together we call for the immediate prophecy of a new Chosen One," she proclaimed. The people under Seth's window began to cheer and rejoice over this news. "We will do our utmost to find your Chosen One," the Queen vowed as her voice diminished, leaving the people to their jubilation.

Seth frowned slightly and shut the window, blocking out the loud, joyful yelling. "Why are people so stupid?" he asked, turning to Biz and Shadow. "Don't they know the time of the Chosen Ones ended thousands of years ago?"

"People are slow to remember the past," Biz said simply, as he rested next to Shadow.

"I guess so," Seth shrugged, walking over to his bed and sitting next to his friends. He reached for one of his books and looked at the title, wanting to forget the war that raged on beyond the safe walls of Remtaya. Seth opened the book and began to read about more important things.

CHAPTER THREE

LOOKING

Hello! I'm the narrator of this story. I'll be going on this journey with you, and that means I'll be interrupting once in a while. I'll give you some background on the world of Terinta, and the city of Remtaya. Every time I want to say anything, my words will appear right below the chapter title. So, if you don't want to learn more about the book you're reading, you can skip it and continue on. However, if you do want to learn more, you'll get some juicy tidbit like this: Seth is the main character. (I know, I finally confirmed it.) He is also a member of the Chosen Race. What is the Chosen Race, you ask? Well, here is a short history lesson.

In the beginning of the human race, there were two sub-races. The races were called the Chosen Race and the Wanted Race. The Chosen Race were all born with gloves on their hands, and these gloves would stay on their hands for the rest of their lives. That is really the one and only difference between the two sub-races of average humans. On Terinta, around fifty percent of humans have gloved hands; this is completely normal, for if no one knew this it would simply seem like half the world's population wore gloves all the time.

I'm done with the lesson. I hope you enjoy the next chapter.

E van stood in his doorway looking down the long hall. He had been awake since four o'clock that morning due to the emergency senate meeting. He was tired and irritated over the assembly's decision. No one in the senate truly understood how hard it was to sift through prophecies, trying to find something that wasn't even there. Yet, he knew they had no choice now; when the senate commands, prophesiers must obey. He simply wished there was another way.

The sound of footsteps reached his ears and he turned his head to find the chief prophesier walking toward him. The man had soft gray hair that hung from his head like falling wispy clouds. His eyes were lively as he focused on Evan with a smile. Evan left his doorway and smiled back kindly at the prophesier. "Chief Prophesier Rogan, you asked me to join you?" Evan questioned, bowing to him in respect.

The old prophesier nodded and walked closer to Evan. "Yes," he said in a calm and clear voice. "Evan, you are one of my most trusted prophesiers." he said with an intent stare, "and I think it's time for you to find the next Chosen One."

Evan's eyes widened. "Me?" he stammered, "Master, I'm flattered but…" He stopped, not sure how to express himself while also sounding grateful.

"Speak your mind, Evan Simhart," Rogan expressed kindly.

Evan nodded slowly. "I'm truly glad that you have faith in my ability to look that far into the Timelines but," he looked at his master with worry, "there are no more Chosen Ones. The last one was killed many years ago. The prophesiers of that time foretold there would be no others."

Rogan nodded with understanding. "Evan," he said gently as he slowly started to walk down the hall as Evan followed, listening closely, "what is a prophecy?"

Evan thought about his studies to become a full prophesier before responding. "They are ripples in time and space, preordained events that will happen no matter what," he offered.

"Yes," Rogan stated, still walking slowly. "And what do we, as prophesiers, do?"

"We look into the future with the help of the prophecy orbs, to perceive possible events in order to make a record of them and protect the people," Evan expressed easily.

"Precisely," Rogan said, nodding again. "As I've told the senate time and time again, the people we send to kill the evil King are not prophesied ones. They are simply people who might succeed in killing our foe. I've not felt a strong prophecy myself in many years," he admitted.

Evan sighed and looked ahead as they continued to walk. The light from the windows fell into the hall, giving off a light blue glow. "Then why are we doing this?" he asked, feeling utter uselessness.

"To bring hope," Rogan explained, looking at him. "The people of Remtaya are those we serve, and we do this for them. Not just the ones in the city, but those fighting the armies of Kondoma, and the villages and settlements outside our walls that are still part of our nation. The idea of a Chosen One gives them all hope."

Evan looked at his wise master and nodded. "I suppose that's right."

They continued down the hall past the prophecy chambers, walking slightly faster to the transport room. Evan walked in silence with the chief prophesier until he remembered something he wished to ask him. "Have you considered my request?" he asked calmly.

Rogan looked up at him. "What request was that?" he asked.

"About my friend," Evan clarified.

Rogan smiled. "If he chooses, your friend can come to the castle and will be very welcome," he expressed.

"Really!" Evan said, surprised. "What did the other prophesiers say?" he asked.

"Your friend Seth is an odd one; he seems to be very shy and he also appears to be a hypochondriac. But he is very skilled with magic and is approved." Rogan said.

"Thanks, I know he'd be happy to hear that," Evan replied.

"Do not thank me," Rogan continued, "thank Senator Russell Healey as he was the one who had the final word."

Rogan looked away from Evan. "As I recall, Senator Healey said that your friend seemed to have great potential."

Evan grinned. "I always knew Senator Healey was a good judge of people," he said happily. "I will tell my friend the good news during my break."

When Evan and Rogan got to the prophecy chamber, they both looked at the massive, luxurious doors. The wood was red and glistened slightly, showing off its clean lines and craftsmanship.

"Are you ready?" Rogan asked.

"I guess," Evan said. They both made their way up the stairs to the chamber doors. Evan pushed one of them open, feeling the change in air as he did so.

The chamber was surprisingly quiet as Evan and the chief prophesier entered. A few prophesiers stood in the massive corridor that separated the rest of the chamber from the large, towering bookshelves nearby.

A young prophesier walked up the chamber stairs and greeted both of them. "Chief prophesier, we have been waiting for you," the young woman said, bowing to Rogan.

"Of course," Rogan said to her, before looking at Evan and smiling. "You know you must do this yourself. I will look into the Timelines with you," he told him with a smile and a pat on the back.

Evan nodded and looked out onto the prophecy chamber. The massive, never-ending, round hall suddenly looked intimidating to him. He had looked into the Timelines before, but this time he needed to go deeper. He wasn't sure if he could do it.

Evan closed his eyes and concentrated. "*Lordren?*" he spoke with his thoughts.

A ball of blue light appeared around one of the tall bookcases and moved quickly toward him.

"Hello, master Evan," the ball of blue translucent light spoke telepathically. Its voice made Evan feel slightly relaxed, having a calm, nearly emotionless sound like that of a man gently reading poetry.

Evan opened his eyes and smiled at his friend. "How are you today?" he asked out loud.

"I am fine," Lordren expressed in a calm and peaceful way. *"You seem stressed,"* the orb observed.

Evan nodded slowly. "I am. Sorry for the discomfort I'm giving you." He walked down the stairs while Lordren floated beside him. Rogan approached another prophecy orb that had floated over to him. Evan stopped as he got to the middle of the chamber and looked at the blue glowing orb. "Rogan wants me to help him find someone to be the next Chosen One," he explained to him.

"The further you go into the temporal strings, the more powerful they may become. I'll try to help even them out for you," Lordren promised.

"Thanks," Evan said, holding out his blue-gloved hands to the orb. Suddenly, images began to appear in his head. He and Lordren moved through the strings of present events and moved deeper into the depths of temporal reality. Everything was so chaotic. Evan knew if he didn't have Lordren showing him the way, he would get lost and lose his mind. Places like these were not meant for mortals' experience alone. Evan suddenly saw a boy sitting in a tree; he fell, but appeared to be safe. The image fragmented slightly as Lordren checked to see if it was important to catalog. Evan felt him push away and move deeper into the confusing realm of time. Evan could see a woman crying by herself, before a knock came to her door. Lordren pushed that aside as well and led Evan even deeper. He saw a dog eating food while wagging his tail. The dog looked familiar when suddenly, a loud noise snapped Evan out of his concentration. Lordren quickly aborted their journey and pulled them out of the trance they were in. He looked around with confusion as everything came into focus. People were running around him, concerned looks on their faces. Evan turned to see the chief prophesier writhing on the ground, holding his head with both his hands. He suddenly gave a loud yell of pain as prophesiers stood and knelt near him. Evan gasped and ran over to him to see what was going on. "Rogan, are you alright?" Evan asked in horror as he got closer, kneeling down next to him.

"I... I... kn... know who the Chosen One is," Rogan said faintly. His eyes slowly became lifeless, and they quickly rolled to the back of his head. His body went limp and he fainted.

"Get the doctor!" Evan cried to the others around him.

CHAPTER FOUR

WHAT MAKES EVIL, EVIL?

*If it is not already clear, the Kingdom of Remtaya is at war with the King-
dom of Kondoma. This is why the Remtayans believe they need a Chosen
One, so they can kill the King of Kondoma, affectionately known as the
evil king. How did this conflict begin? It all began at the end of the Kry
Wars, which will be explained later. After a horrible war reached an uneasy
stalemate, the two largest kingdoms on the continent began to expand their
lands and rebuild. Remtaya lost little from the war, but it did feel some of
the brunt. Remtaya felt the need to retake some of their territory that was
abandoned, only to find Kondoman settlers already on the land. Remtaya
asked for their relocation, but Kondoma ignored their request, seeing as the
land was on the border of the kingdoms. Despite attempts for diplomacy,
neither kingdom could see eye to eye and war ensued. The two kingdoms
are fighting over more than just land, however. They are both fighting over
moral disputes, such as who is good and who is evil. What can you expect
from a war that has lasted for over fourteen years?*

K ing Korson sat on his throne, anxiously thinking about
the state of his kingdom. His people were starving, the
nation was at the edge of bankruptcy, and the war had no
end in sight. Remtaya was no longer being reasonable.

They had sent seven Chosen Ones to kill him. Not only was this an insult, it was purely ridiculous. Killing one Chosen One would have been enough to prove that he was an unstoppable warrior, but sending seven? Remtaya was mocking him; they thought they could catch him off guard, but they were dead wrong. He was already prepared for the next one.

The empty Throne Room was quiet as he stewed over what the city of the Remtaya might do next. How many citizens did they want him to behead before they surrendered? He'd happily behead them all if he had the chance. His head was wracked with the possibilities of what could happen when the next Chosen One came to him. Suddenly, a horrible thought occurred to him. *I'm obsessed with this*, he thought to himself.

Korson stood from his throne and looked around the empty chamber. "Orson!" he shouted loudly. A man emerged from the darkness.

Korson looked at him. "Brother," he said happily.

"Yes, my older brother. What is it?" Orson asked simply, walking closer to him.

"All I can think about are the Chosen Ones," Korson said as he frantically paced around the Throne Room.

"They are your greatest threat," Orson acknowledged. "You should always think about them, so you are not caught off guard," he suggested.

"No!" Korson said anger and determination in his voice. "I need to find a way to make the Chosen Ones stop coming. I'm not going to let the threat of the Chosen Ones rule my life."

"You have done all that you know how to do," Orson stated. "Is the orb not enough to stop the Chosen Ones from killing you?"

"It is, but I need to stop them once and for all," Korson expressed impatiently.

"Then perhaps we should use my suggestion," Orson replied hopefully.

Korson turned to look at his brother. He was shorter than him, with paler skin and a more high-strung disposition, as if he were always afraid of getting into trouble. "No," Korson said forcefully. "We cannot use that! I WILL not use the mirror! It is too dangerous."

"Why is it too dangerous?" Orson asked. "It's a mirror, albeit a powerful one, but it's still just a mirror. I don't see how it can truly harm anything."

Korson walked to the wall and looked at a portrait depicting his mother, father, Orson, and himself standing proudly by the throne that he now occupied. Life seemed so simple back then; there were no problems to occupy him. All Korson had to worry about was watching over his younger brother who had a talent for getting into trouble. Once he was punished by his father for not preventing Orson from wandering down to the basement that was strictly off-limits, due to a very evil thing that was said to be down there. Later, Korson discovered that his brother would rise in the middle of the night and go to the basement. One night when Korson followed Orson, he found that he was looking and talking into what seemed to be a mirror. When Korson looked at the mirror, he could see what looked like two red eyes gazing back from the reflective glass. He was far enough away that he couldn't discern any definite form, but he could tell that they were dark, evil eyes. As he watched in fear, he remembered his heart racing and his throat constricting with fear as a terrible voice spoke from the mirror. What the voice told his brother was frightening, Korson remembered; after he had sneaked away, he couldn't sleep the rest of the night. A day later, Korson's uncle told him that the mirror was called The Mirror of Night. After that, Korson tried to stop Orson from going back there. Luckily, the mirror was taken by his uncle for a while.

"Korson?" Orson asked. Korson snapped out of his rumination and turned to look at his brother.

"That mirror is not the answer, you know what it did to our uncle," Korson advised. "He went mad and killed two women and a child all because he said the mirror would give him anything he wanted."

"That is not true!" Orson said harshly. "He said he had nothing to do with our uncle or the people he killed. Besides, he said the child was not killed." Just as the words left Orson's mouth, he quickly stopped talking.

"What did you say?" Korson asked, looking at his brother in shock. "I know it's not my place to know what you do with your spare time, but I have to ask. Have you been talking to that mirror again?" he demanded.

His younger brother looked down at the ground and nodded slowly. "Yes, I have," he admitted.

"Why?" Korson asked.

"Because I can tell it all of my problems and it will listen to me," he said, sadness lacing his words.

"It's a mirror!" said Korson in exasperation. "It has no feelings; all it is, is evil."

Orson faced Korson with a determined look in his eye. "Come down and talk to it," Orson pleaded. "I know he will give you some good advice."

"He?" Korson asked. "As far as I'm aware, mirrors don't have a gender."

"It will give you good advice," Orson reiterated.

Korson turned to look at the painting of his family. He remembered what his father had told him. *Your uncle was misled. As the King, you cannot let yourself be led astray.* "No. I will not be like our uncle and be told what to do by a mirror. We will find another way to stop the Chosen Ones," Korson said with finality as he walked back to his throne and sat down.

"Fine, but I still think you should talk to the mirror," Orson said with a little resentment in his voice.

"I'm sorry, but I will not indulge that infernal thing like you do," Korson said. Orson bowed his head and walked to the far-left side of the massive chamber, disappearing through an open door. Korson sat there, still struggling with indecision. "What am I going to do with the Chosen Ones?" he asked.

CHAPTER FIVE

PROPHESIER

What do the prophesiers do? To put it simply, they use the knowledge they gain from the past, present, and future, and catalog it. The chamber that the prophecy orbs reside in is, in fact, perfect for this great endeavor. Also known as the infinite room, the prophecy chamber is believed to have no end; it simply goes on forever.

A knock came at the door. Seth closed the book that he was reading and sat upon his bed. Biz and Shadow both looked up and gave a quick bark. He shushed them and stared at the door, his head beginning to hurt as the other person's thoughts flooded into his mind from the other side. The thoughts moved randomly at first, lacking any proper structure. He winced painfully as the thoughts began to gather, becoming organized. Names and words formed, becoming full sentences filled with the person's mental voice.

How can I tell Kitty how I feel? a familiar voice asked in Seth's mind.

Seth smiled and moved to the door, ready to open it. He stopped as he heard a deep longing sigh in his mind. He rolled his eyes and opened the door. "Hello, Evan," he said with a knowing smile on his face.

Evan scanned him, his blue eyes widened and his thin lips frowned slightly as he tried to figure how Seth knew it was him. "You were reading my thoughts," he said as a smile formed on his mouth.

"Always," Seth said, happily letting him in.

Evan walked further into Seth's room and looked around at the state of his quarters. Shadow hopped off the bed and walked over to Evan, wagging his tail. Evan smiled and began to pet Shadow on the head, then said to Seth, "You seem to be doing fine," he said, looking at Seth as he sat on his bed.

Seth closed the door and sat next to his friend. Evan was his best friend and one of the only people in Remtaya that he felt comfortable with. "I'm doing fine, but I wish you still lived here. Ever since you left, I've become a hermit." Seth explained, giving a shrug and a fake pout.

"I left around seven years ago," Evan laughed. "You've been reclusive for a very long time."

Seth shrugged again. "Then come back," he begged, smiling and batting his eyes for dramatic effect. "Without you here, I'm a shallow mess. You complete me," he teased.

Evan laughed and nudged him slightly. "You've always been a shallow mess," he clarified. Seth nodded slowly, laughing a little. "Besides," Evan continued, "if I were to come back, then you would be all alone in the Castle Wall."

Seth stopped laughing and looked at Evan, his eyes widening. The thoughts of Evan flowed over him again and he smiled with the pain. "I'm in?" he asked him. Evan nodded slowly. "They let me in?" Seth clarified.

"Yep," Evan expressed, grinning widely.

Seth sat next to him, facing the wall, a look of amazement on his face. "How is that possible?" he asked.

Evan's grin faded and he looked at him with confusion. "What do you mean? I thought you wanted to be a prophesier?"

Seth shook his head. "I want to be an Ethiristicist. Becoming a novice prophesier is the best way to get into the hard sciences. Remtaya is great, but its education system is strange, I was taught how to read, write and do math but after that I was told to go learn for myself" he expressed, looking at Evan.

"Don't change the subject," Evan said, looking at him with concern. "Did you really think you wouldn't get in?" he asked. "You took the entrance exam last month."

"But I basically failed it," Seth stated sadly. "You know I'm not good with tests."

"You passed the magic exam with flying colors," Evan reminded him.

"Sure, if by flying colors you mean the fire I almost started," Seth retorted. "I'll never forget the angry looks I got from the judges when I singed their hair off. I messed up on all of it."

Evan held back a chuckle. "Well," he stated more seriously, "you *did* get in."

"That's amazing," Seth said as he stood and looked out the window. He could hear the wind pick up, a quiet whisper drifted over his ears. He smiled slightly, walking over to the window and opening it. The sound of thunder rumbled suddenly in the distance and rain began to fall from the sky. Seth grinned and held out his gloved right hand, letting the cold rain land on him. "Finally," he said, before turning to look back at Evan who stood, hands on his hips, looking at him sternly. Seth had always looked up to Evan, who was four years his senior. "What?" he asked him.

"I don't think you're taking this seriously," Evan said, tilting his head for emphasis.

Seth looked at the floor with a nervous grin. "I'm excited to get in," he explained as the rain continued to pour outside, "it's just...this is all I know," he explained, motioning to his room. "I don't know if I can leave it," he sighed, looking up with a sad frown.

Evan looked around the room, scanning it carefully with his eyes. "You'd miss this?" he asked, motioning around him.

"It's my comfort place," Seth explained, walking over to the edge of his bed and sitting down. "I hardly remember anything else. My mother's friend dropped me off here when I was just barely four. This is my home."

Evan shook his head. "Seth, I know you're not the adventurous type, but this is your livelihood I'm talking about. You can't stay here forever."

"I'm only fourteen-ish," Seth stated, looking back at the ground as he tried to remember how old he really was. He didn't like to think of aging, so he never really kept track of his age.

"Don't get me started on your age issue," Evan said, walking closer to him. "All I'm saying is that if you don't take life into your own hands, you're going to be left behind."

"Oh," Seth said, slightly annoyed. "If you know so much, then I have one word for you," he said, standing up and folding his arms. "Kitty," he spoke the name as he read it in Evan's mind. Evan's face grew red and his eyes widened when he heard her name. "Yes," Seth nodded quickly, "I hear you think of her all the time. And you must be suffering from head trauma, because you can't even ask her out," he accused. "Why don't you take your own life in your own hands and say something to her, get married, and have a billion gross, runny-nosed children?" Seth's sudden outburst left Evan in stunned silence. Seth closed his eyes and sighed. "Sorry, the whole mind reading thing gets annoying," he apologized, looking at Evan with worry. "I didn't mean what I said."

Evan frowned and sighed. "Yes you did, and you're right. I should stop pining over Kitty and just say something to her."

"Well, I think the whole romantic thing is foolish, but it's your life," Seth admitted with a smile. Evan shook his head and grinned as Seth sat back down on the bed. "I understand what I need to do, it's just hard," he explained truthfully.

Evan nodded in understanding. "I know how you feel. When the Queen and King asked me to come to the Castle Wall when I turned twelve, I was terrified at first. But, as time went on, it became my home just like this place once was," he explained, sitting next to Seth. Evan's freckled face became livelier as he started imagining all the things that they could do together if Seth moved to the Wall. Seth listened carefully and nodded. He realized that Evan was most likely right; if he stayed there long enough, it would probably start feeling like home. "So, what do you say?" Evan asked.

Seth rubbed his head as it began to hurt again. "What happened to Rogan?" he asked, feeling slightly dizzy.

Evan's eyes widened slightly, appearing taken aback. "Can you hear *everything* I'm thinking?" he asked.

Seth smiled a bit while rubbing the back of his head. "Always," he replied.

Evan rolled his eyes and looked outside as the rain continued to fall. "Rogan is the chief prophesier and he was injured a few days ago," he explained looking back at Seth. "He's fine, but he says he saw the next Chosen One."

"That's impossible," Seth said, gaping at him. "The time of the Chosen Ones is over."

"I thought so, too," Evan explained, "but Rogan says he felt a prophecy."

"Is he sure it's another Chosen One?" Seth asked with interest.

"He was peering deep into the temporal reality, looking for any insight about another Chosen One. It's too much of a coincidence to be anything else," Evan described, shrugging. "Plus, Rogan said that he doesn't remember everything about the prophecy, but he'll know who it is if he sees them."

"Why hasn't the rest of the city been informed?" Seth asked, looking out of the window. The rain was falling harder now as the storm drew closer. The steady pattering of the rain began to blend into a fixed, quiet roar.

"For now, they're trying to keep everyone calm," Evan said. "Besides, we haven't found this new Chosen One yet and it's best not to get anyone's hopes up." He watched Seth carefully, a nervous expression settling on his face. "You changed the subject," he noted.

"I know," Seth said looking at him. "I think I want to go, it's just..."

"Change," Evan finished.

Seth smiled faintly and nodded. "I don't know if I can do it," he admitted.

Evan smiled and moved closer to him, giving him a friendly pat on the back. "You'll do fine," he promised. "Think of it as a new adventure."

Seth gave him an uneasy smile. "That's what I'm afraid of."

CHAPTER SIX

KITTY

We now know that Evan and Seth are best friends. Their friendship began early on when Seth came to the orphanage. From an early age, Seth was shy with everyone, yet he felt safe around Evan. The two grew to be best friends, but Evan eventually had to leave Seth behind. His late mother and father were closely acquainted with the royal family, so when Evan came of age, he was taken in by the Queen and King and started his way into being a prophesier. While the change was difficult, Evan was allowed to visit Seth whenever he wished, and while Seth never did, he was welcome to meet with Evan at the Castle Wall.

Seth stood at his door. He looked at the wooden entrance that separated his room from the outside hall. He gazed back fondly at the room that had been his sanctuary for more than half his life.

"I'm going to miss this place," Seth said, gazing sadly at his uncovered and empty bed. It felt strange seeing it so bare. The whole room felt empty and lifeless now. Biz and Shadow looked at each other and then up at Seth. "What?" he asked.

"It's nothing," Biz's high-pitched voice stated simply.

Seth turned back to his empty shell of a room and frowned, feeling ashamed of his mood. This was a new adventure, something he should look forward to. He was going to live in the Castle Wall, a place where no one without a pass could enter. Despite the upside, he still couldn't shake his fear of change. Seth turned away from his room and slowly shut the door. "Well, let's go," Seth commanded, standing straighter as he looked down at Biz and Shadow. He grabbed the bags he was taking with him and began walking down the hall. *Just think, in a parallel universe you're not leaving,* he reassured himself.

As Seth walked toward the stairs, Tom and some members of his gang appeared around the corner. They were laughing at something that Tom had said and one of them punched him in the shoulder playfully.

"Hey, Seth," Tom said, as the group of boys got closer. "I hear you're moving, and to the Castle Wall of all places, congratulations." He and some of the other boys smiled at his felicitation.

Seth gave him a timid grin and nodded. "Yep, Evan is waiting for me downstairs."

"Yeah, we just saw him," one of the boys said as they walked past Seth. "Evan looks so cool as a prophesier," the same boy stated, with a hint of admiration in his voice.

Tom and the boys nodded in agreement. Seth couldn't help but concur with them; Evan was always the popular one. Tom stopped and looked at Seth with a smile. "'Good luck," he told him, patting him on the back before walking further down the hall with the others.

Seth smiled again nervously before making his way across the hallway and to the stairs. Shadow and Biz quickly hopped down the steps with Seth in close pursuit. He held his bags close to his side as he walked across the second floor before turning down the stairs to the first level of the orphanage. When Seth reached the bottom of the stairway, he saw Evan standing next to Mr. and Mrs. Thomson. The old couple smiled kindly as he, Biz, and Shadow made their way down to them.

Mrs. Thomson stepped over to Seth and gave him a big hug. "I hope you have a good time at the castle," she said with a twinge of sadness in her voice.

Seth hugged her back, feeling the same pang in his stomach. The Thomsons were like grandparents to him. It was hard to say goodbye to them like this. After Mrs. Thomson was done, Mr. Thomson walked up to him and patted him on the shoulder.

"You stay out of trouble, you hear," he stated in his grandfatherly way.

"Harold Eugene Thomson," Mrs. Thomson said with a frown, "you give him a good and proper hug."

"Fine, Meredith," Mr. Thomson sighed, grinning at Seth and giving him a good, if not reluctant, embrace. Seth hugged him back gladly. He usually didn't like hugging, germs and all, but the Thomsons were an exception. "Good luck," Mr. Thomson expressed, patting him on the arm as Evan walked over and picked up Seth's suitcases.

"He can come over anytime he wants to," Evan told the Thomsons. "The hugging *was* a little melodramatic," he stated, smiling.

Mrs. Thomson shrugged at Evan before shaking her head. "You'll understand when you have children of your own, dear," she explained, with a motherly tone in her voice.

"You'd best be off," Mr. Thomson advised, looking out the window at the crowd outside. "The people are in a frenzy over rumors of the new Chosen One. The streets are becoming crowded with spectators."

Seth looked at Evan, who nodded in agreement. "You can't keep a secret in this city," he expressed with a wry smile, before walking to the doors and opening them. Seth picked Biz up and walked to the door before turning to wave at the Thomsons one last time. The old couple waved goodbye as he stepped out of the doorway.

The streets were teeming with people. It seemed as if the entire city was going crazy. People were yelling and shouting with happiness, as children ran around, flying kites that soared like large painted birds.

"Come on!" Evan shouted to Seth over the loud crowd. Seth pushed toward Evan. He beckoned Shadow toward him as he held Biz close.

They began to make their way through the crowd as they moved with the large population.

"Why are so many people flocking to the Wall?" Seth yelled to Evan.

"The public just found out about the Chosen One, wouldn't you be excited?" he asked as they waded through the overflowing plethora of people.

"Not really!" Seth answered, shouting over the roar.

"Well, most people would be!" Evan yelled above the noise.

"Well, that is just great," Seth said sarcastically to himself. He hated crowds. They were full of people and people had germs. He was afraid of germs like a cat is afraid of water.

Seth moved along with Evan, trying not to lose him in the mass of humans. His head began to hurt. *Not now,* he thought to himself, clenching his teeth as he unsuccessfully tried to force out the thoughts that were throbbing into his mind. He grimaced as innumerable thoughts blended into a roar that nearly drowned out the yelling and celebrating around him. It felt as though an hour had passed before Seth looked beyond the people around him to see the massive wall that surrounded the whole city. It had seemed large at the orphanage, but now it was enormous.

"We are almost there!" Evan yelled to him.

The Wall seemed to rise up for hundreds of meters. Its silver-gray structure appeared to be made of metal, but Seth knew it was actually constructed of a sturdy, strong substance found somewhere in the Shiv-el'en mountains. The Wall encircled the city, stretching on for miles in both directions. Seth recalled reading that the wall formed an almost perfect oval. He knew it was meant to symbolize the government protecting the people.

As Seth and Evan drew closer to the castle, the crowd grew larger and louder.

"How much farther?" Seth asked, the thoughts of those around him still painfully penetrating his head.

Evan looked back as they continued to walk. "We're here!" he yelled, an excited grin on his face.

Seth looked over the crowd and saw a tall, wide golden gate which separated the swarming multitude from one of the many entrances to the Castle Wall. Seth, Evan, and Shadow pushed their way through the crowd over to the golden gates. Seth saw around fifty Remtayan sentries, steadfastly standing guard within and without the large golden entryway. Some of them held long flagpoles whose banners waved gently in the soft morning breeze. The flags, in Remtaya's official colors, each depicted a light golden tree surrounded by a field of azure, symbolizing steadfastness and bravery.

"Stay here," Evan instructed Seth, holding up his hands. He walked to the gate and spoke to one of the guards and what appeared to be another prophesier. He pointed toward Seth, Biz and Shadow while holding up two pieces of paper. Seth watched with interest as his headache began to fade. The guard looked at the prophesier who smiled and nodded, signaling for the gates to be opened. Evan beckoned Seth forward as the gates slowly began to swing open. Seth held Biz carefully as he and Shadow moved toward the gates while the people still celebrated behind him. Evan stood inside the gate, holding Seth's bags with a happy smile on his face. As Seth moved past the friendly guards and prophesier, he caught a glimpse of the large, gilded insignia over the gates. There was an image of a tree, whose golden branches and roots spread out in all directions. Alongside the roots and branches were neatly designed leaves that each depicted a certain animal or being. He looked closer to see the name for every animal beside each leaf. The names, Seth realized, were the ancient titles for the beings depicted. He saw the names Droco, Conchingda, Vesril, and Kry. He knew Droco was ancient for Dragon and Vesril was ancient for firebird or Phoenix. He had read of the Kry and Conchingda as well. Seth then saw the name of the tree, Ty-Anti, an important part of Terinta's mythology. He could see other characters of the ancient language on the gates, but he could only glance at them as Evan called for him to hurry. Seth swiftly strode to Evan as Shadow kept pace beside him. Evan guided him to a set of doors in the wall that stood high over them. They walked up a few steps that led to the threshold. Seth looked at Evan, Shadow, and then at Biz who was situated comfortably in his arms.

"Are you ready?" Evan asked, looking back at Seth.

Seth stared at the doors with apprehension. "I suppose," he said nervously.

"We'll walk in together," Evan offered.

Seth nodded and smiled. "Together," he said, trying to build up his courage.

Evan opened the door and they moved through the entrance. The light inside the doorway blinded Seth briefly as he walked in with his friends. As his eyes focused, he began to study his surroundings. He had seen drawings of the castle interior, but it was amazing to finally experience it for himself. The room was grand and spacious, its walls lined with statues of past Kings and Queens. Each sculpture had its own distinct design as if created by different sculptors. As they moved deeper into the chamber, Seth looked up to see a giant glass chandelier with ornately carved designs on it. A mosaic of bright colors rested above the chandelier. As light filtered across the mosaic, its glass designs projected a collage of light and shadow that appeared to dance around the entry room. The chandelier shook from air moving around the chamber.

"Beautiful, isn't it?" Evan asked, smiling.

"Very," Seth answered in awe.

"Come on, I have so much to show you!" Evan said excitedly.

Evan hurried to the chamber's end, reaching a wide vestibule with corridors that extended in all four directions. The hall straight ahead led to what appeared to be an exit. Signs rested on each side of the four corners explaining where they were. The walls inside the castle appeared to be made of light brown brick that extended from floor to ceiling. Wide, gray-colored arches spanned the ceiling, holding glass-encased torches that glowed brightly. Evan turned at a sign that read "Section Seventy-Seven—Bottom Level—Outer Wall," and led Seth, Biz, and Shadow down the long, curved hallway. Seth was amazed at the length of the corridors. The curve of the castle created the illusion that the hallway was infinitely long. Every time Seth looked toward what seemed like the end, it would bend a bit to the right and continue on.

"The people who designed the castle wanted it to look like it never ended," Evan explained as they walked down the hall.

"The castle is an oval, and like the world, it appears that you will go on for eternity, but you will eventually return to where you began," Seth stated, realizing the symbolism.

"Exactly," Evan expressed, nodding.

The hallway had countless doors on the right and left. Each door was spaced three feet apart from the next, with flaming, glass-encased torches in between them.

Seth looked at the doors they passed by. "How many people live here?" he asked.

"Not as many as you think," Evan explained. "Most of the people that work here live somewhere in the city."

Seth looked around at all the doors that surrounded them. "How many people are in this area?" he asked.

Evan stopped and looked up for a second. As he did his thoughts flooded Seth's mind. *"Let's see, I know that Orin and Serena live in Section Forty-Five, Kitty lives in Section Fifty-Six Top Level and Coven lives in Section Thirty-`Seven,"* he thought to himself.

"What section are you in?" Seth asked, smiling and raising his eyebrows.

Evan's face blushed. "Section Fifty-Six," he answered, embarrassed. "I believe the number of people in your section is around fourteen," he recounted. "Many of the rooms are empty because that's how the designers wanted it," Evan explained.

"Why would they leave so many rooms empty?" Seth inquired.

"The emptiness of the castle and its oval shape are to show that the people are the most important. The designers made sure that, in the event of an attack, there was a place where all of the citizens could find shelter," Evan explained. "There are approximately 12,496 rooms in the castle and each one can hold four people, so the entire castle can hold about 49,984 people. Plus, the council chambers could probably hold around 79 and the prophecy chamber, or the infinite room, can easily hold everyone in the city and we still wouldn't find the end," Evan expressed with a laugh.

"When will I see the prophecy chamber?" Seth asked, with interest.

"When I'm done showing you your room," Evan explained. He pointed at a door on the left side of the endless hallway.

"Room seven seven nine three," Evan said. The door looked like the others around it, but Seth knew there was something special about it. From now on, it would be the barrier to his room. Evan smiled as he pulled a key from his robe to give to Seth, who stared at it, his eyes open wide. The key was a simple silver color, with short teeth that shone in the torch light around them.

"I get my own key?" Seth asked.

"Just don't lose it," Evan cautioned, with a nod.

Biz sniffed the key in Seth's hand as they moved closer to the door, whose handle was a soft gold metal that appeared clean and unused. Seth carefully took the key and slid it into the lock. He heard a definite click as he turned the key to the left and the door gave a soft pop as if to invite him in. He turned the knob and opened the door, ready for what was on the other side. Seth and his companions stepped into a room about the same size as the one at the orphanage. A bed already fitted with sheets and blankets stood on short wooden legs, its side facing the doorway. Soft feather pillows rested at the headboard and next to the nightstand behind the bed. A window on the right wall adjacent to his bed was raised with soft sunlight glowing through its white shades. Mounted on the wall opposite his bed was a cabinet, from which Seth knew he could obtain almost anything he asked for. The floor was covered with a soft and cozy Berber blue carpet that felt sturdy as Seth walked around, examining everything. He looked down to find a light blue woven mat resting near a simple wooden desk opposite the end of his new bed. Seth looked at the window with the closed blinds and walked over to see what lay beyond his new room. He placed Biz on the floor while Shadow sniffed around their new chamber. Seth pulled back the drapes, looking out the window to see dozens of open grassy fields that extended beyond the borders of the city. To his left, distant mountains lined up like stone-tipped guardians. A dirt road to his right led away from the city toward the rest of the kingdom. Clouds of gray hung in the sky, casting lazy shadows that sluggishly moved across the grassy ground.

"It's so beautiful," Seth said, smiling, as he turned to Evan who had placed Seth's bags near his bed. Biz was still sniffing around the room, his tail curled, while Shadow hopped up on the bed and inspected the fresh blankets.

"Biz and Shadow can stay here while we see the rest of the castle," Evan explained, watching the two animals explore their new living space.

Seth looked up at the ceiling to see a small chandelier made of slightly glowing glass. Two oil lamps rested on the wooden desk and one candlestick stood on the nightstand. Seth walked over to his bed and called Biz over to him. He gently picked the little creature up and placed him next to Shadow. "What do you guys think?" Seth asked Shadow and Biz. "Do you want to stay here or come with?" Biz looked at Shadow and the black dog gave a huff.

"We'll stay here for now. But I'd like to see more of the Castle Wall some other time." Shadow expressed gruffly.

"Okay," Seth agreed. Evan watched the exchange Seth was having with Biz and Shadow in slight confusion as he couldn't hear what the two creatures were saying like Seth could. "Watch out for each other until I come back." He smiled at Biz and Shadow before he followed Evan out of the room. Seth closed the door gently and used his new key to lock it.

"What do you want to see first?" Evan asked him, excitedly.

"You choose," Seth said, knowing he would like whatever Evan chose.

"Okay," Evan shrugged, as he smiled and rubbed his hands together. "Watch this," he stated, smiling. Evan closed his eyes and stood there for a while. "The library," he suddenly said in a loud clear voice. Without any warning, Evan disappeared and a rush of air enveloped Seth, as he felt magic reverberate around him. Seth was amazed. He had seen people transport before, but it typically took a lot of magical energy and years of practice, depending on how far one wanted to go.

Evan reappeared next to him, with a confused look on his face. "That's odd, I can usually transport people around me, if I think about transporting both of us," he explained, gazing at Seth with a puzzled look.

"Perhaps I should give you my permission," Seth joked, smiling at him with an amused smirk.

"Oh, hilarious," Evan rolled his eyes in annoyance, "let's try holding hands."

"Very well," Seth said reluctantly, taking hold of Evan's hand as anxious thoughts about germs passed through his mind. Evan, after all did shake that prophesier's hand before they came inside the castle.

"I also give you permission to transport me," Seth joked again, trying to think of something else.

"Ha ha." Evan feigned laughter, before he again closed his eyes and began to concentrate.

Seth was suddenly bombarded with thoughts and images. He saw thousands of books on row after row of towering shelves. Blue orbs floated about shelves and books. Seth could also see an enormous chamber with a large, ornately designed symbol on the floor. The scene vanished as quickly as it came, and the image of a person suddenly stepped into view. A young woman, with a long, brown ponytail, stood looking up at a massive bookshelf, her face turned away. Evan's voice abruptly echoed in Seth's head; his words filled with longing and passion.

"*Kitty*," he thought fondly.

Seth felt a sudden surge of magical energy swirl around them. The hallway appeared to fade into a menagerie of endless color. A series of never-ending hues rushed around Seth, speeding and wailing like a tornado. Seth gasped as everything suddenly turned a light blue. For a moment, he felt like he was flying aimlessly through a limitless void. Then, the feeling ceased and a sense of being crushed struck Seth in the chest. He couldn't breathe; he felt like grains of sand were filling his body. He felt Evan's grip loosen and then let go as he was filled with dread.

"*I'm going to die*," Seth thought as the feeling got worse. "*I don't think so!*" a part deep-down inside him shouted. Seth felt a force inside him grab hold of what felt like Evan's hand. He tightened his grip and pulled as hard as he could. Suddenly the sensation of clay filling his body subsided and Seth found himself lying on the floor next to Evan.

Both of them were breathing hard as Seth looked up to find a face peering down at him. The face looked very familiar, as if he had seen it in a picture. Then he realized where he had seen it.

"Is your name Kitty?" Seth asked, taking a deep gasp of air, his chest moving up and down visibly.

"Yes it is," Evan answered, getting up off the ground with a groan. He helped Seth get up, coughing as he did so.

Seth stared at Evan, his body still filled with anxiety. "Why did you almost kill us?" he frowned, panting hard.

"I didn't almost kill us," Evan said, defensively. "There hasn't been a transporter death in centuries," he clarified.

"If I might interject here," said the girl, with curiosity, "who is this?" She pointed to Seth.

Evan and Seth both looked at her and then at each other. "He is my friend; the one who has come here to be a prophesier," Evan explained, still trying to catch his breath.

"Oh, it's a pleasure to meet you," the kind and attractive young woman said, holding out her hand. "And yes, I'm Kitty," she said with a cheerful smile. Seth looked at her hand for a second. *I hope this will not become commonplace,* he thought, reluctantly shaking Kitty's hand while trying to be as polite as possible.

"Is this the library?" Seth turned to Evan and whispered. He was still uncomfortable talking in front of unfamiliar people and automatically regressed into his introverted ways.

"No it is not," Kitty verified. "This is the dueling room where people can practice their wand and fighting skills." Kitty motioned to the large, sparse chamber. The floors were matted and punching bags of various sizes stood around the room. Seth saw an assortment of weapons hanging along the wall or laying on the floor. Some of the weapons appeared real, while others appeared to be made for practice only.

Seth's attention shifted as Evan moved closer to Kitty and said something about how nice she looked. Seth noticed that Kitty was at least five inches taller than Evan. She had bright green eyes and light brown hair, almost the same color as his, wrapped up in a ponytail. She sported a dark, sleeveless shirt, showing off her tan arms, while wearing fingerless gloves that extended halfway up her forearm. The knuckles of the laced sports gloves had padding on them which, Seth guessed, made them good for punching. A milky white stone, a few inches in diameter, rested around Kitty's neck, attached to a simple black string. The stone caught Seth's attention and he realized that he was in the presence of a Seer, one of the wisest, oldest races of human in all of Terinta. While Kitty was basically human like anyone else, meeting a Seer for the first time made Seth feel privileged.

"Are you going to the library?" Kitty asked, snapping Seth out of his daze.

"We were, but something happened," Evan replied.

"I've never felt so much commotion in my life," Seth added, still acting shy.

"We weren't going to die," Evan reassured Seth.

Kitty stared at him with an inquisitive look. Her green eyes seemed to burn into his soul. "Superluminous travel is considered very safe," she insisted.

Evan blushed. "It actually was transmatter transportation," he explained, with a hint of shame.

Kitty's eyes widened in surprise. "Transmatter transportation?!" she gasped, dumbfounded. "It takes years to learn how to trans-materially transport other people. It's only used for one person most of the time," she cautioned, her green eyes narrowed. "How could you be so reckless?"

Evan bowed his head sheepishly. "I was trying to show Seth what I've learned," he explained meekly.

"If it is any consolation," Seth began, looking timidly at Kitty and Evan, "I thought it was a fascinating experience, even if we almost died."

Evan looked at him with a partial smile. "Do you really think so?" he asked.

"Of course," Seth insisted.

Kitty stared at Seth for a moment. Her green eyes seemed to be gazing deep into his soul now. At the moment Seth could not read Kitty's mind. His ability to read minds was always fickle. He tried to look away, but his eyes moved back to Kitty's stone; it was a Seer stone. These stones were believed to hold great power, strong enough to protect the Seers from death itself. Seth had learned that although Seers were known for their prophetic powers, most did not actively prophesy. He also recalled that though Seers may be male or female, only females possessed Seer stones, in honor of the Great One. Seth always envied the Seers; they possess powerful magic and are among the leading minds in ethiristics.

"Are you a Seer?" he asked Kitty, shyly, almost without thought. Kitty's piercing regard faltered as she was caught unaware by the question.

"Yes I am," she answered.

"Kitty is also a wandmaker and trainer," Evan said, with obvious infatuation.

A male voice suddenly called Kitty's name, causing each of them to turn toward its source.

"Just a moment, Kroeno," Kitty called back, then looked at the others. "I really must go; try not to kill anyone else," she instructed Evan with a wink.

"Alright," Evan replied, with embarrassment.

"Farewell," Kitty acknowledged both of them, before sprinting toward the man.

Seth followed Evan slowly to one of the doors of the dueling chamber. He watched his friend look at Kitty as she spoke with the other man. Evan sighed as they exited the large room into a long hallway. "She's amazing isn't she?" Evan mused, with a dreamy look in his eye.

"Why is her name Kitty?" Seth asked, with interest. "It's a very odd name to have."

"Her full name is Glennell Kitteara of the White Hills," Evan explained, sighing. "She doesn't like the name Glennell, so she wants everyone to call her Kitty."

Seth imagined a white kitten holding a large, ornate sword in its right paw and a necklace in its left. "I am Kitty of the White Hills, fear me," the kitten announced. Seth giggled under his breath.

"Her name may sound funny, but she is a very formidable opponent," Evan said. "She can defeat the strongest people in the city just by flicking her wand," he explained.

"I don't question her effectiveness as a fighter, I am intrigued by her name," Seth clarified. "What do you find attractive about her?" he asked, curiously.

"Do you not see it?" Evan asked, with shock.

Seth looked at Evan. "She may be attractive, but I still can't see why you're in love with her. You know what I see in most human faces," Seth explained.

Evan rolled his eyes. "I know there's evidence that humans evolved from a species similar to the chimpanzee, but that doesn't mean that we look like apes," Evan expressed with a frown.

"I still see it," Seth stated, smiling.

"There are some who think that evolution is a fraud," Evan clarified, looking ahead with a smug smile forming on his face.

Seth looked up at the ceiling as they walked across the hallway. "All I can say is that people limit themselves if they can't accept evolution," he said.

"I don't think Kitty looks like a chimp," Evan said, forcefully. "She has beautiful emerald eyes, long, lustrous hair and freckled skin."

"If all you focus on is her physical appearance, then I think you're not going to get married," Seth joked.

"She is kind to nearly everyone. She is also tenacious and very witty," Evan continued, his voice almost faltering.

Suddenly, a small, blue sphere descended from the ceiling before settling a few inches from Seth and Evan. The orb swelled to four times its original size, then quickly vanished, revealing a young man dressed in red robes and another man who looked big and muscular. Seth looked at the spectacle with an inquisitive stare. The man in red robes was thin and pale and his head was clean shaven, but for a skiff of light blond hair on his brow. The other man was large with dark brown hair and gray eyes.

"Ah, Evan how are you?" the bald man asked, with a look of disdain.

"I'm fine, Eris," Evan answered, sounding equally perturbed. Evan looked at the other man with slight concern. "Coven." He said with a nod. Seth could tell by how Evan was acting with Coven that he was slightly afraid of the man.

"Evan," Coven said with a slight nod as well.

Eris, whose bare head and priestly robes denoted his position in the castle, appeared to be in his early twenties. Seth knew the priests were responsible for the religious well-being of the people in the city and nation of Remtaya.

Seth believed in a higher power, but due to experiences with judgmental people, he was not actively religious. Seth knew that if he were to tell Eris of his views, the priest would likely label him a blasphemer and try to cast out evil spirits.

Coven wore a tight dark blue jacket with a tunic underneath, a badge of some kind was on his upper right chest. He wore clean brown pants and dark brown boots. The looks of this Coven gave Seth the thought that he was some kind of law man.

"Who's this?" Eris asked, gesturing toward Seth.

"This is my friend, Seth. As you can see, he is of the chosen race, just like me," Evan said, with a mixture of pride and contempt.

Eris glared at Evan and then turned back to look at Seth. "What is your purpose here?" he asked, forcefully.

Seth cringed and faltered in his response. "I, I am here to become a prophesier," he replied softly.

"A prophesier, you say?" Eris chuckled. "I would suggest a career change. They are not as good as they used to be," he expressed, with a dark smile. "You ought to become a priest; at least we have not lost our touch."

Seth envisioned himself in priestly attire, his head shaven, preaching to a group of his peers. "No, thank you," Seth expressed nervously, recoiling from a vision of a universe that likely existed somewhere. "I think I look better with hair," he stated, with shy honesty. Evan laughed quietly under his breath.

"Besides, if I am not mistaken, you would need to be chosen by the high priest and renounce all worldly things," Evan stated. "That's not such a terrible thing, but Russell would have to retract his sponsorship," Evan spoke to Eris while looking at Seth.

Eris's eyes widened. "*You* were sponsored by Senator Healey?" he asked, astonished.

Evan smiled at Eris. Seth heard Evan's voice in his mind, *I got him.* "He will never tell," Evan said, with a laugh. Evan grabbed Seth's arm and pulled him back down the hallway.

"Not so fast." Coven, who was watching the conversation, said with a sharpness in his voice. Evan stopped and looked up at Coven who towered over Evan and Seth.

"How is Rogen?" Coven had no concern in his voice. Instead, he acted like he was waiting for Evan to tell him something important that he could use for himself. Seth felt the mind of Coven and found that he was thinking about him wanting to be the next Chosen One.

"He's still resting," Evan answered looking at the large man with concern.

"Fine," Coven said with a cold voice. "You tell me when he is up." Coven stated pointing at Evan with a demanding finger.

"Seth and I need to go." Evan insisted with a nervous grin. He took Seth's arm and pulled him from the two men.

"What was *that* about?" Seth asked with concern, glancing back to see Eris and Coven who were walking toward the dueling chamber.

"Eris and I have never liked each other. Ever since I have been here we have just…well…" Evan stopped and looked at Seth. "We just hate one another," he explained.

"Well, that is your prerogative," Seth said, shrugging. "Why did you brag about us being of the chosen race?" he asked.

"I heard from a reliable source that Eris always wanted to be a member of the chosen race," Evan explained, smiling villainously.

"Why?" Seth asked.

"I don't know," Evan said, "he just does."

Seth and Evan continued in silence for a while. The hallway seemed to go on forever.

"And what about the big guy?" Seth asked, looking at Evan as they walked.

"Coven is a self-proclaimed law man." Evan explained. "He is mostly unpleasant to be around because he thinks he is the top dog and everyone else is not worth anything."

Seth looked ahead of them worried about the idea that there were unfriendly people around him. "Where are we going?" Seth asked, breaking the awkward silence.

"To the prophecy chamber," Evan explained. He turned and looked at Seth.

"You do realize that you have to take classes to become a prophesier, correct?" he asked.

"I'm completely aware of what I need to do," Seth replied.

"Good," Evan said, walking beside him, "because I have some bad news for you." A concerned look came over Seth's face. Evan stared at him and smiled a little. "You know how most prophesiers must learn how to fight in combat?" he asked.

"Yes," Seth answered nervously, "but, I don't have to do that. I'm just taking the first year of prophesier training and then I'll be moving to the sciences. I won't need to take that class."

Evan shrugged and his smile grew wider. "Well, things have changed. All first-year prophesiers are now required to take a beginners' fight class, and Coven will be your instructor."

"No," Seth groaned, his heart sinking at the news.

CHAPTER SEVEN

LESSONS

Seth stood on a hill bathed in red. He held a sword in his right hand and a napkin in the other. He stared down the hill to see an entire army of fruits and vegetables. Strawberries, lined up from north to south, lay next to the garden-variety Fragaria. A column of kumquats were growing next to a group of large pineapples and other exotic fruits. Seth's attention turned to an approaching horse with a white-robed figure sitting on its back. The horse was black, with blue stockings on each hoof; its rider appeared to have two heads. Seth saw that one of the heads was Evan and the other was Kitty.

"What do I do?" he asked both of them.

"Eat them," Evan said solemnly. "Eat them slowly and make them suffer!" A dark smile grew across his face.

"Nay," Kitty and the horse said together. "Eat them fast and show mercy."

Seth felt the air around him move quickly and he soon found himself standing closer to the army of food. A giant pineapple rolled up to him, tipping on its bottom as it sat upright. It was taller than him and seemed to get larger the longer Seth looked at it. The sky turned orange and the massive pineapple spoke. "We petition for sanctuary inside your stomach," it spoke, with a small timid voice.

Seth looked up at the overgrown fruit. "I'm sorry, but I don't like pineapple," he apologized. The pineapple suddenly exploded, as did the other pineapples in the army.

"I don't like strawberries or kumquats either," Seth insisted. The army of fruits and vegetables burst forth in a massive eruption. The barrage of exploding produce generated a colossal wave that spread over the whole, red-stained field.

"Look what you did," Evan, Kitty and the horse all said at once.

The massive deluge moved toward Seth until it was right on top of him. He closed his eyes and held up his arms as the wave crashed down over him. A voice out of nowhere boomed as everything grew dark. "DO NOT KILL!" it commanded.

Seth awoke from his dream with a gasp. He lay still for a while, pondering what just happened. "Why do I have odd dreams?" he asked himself. Biz, who was resting on Seth's legs, stared up tiredly before resting his head back on the covers.

The air in Seth's room was cold as the sunlight began to inch in slowly through the window. The oil lamp that he kept lit all night was dim as the flame weaved and bobbed in the glass container. Morning had come and Seth realized he needed to get up. His first day of training had arrived and he didn't want to be late. "Sorry," Seth said to Biz, as he moved his legs out of the covers and over the side of the bed. He felt the firm carpet with his toes as he stood up and yawned. Seth moved to the other side of the bed to see Shadow resting comfortably beside it. Shadow's dark head rose, and his bushy tail wagged happily as Seth moved toward the food cabinet.

The familiar sound of wind chimes emanated from the cabinet as Seth requested the usual food he gave Biz and Shadow. After placing their trays on the floor, he quickly ordered a snack for himself.

It had been three weeks since Seth moved into the castle, and everything seemed to be going smoothly. Evan had been showing him around, and the people in the castle seemed kind, the few that he had met at least. Despite Evan's best efforts to help him feel more comfortable, Seth still felt safer in his new room.

Seth downed the last of his zap juice and stood gazing at the robes he received from Evan three days ago. The robes were dark blue and lined with gold around the sleeves and hem. Beside the robe lay what Evan referred to as mandatory undergarments. They were a lighter cobalt color and consisted of a sleek shirt and pants that appeared to be skin-tight. Evan had explained that this was time-honored prophesier apparel, while also subtly hinting that the undergarments were for sparring practice. He was still angry about the change in his study plans. Not only did he dread learning how to fight, but he had also seen the instructor for the class, Coven, judging by how he acted when Seth had met him Coven appeared likely to bully those he deemed weaklings. Seth knew he would certainly fall into that category.

Trying to alleviate his fears, Seth arose from the bed and walked to the bathroom. Armed with a towel and a sponge, he quickly undressed and walked into the shower, making sure to let the warm, clean water wash away any bodily grime. The water seemed to whisper his name as it always did, and he carelessly listened to its calming tones as he rubbed the soap over his body.

After spending a few relaxing minutes under the spray of the warm water, Seth waved his hand in the air, turning off the faucet with the little magic he knew. His head ached slightly as the magic flowed invisibly around him. He stepped out of the shower and moved his hand slowly up to the top of his head. With his eyes closed, the water that dripped from his body gradually streamed upward, into the air. His hair tousled slightly as the water gently gathered into a sphere of liquid, floating between his uplifted gloved hands. Seth's eyes shone a darker shade of blue as he moved back to the shower and dropped the watery orb into the drain. He then turned and wrapped his towel around his waist while wiping any residual water off of him.

Seth opened the bathroom door and moved toward the robes that lay on the small desk against the wall. He quickly grabbed them and walked into the bathroom, keeping a firm hold on his towel. As Seth began to don the clothing, he observed that the undergarments fit his body like a glove. He looked at his reflection in the mirror and realized that he looked decent in the tight clothing; nothing felt exposed or awkward. He turned to grab the dark blue robe and examined it. The fabric felt soft, like a richly made blanket. He slipped the robe over his head, allowing it to fall freely over his shoulders. He turned to the mirror, frowning slightly at how bulky the robe made him look; it was bigger than he was. The sleeves moved past his hands and the robe's hem fell easily to the floor.

As Seth scanned his reflection, he heard a knock at the door. Moving out of the bathroom, Seth walked to the front door and opened it to find Evan standing on his doorstep.

"Are you ready?" Evan asked.

Seth smiled and looked down at himself. "What do you think?" he asked, whirling dramatically.

Evan looked at Seth for a while. "It's okay," he acknowledged, "you need to get one that's a bit smaller though."

"You gave me this one," Seth retorted with a tease, as he let Evan in.

Evan laughed. "I don't keep track of what size you are," He expressed. "Are you ready to go?"

"Yes, I am," Seth said. He looked at Biz and Shadow who were still happily eating their food.

"Do any of you want to come with me?" He asked knowing that Shadow expressed interest in coming with him to his first day. Seth already walked with Biz and Shadow when Evan showed him the Castle Wall Fortress a few weeks ago. Both of his friends liked their new home. Biz was lazier than Shadow so he told Seth he wouldn't join him for his first day of studies. Shadow barked and hurried over to Seth and Evan as Biz kept eating.

"Don't get into trouble," Seth told Biz with a smile. He walked out of his room with Evan and Shadow locking the door, putting his key in his prophecy robes. He glanced at Evan's robes for a moment, noticing how different they were compared to his own. They fit more snuggly and appeared more elaborate in their design. Evan's robe was tied with a fancy golden sash around his waist, while Seth was wearing a slip-on. "When can I get a robe like yours?" Seth asked.

Evan smiled. "Probably never," he said simply. "You said you didn't want to be a prophesier. Besides, you're just taking the basic course and novice prophesiers wear slip-on robes."

"Oh," Seth replied, with a slight frown.

As they walked down the hall, Seth considered what Evan had told him about a week ago: *Your first day will be spent learning the history of the prophesiers and the continent of Terina.* Seth still remembered all that he had learned when he went to school at age four, however, the school system in Remtaya was lacking in many respects. Due to Remtaya's self-sustaining food supply and magic municipal maintenance, the economy was mostly a formality. Therefore, a lot of jobs that would be essential in most cities weren't needed in Remtaya. Schools teach the very young to read, write, and do simple math, but the remainder of their education is determined by the individual. Seth loved to learn, so he was happy to gain as much knowledge as he could in school. The school year lasted only six months, so Seth spent his free time in the library.

As they quickly made their way across the hallway, Seth wondered what he was going to be taught. He was proficient in history; most of Terinta's history was filled with wars, which were easy for him to remember. He also looked forward to learning the history of the prophesiers. Thanks to Evan, Seth knew they had a rich past.

Evan looked at Seth with interest in his face. "You seem quite relaxed," he observed.

Seth's eyes widened with worry. "Should I be concerned?" he asked nervously. "Did you find out who my teacher is? Are they mean?" he asked with panic.

"No," Evan said, holding up his hands with a slight laugh. "I just said you seemed relaxed. I know how you feel about meeting new people."

Seth nodded and looked ahead, thinking about his social anxiety. "You said there weren't going to be a lot of people in the class," he reminded Evan.

Evan smiled and shrugged with a nervous grin. "I must have exaggerated; there are at least twenty people in your class."

"Twenty?" Seth gasped, looking at Evan with growing distress.

"Don't worry," Evan reassured him as they walked down the long hall, the light from the windows shining placidly on the floor. "With more students in the class, you'll be less conspicuous." Seth nodded with understanding. "Plus," Evan explained, "a friend of mine will be in the class, and she's around your age." Evan looked at Seth with a hopeful smile. "I think, if you let yourself, you both could really hit it off," he suggested, raising his eyebrows up and down.

"What do you mean?" Seth asked, narrowing his eyes at Evan.

"I think you two could become good friends," Evan explained. "Then if all goes well, maybe something more," he grinned.

Seth frowned and shook his head. "You're ridiculous," he expressed simply.

"Hey!" Evan defended as they began to turn a long corner. "I felt the same way before I came to the castle, then Kitty…" Suddenly, Kitty appeared around the corner, stopping Evan mid-sentence. His face turned red as he and Seth both stopped.

"Kitty!" Evan said with surprise.

"Evan, Seth," the Seer said, looking at them with interest. She looked down at Shadow who was walking next to Seth.

"Who's this?" she asked bending down and gazing at Shadow.

"This is Shadow." Seth said shyly to Kitty.

"May I pet him?" she inquired looking up at Seth with a soft smile.

Seth had to remember that most people couldn't talk to other animals like he could. "He's friendly." Seth stated with a gentle nod.

Kitty began to pet Shadow who seemed to enjoy the attention.

"Where are you off to?" she asked, petting Shadow with a flair like she knew how to pet a dog, as if she had one herself. She finished petting him and stood up. Kitty wore a brown dress that ended slightly above her ankles. Her hair was again set high in a ponytail.

"Seth is off to his first day of class." Evan explained.

"Oh," Kitty said, looking over at Seth. "Well, you and I will get to spend more time with each other then," she said with a kind smile. "I'll be helping the first-years learn about magic and how to use it."

Seth knew this already, as Evan had talked his ear off, telling him how lucky he was to have Kitty around. "I'm looking forward to it," Seth said shyly, trying to sound sincere. Truthfully, he wasn't sure if he would like Kitty. She seemed nice, but if her smile was just an act, then he couldn't imagine liking her.

There was a rustling behind Kitty, and Seth caught a glimpse of a young man kneeling behind her. He was picking up a white pillow and golden case with a flustered look on his thin, pale face.

"Who are you helping?" Evan asked Kitty, peering behind her.

"She is helping *me*," the scrawny man said from behind the Seer.

Kitty turned to the man and smiled, folding her arms. "Are you alright, Parkens?" she asked, with a gentle smile.

"Yes, I'm fine," Parkens said, still looking flustered. "I can't seem to stop falling today." He held the pillow with both hands. "Soven's going to kill me if he finds out I dropped the Queen's jewelry box."

"I've dropped it three or four times myself," Kitty told him with a shrug. "Albeit, I *was* a child, but Queen Julia didn't seem to mind."

"That might explain why the Queen wanted the box refurbished," Parkens joked shyly.

"Well!" Kitty said, her eyes widening with slight shock. "I guess she might have minded a little."

"I might have dropped it once or twice myself," Evan interjected.

Kitty and Parkens both looked at him as Seth watched the conversation unfold. "When would you have used the Queen's jewelry box?" Kitty asked.

"I was only curious," Evan retorted.

Seth smiled at Evan, thinking that perhaps he may have been too curious. He pictured Evan admiring himself in the mirror, bedecked with diamond necklaces and jeweled rings.

"Parkens, why are you just standing there?" another voice called from a distance. Seth saw a well-dressed man hurriedly striding over to them. He wore a fancy cloak that swept behind him as he walked. His shoes tapped gracefully on the carpeted floor as he moved closer.

"Oh," the man said as he approached, "Evan, Kitty and…." He looked at Seth with an inquisitive stare. "And who might you be?" he asked, walking closer with a wide smile. His teeth were straight and white, almost too perfect.

"I'm Seth," Seth replied shyly.

"Sorry," the man said, holding a hand to his ear, "I didn't quite catch that."

Seth gulped, as he realized he was speaking too softly for others to understand. "Seth," he tried again, still very shyly.

"My goodness, boy," the man stated loudly. "Are you a human or a field mouse?"

"He's Seth," Evan told the senator with a smile. Seth nodded slowly and bowed his head to the man, feeling embarrassed. He knew a senator when he saw one, and the man was dressed just as the ones that campaigned in the city.

"Oh! Well then! Evan, Kitty, Seth, how are you three today?" the man asked cheerfully. His eyes moved down as he stared at Shadow. "What an adorable dog." He said with a wide grin.

"We're fine," Kitty answered, bowing her head to the man slightly. "I was just helping Parkens with this," she said, motioning toward the box. "And that's Seth's dog, Shadow." She explained to the senator.

"Oh, good! Nice to meet you Shadow." The senator said with a slight bow. He then looked over at Parkens and then at Kitty. "I thought you might be having a romantic encounter with Parkens, here. Good thing you weren't," the flamboyant man said, then turned

to Kitty and whispered, "we all know who you really should be with."
Kitty's face blushed.

"How are you today, Soven?" Evan asked, trying to change the subject.

"Incandescently well," Soven said, with a dramatic bow. The senator exuded an air of respect and joy. He appeared to be in his late forties or early fifties, though it was hard for Seth to tell for sure.

Seth looked at Parkens, who seemed to be the perfect specimen of a senatorial servant. He appeared to be in his early twenties, clothed in a simple red tunic and tan pants. He also had red hair and hazel eyes.

"Come, Parkens, let's return this chest to the Queen," Soven said cheerfully.

"Yes, sir," Parkens said, holding the box and pillow carefully.

"I'll come with you," Kitty said, looking at Soven and Parkens with a smile.

"That would be most appreciated," Soven said, turning to walk down the hall.

"Goodbye," Evan said, waving as they walked down the corridor. He appeared nervous when Kitty walked past him. Seth stood quietly watching Evan as he debated whether to say something to her. He could hear Evan's thoughts go wild as he struggled to speak to the Seer. Suddenly, Soven stopped and turned to look at Evan with wide eyes. "Evan, did you hear that Rogan is awake now?" he hollered.

"What?" Evan said shocked. "When did that happen?"

"I'll talk to you later, just go see him!" Soven yelled before he turned another corner with Parkens. Kitty looked back at them one last time, smiling gently before disappearing.

Evan glanced around frantically and then turned to Seth. "You need to get to room 9." he said urgently. He grabbed Seth's hand and began to hurriedly drag him along.

"Hold on!" Seth yelled, feeling rushed.

Evan ran quickly and continued to force Seth down the next hallway.

Seth wrested his hand from Evan's grasp and pulled away. "Come on, hurry!" Evan shouted as he continued to run, leaving Seth behind.

"Wait!" Seth yelled, groaning as he ran after his friend. Evan quickly turned a sign-plastered corner; one of the signs had an arrow labeled "Room Nine" next to it. Seth quickly rounded the corner, to see Evan turn down a hallway to the left. Seth groaned once more, knowing that Evan must be enjoying himself. He sped through the corridor, darting between the other people in the hallway. He tried to keep calm as he hurried around the corner to see Evan standing by a door at the very end of the hall.

Seth quickly walked toward Evan, breathing hard and glaring at him as he got closer. "Was… that… really… necessary?" he panted.

"Why, you don't like to run?" Evan asked.

"You… know… I …hate… it." Seth gasped.

Evan smiled. "Just one of the things I like and you don't," he said with a laugh. Seth took another deep breath and stared at the door. The number "nine" was affixed above the door, while a list of names arranged by days of the week was attached to the wall nearby.

"Let's see," Evan said looking at the paper. "Oh! You have Healey, the same senator that sponsored you," he said excitedly.

"What?!" Seth said, panicking. He looked closely at the paper to see for himself. "Dr. Russell Healey!" Seth said aloud. "Have you ever talked with him before?" he asked, turning to look at Evan.

"I don't know him personally," Evan acknowledged, "but I've seen him performing tasks around the castle."

"Like what?" Seth asked.

"Oh, things," Evan said, shrugging. "Like I said, I don't know him personally," he explained, "though I do recall hearing that he once had a heated debate with another senator about the sociopolitical issues that would arise if some fruit could talk."

Seth looked at Evan skeptically. "You're joking," he insisted.

"Oh no," Evan insisted, "I heard it from a good source." He looked around for a moment as if he were trying to locate something.

"What is it?" Seth asked.

"I need to go check on Rogan," Evan said nervously. "It's time for your class anyway. I'll see you later."

"You're not coming in with me?" Seth asked, with worry in his voice.

"I'm your friend, not your mother," Evan stated as he walked away backward, then turned to run down an adjoining hall. Seth stared at the door in front of him, his stomach churning with worry. He wouldn't have minded having a mother figure with him at the moment, but he knew that chance was lost before he was born. He studied the door as worry continued to gnaw at him. Seth looked down at Shadow who seemed to enjoy the run that Evan sent to them on. Seth sighed and smiled at Shadow before looking back at the door.

"Did you know that this door was made from the wood of a tall, majestic tree?" someone asked from behind him. "It was felled in the forest of Conching, and it sprouted near the highpoint of the Dragon Empire. Oh, if only wood could talk."

Seth turned around to see a young man in his twenties standing behind him with a smile on his face. The man had dark blond hair and striking blue eyes. Seth was drawn to the man's eyes; they seemed to convey the wisdom of many years.

"Hello! My name is Dr. Russell Healey," the man said, coming closer. "And you are?" he asked, smiling.

"My name is Seth," Seth answered, hesitantly.

"Do you have a last name?" Russell asked.

"No," Seth said, nervously.

"Very fascinating. I knew of 47 life forms with only a first name, but now I know 48," the senator stated, then asked, "why do you have only one name?" Russell looked at Shadow and smiled. "Hello there. What a beautiful dog." Russell bent down and looked closer at Shadow. "And what is your name?" He asked him gently. Shadow stated his name and Russell nodded. "May I pet you?" Shadow walked closer to Russell and let him pet him.

Seth was too preoccupied with trying to formulate an answer to this question. He was told, by the woman that cared for him, that his mother wanted to call him Seth; he liked the name, so he accepted it.

"I was told it was my name and so I became Seth," he answered with nervousness.

Russell smiled. "A straightforward answer is always best," he said. The senator walked over to the door. "Class is in session," he said as he opened the door and beckoned Seth inside. Seth entered the room to find chairs arranged in a five-by-five formation. "Choose any seat," Russell instructed him. Seth and Shadow moved across the room and selected the third chair on the far-right side. Russell seated himself at the desk at the front of the room. Directly behind him sat a chalkboard equipped with a piece of chalk floating in the air. The door again opened and a girl entered the room. Russell looked up at the girl and smiled. "Hello, Serena," he said, with a pencil dangling from his mouth. He removed the pencil and motioned for her to find a seat. Serena looked around nervously, tugging at her brown hair as she walked over to a seat near Seth. He noticed that her right hand was gloved but her left was not, an uncommon, but not unheard of, trait. Serena glanced around the room before her eyes rested on Seth and Shadow. He awkwardly looked at her and smiled nervously, feeling more uncomfortable by the moment. Serena smiled back and blushed turning away.

Slowly, more students began to file into the room. Within a few minutes, half the seats were occupied.

Finally, when the room seemed to be filled to capacity, Senator Healey stood and looked at the students. "Hello," he said dramatically, "My name is Dr. Russell Healey, and I am here to teach you about prophesiers and the history of Terinta." The senator snapped his fingers and small desks appeared in front of Seth and other pupils. On each desk sat a book entitled "A Fun Way to Think of History."

"Now, before we start, please take the book and examine it. Do not worry; the books are very clean," Russell said happily. Seth opened his book and began to flip through the pages. He reached the end and studied the inside of the back cover. The page appeared blank at first, but Seth soon spotted some faint writing near the edge of the cover, "chaos is coming."

Seth pondered the words for a while then shrugged and turned to the beginning of the book again.

Russell looked at everyone, his face filled with excitement. "Each of you has a goal of some sort in this class," he began. "I'm here to help you find the best way to accomplish them. For now, it is best that we learn the basic history of Terina. This class is but one of four to five courses in which you will learn more mathematics, battle skills, magic, writing, science, and many other subjects, depending on what you desire to do, of course," Russell said with a friendly smile. "Each of you will take history from me, the art of battle from a man named Coven, and magic and the art of wand-making will be from an expert in that subject named Kitty," he went on. "Now, I don't want any of you to hate these classes," Russell said, pointing his finger in the air. "Learning should be fun, but informative. I plan to make this history class very engaging, and I know each of you will enjoy the rest of your other classes. However, I must warn you," Russell stated, fixing them all with a stern gaze, "these classes will be vigorous and demanding. If you stay current with your work, you will succeed, but if you fall behind, you will likely fail. Now, shall we get started?" Russell asked rhetorically, clapping his gloved hands with glee. "Good," Dr. Healey answered himself with a flourish.

"Prophesiers 101," he stated. As he spoke, the chalk moved across the board and wrote the title. Russell cleared his throat and continued. "Long before Terina was discovered, there was a group of wizards known as the Order of Nog." Seth listened carefully, while others, like Serena, began to take notes. "These wizards could foresee the future thanks to a life form known as a prophecy orb." Russell studied the class and smiled. "Who can tell me what a prophecy orb is?"

One of the students raised their hand, allowing the senator to call on them. "Prophecy orbs are balls of energy, said to be the oldest form of magic in all of Terinta. They are highly empathic, which means they feel others' emotions."

Russell nodded in agreement. "That's correct," he congratulated the student. "Because they are so empathic, the prophecy orbs have a policy of nonviolence. You'll never see a prophecy orb fight or hurt anyone. In the most extreme circumstances, prophecy orbs may die if the pain of others around them is too much to bear," he explained. "Now, let's fast-forward to the humans of Terinta. By this time, prophesiers are barely emerging. The wizards of Nog were fractured by infighting long ago, and a large faction of them are trying to begin a new life in a new world. This marks the beginning of the time of recording," Russell explained as the chalk continued to write words on the board. "Who knows what the time of recording is?"

Serena raised her hand and Russell called on her. "The time of recording is when people began to record their history for future generations. It started with the fable of Terinta's creation to the beginning of the Dragon Wars."

"Yes," Russell nodded. "The time of recording is when the calendar that we currently use was adopted. It was during this time that much was created and much was destroyed. The first of the prophesiers fought in the Dragon Wars while trying to find a new place to call home. At the end of the wars, the prophesiers discovered an abandoned city once ruled by mighty dragons of many colors, or the rainbow dragons. This city was ideal for them, so they made it their own." Russell walked to the front of his desk and put his hands behind his back. "This city was later named Remtaya, for unknown reasons. Some say it was a password for something, while others believe it is the name of the Great One himself. Yet, many hold that the name was a joke from one of the founders." The class laughed knowingly.

The senator continued to explain how the prophesiers were a racially diverse part of the creation of Remtaya, and how they helped develop most of the city's laws and beliefs. Seth listened intently, keeping mental notes of anything important. Occasionally, Russell would ask the class if they knew specific dates in Remtayan history or to explain why certain time periods had specific names. While Seth knew most of the answers, he never raised his hand to answer the senator's questions.

"Now," Russell said, looking at an outline of Terina the chalk had drawn, "Remtaya is here." As he spoke, the chalk drew a star at the top right edge of the map. "And, the current year is two thousand three hundred sixty-nine ADW," he said before turning around to stare at the class. "Who can tell me what is so important about this date?" Seth wasn't surprised as nearly everyone raised their hands; anyone who paid attention to basic information knew that date very well. "Yes, Literasaya," Russell said to a girl on the other side of the room.

"That day is when the wizard saved our city from destruction," she said with a smile.

"We don't know who it was exactly," Russell said, with a nod, "but, you're right. That day marks the transformation of our great city from a place of poverty and death, to one of the most beautiful, prosperous cities in the world." The floating chalk hovered idly behind the senator before he waved his gloved right hand and it drifted down to the desk. "Thanks to this power, we are able to live our daily lives. It definitely helped the city's prophesiers." Russell turned to the chalkboard and rested his hand on its surface. With a swift, sweeping motion, he moved from the board, holding both his hands out in front of him. Seth and the rest of the class gasped as the drawing of Terina quickly flew off the chalkboard into the middle of the room. The image floated in the air as Seth and the others tilted their heads to get a better look. Professor Healey moved his hands together before slowly spreading them apart again. As he did, the image appeared to zoom in toward the chalk star. Seth watched as the star slowly morphed into a small oval that grew larger and larger until a bird's eye view of the city came into view.

Countless buildings, homes, and shops that rested safely inside Remtaya appeared. In the heart of the city, Seth saw the castle citadel where all city planning and ceremonies took place. The citadel was connected to the border wall via a partition which bisected the city. Remtaya still appeared to be drawn by chalk as the senator zoomed in further, slowly pulling his hands apart. Seth looked up at a seemingly unimportant section of the wall that guarded the city. "Who can tell me how Remtaya's wall was built and, more importantly, who built it?" Russell asked, as they all looked up at the image. A boy sitting near Seth raised his hand, allowing the senator to call on him.

"I know it was designed by architects who were also prophesiers," the boy stated. "Building started before the city was given its great gift, but construction was halted for being over time and over budget."

Russell nodded. "Correct. Before the gift, the King and Queen ordered the prophesiers to build a wall around Remtaya. This was a last and desperate attempt to keep people out of the already overpopulated city. However, after we received the gift, construction was ordered to continue. This was mainly to protect the people and the city from the war that followed. The prophesier builders found that not only was construction easier and safer, but the city itself seemed to come alive as the citizens helped build the wall. The most prominent place where this occurred was the prophecy chamber, which you are currently viewing aerially," Russell explained. "While the chamber was built before the barrier, the city somehow constructed the wall around the compartment, reinforcing and strengthening it."

One of the class members raised their hand, causing the senator to call on them. "I thought the prophecy chamber was built by the prophesiers," they said, with confusion in their voice.

Russell smiled and shook his head. "While the prophesiers filled the chamber with history books and documents, the chamber is actually much older than that. Some historians believe the dragons built the chamber long ago. Others assert that the chamber may be much older, making it one of the most ancient structures on this planet. Some even contend that the Kry may have built it," he clarified. Seth looked around the classroom as some students whispered the word Kry under their breath. A sense of anxiety settled over the class. "But," Russell drew the class's attention back to their lesson, "that will be a lesson for a later time. For now, let's discuss how the prophesiers finished building the wall."

The chatter subsided and the students again listened intently as Russell related how the prophesiers shaped Remtaya. After explaining how the spell over the city helped with the wall's construction, the senator waved his hand in the air and the chalk image again appeared on the chalkboard behind him.

"Now," Russell said with a kind smile, "before the end of class, we are going to discuss modern Terinan history." He looked around the room with his kind blue eyes and walked to the front of his desk. "Prophesiers have a deep understanding of the past, but they are holders of the present. As guardians of knowledge, one of their most important tasks is to chronicle the history of the world, as it is happening or about to happen. Therefore, at the end of each class session, we will discuss current events, and debate their importance in the present and future." The senator straightened his back as he sat at the front of his desk. "Because this is our first class together, I'll begin this discussion, but next time I'll call on one of you to start," he promised. Seth gulped nervously. He was afraid of that.

"Let's get the big event out of the way. We are at war," the senator said bluntly. "Now, the question is, with whom?"

"Kondoma," most of the class said in unison.

"Correct, and why?" he asked calmly, nodding his head.

"Because of the evil king," a boy with black hair stated. Many of the others in the class nodded in agreement.

"Why are we fighting the King of Kondoma?" Russell asked simply, moving the discussion along.

"It's a battle against good and evil," the same boy stated.

"I disagree," a girl next to him said calmly. The rest of the class watched closely. "This war is based on a failure to listen," she expressed. "After the end of the Kry Wars, Terina was fractured and Kondoma was suffering. While I believe it is our right to fight them, I also think that the violence could have been stopped if people would have listened."

"You can't listen to Kondomans, they're all liars!" another boy interjected. Some of the students nodded while Seth and the others watched the discussion unfold.

"I think it was Kondoma's fault that the war started, but I also see that the fighting could have stopped if people could have deliberated reasonably," another girl in the class stated.

"There were peace talks, many times in fact," Russell explained to the class, "however, due to differing ideas and growing conflict, our respective kingdoms were unable to resolve their differences."

"I think the Kondomans are barbarians!" a girl sitting next to Serena said passionately. "My cousin is part of the Remtayan army, and he writes to my family often about the awful things the Kondoman army does."

"I agree," the boy to the right of Seth replied. "My two older brothers are in the army. Last winter a good friend of theirs was killed and based on the story they told my parents it proves they are monsters."

"That is an interesting, real scenario you have shared, Eathsen," Russell said. "As war drags on, people are being killed on both sides. Our army is actually smaller, but it is supplied and trained well, while the Kondoman army is larger but more poorly trained. This means we are fairly evenly matched. When do you think it is appropriate to fight, and when is surrender in order? Is it worth losing lives?"

Seth listened to most of the conversation as his fellow classmates discussed various topics about the war. He knew Russell expected everyone to participate, so he made a few comments, making sure nothing was too controversial. Seth shared many of his opinions, so he felt his view was thoroughly expressed.

After a good thirty minutes passed, Russell stood and nodded to the class. "Unfortunately, that is all the time we have for today," he said with a slight frown. "Your journey to the future is just beginning. We will meet each Tuesday to learn about all sorts of wonderful things. Next week, we will learn more about the aftermath of the Kry Wars and their effect on Terina," he explained excitedly.

Seth rose from his desk and waited for most of his new classmates to exit before he walked to the door.

"Have a good day, Seth and Shadow," Russell called from behind him.

Seth turned and thanked the senator before leaving the room.

CHAPTER EIGHT

A Talk with Friends

K itty stood beside Seth watching his every move. Seth held the simple wooden wand in his gloved right hand and pointed it at the target. Kitty studied his form and nodded, showing approval of his stance.

"Think of the spell carefully. Let the words flow through your mind before speaking," Kitty instructed.

Seth concentrated on the spell he wanted to use and let it move through his mind like a trickling stream. The words were there, but he was unable to concentrate on them due to the feeling of magic moving over his body. The rivulets of energy moved quickly as he heard himself utter the words with more force than he preferred. The wand he held vibrated rapidly as it came to life, shooting a blue burst of magic at a bullseye across the sparring chamber. The magic whistled violently through the air and hit the sack of straw, causing it to burst.

"Wow," Kitty said, looking at the demolished sack. "There's no doubt that you have a powerful proclivity for magic." She looked at him closely, her green eyes examining him. "Do you suffer from headaches when you use magic?" she asked.

Seth nodded. "I also have them when I read others' minds. Is that bad?" he asked nervously.

Kitty's eyes widened slightly. "Most humans must learn to read others' minds. You have a rare gift," she responded. "Have you had this all your life?"

Seth nodded again. "Is that bad?" he asked once more.

"No," Kitty told him with a smile, "it's rare, but not unheard of." She put her hands on her hips and appeared deep in thought, her eyes gazing off into the distance. "Biz and Shadow are the two dogs you brought here, right?" she asked him.

"You remember their names?" Seth asked her in surprise.

"Sure," Kitty stated. "You're friends with Evan, and a friend of his is a friend of mine. I like to keep track of what my friends like," she expressed.

"You think of me as your friend?" Seth asked shyly.

"Of course!" Kitty clarified. "You've been here for about three months now, so I'd like to think of us as fairly well acquainted. Now, I was going to ask, can you hear Biz and Shadow talk to you?" she asked with interest.

Seth nodded slowly. "Yes, I think I'm an Ayomancer. I can hear all animals." he stated with a nervous grin. Being an Ayomancer was a pretty rare gift to have so Seth wasn't sure how Kitty would take it.

Kitty simply shrugged and held up her own wand, its entire wooden shaft covered with elegant etchings. "As I said during class, magic is everywhere," she explained. "Experts have discovered that an invisible energy field covers the entire earth. It seems to flow through and around all things, and it's considered to be the basic form of mystic energy," she explained. Seth nodded as he recalled that class session a few weeks ago. "Do you remember how we use spells?" Kitty asked.

"Singing," Seth stated tentatively.

"Basic rhythmic harmonics," Kitty clarified. She put her wand away and held out her hands. Closing her eyes, she slowly started to move her hands up and down. As she moved her hands through the air, she began to hum a simple tone. Seth watched as tiny wisps of gray sparkling magic formed around her hands. She stopped her humming and moved her hands up and down one last time before folding them, the wisps of magic fading away. "It's thanks to the simple rhythm that is created by someone's voice that causes the energy around us to vibrate and take visible form," she explained. She took out her wand and pointed it at another bullseye. "When we use a spell while using a wand, the magic is translated through the wand and becomes more focused. Plus you don't have to sing out the words like a magician would." Kitty gazed at the bullseye with confidence. "Infirnate," she incanted. A burst of fire launched out of the wand and zoomed at the bullseye. Unlike Seth's target, the mark didn't explode. Once the fire hit the goal it burst into flames. "When you become better trained you don't even have to speak words aloud" Kitty explained to him.

"Which is better, harmonic or nonharmonic magic?" Seth asked.

"They both have their strengths and weaknesses," Kitty explained. "Most wizards and witches use harmonic magic because it is far more powerful than static spell casting."

"Are you considered a witch?" Seth asked, curious about the subject.

Kitty laughed and shook her head. "No," She chuckled. "I'd be considered as a sorcerer or just a practitioner of magic. However, being a wandmaker by trade I'm in a classification all my own. I learned most of the facts of harmonic and static magic use when I was studying to become a wandmaker. Harmonic magic is all about vibration through a voice or a special instrument, while static magic is using mystic energy that is inside a magical object. I personally like static magic because I'm a wandmaker, and I'm not a good singer." She joked with a wink.

Seth chuckled and smiled with a nod. "Neither am I." He stated. "I have a terrible singing voice."

"Really?" Kitty asked, looking at him with confusion. "The higher pitch to your voice might make you really good at it." She observed. A twinge of hurt came over Seth as Kitty mentioned the pitch of his voice.

He supposed it was just a reflection of the times Zimpher and his gang had bullied him over it. "You okay?" Kitty asked, noticing Seth's slightly hurt expression.

"I'm fine," he told her with a smile. "You just caught me off guard for a second."

"I'm sorry," She apologized kindly. "That observation wasn't an insult."

"I'm fine with the way I sound," Seth explained truthfully. "I'm just used to most people older than me teasing me about it."

Kitty nodded. "I get that," she said. Kitty looked over to a section of the chamber where Evan and Shadow were sitting. He had brought Seth over to practice and was waiting for him to finish up. "Evan told me that you were teased before you came here," Kitty said looking back at Seth. "He seemed worried about you."

Seth smiled and nodded. "We all were bullied once in a while." He explained. "A group of other orphans at another home liked to pick on younger kids. But it's never been serious." Seth said looking over at where Evan was sitting. "When Evan was still with me at the orphanage, he would help keep the bullies away. But, Remtaya also has a no violence policy so the law enforcement kept me and the others safe."

"You can thank the Queen for that," Kitty told him with a smile. "She observes that while Remtaya was a very safe place, there was still crime in the city. She set down laws that have helped keep Remtaya a better city to live in." Kitty looked up at a window that had light shining down to the floor close to them. "Times almost up," she told him with a smile. "Let's practice some more of your magic using.

Evan looked across the court, watching Seth and Kitty dueling with wands. Kitty laughed as one of Seth's spells shot the wrong direction.

"What is so funny?" Evan asked himself out loud.

"What is?" Someone said behind him. Evan looked back to see a young girl with long, dirty brown hair standing behind him.

"It's nothing, Serena." Evan lied.

Serena looked at him as she sat down. Shadow gave a happy whine and moved closer to Serena. She smiled and stared to pet him as she looked at Evan. Her eyes had a passive contemplation to them, it made her appear to always have something calming yet important on her mind. "When did you first have a crush on Kitty?" She asked simply. Evan looked at her, not sure what to tell her about his feelings for Kitty. Serena smiled and shook her head, "you do not have to answer," she said.

"I do find her attractive," Evan said with nervousness. His nervousness was mostly due to Serena's father, who until around two years ago was courting Kitty.

"I never wanted to get in the way of Kitty and Orin," Evan explained, shrugging his shoulders.

Serena laughed slightly like she found what he said funny. "Dad is very observant about almost everything else but romantic feelings, he has no idea." she clarified. "Plus, I think he'd be fine with it."

Serena looked over at Seth and Kitty as they dueled unaware of what they were talking about. They both watched for a while as Kitty seemed to be explaining how to focus his energy more. "Remember, magic is like music," Evan heard Kitty explain. He saw Seth watch as she pointed at her wand and used a small spell as an example. Serena sat still watching the discussion with an understanding look on her face. Suddenly, she straightened as if she forgot something. As she turned her head looking behind the other direction, a smile formed on her mouth. Evan turned as well to find a man with messy raven black hair walking up to them. The man had broad shoulders and a lean waist with muscular arms. He had a wide smile across his handsome face as he calmly moved toward where Serena was sitting.

"Dad!" Serena yelled happily. She hopped off the bench and ran excitedly to the burly man before she jumped at him with her arms wide.

"Woho." Orin stated as Serena almost pushed him over when he bent down for her to hug him. "I wasn't gone for that long." He said, giving a soft chuckle while patting her lovingly on the head. "How've you been?" He asked Serena, his voice warm and soothing as he tousled her hair with his hand.

Serena chuckled as Orin showed his affection for his daughter. "Good, but better now," Serena said as Orin stood up. Her nose barely reached her father's broad chest.

The sound of Kitty laughing once more caught Evan's attention and he looked back to see what she was laughing about.

"Hi, Evan," Orin said as he and Serena walked over to him.

"Orin," Evan said standing, looking up at his tall well-built friend. He shook his hand happily before they all three sat back down. "How was the mission?" Evan asked Orin as he sat next to him and Serena.

Orin looked at Evan kindly. His sapphire blue eyes seemed to gleam with life, giving Evan the feeling that Orin was an intelligent and wise man. Orin shrugged his large shoulders while also pressing one side of his lips together to give a short hum sound. His head was slightly tilted to the right and his good-looking face gave the appearance of calmness mixed with unsureness. "Everything went fine for the most part." He explained as he stroked the black three-day-old stubble under his chin. His facial-hair seemed to perfectly complement his natural handsomeness. "But, Coven shouldn't have come with us, his war happy attitude almost ki…" Orin stopped and turned his stare on Serena giving her a nervous smile. "Almost compromised part of the mission." He restated turning his nervous grin into a happy expression. He was obviously trying to make Serena feel more comfortable.

Serena frowned and punched him on his upper arm. "What happened?" She asked with a scowl, worry in her voice. "You told me the mission wasn't going to be dangerous."

Orin gently rubbed his right arm and shrugged. Evan had to smile a little as Orin was playfully pretending that Serena's punch actually affected him. "It wasn't." He defended, smiling at her in an attempt to soothe her apparent distress. "It was a simple map tracking operation; we also were sending supplies to the troops about to ship out past Selsen. We all thought the trip would be uneventful, but Coven got a little antsy when a group of bandits jumped us on the way home."

"Bandits!" Evan and Serena both said with shock.

"I had the whole thing under control," Orin said, chuckling, finding their shock amusing. "Coven, however, got overzealous and started threatening them. I had to wolf out and scare away the bandits before anyone got hurt." He explained.

"You became a wolf?" Evan asked, interest crossing his face like that of a rising breeze. He loved hearing stories of Orin using his werewolf abilities. The thought that one of his friends was a big strong lycanthrope always amazed Evan. However, the thing that really made Evan feel lucky to be friends with Orin was that he was a legend. There was always talk of the tales of the mighty Orin Wolfhart, one of the most honorable men in all Terinta. Evan loved to hear the tales from the actual source, Orin himself.

One of the fun things Evan enjoyed hearing about from Orin, was his adventures he had when he was looking for Serena. It was a surprise to Evan to hear that Orin was actually not Serena's biological father. He was her uncle. Orin took care of Serena after her parents died. He thought it was sweet of Serena to call Orin her father and he called her his daughter. It showed how much they cared for each other.

Orin like most werewolves was very handsome. Even noticed it was a type of rugged handsomeness. Many compared the werewolves to the legends of the elves, where the elves were believed to be very fair and beautiful. However, Evan didn't agree with that comparison. The werewolves he had seen namely Orin were very striking, but their beauty felt more of the earth not some ethereal magical beings.

"Ya," Orin said with a mischievous and attractive smile. "I scared the crap out of the bandits and Coven, but I also spooked the horses which almost hurt others in the group. But, I must admit, freaking Coven out was almost worth all that hassle." He stated, still grinning.

Serena smiled and giggled under her breath. "Well, I'm happy you're okay, it seems like you had everything handled."

"I always do." He told her with a wink. "Plus, Coven wanted to get back here as soon as possible. We got word that Rogan was close to discovering who the next chosen one is." Orin looked at Evan with concern. He was asking if Rogan had discovered anything more about the next chosen one. Evan sighed and shook his head no.

"Rogan is awake but still weak. Agatha doesn't want him to overexert himself yet." Evan explained with a frown. "Whatever he saw in his prophecy orb was very powerful. Not even Llivenar, Rogan's orb, is able to understand the prophecy."

"I better go see him eventually," Orin said, looking more concerned than cheerful.

Serena cleared her throat, Orin's words clearly worried her. "I'd prefer you'd wait until he finds the new Chosen One," Serena said sitting up straight.

"Why," Orin asked, a hint of laughter in his voice.

"They say he'll know who the Chosen One is when he sees them," Serena explained with a shrug. She was still sitting straight, and Evan started to consider that she was trying not to show how much this was worrying her.

"Kiddo, I'm certain it's not me," Orin said with a sure smile as he scooted closer to her and gave her another half-hug with his arm.

"Actually, you'd be perfect," Evan stated nonchalantly, forgetting that Serena seemed to be worried about her father possibly being the next chosen one.

Orin looked down at him. "But I'm not," he said through his teeth, motioning at Serena covertly with his eyes.

Evan suddenly realized what he said was a bit insensitive. "You're right," He recounted with a forced smile. "It's not that possible."

There was a slightly awkward silence as they continued watching Kitty help Seth with his magic. "Is that the new kid you were telling me about?" Orin asked Serena, finally breaking the growing uncomfortable silence.

"Yep, he's the one that's really good at the science and magic side of our studying," Serena said with a hint of jealousy in her voice.

Shadow gave a huff sound and Serena and Orin both looked at him. Orin laughed at something the dog said. Being a werewolf Evan knew Orin could understand dogs, cats, and wolves.

"I don't think we've met." Orin said to Shadow with a kind smile. He asked what Shadow's name was and then nodded when Shadow appeared to somehow answer him.

"Nice to meet you Shadow." He said scratching the dog's right ear. "I think you're right, Seth does seem good with magic," Orin said as they all watched with slight interest. "Not that I know much about how to use magic." He stated with a disinterested shrug.

Evan watched Seth use a spell that shot a blue light at a target, hitting it right in the middle.

"Seth has always been good with magic," Evan said with a bit of pride in his voice. He was happy that Seth was good at something, he knew how depressed Seth could get when he felt worthless.

"You know him?" Orin asked, turning to Evan with interest.

Evan looked back at Orin and Serena giving a positive nod. "Seth and I were friends before I came here." He explained as he folded his arms.

Orin looked over at Seth with an inquisitive stare. "He's *that* Seth?" He asked pointing over to him with surprise showing in his powerful blue eyes.

"Yes," Evan said. "Why are you surprised?" He questioned, raising his eyebrow slightly.

Orin shrugged. "When you told us about Seth I imagined a scrawny boy who was shy and had severe social problems." He characterized, continuing to watch Seth practicing with Kitty. "I mean he's not muscular or anything, but I wouldn't describe him as scrawny," Orin expressed observing Seth closely.

"I never said he was scrawny." Evan defended. "You are right about him being shy." Evan chuckled a little while thinking about Seth's issues. "And he does have some social problems."

"Like what?" Serena asked looking over at Seth and Kitty. "All I've noticed is he's really shy."

"He has a problem with shaking people's hands, gets nervous in large crowds and thinks all humans look too much like monkeys. Oh, and to add to that, he hates monkeys." Evan explained.

Orin's eyes widened. "Really?" He asked in disbelief. Orin rested his forearms on his legs still giving Evan a disbelieving stare.

Evan smiled a little mischievously at Orin. "If you find Seth coming down the hall, see what happens if you hold out your hand for him to shake. He will be perfectly polite to you because he doesn't want to hurt anyone's feelings, but he will hesitate when you naturally insist." He explained, still smiling.

"I can see how people could look like monkeys," Serena commented randomly.

Evan and Orin both looked at her for a second. Suddenly there was a sound of a giant bell in the distance.

"Oh, sorry I have to go," Evan said, getting up and waving Seth toward him.

"See you later," Evan said to Orin and Serena as he walked over to Seth.

CHAPTER NINE

THE COMING OF SETH

Time is a very mysterious and beautiful topic to discuss. Ethiristicists, philosophers and all other inhabitants of the universe have contemplated the meaning of time.

Let's quickly review what is currently happening in Seth's life. Four months have passed since he left the orphanage. It has been a time of vigorous training and study for him. During his matriculation, Seth has been throughout the castle, studying history and science with Senator Healey, honing his fighting skills with Coven (at which he is failing miserably) and mastering the art of magic with Kitty. Seth has been busy these last few months and it only took nine chapters to tell the tale thus far. Time is such a fascinating concept, isn't it?

S eth sat at a long table in what appeared to be a spacious and elegant dining room. He looked around and noticed that he was holding a cloth napkin in his gloved left hand and a sword in his right. All around him lay the remnants of fruits and vegetables. He looked up again see the black horse with blue stockings mounted by the same two-headed figure.

"Oh no, not again!" Seth groaned.

"Look what you did," the face of Kitty said solemnly.

The face of Evan smiled and laughed. "They didn't have a chance," he said gleefully.

Seth looked around the room still dripping with splattered food. "Why am I having this dream again?" he asked angrily.

Evan, Kitty, and the horse looked at him with shock. "You're aware of this place?" Evan asked in horror.

"How do you know of the Tesseract?" Kitty asked.

Seth rolled his eyes in annoyance. "I heard Senator Healey speak of Tesseracts, and this place is definitely not a Tesseract. I am only dreaming," he explained wisely. Suddenly, a floating object appeared in the sky. It continually twisted and folded, never maintaining a defined shape. "That is a Tesseract," Seth explained.

"Neigh, liar!" the horse yelled.

"Sure, Senator Healey did mention that Tesseracts aren't visible to the naked eye, but that *is* a shadow of one," Seth replied. He turned to look at the two-headed monstrosity and the rather adorable horse. "Well, goodbye," he said happily with a feeling of complete confidence. "I'm leaving this madness." As he turned to leave, Seth could hear the pulverized produce crying. The entire room began to shake and the food fragments, along with the two-headed figure and horse, were thrown into the air. As the room's contents began to plummet toward the ground, Seth held up his arms and stopped the falling objects in midair.

"You have taken over the realm," the floating horse and figure said together.

"I have taken over my dream, you mean," Seth clarified. Suddenly the room plunged into darkness and a booming voice erupted out of the void.

"Do not kill!" the voice screamed.

Seth awoke, startled by the intensity of the dream. He laid still, pondering what had just happened. The chirping of birds echoed outside his window as the light from the rising sun filtered into his room. Seth sat up and saw Biz and Shadow snuggled up at the end of the bed.

"Well, that's the first time I've ever had a lucid dream, but I like it," Seth said with wonder. He moved to the edge of his bed, stretching and yawning. An aching soreness moved across his arms and waist as he stretched. He sighed and stood to walk toward the bathroom to prepare for the day.

The last few weeks had been both exciting and difficult. He enjoyed his lessons with Senator Healey and Kitty, but Coven was cruel. Although he was known to be a stern and intimidating teacher, Coven seemed to take extra pleasure in Seth's discomfort. After showering and dressing, Seth emerged in his blue robes, feeling prepared to face the day. Biz and Shadow were resting on the bed, still exhausted from a long walk the day before.

"I have your food and water ready. Don't get into trouble." Seth smiled at his friends and shut the door.

Seth turned and began to walk when someone called to him from behind. He glanced back to find Soven approaching him. The chief judge's attire had changed since the last time Seth had seen him. Soven was now wearing an orange robe and a black cape. Seth also noticed that his eyes were a different color as well. They were a bright shade of green. He knew that the elite people in the city used magic to change their eye color, but this was the first time he had seen it for himself. He had noticed that his own eyes changed color when using spells, but this seemed overly excessive.

"Hello, Seth! Hitting it hard?" Soven asked, smiling widely as he approached.

Seth felt uneasy and awkward. He hardly knew Soven, and his remark didn't help. He looked down at the ground. "Hit what hard?" he asked quietly.

Soven's booming laugh echoed through the halls while Seth smiled nervously still confused by the first question. "It is an expression. It means 'are you ready for the day?'" Soven explained, still chuckling.

Seth kept his nervous smile as he tried to think about what to say to the senator. "Forgive me," He explained very timidly, "but it sounds like abuse." He mumbled.

Soven chuckled. "As I said, it is an expression." He explained with a shrug. Soven moved closer to him and smiled. "You're still very quiet Seth." He expressed with complete honesty. "I was once like you, weak, scrawny, squeaky, unimportant, unsure." He said standing up straight and looking off into the distance. Seth listened to him, trying not to feel too insulted by the words he was using to describe him. "I was completely replaceable, just another human in the long run of boring generic people." He expressed with a wise sulk on his face. Seth frowned a little as he stared up at the senator. *Thanks, how flattering*, he thought sarcastically. "But," Soven said looking down at him, "then I learned that I could do more, all that was holding me back was myself." He smiled down at him with perfectly straight, white teeth. "You know what I'm saying?" he asked. Seth nodded unsure what to actually say. "Oh right." Soven suddenly snapped reaching into his robe pocket. "I was supposed to give you this." He said, holding out his hand. Seth looked at the hand to find that Soven was not holding anything. "Oh. Pardon me." Soven said with a chuckle. "Parkens must still have it." He said looking behind him. "Parkens, where are you?" Soven yelled loudly. The same man that Seth had seen a few months ago ran stumbling around the bend. He was panting and had in his hand what looked like a letter. "Where were you?" Soven asked with what sounded like anger, yet Seth could empathically sense that he was joking around with Parkens.

"Sorry, sir." Parkens apologized breathing hard. "I cannot keep up with you when you run." He panted.

"Well, then you need to get into shape." Soven accused him, swiping the letter from his hand.

Seth chuckled under his breath at seeing this odd behavior.

"What is funny?" Soven asked Seth interested in the humor.

Seth smiled shyly and shrugged it off. "It's nothing," He instead now felt nervous and bashful.

"Its Parkens isn't it," Soven said looking at his servant. "His clumsy attitude and his wholehearted need to please make him a fun-loving clown." He stated while nudging Parkens in the shoulder.

"Thank you, sir," Parkens said with a wince and a bow.

"Now here you go," Soven said, holding out the letter to Seth.

Seth graciously took the letter and opened it trying to not feel as unsure of himself.

I, Senator Russell Healey, do sponsor the training of Seth and do support his choice to learn on becoming an Ethiristicist.

Seth looked at the letter with wide eyes as he read it to himself. He looked up at Soven who was gazing down at him with a wide smile. "What does this mean?" he asked, holding the letter up to him.

Soven took the paper and read over it while nodding. "Congratulations." He said happily. "It is official. You are now being sponsored by Senator Healey."

"What does that exactly mean?" Seth asked nervously.

Soven moved closer to him putting his arm around his shoulders as they started to walk down the hall.

"It means that if you ever need help with something that has to do with you reaching your dreams, Russell will help you." Soven said. "So where are you going?" He asked his arm still on his shoulders.

"Evan wants to show me his prophecy orb," Seth explained bashfully.

"Oh, well good luck with that." Soven began. "You know I once…" Soven started but then was interrupted by Parkens.

"Sir, I am sorry but you have a meeting with the King and Queen right now." Parkens insisted.

"Oh my, you are right." Soven said taking his arm off Seth's shoulders and walking back the way they had come. "It seems like there is never enough time in the day," Soven said looking at Parkens. "I wanted to drop off the letter personally, but now I'm late." He complained. Soven turned around and looked at Seth again. "Oh, say hi to Evan for me, and make sure you meet Rogan if he's up and about over there." He told Seth before running the other direction leaving Parkens alone to catch up.

"Sorry," Seth told Parkens.

Parkens shrugged. "It's all good fun." He said before he ran after him.

The hall was mostly empty as Seth walked alone, thinking about what he was going to do for the day. The light from the top of the ceiling shone gracefully through the glass chandeliers that hung like motionless icicles. Making sure he was going the right direction Seth turned to the left and looked down a hall that didn't bend like the long hallway his room was in. A sign at the corner where Seth was standing read "Section Transport Room." He walked down the hallway looking down at the blue carpet on the floor while hearing how the sound of his foot beats seemed to echo louder than he thought they would have.

Seth walked down the long hallways alone thinking about how it would feel when he first looked through a prophecy orb. He then turned left and then made a quick right. He found himself at a dead end with a door at the very end of it. Seth calmly walked to the end of the hall with his hands behind his back. When he reached the door he opened it and walked in. Inside was a room that was as big as a medium-sized closet. Seth calculated that around seven grown people could fit comfortably inside. He looked at a paper that was attached to the back of the door that he just opened. The paper had various names on it. Seth looked down the paper until he saw the words library/prophecy chamber. Seth then looked at the brown door.

"Take me to the prophecy chamber please," Seth said clearly. There was a flash of light and a noise that could be described as beeping. He opened the door to find himself in another section of the castle. He was looking down a hallway that ended abruptly showing another part of a larger hall perpendicular to it. He sighed and smiled marveling at how convenient the transporter rooms of the castle were. As he started walking down the hall, a few other prophesiers caught his eye as they walked past his viewpoint. His nerves began to increase a little at the sight of people that appeared to be going where he was. He turned the corner and into the next hallway to find two very complex massive doors to his right. Seth silently and shyly followed the two prophesiers as they walked over to the massive doors, opening one of them by pushing on it. As they did, Seth was bombarded by a cacophony of voices in the chamber. He saw that there were a lot of prophesiers talking to one another before the door closed and all fell silent again. He stood there looking at the ornate doors with nervousness growing inside of him. There were a lot of people in the chamber, people that he definitely didn't know. He stood staring at the massive doors for more than a while thinking about what he should do. *I could always leave and come back later.* He thought to himself. *No, Evan is waiting for you in there, go in, they're just people.* He argued mentally. *Yes, people that are germy, and loud.* He countered his own argument. *Fine go, you can explain to Evan why you didn't show up. Think how sad he'll be.* Seth suddenly imagined Evan weeping at his door and saying how his life was useless since he couldn't show him all the amazing things in the prophecy chamber. His visions changed to Evan lying in a coffin while Kitty wept over his lifeless form. *"If only you would have just let him show you all that cool stuff."* She sobbed while glaring at him. Seth's imaginings quickly faded, and he gave a soft sigh of concern before he walked over to the doors and pushed one of them open. He was slightly amazed at how light the door felt as it slid open, but his interest in the door quickly changed to stress. He looked around the noisy crowd at all the prophesiers, voices of many people started to flood his head making him cringe and look around frantically for Evan. As he scanned the massive chamber, he saw that along with the people in the chamber were blue orbs of various sizes that floated calmly in the air. He also saw some human-shaped blue colored entities talking with some of the prophesiers in the chamber. His eyes moved over the crowd until he spotted Evan talking to a floating blue orb.

He quickly walked down the few steps that led to the floor of the chamber before making his way through the crowd of prophesiers. "Evan." He yelled over the loud room.

Evan turned to see Seth and beckoned him over. As he moved toward him Seth heard some of the prophesiers asking each other if a new Chosen One had been identified yet. Seth passed the people and hurried over to Evan and the blue orb.

"What is going on," Seth asked, trying not to listen to the voices that were outside and inside his mind. "It was not this crowded last time I was here." He stated.

"Sorry." Evan apologized. "The last time you were here all the prophesiers had gone, but it has been very busy and loud ever since Rogan foresaw the next Chosen One." He explained.

Master Evan, the orb next to them spoke calmly. *May I suggest we find a quieter location?*

Seth's interest grew as he heard the voice of the orb both in his mind *and* with his ears.

"A good idea Lordren," Evan said.

Seth followed Evan and Lordren deeper into the prophecy chamber, moving into one of the passages created by the massive bookshelves standing high over them. Seth stared at one of the tall bookshelves, marveling at how many books one of the enormous mantles held. It almost seemed like the whole shelf was completely full. He noticed a book with silver edging inscribed on its spine as they walked past it. *The Life and Extinction of the Elves,* he read to himself.

They eventually stopped as they came to the middle of the two bookstands. Seth looked up at two other bookshelves that were in front of them, the four shelves only separated from each other by a few meters. Seth stared left to right noticing that in both directions, the massive bookshelves appeared to go on forever. Without speaking he formed the word "wow" with his mouth, amazed at the endless massiveness of the prophecy chamber.

"Allow me to introduce you two," Evan said acknowledging Seth and Lordren. "Lordren this is my best friend Seth and Seth, this is Lordren my prophecy orb." Evan introduced.

Seth turned to the blue, shimmering orb. It appeared to have some kind of substance, but also looked mostly translucent. The orb's edges seemed perfectly round like someone had sculpted it out of one piece of glass. "Hello, Lordren," Seth said with a shy smile, bowing to it.

Greetings Master Seth. Lordren spoke calmly. The orb's voice was clear and soothing, both in Seth's mind and to his ears.

Evan turned to Seth and smiled. "Lordren has agreed to let you look into him so you can get your first feel for a prophecy orb." He explained.

I will guide you through the visions so you do not become overwhelmed. Lordren stated in the same calm, male-sounding voice.

Seth looked at Evan with concern. "Are you sure?" he asked. "I'm not in training to be a prophesier, don't I need a permit or something?"

Evan laughed a little and shook his head. "You need to have permission from a prophecy orb," Evan said motioning at Lordren. "And, didn't you want to come here to learn new things in the first place? Trust me, you haven't lived until you've seen into a prophecy orb."

"Okay," Seth said nervously. He turned to Lordren and smiled shyly at it. "I do have some questions if that's okay?" He asked.

That will be acceptable. The orb calmly complied.

"I hear your voice in my mind, but I can also hear you with my ears. How are you doing this?" He asked.

All prophecy orbs speak to all living things through telepathy and a common speech. It allows us to speak with clarity and without confusion. Lordren explained.

"Fascinating," Seth admitted feeling more comfortable with the orb. "I've read about prophecy orbs but there is much I do not know. Like do you have a gender, and can you feel emotion?" He asked, interested.

All prophecy orbs are born without a gender, we then decide what we want other life forms to see us as. I sound and look male but in all the things that matter I have no gender. All prophecy orbs do have emotions. We can feel happiness, joy, and even sadness. We also can feel anger and pain but only a few of us can relay these emotions to others. I am not one of these few. Lordren explained.

"Amazing," Seth stated with an interested smile.

"Are you ready to try to see the future?" Evan asked, putting his hands on his hips.

Seth stared at him and nodded, though he was feeling a little jittery "I believe so."

Do not be afraid, I will keep you safe from the most powerful of visions. Lordren's voice stated gently.

"Okay," Seth said with a nod while walking closer to the orb.

"Good luck," Evan said smiling.

Seth lifted both his hands to the sides of the orb and instinctively closed his eyes. Suddenly his mind was conveyed to a place where he felt like he was floating. He saw what seemed to be colored strings stretched out to incredible lengths, the long strings appeared to hum pure music. Seth could hear the music move around him, filling him with energy and joy.

There was a slight shaking that startled Seth for a second, but it stopped as soon as it had started and the music around him became stronger. *Seth, can you hear me?* Lordren asked calmly.

"Yes," Seth said, feeling tranquil. "What is this place?"

Focus on one of the strings near you. Lordren instructed. Seth turned his stare on a red-looking string and focused on it. The string began to vibrate, the music changed frequency and suddenly it unraveled, opening into a spiral of light. Seth found himself looking at a dog getting a drink.

"I did it," Seth said excitedly.

Do you know this animal? Lordren asked.

Seth looked closer to find that it was Shadow. "It's Shadow, my dog." He said with interest. "Is this the future?" He asked, feeling amazed.

No. This is the present. People who look through a prophecy orb for the first time will not see the future. They will see the present state of someone they care for. Lordren explained.

The image faded away and Seth found himself with the hundreds of singing strings again.

"What are these string things?" Seth asked, looking around, noticing how his voice echoed.

Most prophesiers, or anyone who has seen the strings call them Time Lines. They connect all time together. Lordren explained.

"Time Lines," Seth said smiling. "I like that."

Focus on another one. Lordren instructed.

Seth focused on a blue Time Line. The string did the same as the other one and Seth found himself looking at the entrance to the prophecy chamber; there were still a lot of people talking. The giant doors opened and a boy wearing clothes similar to Parkens walked into the chamber. He held a small pillow with a rectangular wooden box on it. One white-haired prophesier walked over to the servant and opened the box after bowing and thanking the boy. Before Seth could see what was in the box the vision stopped. He found himself back where all the Time Lines were.

"What happened?" Seth asked.

The vision closed. It was to be expected. Lordren explained. *It is time to return.* Lordren stated calmly.

Seth found himself looking at the blue prophecy orb, his hands still holding onto it.

"So how was it?" Evan asked.

"Very fun," Seth said with a smile as he let go of the orb and turned to Evan. "I want to do that again." He said laughing.

"Did you see into the future?" Evan said, still smiling at Seth's obvious joy.

"I think so. I don't know." Seth looked at Lordren for an answer.

The last vision you saw will most likely happen in two minutes at the entrance of the prophecy chamber. Lordren predicted.

"Then let us see if you saw the future," Evan said, walking back to where they had come from. As they got closer to the entrance of the chamber, they could hear the voices get louder. The three of them waited at the end of the crowd to see if Seth's prophecy would come true. Soon the giant doors opened and the boy Seth had seen came in holding a small, square box. The white-haired man walked over and opened the small box, pulling out a piece of paper.

The man held up his hands and the entire room grew quiet.

"The Queen and King have met with Rogan and the Council and have decided to find the new Chosen One immediately." The man said. Some of the people in the chamber clapped and nodded, but most of the prophesiers appeared to be underwhelmed by the news. Seth heard someone say it was another death sentence.

"Oh great," Evan said, folding his arms and rolling his eyes in annoyance.

"I don't understand," Seth said, looking at Evan while feeling the anticipation in the chamber.

"You don't understand what?" Evan asked.

Seth looked at Evan and Lordren. "I saw the same boy and white-haired man, but the box was wrong, and I saw the boy holding a pillow, and there was a rectangular box on it, not a square one." He explained.

You saw a possible future. Lordren explained. *Contrary to popular belief what we see is not always correct.*

"That is what makes the Chosen Ones a chance also." Evan began. "So many people think that a prophecy is one-hundred percent. The Chosen One will look like this, the Chosen One will go on a great journey, and the Chosen One will kill the evil king. When in fact it is more like the Chosen One could look like this, the Chosen One could make a great journey; the Chosen One has a fifty percent chance of killing the evil king. It's just the Senate and the rest of Remtaya want to have the evil King killed so badly they will not see the truth." Evan explained sadly.

Seth nodded his head. "I understand." He said solemnly. He, Evan, and Lordren stood there watching in silence as the chamber began to become lively once more with conversation.

I feel sorry for the next Chosen One. Lordren said calmly with no tinge of emotion to what he just expressed.

Two Days Later

Seth pointed his wand at the target.

"Inferno." Seth incanted trying to move his voice up and down as Kitty had taught him. His eyes turned red and fire shot from the wand, hitting the middle part of the target.

"Good job," Kitty said behind him. "You've improved."

"I have not improved with my fighting skills," Seth stated with a frown. "I am obviously not a fighter, and I am perfectly fine with that." He added with a smile and a shrug.

Kitty laughed. "You are a person who likes peace aren't you?"

"I believe so," he said. Seth had become good friends with Kitty, there was a lot about her that reminded him of Evan, and she had become like his big sister. He never had any other siblings, but Kitty seemed to be what a sister would be like.

"I think that is all for today," Kitty stated while putting her wand away. Seth gave her the wand he used for practice and followed her out of the arena.

"Where are you heading?" Kitty asked as they walked into the western hallway.

"My room," Seth said simply. "I need to check on Biz and Shadow."

"I've been meaning to ask you," Kitty said looking at him with interest. "How did you come to have two dogs of different sizes?" She asked.

Seth smiled and looked ahead. "It happened so long ago I can hardly remember." He stated. "All I know is Biz and Shadow came to me when I was the loneliest. It was before I was sent to the city."

"Where did you live before?" Kitty asked him.

"Some small village on the border of the Conching forest," Seth explained. "I hardly remember it."

"And you never knew your mother or father?" Kitty asked, a hint of sadness in her voice.

Seth shook his head. "The woman who took care of me before she sent me to her grandparents did." He stated. "I remember her telling me that they were good people."

"It must have been difficult for you," Kitty said with a kind sisterly smoothness.

"Not really," Seth admitted. "I wish I knew them, and I have felt sad that I'll *never* know them. But," Seth stopped and looked up at the ceiling thinking about what someone else said to him once. "I've always known they loved me, which seems to be enough." He stated with a smile.

Kitty smiled down at him seemingly moved by what he said. Before she could say anything else a tall burly man walked around a nearby corner. His eyes narrowed on Seth but softened when his look turned to Kitty.

"Kitty, and Seth," Coven said with mild interest in his voice. A feeling of nervousness moved over Seth as his fighting teacher moved closer to them flashing a cocky smile. His walk was full of self-confidence and swagger as he strolled in front of them.

"Coven," Kitty said folding her arms and frowning a little. "It's been a while, I hear you didn't do so well when you went with Orin on that mapping mission."

Coven stood over both her and Seth as he grinned and laughed. "That's Orin's version, you know how he likes to make up stories." He said with his deep, loud voice. Coven flashed his brown eyes down at Seth and folded his arms over his chest. "What are you doing with her, squirt?" He boomed, sounding more accusing than inquisitive.

"He's been practicing magic with me," Kitty interjected. "Seeing as I'm his teacher in such things?"

"Too bad you can't use magic in my class," Coven said punching Seth in the arm. Seth smiled but deep down wanted to say ouch.

"If he could use magic, you wouldn't be able to touch him." Kitty jokingly countered by punching Coven back just as hard. Coven smiled at the tease but seemed to find Kitty's punch almost threatening.

"So," Coven said, changing the subject while gazing deeply at Kitty. "I heard that they are very close to finding the next Chosen One." He stated, a cunning smile forming on his face. "In fact I heard that Orin could be the next one." He said looking at Kitty intensely. He obviously wanted to see how Kitty would react.

"Now you're just being petty Coven, and cruel," Kitty said, glaring at him. "Do you really want to see a friend of yours get chosen?" She asked.

"I've heard that it could be any of us." Coven restated, evading the question.

Kitty nodded slowly in agreement. "Rogan has said that he is fairly certain the Chosen One lives in the castle. Poor soul if you ask me." She said, shaking her head.

"Well, I hope it is me," Coven said, punching out his chest. "The Great One knows we need a real warrior to kill that King, and that warrior is me." He expressed with a dark smile.

"The evil King would most certainly die from your overconfidence." Kitty muttered so only Seth could hear it.

"What?" Coven asked, gazing at her with a deep stare.

"Nothing," Kitty said, waving her hand and smiling. "I just said the evil King would not be able to handle your authoritarian might and stout will." She choked back a laugh from under her breath.

Coven looked at her, more confused than angry. The words she had used in her compliment had obviously flown over his head, which Kitty knew very well. The man may be strong, but not wise.

"Coven lifted his head higher to keep up appearances, looking at Seth with an even darker smile.

"Seth, run along please, you and the rest of your class have training with me tomorrow." He said using the same commanding tone he used in his classes. It was not a secret that Coven had been trying to court Kitty for some time, and this was just another attempt. Despite Coven's efforts, Seth felt like Kitty could handle his attempts to infatuate her with his masculinity.

"Bye," Seth said looking at Kitty who winked at him and waved farewell.

"See you later." She said as Seth walked away from them.

He walked down the hall before hearing Kitty tell Coven goodnight and walk away from him. Seth smiled and shook his head as he turned the corner where the transport room was. He had no stake in Kitty's relationships, but he knew Evan would like that she wasn't interested in Coven. He walked into the room and closed the door with a click. "Take me to Section seventy-seven please." He requested.

There was a flash of light and the sound of beeping. Seth opened the door and walked out toward his room.

As he walked, two girls walked toward him. "I heard that the chief prophesier is in his room meditating right now about who the Chosen One is." One of the girls whispered to the other one.

"I heard that they already found the Chosen One and are keeping it a secret because they are teaching them to be a master killer, so they will be ready to kill the evil king." The other girl whispered back.

Seth walked past them as they continued to gossip. *The Chosen One, that's all everyone is talking about, why are people so obsessed with another Chosen One?* Seth asked himself as he walked to his room. He opened his door to find Biz and Shadow standing on his bed.

"Hi. What are you doing?" He asked both of them.

"Did you forget to do something today?" Biz squeaked.

"What was I supposed to..." Seth stopped when he remembered. "Oh, let's go." He said beckoning Biz and Shadow out of the room. Biz and

Shadow both hopped off the bed and ran out of the room. They all three quickly walked to one of the exits that led out to a grassy section outside of the city. Seth walked up to one of the guards standing at the exit.

"Can I take my friends out for a second?" He asked. The guard looked at the other guard standing on the other side of the door before nodding at him.

"Be quick," He said with a steadfast expression on his face.

"It is not safe outside the city at night." The second guard warned.

"Thank you. We will not be long." Seth assured them shyly. He, Shadow, and Biz walked out of the doors and stepped out into the beginnings of the world that Seth had only known about through books and stories. As Seth waited for Biz and Shadow, he felt small looking out at the low wall that covered this section of the larger wall behind him. He could see over the bricks out to the long grasslands to the south. The world was so big, and he had no idea what was really out there. He felt safe in the confines of the city, and had never actually been outside of the castle walls until recently. Biz and Shadow walked up to him and they went back inside. Seth thanked the guards and walked back to his room, this time slower.

As he sat on his bed questions began to rummage through his mind. Outside beyond the city, there was a war going on. People, good people were dying on both sides. He never really thought too hard about the war, it had been going for so long and the city never got attacked, but now it was all he could think about. "The world is so big." He said out loud as he stood up from his bed and walked over to his desk. Books from his classes sat on the wooden stand cluttering up the small space. One of the books lay open with a parchment laying on the open pages. Seth looked at his own writing.

The Kry wars began when a mighty King, the King of the lost city of Ki, was murdered by a demi-Kry assassin.

Seth sat down by the desk and studied the rest of his writings as he rubbed his head, an aching feeling started to form over his brow.

Sely voge alon Anti. Meaning I serve the King of Life. Because most kings are called the King of Life, the rulers of Ki declared war on all of Terina and began the Kry war. The King of Life could also mean master of life.

Seth clenched his teeth and frowned at the words he wrote. "Why can't I write fast enough?" He asked himself while looking at the words he missed and spelled wrong. His headache was starting to get worse as his anger at the missing and wrongly used words got to him. Feeling like he wasn't going to get rid of his growing headache looking at his mistakes, he stood up from his desk and walked over to his bed resting by Biz and Shadow. *Why did that demi-Kry all those years ago kill the King of Ki? Who was the Master of Life? Why do the people of Remtaya want a Chosen One so bad? We are doomed.* Seth thought. His head started to pound more. It was like his head was getting mad at what he was thinking about, moaning in frustration he got up from his bed and walked over to the food shelf, his head throbbing harder.

"A glass of water please." He said holding his hand on his forehead. The shelf made the usual sound of magic that resembled the sound of wind chimes. Seth opened the shelf and grabbed the glass of water that was now there. He took a drink and squinted his eyes as coldness filled his head.

"Brain freeze," Seth said, trying to make his way to his bed. He hobbled over as the cold seemed to make his head want to burst. Suddenly his foot made contact with an unknown object, he tried to regain his balance but it was too late. He gasped as his body fell hard on the sturdy carpeted floor, sending his glass of water skidding across the floor, spilling water everywhere. Seth's head hit the corner of his cupboard, sending him reeling with pain.

"Ouch." He yelled as his head collided violently with the cupboard. Suddenly Seth found himself falling from the sky. The wind blew all around him and the sky was dark with clouds as the rain began to fall.

Seth screamed as he realized this was not a hallucination. He looked down to find that he was high above the city of Remtaya but rapidly falling to his imminent end.

"Oh, my Great One!" Seth screamed in horror. He was doomed as he fell ever down to the top of the castle wall.

The rain fell gently beside him. *Seeethhh.* A voice whispered beside him.

"What, who is that?" Seth demanded as he kept falling closer to the Castle wall. The voice sounded familiar like he had heard it before.

Seeethh. Look out, you are falling. The rain whispered quietly as the wind blew in Seth's face.

"I don't want to die." Seth cried out as he got closer to the walls.

Then don't. The rain whispered calmly. Seth closed his eyes as he got closer to his death.

"Nooo!" He screamed as he was inches away from the wall. He held his hands up in a futile attempt to stop himself. Suddenly, his head banged with pain and he found himself holding on for dear life to a stone rod. He looked around to find that he was somehow back in the castle but was hanging precariously high above the floor.

"What is happening?" Seth asked, panicking looking down at the hallway beneath him. "If I let go I will surely die." He said in near panic.

Then don't. A group of voices sparked as one.

"Who is there?" Seth asked, looking around in fear. There was no answer. The torches flickered harmlessly beneath him.

"Help!" Seth yelled. No one was there.

Seth began to cry. His arms were growing tired of holding on for dear life "Help me." Seth's tears falling from his face and to the faraway ground. "Please someone help me!" He sobbed.

"Is there someone there?" Someone asked below him.

"Yes!" Seth yelled looking down at the floor to see who was there. "Help, I am up here!" He yelled with vigor.

An old-looking man with gray hair and blue robes walked below him, looking around him with interest. "Where are you?" The old man asked while scanning in front of him.

"I'm up here!" Seth shouted.

The man looked up at him, his eyes growing wide with shock. "Oh my, how did you get up there young one?" He asked.

"It's a long story. Please, can you get me down?" Seth begged.

"Of course." The man said hurriedly. He held up his blue gloved hands and moved them slowly to the sides. As he did this he began to hum a soft tone. A blue fog formed around Seth until he was completely surrounded by a blue mist.

The old man held up both his hands higher and stopped humming, seeming to focus more on the magic he was wielding "You can let go now I have you." He said with confidence. Seth closed his eyes and let go, half expecting to fall. When he didn't, he opened his eyes to find that he was floating. The old man began to softly hum as he moved his hand slowly down and Seth gradually descended until he reached the floor. The blue haze around Seth dissipated as the man stopped humming. He waved his hands in the air and the mist vanished completely.

"Thank you," Seth said with happiness, gazing at the old man.

"Thank the Great One I heard you." The man said walking up to him. He wore prophecy robes and appeared to be in his late seventies, his wispy white hair was well combed, and he held an air of wisdom in his figure. "Why were you up there, can I ask?" He inquired.

"I'm not positive," Seth stated, still feeling very relieved that he was saved by the man. "I was in my room, then I slipped and hit my head and I was falling from the sky, then right before I hit the castle, I found myself hanging here." He stated thinking about his near-death experience.

"How strange." The old man said looking at Seth with his worn down, blue eyes. "You must have accidentally been transported. It is rare, but it can happen." He hypothesized. "We should get you to the hospital wing. To make sure you do not have a concussion." He decided with a kind smile.

"Okay." Seth agreed, feeling unnerved over his experience.

"My name is Rogan." The old man said, holding out his hand.

Rogan. I've heard of a Rogan. Seth thought to himself. He looked at the man's outstretched gloved hand for a second. *He did save my life.* He thought. *Plus, I think he's the chief prophesier.* "I am Seth." He said holding out his right gloved hand shyly. As both their hands touched there was a sudden flash and a bang. Seth and Rogan were thrown backward from one another. Seth slid across the floor before stopping with a pained moan. He laid there for a second, the air knocked from his lungs. His vision blurred and everything became warped. Faces and voices he didn't know or understand started to flash over his eyes and mind. A familiar woman's face looked kindly down at him before her face bent into the shape of Kitty's face. "Seth." He could barely hear her as his ears were ringing from the bang. He opened his mouth trying to get the air back into his lungs. As he was gasping for air Seth felt Kitty help him up, she looked at him with worry in her face.

"Seth, can you hear me? Are you okay?" She asked nervously. The ringing in Seth's ears grew quieter.

"What happened?" Seth gasped.

Kitty looked behind her. "Is he alright?" She asked someone else.

"I don't know." A voice that sounded like Evan's said.

"Can you get up?" Kitty asked Seth, scanning him with her green eyes. "I think so," Seth said, getting up with help from Kitty. He looked over to where Evan was helping Rogan up. All four of them walked toward each other. Rogan looked around, obviously dazed and confused.

"Rogan are you okay? What happened?" Kitty asked. Rogan looked around ignoring the question. "Rogan?" Kitty asked again.

Rogan turned his eye on her for a second and then smiled. "Kitty where am I?" He asked.

"You are in Remtaya," Evan explained.

Rogan turned and smiled at Evan. "Evan I think I just met your friend Se..." He suddenly stopped and gazed at Seth intensely, his eyes widening. "Oh, Great One." He exclaimed pointing at Seth.

"What?" Seth asked, taken aback at the attention. He still felt faint and confused.

"It's you," Rogan said with amazement. The thunder boomed outside. "It's you." He said again this time more frantic.

"It's him what?" Kitty asked, looking at Seth and then Rogan with concern.

Rogan gawked at Seth, his eyes wide. "You are the…" The old prophesier gasped.

"The what?" Evan asked, looking at Seth.

"You are the … Chosen… one." Rogan said pointing at Seth, giving a loud gasp and putting his hand over his mouth.

Seth stood there in shock. "What?" He asked dumbfounded.

CHAPTER TEN

NOT ME!

It's time for a quick history lesson about Terina. Long before Seth was born, and when Remtaya had just gotten its gift, there were three main kingdoms on the continent. Remtaya, Kondoma, and Ki. Remtaya was by far the richest and therefore more powerful, but Ki was wealthy as well, Kondoma had its issues but was powerful in its own right. The three kingdoms had a steady but uneasy peace between them. Each kingdom knew that war would be costly, but when a mysterious assassin snuck into the Throne Room of Ki and killed the King, such unrest quickly escalated. This is not unlike what Seth is going through at the moment. Due to being branded the next Chosen One, unrest for him will most certainly escalate as well.

S eth paced next to his bed. Biz and Shadow watched him calmly. "What am I going to do?" Seth said nervously. "I cannot be the Chosen One I am t…t…too." Seth stopped and looked up at the ceiling of his room. "Dead." Seth cried out, putting his face in his hands.

"Tell us what happened again," Shadow asked in his low gruff voice. Seth sat down on his bed and looked at both Biz and Shadow.

"Well to put it simply I was transported out of this room, was almost killed by falling, then was transported above the hallway and almost died again, or would have if Rogan had not found me. Then I shook his hand and now I am the next Chosen One." Seth explained.

"Sounds like an eventful night to me," Biz said.

"Thank you for your understanding," Seth said sarcastically. He began to breathe faster and faster, his nervousness reaching a new level of stress.

"If you keep doing that you will start to hyperventilate," Shadow explained. Seth closed his eyes and concentrated on slowing his breathing.

"What are you going to tell the King and Queen," Biz asked quietly.

Seth opened his eyes. "I will say that I will not go on a suicide mission and they cannot make me." He said with false confidence.

"I can't see that going well," Biz said.

Seth sat on his bed in silence with horrible thoughts of how he was going to die running through his head. A knock came at the door causing his heart to beat faster in fear. "Come in." He said nervously standing up and gazing at the door. Evan and Kitty walked in, looks of concern on their faces.

"Well?" He asked them, shaking his head nervously.

Kitty looked at Evan concern showing on her face. "We just got done talking to the King and Queen." She said, turning her eye on Seth. "They want to meet you, but not tonight, it is too late for that."

"Go on." Seth bade them nervously.

"We need to get you to the doctor," Evan said his voice sounding worried.

"The doctor, why?" Seth said apprehensively, gazing at both of them frantically.

"You hit your head; the King, Queen, and Rogan want to make sure you don't have a concussion or something," Kitty explained. She smiled a little, but it came out more as a concerned twitch over her mouth.

"No, no, no," Seth said, his panic rising more. He stood where he was, his muscles grew stiff, and his legs froze in place. "I'm too scared to move." He told them in a shaking voice.

Evan frowned slightly. "Seth, you're not going to fight the evil King right now. It's just the doctor, relax. Kitty and I will be with you the whole time." He told him, trying to sound comforting, but there was a tone deep in his voice that echoed with worry.

Seth gasped loudly and started to pace his room back and forth. "I can't do this." He said mostly to himself. "One minute I just had a headache now I'm being sent to my death. By the Great One, I'm cursed." He cried looking at Evan and Kitty and his hands started to shake.

Kitty gave a slight sigh and walked closer to Seth. "Do you want me to carry you out of your room and to the doctor?" She asked with cynicism in her voice.

Seth frowned at Kitty. "This isn't funny," he told her, still shaking. "I was just given a death sentence." He told both of them.

Kitty nodded slowly. "Seth, I understand what you are going through. And I know that this isn't a joke, but you need to come with us to the doctor. Perhaps she can give you something to help you feel better for the time being." She stated kindly.

Seth sighed and closed his eyes. He knew they were trying to help him, he just needed to relax. "Fine," he said, opening his eyes to them. "Let's get this over with." He, Evan, and Kitty walked out the door before Seth turned back around and looked at Biz and Shadow. "I'll be back," Seth told them both before shutting the door.

"Don't worry; Dr. Agatha is the best medical doctor in all of Remtaya," Kitty told Seth. Evan, Kitty, and Seth walked down the halls, many people standing quietly as Seth and his friends passed them. Seth saw that some looked happy and excited while others looked worried and sad, one resident even went as far as to throw a rose on the floor as they passed by.

"Some of these people are already thinking I am going to die," Seth whispered accusingly at Evan and Kitty.

"Just ignore them," Evan instructed. Seth sighed and tried to keep his eyes to the ground.

They turned another corner to where the transport room was located. Kitty opened the door to find Serena inside.

"Oh, Hi?" Serena said looking at them with a questioning look.

Kitty, Seth, and Evan walked into the room and shut the door. Kitty looked at Serena with a kind smile. "Where are you going?" She asked cheerfully.

"Section 4, I guess when you opened the door it sent me here instead." Serena deduced. "Where are you guys going?" She asked, interested.

"We are going to the hospital with Seth," Evan explained. Serena looked at Seth; he still was looking at the ground and was only partly paying attention to the conversation. He was thinking too much about how he was going to get out of this.

"Are you okay?" Serena asked Seth.

He looked up at Serena with confusion. "What? Sorry I was not paying attention." He apologized.

"Are you okay?" Serena repeated.

"Oh, yes, I am just contemplating my imminent demise," Seth said bowing his head.

"What?" Serena asked in horror. "You are dying?" She inquired nervously.

"No, Seth has just been diagnosed with a potentially fatal condition sometimes called Chosen One syndrome." Evan teased. "It has been going around lately." He ended with a smile.

"Haha." Seth and Kitty said at the same time, not impressed by Evan's attempt to lighten Seth's mood with humor.

Serena looked at Seth with shock. "You are the new Chosen One?" She asked, her eyes wide.

"It seems that way," Evan said. Serena kept looking at Seth. He looked back at her and noticed that one of her eyes was ocean blue and the other was a dark forest green.

Interesting. Seth thought to himself. Serena was still looking intensely at him. He raised his right eyebrow inquisitively.

"Oh," Serena said, realizing that she was still looking at him. "I am sorry. I have never met a Chosen One in person before." She explained.

"Well, I am holding out the ever-fading hope that Rogan is either mistaken or insane," Seth said truthfully.

"I doubt that he's insane," Evan said strongly.

"We need to go." Kitty insisted. "The hospital," Kitty commanded.

"Please," Seth whispered under his breath.

"Section four," Serena said.

"How is it that you don't know Seth is the Chosen One?" Evan asked Serena. "The news traveled quickly."

"I was practicing with my dad in the...." Serena was cut off short by the flash of light and a beeping noise. Seth looked over to where Serena was but she was not there anymore.

"Where did she go?" He asked, confused.

"She was going to section four," Kitty explained.

Seth looked around. "But she didn't finish. What was she going to say?" He asked annoyed. He had a big problem when certain conversations just abruptly ended. He needed resolution.

Kitty opened the door and they walked around the corner to find two glass doors in front of them. Through the glass doors was a chamber with beds on the left and right sides of the room. Next to every bed was a curtain that was attached to the metal rods that encircled each bed. Evan opened the glass doors and all three walked inside.

"Agatha, are you in here?" Kitty asked looking around.

"I'm here." A woman said, opening one of the curtains revealing Rogan who was getting up from the bed. Agatha had a slightly tan face, brown eyes, and very black hair. She wore a blue dress and had a white apron around her waist.

"Hello, Evan and Kitty." She greeted them. Agatha's attention fell upon Seth. She looked him over for a second.

"You must be Seth," Agatha asked happily. "Please this way." She beckoned them to a bed on the right side of the room.

Seth walked over to the bed and sat on the edge and looked at Agatha.

"How are you doing Seth?" Rogan asked, walking over to him and the others. Seth was secretly mad at Rogan for making everyone think he was the Chosen One, but he would not let that emotion show.

"I am okay considering I might be the next Chosen One," Seth said humbly. "How are you?" He asked Rogan.

"He is fine," Agatha stated kindly. "The energy burst that Rogan described to me did seem to leave an odd signature around Rogan's body but that is all." She explained. She smiled at Seth as she pulled out a wand from her apron and began to move it slowly around him.

"What kind of signature did you find?" Evan asked.

"It was an odd energy signature. It's something that I do not usually see in my line of work." Agatha explained moving her wand to Seth's left. The wand had a green haze around it, but it turned a very dark blue and then turned black. "Well you also have the same energy signature as Rogan does but yours seems to be stronger," Agatha said smiling at Seth.

"Is it serious?" Seth asked nervously.

"No, the energy is harmless." She explained. "It must have been an aftereffect of the energy that was released when you two shook hands." Agatha theorized.

"Why was there so much energy released in the first place?" Kitty asked.

"If I had to guess I would say that it had to do with how Rogan said he would know who the Chosen One was when he saw them, or in this case touched them." Agatha explained.

"I would agree." Rogan concurred.

Agatha looked at Seth. "You have to be the youngest Chosen One they have sent to me." She stated.

"I don't want to be the Chosen One," Seth said sadly.

"Well, it is a great honor," Rogan said. "You will be considered a hero." He emphasized.

"Perhaps what we need is someone like you," Agatha said. "All of the other Chosen Ones that I have seen all were very eager to go and kill the king. Maybe what we need is someone who will try something different." She suggested.

"Like negotiation?" Seth asked.

"Precisely." Agatha insisted.

"I like that plan, but I would be a terrible negotiator," Seth explained. "I can barely talk to people I have never seen before." He said shyly.

"You are talking to me, okay," Agatha said. "I just think that all of Remtaya needs to look at the big picture. If we kill Kondoma's King, then his brother would just take over and we would be in the same mess we are in already." She proclaimed.

"I agree," Kitty said. "But we have tried to send people to negotiate, and they suffered the same fate as the Chosen Ones." She explained.

"It is a tricky conundrum," Rogan said.

Agatha waved her wand above Seth's head, the wand glowed blue.

"Well, the good news is that you do not have a concussion. In fact, except for a bruise on your head you're perfectly healthy." Agatha said happily. "You are ready to go and have a good rest, both of you," Agatha said looking at Seth and Rogan.

"I think that is a good idea," Kitty said. "Seth, you have to go see the King and Queen tomorrow, so you should get some sleep." She insisted.

"I can't sleep with this worry over me," Seth complained.

"It's okay, Seth," Evan said, walking over to him. "I will take you to your room." He offered.

"Okay." Seth complied.

"Good luck tomorrow," Agatha said waving goodbye.

Seth walked to the transport room with Evan, Kitty, and Rogan feeling very stressed.

CHAPTER ELEVEN

THE PRICE OF BEING THE CHOSEN ONE

Look around you. Where are you? Is there anyone else nearby? What if I told you, that no matter where you are, there is at least one Kry? The Kry are still very mysterious creatures to you, aren't they? Well, what do you know about them? To begin with, you have learned that they are all-powerful, omniscient beings. They also have a war named after them and this entire story is named in their honor. Now, I will not tell you everything about them--you will have to keep reading. However, I will give you one more piece of the puzzle. The Kry are mischievous; they love to play pranks on everyone and everything. Sometimes the Kry don't even have to do anything to humans or any other lifeform in order to be mischievous. Suffice it to say, the Kry could be having a good, hard laugh at what Seth will have to face next.

Korson stood at his throne, thinking about the state of his kingdom.

The war is taking its toll on the people. I need to find a way to win this costly war, he thought to himself.

Orson stood just out of view, watching his brother toiling in thought. He looked down with sadness. "This war is killing him," Orson said quietly.

Your brother refused my help. Let him fester, a dark voice spoke inside Orson's mind.

"That was not our agreement. You promised me that my brother and I would defeat the Chosen Ones and the war would be over," Orson whispered to himself.

I promised that your brother would not be killed by the Chosen One. I will keep my promise if you keep yours, the raspy voice hissed. Orson looked around and then hurried into a closet.

"My brother has what you want, but he will not let me in his personal treasury," Orson said, with panic in his voice.

Fool! I did not help you find the orb of prophecy for nothing! The voice caused Orson to cringe in pain as the sensation of hot pokers shot through his head. *The orb will help keep your brother alive. Just obtain the item and follow what I say. I promise you, your brother's enemies will wish they were never born,* the evil, raspy voice declared.

"Orson!" Korson called.

Orson quickly stepped out of the closet and walked casually into the Throne Room, making sure to appear nonchalant. "Yes, brother?" he asked calmly. Orson noticed that there was another man in the room. The man was holding a scroll and wearing the garb of a palace messenger.

"This man has given me the most wonderful news," Korson said happily.

"What is that, my brother?" Orson asked with interest.

"The Kingdom of Remtaya has found the next Chosen One," Korson said, laughing.

"Is he on his way here?" Orson asked.

"No, not yet, but that will soon change," Korson explained. "I grow tired of the long journey the Chosen One must take to get to my city. Get my assassins," Korson commanded, with a dark smile.

"Yes, brother," Orson said, before running out of the Throne Room. He ran down hall after hall until he reached a chamber to the left. He stopped running and turned to the closed doors. Inside he could hear a pleading voice. Orson opened the doors to find four women standing over a ragged-looking man kneeling painfully on the floor. Three of the women had bright red hair and were wearing red dresses. The other woman had inky black hair and wore a long black dress. She knelt by the broken man. The woman reached out a hand adorned with long, pointed nails. She extended her index finger and wiped some blood off the man's lip. The woman looked at Orson.

"Yes, my lord?" she asked, licking the blood off her finger. Orson held back the urge to gag.

"The King wants each of you," Orson said, trying to look brave against these monstrous women.

"Very well," the black-haired woman said. "Seapa, Septa, and Seala, come. Our King has summoned us." The women all stood in a circle. The black-haired woman held up a wand and with a flash they all disappeared from the chamber. Even the haggard man had vanished.

Orson rolled his eyes. "Witches," he said with annoyance at the disgusting behavior of the dark haired witch. He ran back down the halls until he was back in the Throne Room. The four women were already there.

"What do you want of us, my king?" the black-haired woman asked.

"Loral, I have received word that a Chosen One has been found once more," Korson began. "I want you, your assassins, and some of my soldiers, to go to Remtaya and capture this new Chosen One. I understand your sister is a doctor in Remtaya. I hope that will not be a problem?" Korson asked.

"Agatha and I may be sisters in blood, but I assure you, she is not a problem. I would gladly kill her if I got the chance," Loral said.

"Very well. Prepare to go," Korson commanded.

Loral smiled sinisterly. "What is this new Chosen One's name?" she asked.

"Seth. His name is Seth." Korson said, smiling darkly.

CHAPTER TWELVE

WILL YOU BE THE
NEXT OF THE CHOSEN?

The King and Queen of Remtaya are truly wonderful people. King Leo Trotory Delany is a brave and strong King who sees that without laws there would be chaos. He also believes that the greatest values some could have are humility, loyalty, kindness, strength, and love. He was married into the crown of Remtaya but is a great ruler who has kept a very cool head in times of war. Queen Julia Long-coat Delany is most likely the kindest and most warm-hearted person one could ever meet. Being Queen by birth she has the knowledge and wisdom to make swift but accurate decisions about a scenario. Her ability to see all the sides of a problem is what makes her so wise. Not only is she a good diplomat but she is considered a very formidable fighter on the battlefield and the courts. She is a perfect role model for all girls and women out there. The King and Queen are good and very kind people and are considered to be the best King and Queen in Remtaya for a century. Unfortunately, even the benevolent King and Queen of Remtaya would have to send a boy who looks only around fourteen on a very dangerous and potentially life-threatening journey even if the said boy does not want to go.

Seth got up with a start, surprising Biz and Shadow. He sat there gasping as the nightmare he just had left his memory. He looked around his room as tears filled his face and feelings of butterflies filled his stomach.

The memories of what was going on in his life started to flood back in. "I'm going to die!" Seth sobbed as he laid on his bed. He covered his face in his soft pillow and gave a loud moan. He stopped his groan of fear and took a deep breath before he screamed in his pillow. Just then a knock came at the door, making Seth feel self-consciousness. He quickly looked up from his pillow and wiped the tears from his face. Getting up from his bed he sat at the edge trying to make it look like he had been up for a while.

"Come in?" Seth asked nervously, his voice still shaking. The door opened and Evan and Kitty walked in. Evan was wearing a blue robe, but it looked more prestigious than the one he normally wore. Kitty, however, looked like a completely different person. She usually wore a white, long-sleeve shirt covered up by a brown buttoned-up vest accompanied by white pants, but today she wore a very flamboyant, light blue dress. The dress was so big around the bottom part that it almost couldn't fit through the door.

"Are you ready?" Evan asked Seth.

Seth looked behind Kitty's enormous dress and at his empty doorway behind them. "No guard escort so that I don't try to run away?" Seth asked them with a frown.

"No," Evan told him simply. "The Senate wanted you to have an escort, but the King and Queen decided that wasn't a good idea for you."

"They sent us to get you since we are your friends," Kitty told Seth with a forced smile. She seemed very annoyed at her massively sized dress.

"Now," Evan said again. "Are you ready to go?"

Seth looked at both of them and took a deep breath. He felt like screaming again. "I don't want to." He said, forcing himself not to let his fear and anger out.

"Well, you have to," Kitty said, sounding irritated now. She gave a loud groan and looked like she was going to yell as well.

"What's wrong with you?" Evan asked her. "You look good in that dress," he said.

"I may look good in it, but I hate this thing. It is so big and restricting." Kitty said angrily, pulling at her dress so it would all come into Seth's room.

Seth stood up and walked over to the bathroom and quickly took a shower making sure that he was as perfectly clean as he could get. He then put on a dark gray tunic and some brown pants. He walked out of the bathroom to find that Shadow was playing with the bottom part of Kitty's dress. Kitty twirled softly to offer some challenge to Shadow, then looked up and smiled.

"Seth after today I am giving this dress to you, okay? It will be our little secret to have Shadow tear it to shreds." Kitty insisted.

"Okay." Seth shrugged, not really caring. He slipped on his shoes and walked over to where Kitty and Evan were standing.

"I am ready to say no," Seth said, very ready to actually tell the King and Queen that he would not like to be the Chosen One.

Kitty shook her head and walked over to Seth. She started to straighten any wrinkles that she saw around Seth's attire.

"I know the Queen and King very well, and I know what they are going to ask you." She explained. "Make sure to keep eye contact with them and the social convention is to bow when they stand up," Kitty said looking at Seth's hair and frowning. She pulled out a wooden comb and started to brush his messy hair.

"The King can be a little intimidating, but he really isn't. The Queen will most likely have a worried expression on her face all the time, so don't really worry about it. She worries over the entire kingdom like they're her children." Kitty said smiling. She stopped brushing Seth's hair and looked him over one more time until she nodded with approval and walked back to Evan. Kitty then looked at Evan's hair and sighed softly as she combed his hair also.

"Why do you have a comb in your dress?" Evan asked.

"Contrary to popular belief I do like to have nicely combed hair," Kitty said.

"Well, it is time to go," Evan said looking over to Seth.

Seth sighed and walked to the door. He waited for Kitty to get her unnecessarily gigantic dress out of the door and into the hallway and then he turned and looked at Biz and Shadow.

"I will come back and feed you soon." He said before shutting the door.

"Have you ever been to the Throne Room?" Kitty asked.

"No," Seth said, starting to feel scared. "I have only seen the King and Queen in their drawings." He said looking around the corner. Seth could hear what sounded like cheering.

"Can you hear that?" Seth asked Evan and Kitty. They both looked at each other as if they had a secret. The cheering got louder.

"What is that?" Seth asked, more adamant. They were walking toward a window that overlooked the city. As they got closer, Seth heard what sounded like hundreds of people shouting his name. He ran over to the window and looked down to the street. The people of Remtaya were everywhere, shouting Seth's name.

"Oh no," Seth said in horror. "Why are they shouting my name?" Seth snapped angrily at Evan and Kitty.

"They are excited that you are the Chosen One. You are giving the people hope." Evan explained. Seth turned away from the window and the applauding crowd.

"Hope!" Seth said. "I never wanted to give people hope!" He yelled and the power of his voice exploded out in the air, sending Evan and Kitty flying backward and shattering the windows.

"Seth?" Evan asked snapping Seth out of his graphic daydream. "We don't want to keep everyone waiting." He said looking at Seth with concern. Seth nodded soberly and turned away from the window to continue to the Throne Room of the King and Queen, leaving the cheering crowd behind him.

"The Throne Room is actually in the center of the city so we will definitely have to take one of the transport rooms or it could take us almost two weeks to get there," Kitty explained as they turned a corner.

"I sometimes forget how big this city really is." Evan marveled. Seth walked quietly behind them thinking about his rather odd daydream. Seth had daydreams before but never like that. The anger he felt was strong and powerful. He was so mad and wanted to do more than yell at people. In that particular daydream, he wanted to do something much worse than push Evan and Kitty away. Seth tried to get his mind on something else. He looked around trying to find something to fixate on.

Wait, you are going to the Throne Room because you were called as the new Chosen One and are probably going to die because of it. So you can just fixate on that. Seth thought to himself.

The knots in his stomach grew as they walked closer to the transport room. As Kitty and Evan walked into the room Seth stood there looking at both of them. They looked back.

"Seth, come on you can do this," Kitty said, smiling and holding out her hand. Seth sighed and walked into the room with them. Even though the room could hold five people very comfortably, Kitty's dress took up half the space in the medium-sized room.

"I hate this thing," Kitty said with anger.

"The Throne Room," Evan said, chuckling under his breath. There was the usual flash of light and then the familiar beeping noise. Seth and Evan waited for Kitty to get her oversized dress fully out the door before they walked out. Seth found himself in a very unfamiliar part of the castle. Unlike most of the castle, which was like a giant wall that encircled the entire city, this place looked more like a very luxurious palace, with enormous chandeliers and windows that were at the top of the very high ceiling that Seth, Kitty, and Evan were walking under. All around them were statues of all the Kings and Queens of Remtaya. Unlike what Seth had seen when he first entered the castle, these statues stood around twenty feet tall, and each statue was holding some kind of object. Some of the kings were holding different kinds of swords in certain ways. Some of the Queens held round, ball-like objects while others held stone renderings of paper or scrolls. Seth and his friends walked past many other statues until they reached what looked to be the middle of the enormous chamber. Seth looked up in wonderment at what he was seeing. It was a glass tree in the middle of a small pond. The tree was very big in both length and width. The glass branches elegantly twisted upward to an enormous glass chandelier right above it. The chandelier was attached to a big skylight. The sun's light shone through the skylight and hit the chandelier, sending fractured light of many colors beaming down on the floor and the glass tree.

Seth stood there, his eyes wide as he looked at the very beautiful view. The light shone on the crystal formed tree in such a way that it almost made Seth cry. The water that surrounded the beautiful tree had small leaves and flower petals on the surface. In the water were fish of various colors, sizes, and forms swimming around freely. At the bottom of the small pond was writing.

In honor of the great tree Ty-Anti and the purity of its roots.

Seth recited out loud.

"Beautiful isn't it?" Evan rhetorically asked. They all three stood there for a second basking in the wonderment of the spectacular tree.

"We have to go," Kitty whispered, still looking at the wondrous view.

"Right," Evan said reluctantly, turning away from the glass tree.

Seth kept looking at the tree as Evan and Kitty started to walk to the right side of the room.

"Seth come on," Kitty shouted.

Seth ran to them. Behind the glass tree was a giant staircase that led up to a giant stained-glass window. The rendering on the window was of the current King and Queen. The King was wearing a long robe with different colors that complemented the image. He held in one hand a round ball that had a small tree on top, and in the other hand he held a beautiful orange paper that had writing on it that Seth was unable to read. The Queen wore a dress that seemed to flow all over the painting.

She held in her left hand a sword and in the right, a golden rod that also had a small replica of a tree on the top of it. To the left and right of the giant stained-glass window were other staircases that went up to a second level of the chamber. The floor where Seth and his friends were contained doors to the side of the first staircase. Evan and Kitty moved to the right staircase and beckoned Seth to follow them. As Seth walked to where they were standing, they both stood there looking at him.

"Are you ready?" Evan asked Seth.

"Do I have a choice?" Seth asked with annoyance.

"Inside is the Throne Room, just remember what I told you to do and you will be fine," Kitty explained, sounding more nervous than she did before they left Seth's room.

Suddenly the doors they were standing next to opened slightly and Soven walked out.

"Oh, Seth, Kitty, Evan," Soven said, sounding both startled and relieved. "It's good you're here. The King and Queen just sent me out to find you. Everyone is inside." He explained looking at Seth, smiling as if he was planning something.

"Seth before we go in I would just like to know. On a scale of one to ten, with one meaning you are dreading being the next Chosen One and ten meaning you are super excited, which one are you?" He asked.

"I would have to go to the negative numbers to indicate how I feel," Seth explained, folding his arms, a look of annoyance on his face.

"Well, then I win," Soven said happily.

"Soven did you bet on how Seth would feel about being the Chosen One?" Kitty asked, shocked. Soven shrugged. "Well yes and no," he said. "There was a bet that if another Chosen One was found we would see how he felt about it. I bet that the next Chosen One would not be happy about it. Now I get some friendly game money." Soven explained happily.

Kitty shook her head in disapproval and put her hand on Seth's shoulder.

"Are you ready?" Soven asked Seth.

"He is." Kitty reasoned. Soven then nodded and opened the two doors. Seth was bombarded by people talking in the lights of a very big chamber. He, Evan, Kitty, and Soven all walked in together. Seth walked across a red carpet that was on the floor. The carpet curved left to another red carpet that was at the left side of the chamber. The two carpets met each other until they became one carpet that then moved through the center of the room to where the King and Queen were sitting. There were long, bench-like chairs that were lined up in rows of five that were on both sides of the room. The people that were sitting in the chairs were unaware of Seth and his friends' presence. Soven motioned to the King and Queen to show that Seth was here. The King and Queen stood up and suddenly the people sitting at the benches stopped talking. They all rose and turned to look at Seth; he stood there looking at the now very quiet people who were all there because of what an old man saw in a shiny blue ball. Kitty softly nudged Seth forward. Seth started to walk past all the people who were looking only at him. Seth suddenly thought about something he had read about called stage fright. He thought about how some people can get sick or faint if they are around large crowds. Seth suddenly had the urge to run. He kept walking, though. Seth was halfway there, and could see the King standing there looking so tall.

But the King is not tall. Seth thought to himself. *In fact, King Leo is one of the shortest kings that Remtaya ever had.* Seth told himself. *Then why does he look so tall?* Seth thought. Seth's attention shifted to the Queen. She looked very worriedly at him. Her face seemed to grow more worried the closer he got to them. *Kitty was right about that.* Seth thought.

Suddenly thoughts that were not his own flooded into Seth's mind. *He looks so young.* Seth heard the Queen think. *Why does he have to be so young?* She thought.

We cannot think that honey. The King reasoned telepathically to his wife. Seth suddenly stopped, shocked as he realized what he was hearing.

They can communicate with each other telepathically. Seth mused. *They are using Dyomancy! That is so cool.* Seth did not realize it, but he had stopped exactly where he was supposed to stop. Unfortunately, because Seth was too enthralled by this new discovery he forgot to bow.

"Seth," Kitty whispered. Seth snapped out of his amazement and looked over to Kitty who was already bowing. Seth realized what he was supposed to do and bowed to the King and Queen. The King gestured for the people to stop bowing. Seth stood up and looked at the King and Queen nervously.

"Seth, you have been foreseen by Rogan the chief prophesier to be the next Chosen One," the King said loudly.

"To go and vanquish the King of Kondoma and bring this horrible war to an end." The Queen finished.

"Let us hear the prophecy itself," the King said loudly. Evan walked up and took a scroll that was handed to him by a servant. Seth looked at Evan questioningly. Evan winked at Seth and then looked up at the Queen and king.

"Dear King and Queen. I have been asked by The Chief Prophesier Rogan to recite the prophecy of Seth." Evan said. He opened the scroll and began to read.

When the bird begins to make its nest.
Fate calls for Seth to take this quest.
Fear and danger will place him there.
A warning for the evil King to be aware.
Seth's quest will be Korson's dread.
As the Chosen one strikes the King, and he falls dead.

Evan recited the prophecy. Seth and everyone else just stood there. Seth was shocked. His name was in the prophecy. *"What if I am the Chosen One?"* Seth thought to himself.

"The prophecy has been read, now we will ask the Chosen One if he will accept the role of the Chosen One," the King said to the entire chamber. The Queen looked at Seth with worry in her face. She had a very kind face, like a mother worrying about him as if he was her own child.

"Seth, do you accept the role of the Chosen One to go and end the war by destroying the King of Kondoma?" Queen Julia asked. Seth stood there unable to say anything. The worry filled him and stopped him from talking.

What am I going to say? Seth thought to himself. *I am not the Chosen One, but you have a prophecy that has my name in it?* He said to himself in his mind. Seth was in conflict and was completely speechless.

"Yes." Someone said quiet enough so that Seth couldn't know who it was, but loud enough for most of everyone to hear the answer.

Seth looked around the room to find out who had spoken.

"Very well," the King said, looking more relieved. The Queen, however, looked more stressed. The Queen and King stood up and walked out of the room, and the rest of the room began to leave. Seth stood there in shock at what had happened. He did not accept, someone else did. Seth looked at Evan and Kitty when it hit him.

Kitty. The voice I heard was Kitty. Seth thought angrily.

Three hours later

Seth stood next to one of the many humongous bookshelves that stood very high in the prophecy chamber. Seth looked at all of the books that were neatly stacked upright with the title of the book showing on the spine. Seth looked closer at one of the books.

"There you are," Seth said feeling determined.

Seth had left the Throne Room around three hours ago and fed Biz and Shadow and then went to the prophecy chamber because he was determined to find proof that he was *not* the Chosen One. Seth pulled out the book. *"The History of the Chosen Ones."* Seth read out loud. He sat down on the floor and started to read.

There are 75 Chosen Ones that have lived on the planet Terinta. The book began. *This is the history of how they became the Chosen Ones and what they did. There are also other names for a Chosen One. Some are called Seekers or Heroes, others are called the Prophesied or Prophesied Ones, and some were called the Saviors.* Seth read to himself.

The first Chosen One was born before the construction of the great city of Centila on the continent of Celesta. The ancient priests of the order of Nog foresaw a time of pain and death. The prophecy that subsequently followed showed a man was to rise up and kill this great evil. The man was named the Savior. All that is said of the Savior was that he would be born in a humble place and would save the world from a great evil. The mans actual name was never found, and it was said that this Savior trapped the evil and did not kill it. Some religions believe that this Savior was, in fact, the son of the deity known as The Great One. Seth was very much aware of this Savior, having been brought up in a religion that believed this and living in a city where the city priests held a week-long celebration/fasting in commemoration of this Savior, and also the traditional warning to all who do not repent when the Savior returns. Seth had always believed to an extent this religion but always thought that the priests of the city of Remtaya liked to use fear and ignorance to accomplish their so-called righteous goals. Seth turned the page.

The second Chosen One was born three hundred years after the events of the first Chosen One. The prophecy of the second Chosen One was made four years before he was born. This Chosen One was said to defeat an unknown enemy. This enemy turned out to be the Eanawly. With their ability to control other life forms' thoughts and actions, added to their bloodthirsty nature, the Eanawly were truly deadly foes. The Eanawly invaded the continent of Celesta and began to subjugate the people. That was when Thermin Grian was determined that he was the next Chosen One and through a great war and master planning, Grian was able to defeat the Eanawly. Seth stopped and looked at the name Eanawly.

"What an odd way to spell a name," Seth said to himself.

Seth started to read again. He read for what seemed to be hours. Seth scanned each chapter trying to find anything that could show that he was not a Chosen One. Seth then got to the last few chapters.

The Time of the Dark Chosen Ones.

The section read:

A Dark Chosen One is a prophesied individual that is chosen by a prophecy to defeat a great evil and does, but the person then becomes what they were chosen to defeat, the book defined. *The seventy-first Chosen One started the line of dark Chosen Ones. He was prophesied to be born with a birthmark that was shaped like a sun and moon put together. He was chosen to defeat an evil King that was terrorizing the continent of Terina. The prophecy said,*

One will be born with The Great Ones thumb.

The mark will be the shimrock.

A life and lie will come.

To bend to the will of a Timpnock.

The shimrock was what the sun and moon together were called. Timpnock refers to a tribe of people that were one of the first to settle Terina after the dragon wars. A member of the Timpnock clan was born that had the makings of the shimrock on his right arm and he was trained to be, as the people called it, The Great One's thumb so that he could defeat the enemy that was terrorizing Terina. He did so and became king. Unfortunately, he became too power hungry and was more terrible than the other King was. So five years later another prophecy was made about twins who would rise up and kill this new threat. The King tried to stop the prophecy from happening by killing any newborn twins in his kingdom. Later, his Queen was told by a cleric that she would have twins and they would be the Chosen Ones. So, for fear that her husband would kill her children, she faked her own death and went somewhere, where her children could learn to fulfill their destiny. When their twenty-sixth birthday came, they went to the kingdom. After a fierce battle with their evil father, he was ultimately killed by his own daughter. Again, it seemed as if the peace had won, but feeling cheated by his sister, her twin brother poisoned her and made himself the new king.

Seth read on.

Fifty years later a farm boy named Ky would be called as the next Chosen One. Seth looked at the name Ky. "I wonder if that has to do with the city of Ki," Seth asked himself.

This prophecy foretold of a Chosen One coming back as a spirit and possessing a farm boy to be the next Chosen One. After a fire burned down the barn where the farm boy Ky had been, he was believed to have been killed, but a few days later he emerged from the ashes unharmed. He did not know who he was and did not know his name. After doing three things that he had been prophesied to do, Ky was discovered as the new Chosen One. He later renamed himself Ki and went and killed the other corrupted Chosen One. After that, he became King and renamed the city, Ki. For a while it seemed as if everything was fine. Then the King began to lose his mind and started to kill innocent people.

Seth had reached the last chapter.

The last Chosen One.

Seth read smiling. "This is promising," he said. Seth began to read the chapter.

A Chosen One was prophesied to come and stop the King of Ki but it was also said that this Chosen One would have to start a war and would be the last Chosen One to come to the world of Terinta.

"Aw ha," Seth said. He quickly pulled out a piece of paper and wrote down the last line that he had just read. He continued to read.

This last Chosen One had to start a civil war in order to kill the king. Afterwards, this new Chosen One became the new King and kept the name of the city Ki, in order to commemorate the last King before he went insane. This Chosen One was number seventy-five and was called the last Chosen One.

"I knew it," Seth said with happiness.

"Knew what?" Someone asked. Seth turned to see that it was Evan.

"We were looking everywhere for you," Evan said, walking to Seth.

"Look at this," Seth said, holding up the piece of paper he had written on.

Evan took the paper and read it. He looked at Seth and smiled.

"I know about this stuff," Evan said, giving Seth the paperback.

"Then you know that I can't be the next Chosen One. Because there will be no more Chosen Ones." Seth said frantically.

Evan shrugged. "I do not know why but that prophecy was very convincing," he said.

Seth held up his arms in distress. "That poem was so convoluted that it is nothing but words," Seth said angrily. "It was so hackneyed that it just left everyone confused." He explained.

"Let's go back to your room. You still have a big day." Evan announced.

Seth looked at him with distress. "What do I have to do?" He asked nervously.

"Just say hi to some senators. Then you have to get ready to go to Kondoma." Evan said walking with Seth back to the entrance of the prophecy chamber.

"I am not the Chosen One!" Seth cried out in protest as they left the chamber.

CHAPTER THIRTEEN

GATHERING TEAM SETH

Why did Kitty say yes for Seth when the King and Queen asked Seth if he would go and defeat the evil king? Well, it had to do with Chaos theory. For those that do not know what Chaos theory is, think of it this way. If you were to clap your hands the concussive force of that action could have a chaotic but mathematically measurable effect on the planet's weather. So, you may ask how does Chaos theory have to do with Kitty saying yes to the King and Queen? The actual action of saying yes was Kitty's choice but the outcome of this has set a chain of events into motion. Events that could do more to the world of Terinta than just change the weather.

You may also be wondering why the King, Queen, and most of the other people in the Throne Room think that it was, in fact, Seth who had said yes. That has to do with the voice of Seth and the ability of the human mind to make connections to two things that actually have really nothing to do with each other. For example, if I were to ask, how many penguins live in the North Pole? What would you say? If you had to think about that for a second or two do not worry you have just experienced what your brain does in order to be more efficient. This is what happened to the people in the Throne Room. It is just another example of what is really going on in the human mind. The senators simply heard what they thought they were going to hear and did not question who actually said it. There was one other reason why this worked. Unlike what usually starts to happen to fourteen or older boys is the vocal oscillations lowers. This has not happened to Seth. He did not have a super high voice, but it was sufficiently high enough to be considered a girl's voice if people did not know Seth very much. Seth had actually been called a girl on more than one occurrence. Mostly, because the outside observer will make a quick and inaccurate decision about something without giving any other thought about it. Seth was not fond of this, but he had considered that in a biological sense, the female is more important to nature than the male, so it was not that bad. Plus, Seth knew that he was male and no one could tell him otherwise.

Seth stood on a black field. The ground seemed to be made of ash. Suddenly, a shadowy figure rose out of the field and grew to the size of a tower.

"Face me, Seth, if you dare." The shadowy figure challenged.

"I do not acknowledge your existence," Seth said, not even looking at the massive figure. The shadowy form then yelled and pulled out a very big shadowy sword. It swung the sword at Seth. Seth agilely dodged the sword and produced a sword of his own.

"I still don't acknowledge your existence," Seth said stubbornly.

"I am the evil King, and you are the Chosen One. You will die." The shadow said evilly.

"No," Seth said calmly. "I will not speak to you anymore," Seth said, folding his arms.

"Then you will die!" The shadow screamed and swung the sword down on Seth. Suddenly Seth was jarred awake by knocking.

"Come in," Seth said automatically. The door opened and Kitty walked in.

"You!" Seth pointed dramatically at Kitty. "Why have YOU come?" Seth asked angrily.

Kitty held up her hands.

"Seth, can we talk?" She asked.

Seth looked at Kitty with anger. "Oh sure. Why don't we talk about why YOU said yes and doomed me to die, and why YOU obviously hate me, and why YOU want me dead?" Seth asked accusingly at Kitty.

"Can you stop emphasizing your 'yous'? It is unnecessary." Kitty said, walking over to Seth's bed. She sat on the corner of the bed making sure to not sit on Biz and Shadow. Shadow looked up at Seth with sleepy eyes.

"Just forgive her," Shadow said sleepily.

"Stay out of this Shadow." Seth pouted. Kitty smiled and started to pet Shadow.

"Seth I am sorry about what happened." She began. "I knew that if you had said no, the Council would start to ask you very hard questions and even accuse you of being a traitor to Remtaya," Kitty explained.

"Yes, but it is all a lie. First, I am not the Chosen One and second, I am getting credit for something that I never even said." Seth said sadly. Kitty looked at Seth with kind eyes.

"It is not a matter of debate that you are the Chosen One," Kitty said. "You may not think of yourself as the Chosen One, but I know you have the potential to be the Chosen One." She said smiling softly.

Seth moaned and covered his face with his gloved hands. One thing that Seth could never really do was hold a grudge. He would always just forgive people who did something that he did not like. Seth was not sure if that was a strength or a weakness.

"Why?" Seth moaned his hands still covering his face.

"Why what?" Kitty asked.

"Why me?" Seth asked, uncovering his face and looking at Kitty.

"Maybe this is your destiny, to kill the evil king." She said.

"I believe we set our own destinies," Seth said, getting up from his bed and walking over to a shelf to get Biz's and Shadow's food ready.

"What is going on? Did you just come here to apologize?" Seth asked.

"Yes and no," Kitty said. "The King, Queen, and Council have decided that you will be leaving for Kondoma in three weeks," Kitty explained.

"Three weeks!" Seth said with horror. "I am going to die sooner than I thought." He said bowing his head.

"You will not die if I can help it," Kitty said. "I am coming with." Seth turned around and looked at Kitty.

"Just you and me?" Seth asked not really wanting to be with Kitty all that time.

"No, the last Chosen Ones left with no more than three companions so that they could sneak up on the King without him noticing, but that has not worked so the Council has decided to send six people with you," Kitty explained. "I volunteered to go and so did Evan. I also know that Coven had volunteered to help the next Chosen One, even before we knew it was you and Orin was 'asked, slash volunteered' to go." Kitty said, trying to remember the others she knew were going.

"What does it mean when you are asked, slash volunteered to go?" Seth asked.

"It is pretty much what happened to you. Orin is happy to come. The only thing is that he has Serena. Despite that, he is coming." Kitty said looking dreamily out into the distance. Seth did not need to have telepathy to know what Kitty was thinking about at that very moment.

"Will Serena be coming with us also?" Seth asked. Even though Seth, Evan, and Kitty were good friends, both Kitty and Evan were older than Seth and Serena. Serena was the same age as Seth. If Serena went then Seth could be around someone closer to his own age if he was tired of being around all the grownups.

"No, she volunteered but was denied by Orin and the King and Queen because it is too dangerous," Kitty said, snapping out of her fantasy about Orin.

"What?" Seth said looking at Kitty with shock. "They tell Serena, a person who is my same age, that it's too dangerous and then they want me to go," Seth complained.

"Serena had the same arguments," Kitty explained.

"At least someone is on my side," Seth said.

"We have to go," Kitty said. "Everyone is waiting at the arena." She explained hurriedly.

"Right now?" Seth complained.

"Yes." Kitty acknowledged.

"Fine," Seth sighed. He gave Biz and Shadow their food and then went to get dressed.

Seth walked down the hall with Kitty to the arena where everyone was talking around chairs and a chalkboard that was floating. Seth assumed this was the center of the discussion area. As Seth got closer, he could see the faces of the distant people. He noticed Evan was talking to a man that was looking amused at something. Suddenly, Seth began to hear the voices of the people around him. Seth stopped and closed his eyes, not in the mood to hear what people were thinking. It took him a second but soon the pain in his head slightly subsided. Kitty stopped and put her hand on Seth's shoulder.

"You need to learn how to control your mind reading." She insisted gently.

"I know," Seth admitted the pain in his head lessening even more.

I may not be a powerful telepath like you, but I can teach you how to better deal with those headaches." Kitty promised.

"Thanks," Seth stated looking at Kitty. Seth and Kitty continued walking toward the group of people. When they got to where everyone was Seth was bombarded by humans he had never met. They all walked over to him, said something joyfully, and then patted him on the back before walking back to where everyone else was. Just when Seth thought he was done with having strangers talk to him a man walked up with a glad, handsome smile. The man was definitely taller than Seth, so he had to look up to see his face. His eyes beamed with life and vigor that Seth could only describe as calm excitement. The features of the tall man were striking, he was well-built and had an attractive symmetry to his face.

"Hello, Seth." The man said, holding out his right hand while smiling kindly. "I'm Orin Wolfhart, it's a pleasure to finally meet you." Orin gave him a friendly wink. Seth observed Orin's kind but piercing sapphire blue eyes, almost getting lost in them. The name Orin was already well known to Seth, but this was the first time he had met the man. He couldn't fault Kitty for still finding her old boyfriend dreamy. Orin had his hand still out ready to shake Seth's unoffered hand. He looked at Orin's right hand for a second.

What's one more handshake? Seth thought to himself. He reached out and shook Orin's hand.

Evan was right. Orin thought with a feeling of humor. He smiled friendly at Seth once more before walking over and taking a seat.

What did Evan say? Seth asked himself.

Coven walked over to the floating board and held up his hands to get everyone's attention. Seth walked over to a seat at the back where Evan and Kitty were sitting. He looked around at the people that were sitting in front of him. He only knew Evan, Kitty, and Coven and he had just met Orin. Seth did not know any of the others that were apparently here to help him defeat the evil king. Seth thought about how he should feel very glad that these people would just drop what they were planning and help him. Then he remembered that most likely these people were all here because he is the Chosen One and if he was not, then these people would probably not even notice him.

"Hello, thank you for coming." Coven began. "As all of you know we have either volunteered or were asked to go to Kondoma and help the new Chosen One kill King Korson," Coven said, gesturing toward Seth when he said Chosen One.

"We will come here for the next two weeks and practice to defend ourselves and learn to fight against the enemies we will face," Coven explained, walking back and forth as if he were talking to a group of soldiers.

Seth realized that in fact most of the people here are or were probably soldiers or guards of Remtaya. So the way Coven was addressing them would seem natural to most of the people in the room.

Seth turned to Evan. "Is this called a debriefing or a briefing?" Seth asked quietly. Evan shrugged and turned to Kitty and asked the same question.

"I don't know I was never in the military," Kitty whispered to both of them. As Coven was still talking, Kitty tapped on Orin's shoulder. He was sitting in a chair right in front of her. He looked back at Seth, Evan, and Kitty and quietly chuckled.

"You three look like two brothers who are with their big sister sitting behind everybody else." He said smiling. Kitty laughed quietly and asked the question that interested all three of them.

"This is a briefing." Orin clarified.

"Then what is a debriefing?" Evan asked, trying to speak softly.

"That is when someone is asking for information that was gained after a secret mission or something similar to that," Orin explained.

"Do you four have any questions?" Coven asked, interrupting their conversation.

"Yes, I do," Kitty said, getting up from her seat. "When are you going to be done with your monologue about how we are the first and last defense for Remtaya and actually start the briefing?" Kitty asked smiling impishly at Coven and winking at Orin. Coven folded his arms and shook his head with a smile of amusement on his face while the other people in the room softly chuckled out loud.

"Very well," Coven said looking at Kitty. "Kitty if you will please show us the intelligence we have of Kondoma?" He asked. Kitty pulled out her wand and waved it in the air. A picture began to form on the chalkboard. It was a map of Terina with lines that marked the property of the various territories of the different countries that were in Terina. On the northern side of the map was the name Remtaya. Most of Remtaya's people lived in the city but some of its people lived in outlying villages in the territory that it claimed. The territory that Remtaya claimed looked to be just as big as the territory that Kondoma had. Kondoma was south of Remtaya and closer to the Gulf of Terina. As the map grew in complexity, Seth saw many of the other countries and cities that all lived on Terina. He could see the southeastern City of Night and its sister city, the City of Light. On the north-western side of Terina was the name of one of the most mysterious cities ever. The city of Krydom, Seth had learned in history classes with Senator Healey that Krydom was built by the Kry on the ruins of the city of Ki. It is said that only certain life forms are allowed to enter and live in the city. Humans were not one of them. Krydom was close to one of Terinta's five wonders, the Forest of Conching, where the very mysterious and elusive Conchingda were rumored to live. The forest was the biggest forest in all of Terinta and mostly unexplored. Seth watched as Coven began to point at the now-finished map.

"All of you should already know why we are at war with Kondoma but, I will explain anyway." Coven began. He pointed to a section of the map that was in the middle of Remtaya and Kondoma. "This is called the disputed territory." Coven explained. "This belongs to Remtaya, but Kondoma really wants it," Coven said bluntly. Seth waited for Coven to start telling how this dispute began but he then began to talk about what the city of Kondoma looks like and where its defenses were.

Seth looked around to see if anyone was going to protest but no one did. Seth had an overwhelming urge to raise his hand but the shy part of him stopped him, saying that it was too risky. Then, in an act of pure randomness, he raised his hand. Coven stopped and looked at Seth.

"Yes, Chosen One Seth?" Coven said with a hint of resentment. Seth had to try to ignore the title that Coven gave him in order to concentrate on the matter at hand.

"I was wondering if you were going to explain to us how Kondoma also has a valid claim on that territory?" Seth asked nervously. There was silence in the room. Seth looked around to see that many of the people in the room were looking at him with shock.

"What do you mean?" Coven asked with a waver in his voice. "That territory belongs to Remtaya." Coven restated.

"That is not completely true," Seth said. "Before the war began there were many people in that territory that belonged to Kondoma, then, when the Kry wars happened, they had to evacuate. When it was safe to return, Remtaya had claimed that land. So in a way, Remtaya actually started the war with Kondoma." Just as Seth finished, he realized that he should have listened to his shy side.

"That could not be farther from the truth," Coven said angrily. "That territory was always Remtaya's and will always be Remtaya's," Coven said with a cold rage. Seth knew that he should sit down but something kept him up.

"But that is not consistent with history." Seth countered. "The territory was actually unofficially claimed by Kondoma but during the war, it became too ravaged, and everyone forgot about it until the war was over," Seth explained feeling more and more anger and disbelief in the people that were around him. Coven threw up his hands in frustration.

"I can't believe what I am hearing," Coven said looking at Seth with anger in his eyes. "You are the next Chosen One, you are destined to kill the evil King of Kondoma, and you are defending them. You are defending him," he accused. Seth was going to say something, but Kitty calmly gestured at him to sit back down. She then told Coven to continue. Seth was sweating and almost started to cry. He understood why Kitty had him sit down. Coven was becoming very angry, in fact, Seth was almost certain that if Kitty had not asked him to sit down Coven would have gotten physical.

"Are you okay," Evan asked Seth as Coven continued to explain the defensive capabilities of Kondoma. Seth nodded at Evan, Kitty, and Orin who were looking at him with worried faces.

"I am sorry I told you to sit down." Kitty apologized. "I just know how fanatic Coven can get," she said.

"It's okay. I understand why." Seth whispered to her.

"Good job standing up to him for as long as you did," Orin whispered to Seth before turning and looking at what Coven was pointing at.

"Now we will have to keep planning as the weeks go on, but the plan right now is getting into the Kondoman castle undetected, then our primary objective is to keep Seth alive at all costs and to get him close to the King for him to kill," Coven explained. "We will hold off as many of the guards as we can while Seth makes the kill," he said. Seth was hit by the sudden realization that he was supposed to kill the King of Kondoma.

Seth immediately raised his hand. Coven looked at Seth with a fake smile plastered on his face.

"Yes," Coven said, obviously trying not to sound angry.

"I am sorry but is there a plan where I *don't* have to kill the king?" Seth asked. Coven rolled his eyes.

"What do you mean?" He said, annoyed.

"The only things I have ever killed were some unfortunate spiders that found their way into my room. And I felt bad after killing them. So, I do not think I can kill a human." Seth explained.

"You have no choice, Seth, you have been prophesied to kill him," Coven said smiling a dark smile.

"Well, that is not exactly true. Prophecies do not always come true." Seth said. "And I have seen my prophecy, sure it says that I'm going to kill the King of Kondoma, but prophecies can be wrong." He added.

"So you will not kill the evil King ?" Coven asked.

"I hope not," Seth said truthfully. Evan slapped his hand on his face in exasperation. Coven's face became very red.

"Sit. Down." Coven said with barely concealed rage as he stared down the young Chosen One. Seth sat.

"Now there are some people that all of you should know about," Coven said, calming himself. He motioned for Kitty to change the chalkboard's picture. Kitty flicked her wand in the air and the map began to change into a new picture that was colored. The picture that formed was a full-body portrait of a woman in a black dress who had long, black hair. The form of her body was so gaunt she looked sickly.

"This is Loral," Coven said. "She is a very powerful and dangerous witch. We will try to keep away from her. She has been known to eat some of the people she tortures." Coven explained. "If we get the chance, we should try to kill her but if we can't or if you find yourself alone and you know where she is, do not engage her and run back to the group." Coven advised. Coven nodded at Kitty to change the picture, and she waved her wand. The next picture was of three women, all three with long, red hair and wearing red dresses. The woman in the middle of the others looked taller and the woman to the left had red paint in the shape of a flame on her right cheek. The three women's faces looked similar to each other; they were handsome faces, but they looked so cold. Seth had an uneasy chill when he looked at them.

"These three are rogue Phoenixes." Coven began. Many of the people in the room began to whisper quietly when they heard that.

"I hate rogue Phoenixes," Orin said under his breath. Seth had learned about rogue Phoenixes. Contrary to their name, rogue Phoenixes had nothing to do with actual Phoenixes. The only way in which they were similar to real Phoenixes was their ability to make fire.

"These women are also very dangerous. Their names are Seapa, Septa, and Seala." Coven said. "They are known as the three sisters and they have killed many. They usually follow what the witch Loral tells them to do." Coven explained. "Together, with Loral, these women are called the assassins," Coven added. "The three sisters are considered just as dangerous as Loral and should not be fought alone." Coven warned.

"Can't we just splash water on the rogue Phoenixes?" Someone asked.

"It is true that if a rogue Phoenix is exposed to water they will blow up, and if any of you get a good chance to kill these three abominations feel free to. I will just add that they have gone this long without being hit by water so I think they do know how to stay dry." Coven said. The picture changed again. This time it was a full-body profile of a man. The man wore a black cloak and a blue tunic under it, and he had brown pants on. His hair was dark, and his eyes were brown.

"This is Orson. The evil King's younger brother." Coven said. "Not much is known about Orson. He is a recluse and is rarely seen in public. He is considered to have no fighting skills and could possibly be a diplomat for his brother, or he could be some sort of scientist. If what we know about him is accurate then he will be very easy to eliminate." Coven determined. Seth looked at the picture of Orson.

He seems a lot like me, Seth thought to himself. Kitty waved her wand in the air once more and the image changed. The new image showed a man wearing nothing but black clothes. He had short black hair and looked very angry in the picture; he was also sitting on a throne with steps leading up to it. As everyone looked at the picture many began to whisper and mutter quietly.

"As many of you already know this is Korson, or as we call him, the evil King," Coven said pointing at the drawing. "Seth," Coven said. Seth looked at Coven, hoping he wasn't still angry with him. However, when Seth looked at Coven's face, he appeared to be serious, not mad.

"I want you to study everything about Korson. I want you to memorize everything we know about his strengths and his weaknesses. Make him your life and learn all you can because it will all come down to you." Coven said seriously.

"Okay," Seth said quietly and nervously.

Coven looked back at the board. "We know that Korson is fluent in all known forms of fighting and that he is known for collecting rare and deadly weapons. He is also good at magic and is considered one of the deadliest men in all of Terina.

"We all know what he does to the innocent and good," Coven said bowing his head in sadness. Seth noticed that everyone except for him was bowing their heads.

"So I will say one more time," Coven said when everyone raised their heads. "We will do this, we have the Chosen One and if we put ourselves to the test and are prepared I know we will win. We will win this for the King, the Queen, and for all of Remtaya." Coven's voice began to get louder. "We will win for all of the free people of Terina, and WE WILL WIN THIS WAR!" Coven shouted, raising his hands in victory. Almost everyone got up and started to clap and cheer. Orin was sitting still; he was clapping but didn't seem to be as excited as the others. Seth heard him think how cruel it was to send a child to kill someone. Seth looked at Orin behind him feeling the thoughts that flowed from him. He heard him think how he would do anything to prevent Serena from going on the mission. Seth felt how deeply Orin cared for Serena. Seth heard Orin think about how he disagreed with the idea that Seth should go, but since he wasn't Seth's care giver there was nothing he could do to prevent it. Seth's attention was taken off Orin when Kitty and Evan stood up and continued clapping.

"He certainly knows how to give a speech," Kitty said to Evan as they both clapped. Seth sat on his chair, feeling like there was no hope. What would this demand for him to kill another human do to him? Seth sat there for what seemed like hours as most of the people that were in the arena left. The only ones left with him were Kitty, Evan, and Orin.

"What is the matter?" Evan asked.

Seth sat there, thoughts filling his mind. "How am I going to kill someone?" He asked. "I can't." He bowed his head. "I would rather die than kill."

"You will have to decide what to do when you are faced with the decision," Evan said to Seth.

"I don't stand a chance. I'm going to be killed by the King." Seth said feeling completely drained of energy.

"No, you won't," Kitty said with a determined sound to her voice. Seth was staring into Kitty's eyes. They gleamed with more than determination. They shined with a willpower that Seth had never seen before. "I will not let him kill you." She promised, her voice clear and simple. Seth didn't know how, but he knew that what Kitty said was more than just a promise to him, it was law, and she would never break it.

CHAPTER FOURTEEN

ATTACKED

What do you think? Should Seth kill the King of Kondoma? Is that right? Well, think about it for a second...

Are you done? Let's talk about Orin for a moment. Orin is a good man, who has been through a lot. I'll let the story you are reading tell you more about that. But let's just say Orin has been through the ringer of bad luck. Despite how he looks Orin is in his sixties, so he's seen a lot throughout his life. And before you think ew, gross, didn't he date Kitty? First of all, that's what many werewolves have to do if they pair with a non-werewolf. Because they age slower than most other humans, they have to find people who match their physical age rather than their biological phase of life. And second, the main reason why Orin started dating Kitty was because he saw how much Kitty cared for Serena, and he fell in love with her for that reason. Also remember they are no longer together so it really doesn't matter anyways. Orin and Kitty both had to deal with people who would not understand what was happening. While most liked Orin and Kitty. Some did find their courting wrong and made sure to tell them about how they felt. That's a little history about Orin for you, now let's see how Seth's training is going.

"**G**et into a fighting stance," Coven commanded. Seth spread his feet and lifted his arms and hands to his chest. He looked around to see Coven, Orin, and Kitty all surrounding him. Coven unexpectedly pounced on Seth. Seth tried to dodge but Coven got hold of his leg and pulled him down. Seth slammed to the floor and then quickly rolled away before Coven could get him. Seth stood up just as Orin ran at him. In self-defense Seth held his hand up to block Orin's tackle, there was a flash and Orin was sent flying the opposite direction. He crashed into the ground of the arena.

"Sorry," Seth shouted to the downed man. Kitty was suddenly right on top of him; she grabbed Seth's right hand and flipped it around so that it was behind his back. She wrapped her left arm around his neck and held him there. Seth tried to move his left arm up to Kitty's arm that was around his throat.

"You should know that I gag easily," Seth tried to say.

"Do you really?" Kitty asked, concerned, releasing her grip around Seth's throat.

"Yes, but I will le…." Seth stopped talking to gag. "Sorry," Seth said.

"Do you want me to stop," Kitty asked.

"No," Seth said his teeth clenched so he would not gag again. Seth's head suddenly pounded and Kitty was sent flying backward from him. "Sorry," Seth shouted to Kitty. She got up and waved it off. Orin and Coven were on top of him, Seth ducked and ran past them as they leaped at him. He turned to see them right on him again, they both tackled him. Seth bent down and quickly braced himself. Seth's head pounded again, suddenly before Orin and Coven could get on him there was a flash of light around him which repelled Orin and Coven away from Seth. Seth got up to see Orin and Coven sprawled against the floor.

"Sorry," Seth said to them. Coven and Orin both were helped up by Kitty.

"Stop saying that," Coven said to Seth. "But I thought I told you this was a combat exercise, not a magical one," Coven said with anger in his voice.

"Why can't he use magic?" Kitty asked. "He is kicking all of our butts with his magical abilities." She marveled.

"I can't help it," Seth said. "When someone attacks me, I get a big headache and then I use magic." He explained.

"You are not doing that on purpose?" Kitty asked in shock.

"No, Coven told me no magic before we started," Seth reminded her.

"What does that mean if Seth is not doing it on purpose?" Orin asked Kitty, concerned. Seth looked over to where the other groups were training. Evan was in the closest group and was doing very well keeping three people off of him.

"We should go see Agatha and find out why you are getting head-aches every time you inadvertently use magic," Kitty said to Seth.

"Okay, but only Seth, we need to keep training," Coven said. "Seth when you are done come back here." He commanded.

"Okay," Seth said reluctantly. He wished he could just go to his room and read a good book and not have to sweat and train for a mission that was probably going to kill him.

Seth walked past Kitty who nodded at him encouragingly. He then looked up to see Orin walk past him.

"Good luck." Orin winked at Seth as he went by.

Seth left the arena chamber and walked to one of the transport rooms.

"Hospital please," Seth said to the transport room when he entered it. He stood there feeling very tired and stressed. The room flashed and Seth was surprised to see someone next to him.

"Oh. Seth, I was just thinking about coming to see you." The woman said, smiling kindly at Seth. It took him a while to realize who it was he was looking at. Then it hit him.

"Your majesty," Seth said, quickly bowing his head.

"Please, Seth that bowing is only when people are watching." The

Queen said lifting Seth's head with her hands. "And call me Julia." The Queen insisted.

"I don't think I can," Seth said, wondering if there could ever be a day where he and the Queen would be on a first-name basis.

"Do you want me to call you Chosen One every time we meet?" The Queen asked.

"No." Seth acknowledged as he realized what she was saying.

"Are you going to the hospital?" Queen Julia asked.

"Yes. I have been using magic without meaning to. I'm not in control of it." Seth explained.

"You poor dear," Julia said. "Well come, I will accompany you." She said walking out of the transporter room. Seth followed in close pursuit. They walked toward the glass door that was the entrance to the hospital. Seth could see Agatha standing over an empty bed and straightening the sheets. The Queen and Seth entered the chamber just as Agatha was finished.

"Hello, Agatha." Queen Julia said cheerfully. Agatha turned and smiled at the Queen.

"Julia, it's been a while since you have come to the hospital," Agatha said walking over to the Queen and giving her a big hug.

"Well, I am just so healthy." The Queen said, reciprocating the hug. Agatha noticed Seth while she was hugging the Queen.

"Seth, it's nice to see you again," Agatha said as she walked over to Seth and patted him on his back.

"I enjoy your company, but I have to ask who's not feeling their best here?" She asked, looking at Seth and the Queen.

"I was just looking around the castle. It has been a while since I just walked around the fortress. Then I met Seth and he said that he has been having trouble controlling his magic." The Queen said looking at Seth with worry in her eyes.

"I have been training with…" Seth stopped and sighed. "Team Seth." He said rolling his eyes in annoyance.

The Queen and Agatha laughed at the very obvious name.

"I loathe that name almost as much as I hate gravity," Seth said.

"Why do you hate gravity?" Agatha asked with interest.

"It has tried to kill me three times and its constant nature is helpful but also very annoying. It is like gravity is taunting science to find out its secrets but will not reveal them. Gravity is the bane of my existence." Seth explained.

"Well, you definitely are not like the rest of the Chosen Ones," Agatha said smiling at Seth as they walked to a bed. Seth sat on the edge of the bed and the Queen sat next to him. Agatha took out her wand and moved slowly around Seth's head. The wand turned a light blue as she moved it around Seth.

"Have you been having headaches accompanied by this magic?" Agatha asked.

"Yes," Seth said. "Why?" He asked.

"People with potential for great magical abilities can have headaches because their power is trying to reach its full potential," Agatha explained. "I would suggest that you learn how to control your power and then the headaches should subside." She said softly.

"I am wondering if it is possible for my magic to try to protect me?" Seth asked. The Queen and Agatha looked at each other questioningly.

"What do you mean?" The Queen asked.

"When I was training with my group, I would only use magic when I was being attacked by someone. Could my magic be protecting me?" Seth asked again.

"I do know a lot of magic, but I don't suppose that magic can think. It is just energy that is all around us and some can manipulate it. I have never heard of magic saving someone's life or protecting people that have it." Agatha said.

"Okay, thank you," Seth said, feeling relieved that it was nothing serious. He and the Queen got up, thanked Agatha, and then walked out of the hospital and back to the transporter room.

Loral looked up at the giant wall that surrounded the city of Remtaya. Behind her were Septa Seapa, and Seala and behind them were five soldiers that the King had given her. They were hiding in a small forest overlooking the Kingdom of Remtaya.

"How are we going to penetrate that?" Seapa asked with a high, pinched rasp.

"Silence," Loral hissed at Seapa. "Getting into the Castle Wall fortress is easy, it's getting out with the Chosen One that will be difficult," Loral explained to the group.

"Oh, I hope he is as good looking as the other ones were." Seala screeched with glee. Loral rolled her eyes.

"You can play with the Chosen One once we have him, but for now keep your head in the game," Septa said, slapping her sister hard on the head. Loral stopped when she found what she was looking for.

"There, do you see that guard?" Loral pointed at a part of the wall where there was a lookout post. "In a few minutes the guards will change their posts. For a few seconds there will be a blind spot where that guard is." Loral explained to the rest of the group.

"What do we do when we get inside?" One of the soldiers asked Loral.

"We kill everyone." Seala said laughing excitedly.

"No," Loral said, staring down Seala. "We do not have time for fun. We will get into the castle and try to extract the boy quietly. If all goes to plan no one will know we were even there." Loral said. "If we do attract unwanted attention, that is when you and your men will distract the resistance." Loral said pointing at the team leader of the soldiers. "While I and two of your soldiers go get the Chosen One." Loral added.

"How will we find this Seth?" Septa asked.

"I have ways of finding people." Loral said darkly. She looked up and saw the guard move away from the lookout post.

"It's time." Loral said. "Quickly, follow me." She commanded. They left the concealment of the trees and moved into the open, keeping low to the ground as they moved to the wall where the blind spot was. Loral looked at the gray stones that made up most of the castle. She pulled out her wand and began to spin it around in a circle while she chanted a spell. Magic sprung from the wand and at the wall, causing a portal to form. The spinning portal blazed blue and red and made a whooshing noise like wind.

"Get in." Loral commanded. Seala, Seapa, and Septa all went through the portal along with four of the five solders. Loral stopped the fifth soldier before he went through.

"I need you to wait for my signal and then come out with the wagon. We will need to get out of here as fast as possible." Loral said.

"Understood," The soldier said running back to the woods. Loral stepped into the portal and was inside the castle wall. She looked around to make sure everyone was here.

"Let's go." Loral commanded as they walked down the hall.

"Won't people notice us?" Septa asked looking around with apprehension.

"This castle is so big there are places that rarely have anyone in them." Loral began to say when a prophesier turned the corner. The prophesier looked at them, shock on his face.

"I have been wrong in the past." Loral acknowledged.

"Who are you?" The young prophesier asked. Loral stepped closer to the boy.

"What is your name boy?" She asked harshly.

"I am Lowden." He answered looking at the others with a questioning look.

"Oh. Well then run along Lowden, my friends and I are just exploring the castle before we..." Loral looked behind her at her group that were still holding swords and other weapons. "Before we get to the arena to practice our skills." Loral lied. The others behind Loral nodded their heads trying to make the lie seem more truthful.

"I thought we came here to kidnap the Chosen One." Seala said, sounding confused. Loral closed her eyes and sighed.

"What?" Lowden said with shock. "You're here to kidnap Seth!" Lowden shouted. He quickly ran the opposite direction.

"Really," Loral shouted at Seala angrily. She and the three rogue Phoenixes ran after the boy. Loral shot a spell at the boy making him lose his footing, causing him to fall to the ground. Before Loral could get to him the boy shot a spell into the air. A small green ball of light rose in the air and then quickly moved out of sight. Loral heard the ball start to screech the word "intruders." She knelt by the boy and smiled.

"You should not have done that Lowden." She said before taking her knife and slitting his throat.

"Oh! Killing, we get to kill people now!" Seala said running over to the now dead corpse and looking at it. "Can I keep him?" She asked, smiling.

Loral grabbed Seala and pushed her against the stone wall. "Because of your stupidity this just became much harder." Loral shouted at Seala. Seala began to moan and tried to twist out of Loral's grasp.

"Let her go, we do not have time for this." Septa said to Loral. Loral spat on Seala's face and then let her go.

"Come on." Loral commanded.

"The guards of Remtaya will be on top of us now, not to mention prophesiers." Septa said walking up to Loral. "There is no way we can get to the Chosen One now." She complained.

Loral smiled. "Like I said before I have ways of finding people." She began to chant a spell waving her wand around her left hand. A small blue ball emerged from nowhere and floated there. "Find the Chosen One named Seth." Loral commanded. The blue ball winked twice and then zoomed away just as Loral could hear the sound of running coming closer.

"Get ready to fight." Loral commanded the soldiers.

Seth and the Queen walked down the halls so Seth could get back to the arena.

"Seth, can I ask you a question?" The Queen asked, looking at Seth with her kind green eyes.

"Of course, Queen Julia." Seth said nervously.

"Do you really want to be the Chosen One?" She asked. Before Seth could answer there was the sound of someone screaming something. Seth and the Queen turned around to where the noise was coming from. A small green light suddenly zoomed past them screaming the word intruders. The Queen looked around nervously.

"Seth come, let us get to your friends." She said as they both ran to the arena. "We must hurry."

They ran into the arena to see that most of the people in the chamber were grabbing weapons and running out after the green orb. The Queen and Seth ran to where Kitty, Evan, Orin, and Coven were.

"My Queen." Coven said bowing.

"Get up Coven we do not have time for that." The Queen commanded.

"What is happening?" Evan asked.

"I am not sure, but by the sounds that I have been hearing I would say we are under attack." The Queen said. "I can also safely assume that they are here for Seth," she said.

"What? Why me?" Seth asked.

"You are the Chosen One." Evan explained. "The evil King most likely wants you to be killed or kidnapped," he said.

"We must stop them." Coven said grabbing an ax and running after the others.

"Queen Julia you need to go to the safe room." Orin said looking at her.

"Seth needs to get there too." Kitty acknowledged.

"Agreed, Kitty and Evan you need to give Seth and I time to get to the safe room." The Queen determined. "Orin you will escort us and my husband there," she said.

"Understood," Kitty said, pulling out her wand. The Queen looked at Evan and Kitty. "You two are like the children I never had. Do not take any unnecessary risks." The Queen told both of them with tears in her eyes.

"We must go." Orin said. The Queen hugged Kitty and Evan and then left with Seth and Orin.

Seth looked back at his two friends.

Be safe. Seth thought as they left the arena chamber.

"What is the safe room?" Seth asked Orin.

"It is a place where the Queen, King, and Senate can hide and be safe if Remtaya is ever attacked or intruders break in." Orin explained.

"It is protected by a powerful enchantment. We will be safe there." Queen Julia said.

"What about Evan and Kitty?" Seth asked, feeling very worried for them.

The Queen was going to answer when suddenly Orin held his hand up motioning for them to stop.

"What is it?" The Queen asked.

"I hear something." Orin said tilting his head a little to the left.

"I can't hear anything." Seth whispered quietly to the Queen.

"Because Orin is a werewolf, he can hear much better than other humans." The Queen explained quietly. Orin suddenly turned around and looked in the direction from which they'd come.

"Something is following us." Orin said.

"What is it?" The Queen asked nervously.

"I don't know." Orin said. "Hurry, we have to go now." He said motioning them to run. They all ran to the nearest transport room. Seth looked behind him as they ran and saw a glimpse of what looked like a small blue orb zooming toward them.

"Faster." Orin shouted. As the orb got closer to them. Seth saw the transport room and ran as fast as he could toward it. They were almost there; Seth could hear what sounded like buzzing behind him. The Queen and Orin opened the door of the transport room and both went inside. They both turned and beckoned Seth to come faster. The buzzing got louder and louder. Seth dared to not look back. He was only a few inches away from the room. Orin and the Queen held their hands out so they could grab him when he got to their reach. Seth felt a warm uncomfortable feeling on his back. The buzzing seemed to be right on top of him.

"Jump," Orin yelled. Seth complied, jumping toward them. Orin grabbed Seth by the arm and pulled him inside. As Seth turned, he saw the small blue ball was right in front of them. Orin slammed the door before the orb could get inside.

"The safe room," the Queen panted. The room flashed as Seth was trying to take deep breaths.

"Come on." Orin urged as the room made its signature beeping sound. Orin opened the door and they began to walk down another hallway. Seth looked around realizing that he had never been to this area of the castle before.

"What was that thing that was chasing us?" Seth asked, still breathing hard.

"I think it was a tracking spell, and it was tracking *you*." Orin said looking at Seth as they kept walking.

As they turned a corner they ran into a group of people. Seth realized that most of them were senators, including Senators Soven and Russell. Along with the senators were the King and some guards.

"Julia," the King said, walking over to her. "Thank goodness you're safe," he said.

"We have to keep going." Orin insisted. "I can hear the tracker." He warned.

"Tracker what tracker?" the King asked as the group began to run toward the safe room.

"The people who are attacking apparently are looking for Seth." The Queen explained.

"We are almost there." One of the senators shouted pointing to a brownstone wall. Seth suddenly heard the same buzzing that he had heard before. He looked back to see the small blue orb flying toward them.

"It's here." Seth shouted. The group all stopped at the brown wall. The King hurried and whispered something at the wall. As he did the wall opened and all the senators quickly ran in. Seth turned and saw the blue orb quickly shooting toward them.

"Seth get behind me." Orin said. Seth walked behind Orin and into a small hallway that was where the brown wall used to be. The senators were all going into another room on the other side of the small hall.

"Quickly follow me." The Queen said to Seth. Seth looked over to see Orin standing in front of the small hallway, his back turned.

"What is he doing?" Seth asked as he heard the buzzing get louder.

"Seth get in here!" The Queen shouted. Seth turned to see that the Queen, King, and all the senators were inside the room and the stone doors that protected the room were closing.

"We can't leave Orin out here." Seth said as the buzzing noise got louder. Seth suddenly heard growling and turned to see that Orin was making the noise. He had his fists clenched as he stared down the tracker. The small blue ball zoomed at him and shot a burst of light at his chest. Orin was thrown backwards. Seth dodged his body as it flew by him. Orin's limp body then flew into the room, knocking the Queen down. Seth quickly ran to the room, trying to get there before the stone doors closed.

He was too late.

"No!" The Queen shouted as the doors closed. Seth turned around to look at the small blue ball. It flew toward him, its buzzing sound getting louder. It stopped right at Seth's face and flashed three times. Seth ran the other direction, trying to avoid the tracker. He ran out of the small hallway with the tracker in close pursuit. The ball flew in front of him, he gasped as the ball buzzed extremely loudly. Then it zoomed straight toward him. Seth held up his hand as the ball enveloped him.

Loral pointed her wand at a prophesier, shooting a blast of energy at the person sending them spiraling to the floor. Kitty shot a spell at Loral, but she deflected it.

"That little Seer." Loral said angrily. The hallway was erupting into a full battle. Remtaya soldiers were holding up their shields constantly driving Loral's group back to where they had come from. The prophesiers were firing constant spells at the three sisters and the Kondoma soldiers. Kitty and Evan shot spell after spell at the invading force.

Loral called two soldiers to come to where she was.

"Yes ma'am." One of the soldiers asked.

"You two will follow me while the others keep the way clear for us." Loral commanded.

"Where are we going?" The same soldier asked. Loral smiled darkly.

"To get the Chosen One," She smiled maliciously. They suddenly vanished from the battle.

Kitty and Evan looked at each other.

"Seth." Evan said worriedly, running the way they had come, Kitty following close behind.

Loral and the two soldiers appeared next to the ball that was confining Seth. He pounded on the round, blue barrier that surrounded him. Loral walked over to Seth and smiled.

"You must be Seth," she said. "I have to admit I did imagine you to be older and taller."

Loral looked at one of the soldiers.

"Come here," She commanded. "I am going to release him. When I do you need to tie him up so he can't go anywhere." Loral said to the soldier. She waved her hand and the barrier that was holding Seth dissipated. The soldier took Seth's gloved hands and tied them with some rope.

"Ouch," Seth said as the soldier tightened the knots around Seth's hands.

"Sorry," The soldier apologized sincerely. He then tied up Seth's feet.

"Is he ready?" Loral asked impatiently.

"Yes," The soldier said, picking Seth up and putting him over his right shoulder, so that Seth's upper body was facing toward the man's back.

"Good, Now let's…" Loral stopped and turned her wand on someone who was behind her.

Seth realized that it was Agatha. She and Loral both had their wands pointed at each other.

"Take the boy to one of the transport rooms and wait for me there. Do not get captured," Loral demanded. The soldier carried Seth away so that he could not see what was going on anymore.

Loral faced Agatha and smiled darkly.

"It's been a long time my sister." Loral said.

"Not long enough." Agatha retorted.

Loral laughed evilly.

"Mom and dad would punish you, Agatha, for saying such a dreadful thing." Loral said faking sadness.

"You were the one who killed them. While I was trying to do something good in the world." Agatha said with deep rage.

"Yes, do what they wanted us to do, become doctors like our pitiful mother." Loral said spitting on the ground. "I was not going to let them make me weak like they did you!" She shouted. "Intanga!" Loral enchanted. Agatha blocked the spell and shouted one at Loral. Loral caught the spell with her wand and deflected it toward Agatha. Agatha quickly dodged and shot another spell at Loral.

"You know you are not as powerful as I am." Loral said smiling impishly.

"I didn't want to be more powerful than you," Agatha panted, drained from the magic she was using.

Loral laughed. "I promised myself that if I saw you ever again I would kill you, and now I have my chance." She said cackling.

"You will not destroy me like you did our family." Agatha yelled. She pointed her wand at Loral and the wind began to spin around them.

Loral chuckled maniacally. "Are you planning to scare me away with the wind that you have conjured inside a building?" She mocked.

Agatha smiled. "That was never my idea." She said, determined. "I needed to distract you for my friends to get here." Agatha said. Loral turned to find herself trapped by Evan and Kitty. Loral turned to Agatha.

"This is not over my sister." Loral said with anger. She waved her wand and vanished. Kitty ran over to Agatha.

"I will ask you about the whole sister thing when we are done rescuing Seth." Kitty said to Agatha. All three of them ran back down the hallway where Seth had been taken.

Loral appeared next to the two soldiers who had Seth. "Let's go." She said transporting them back to where the rest of the team was.

"Get to the exit point." Loral commanded angrily. Loral turned to the three rogue Phoenixes.

"We need some cover." Loral said to Septa. Seala, Septa, and Seapa all raised their hands causing a wall of fire to form in front of them, blocking the Remtaya soldiers and prophesiers. The group all ran to where they had come in. The soldier carrying Seth leapt through the portal first followed by the other soldiers and the three rogue Phoenixes. Loral's path was suddenly blocked by a soldier who was holding a sword at her chest. Loral put her wand on the sword causing it to turn into dust. She walked over to the man and grabbed his neck, lifting him in the air with ease. She caressed his face with her other hand.

"I would kill you properly, but I just don't have the time." She said scratching the soldier's face with her long nails. The man began to scream in pain as she dropped him and walked through the portal. Loral ran to where the carriage was waiting for her. Soldiers on the top of the wall began to shoot arrows at them. Loral held up her wand and deflected the oncoming arrows. The soldier carrying Seth leapt into the back of the wagon along with the other soldiers and the three sisters. Loral got in the front of the wagon and whipped the horse to start moving. She began to wave her wand to make a portal back to Kondoma.

Kitty ran to the wall where she could see the wagon and the portal that was about to be produced.

"Inlinken." Kitty shouted. A giant metal chain erupted from Kitty's wand and moved toward the wagon where it connected with it, stopping the wagon from moving.

Loral looked back at the chain that was stopping the escape. She waved her wand at the giant chain, breaking it. As the wagon got closer to the portal Kitty pointed her wand at the wagon, concentrating.

"Consivitoe." Kitty shouted. A blue light flew toward the wagon, hitting it right when it went through the portal. The portal shut, leaving no sign of the wagon or Seth anywhere.

Seth lay in the back of the wagon as they moved along what seemed to be a dirt road.

"Where are we?" One of the rogue Phoenixes asked. The wagon stopped and Loral uncovered the canvas that was blocking where she was sitting.

"That Seer put a blocking spell all over the wagon. We have to wait a few hours before I can make a portal to get to Kondoma." She said angrily. She dropped the canvas and the wagon started moving again. One of the rogue Phoenixes looked at Seth with piercing red eyes.

"You are even more handsome than I thought." The rogue Phoenix said, giggling. "Maybe when the King chops your head off, he will give it to me and I will get to play with you all day long." She said happily.

Seth suddenly realized that it was too late. They had kidnapped him. He was going to die. Seth began to breathe hard.

"What is it?" The same soldier that had carried him asked.

"I am going to die." Seth said breathing harder, he soon began to hyperventilate.

"Shut him up." One of the other rogue Phoenixes said.

"Just relax, you are safe now, you are not going to die." The soldier said, trying to calm Seth down.

"Yes he is." Seala said looking at the soldier excitedly. "Then I want his head and body." She added. Seth's hyperventilation became worse.

"Oh shut up." Septa said looking at Seth and pulling out a small pouch from her red dress. She opened it and pulled out some white powder.

"Here this should shut you up for at least an hour." Septa said sprinkling the white powder all over his head. Seth's head suddenly began to pound and he began to choke. His breathing became erratic. He then began to convulse with his eyes rolled to the back of his head.

"What did you give him?" The soldier asked, horrified.

"It is sleeping dust." Septa said looking at Seth as the seizure got worse.

"Is he dying?" Seala asked excitedly.

"Shut up Seala." Seapa demanded. "Loral, Septa is killing the Chosen One." Seapa said loud enough for Loral to hear her.

"I am not, he is doing it to himself." Septa protested. The wagon stopped and Loral opened the canvas to see Seth.

"What did you do?" Loral asked angrily, holding her wand above Seth. Seth's convulsions stopped and he began to relax. Soon Seth laid there calmly sleeping.

"What happened?" Loral asked looking at the soldier that was next to Seth.

"He began to hyperventilate, and Septa put some sleeping dust on him and then he just started to convulse." The soldier explained.

"He must have had a bad reaction to the sleeping dust." Loral determined. "Do not give it to him again, Korson wants the Chosen One alive when we get there." She said dropping the canvas. The wagon began to move again.

"I was not aware that anyone could have a bad reaction to sleeping dust." Septa said nonchalantly.

CHAPTER FIFTEEN

FINDING SETH

It is a very strange feeling to realize that you cannot do anything to stop what is happening. It is maddening. You want to stop the future due to uncertainty. The need for control is a very powerful desire for some people. These individuals could be called two things, control freaks or dark soulers. Now, don't be offended if you could be considered a dark souler, or just a dark soul for short; this does not make you a bad person. In fact, you must remember that nothing, and I do mean nothing, is born evil. It is always influenced for bad or evil. Every life form is innocent and good at the out-set, but through certain processes, a good thing could become evil. However, people who are dark soulers were born that way. If you have a dark soul, you are not evil; in fact, you have a great potential to be good. You also have a great potential to be evil, but that will be explained later. For now, suffice it to say, you know at least one person who has a dark soul. That person is Seth. Seth is a dark souler. Shocking, you say? Well, not really. Seth is definitely a person who likes to keep things under his own control. Yet, Seth is not an evil person in the least; he is a very kind and compassionate person. Sometimes, Seth is too compassionate, but he can't be faulted for that.

On the planet of Terinta there are two sub-races of humans, the Chosen Race and the Wanted Race, as you should know by now. Seth is part of the

Chosen Race. About twenty-five percent of the Chosen race are considered to be dark soulers and most of them are perfectly fine people with germ phobias, along with anxiety and compulsions. Some people have social anxiety coupled with obsessive cleanliness, but all in all, these people are just like you. Well, it must be admitted that evidence has shown that individuals with dark souls are fifty percent more intelligent than the average person. Now, don't let this information dissuade you from pursuing the hard sciences. There are some downsides to having a dark soul, but that discussion will come later. Meanwhile, what will Kitty and Evan do to get Seth back?

K itty walked down the hall to the hospital. She quickly opened the door to find hundreds of people lying in beds. She looked toward a bed on the right where Agatha was tending to the Queen. Next to the Queen's bed was Orin who was sleeping soundly, with Serena sitting nearby. Serena held his hand in hers and looked at him nervously. Kitty walked over to Serena, who looked up at Kitty.

"How is he?" Kitty asked Serena.

"Agatha said that if he was not a werewolf, he would probably be dead." Serena said, her voice shaking with concern.

"I always told him to be thankful for his werewolf genes," Kitty said, putting her hand on Serena's shoulder.

"Did they really get Seth?" Serena asked nervously.

"I'm afraid so," Kitty said sadly, "but I have a plan to get him back."

"I hope you find him before the evil King does," Serena said. Kitty walked over to the Queen.

"Julia, are you alright?" Kitty asked the Queen, hoping not to see if she had any scratches or bruises.

"I'm fine. Agatha got nervous when she heard that Orin had fallen on me," the Queen explained.

"Orin is a big, muscular man and he was completely limp when he fell on you. I needed to see if you were injured," Agatha said, walking over to them.

"You should ensure that Orin is well," Julia said to Agatha.

Agatha smiled softly. "He'll be fine," she said to Serena and the Queen. Kitty looked at Agatha for a second.

"What?" Agatha asked, feeling uncomfortable under Kitty's intense gaze.

"I have to ask about your sister Loral," Kitty said, raising her eyebrows.

Agatha shook her head. "We may be sisters, but we hate each other. I have no loyalty to her," Agatha assured them.

"I don't doubt that," Kitty said to Agatha, "I was just wondering if you can tell us anything more about her."

"Well, I can say that she has poisoned her own fingernails," Agatha responded sadly.

"What do you mean?" the Queen asked.

"We found a soldier lying where they had escaped. He was infected with shadow fever from what looked like small fingernail cuts on his face," Agatha explained. "He is in the stages of reversion. He will either die or turn to shadow."

"How do you know Loral did this?" Kitty asked.

"Because this is exactly what she would do," Agatha said sadly. Serena let go of Orin's hand and arose from her chair.

"What will happen to the soldier with this shadow fever?" Serena asked curiously. "What is shadow fever?"

"Shadow fever is a very deadly and mysterious sickness," Kitty explained. "If a person is infected, then, unfortunately, only one of two things happen. They can either die or go to a nether world where they become servants of darkness." she said sadly.

"Is there a way to save him?" Serena asked.

"No," Agatha said, with sadness.

Kitty walked over and looked at the Queen.

"Julia, I placed a spell on the wagon that carried Seth. They have not arrived in Kondoma yet and I have a plan to get him back," Kitty explained.

"Well, then do not waste time," the Queen said. Kitty nodded and left the chamber. She walked down to the transport room.

"Section seven," Kitty said. The room flashed and beeped. Kitty opened the door and walked quickly down the hall until she reached Seth's room. When Kitty opened the door, she saw Biz and Shadow waiting at the door. Shadow barked and both dogs wagged their tails.

"What is it? Do you need to go to the bathroom?" Kitty asked them. Biz put his ears back and walked to the closed door behind Kitty and scratched at it. She opened the door and Biz and Shadow both ran out of the room toward the nearest exit from the city. Kitty ran after them and found them at a door blocked by guards. Kitty let the dogs out and when they were done, she quickly followed them back to Seth's room. She looked around the room and noticed that they had eaten their food.

"Evan must have fed you," she theorized. Kitty walked to Seth's bathroom and looked around for a comb. Once found, she took one of Seth's hairs from the comb and walked toward Biz and Shadow.

"I'll bring him back," Kitty promised, as she shut the door and again walked toward the transport room.

"It's good that Seth combs his hair once in a while. This hair will be a great help to me," Kitty said aloud. She walked to the nearest transport room, opened the wooden door, and walked inside. Kitty closed the door and stood staring for a while. She wondered why the evil King had decided to kidnap the Chosen One now. He had not attempted this on any Chosen Ones before.

"It had to happen to Seth," Kitty said, shaking her head. "Section five, top level," she commanded. The room flashed and beeped letting Kitty know that it was safe to open the door. She walked out calmly and strode down the hallway toward her own chambers and work area.

Kitty had always wanted to be a wand maker. It was the profession of her father, so she always loved working with various woods to craft a perfect wand. She also loved to create inventions for practical purposes and just for fun. As Kitty walked to her workshop, she could see Evan waiting at her door.

"Did you get it?" Evan asked. Kitty held up her hand, showing Evan the hairs she had retrieved from Seth's comb.

"If you were already in Seth's room, why didn't you just get it yourself and then tell me? We could have done this spell earlier," Kitty grumbled to Evan, opening the door and entering the workshop. The room was filled with boxes, and bottles with different colored liquids in them. A variety of strange smells wafted through the air.

"I haven't been in Seth's room since we took him to the Throne Room," Evan clarified. Kitty turned and looked at Evan inquisitively.

"Then who fed Biz and Shadow?" she asked. Evan shrugged.

"It wasn't me," he said. "I should thank this mysterious person, because they were probably hungry." Kitty said clearing off a spot on the table that was being obscured by various papers and books. She grabbed a map and a small, brown clay bowl, then placed the hairs in the bowl and poured in some orange-looking liquid.

"What is that?" Evan asked, looking at the liquid.

"Urine from a troll," Kitty said simply. Evan's eyes grew wide.

"How did you get it?" Evan asked, not really wanting to know. Kitty smiled and pulled out her wand.

"It's not really troll urine, I just wanted to see how you would react," Kitty laughed. "It is a simple catalyst for the spell to work," Kitty explained, still smiling.

"Have you ever done this before?" Evan asked, as Kitty began to chant a spell.

"No, but I have studied it and seen my father do it," Kitty explained. She began to chant. As she did so, the orange liquid began to spin the floating hair, which turned a blue color and began to spin rapidly around the bowl. The orange liquid then began to change into various colors.

"I thought you said that was a catalyst," Evan said, watching warily as the ever-changing liquid and hair began to spin faster and faster.

"It is!" Kitty shouted, as a deafening roar erupted from the spinning solution. "It should not be affected by the spell!" she yelled, right as the bowl shattered. The liquid was now a vapor. The hair and the orange mist then spun around the table until there was a flash and the cloud flew straight toward the map. Kitty and Evan both looked at each other in shock.

"Was that supposed to happen?" Evan asked, looking at the broken bowl that lay in shards on the table.

Kitty looked at the map with surprise, "No, but no matter what just happened, we can find Seth now," she said with joy, holding up the map to show Evan. A small glowing dot appeared on one of the roads that led to Kondoma.

"The good news is, they appear to be closer to the Remtayan side of the border than the Kondoman side," Kitty said. "It also seems that the dampening spell I put on the wagon worked, or they would be in Kondoma by now," she said happily.

"How long will the spell last?" Evan asked.

"For another four or five hours," Kitty guessed.

"We do not have a lot of time, then," Evan said with haste.

CHAPTER SIXTEEN

A WATER SNAKE THING
AND THE WRATH OF SETH

Technology! It is the best thing to ever exist. It can do so much and it keeps getting better and better. People who hate technology will be left behind and eventually they too will have to concede to the realization that this is the future and there is nothing that they can do about it.

What is magic you may say? Magic is surely some sort of opposite property from technology one could say. Well not quite, magic is a wonderful thing and it is no doubt mysterious, but it is not different from technology or science. It is just something that has no explanation about it yet. Magic is like the constant line that is being drawn from the realm of the understood to the place that is still mysterious. One very important author from the planet Earth said, "Magic's just science that we don't understand yet."

That was Arthur C. Clarke who said that and he is absolutely correct. Magic will always have to keep moving into the realm of understanding and then it will not be called magic anymore. That is just how it works. Do not let this ruin your belief in magic though. It is the constant want to know how the trick is done or the desire to marvel at the mysterious that keeps magic and science so close to each other. There is not one without the other. So live in this realm of technology and hope that Seth can somehow get out of the clutches of Loral and her gang of miscreants.

Seth awoke, his eyes still closed. He lay there thinking about the dream he just had. As the dream began to leave his memory, Seth tried to think about what happened in it. Kitty and Evan were using troll urine to try to find a lost puppy. That was all Seth could remember. Seth was suddenly jarred fully awake from a sudden bump in the road, *Oh, I'm in a wagon*, Seth remembered. He looked around as the full realization of where he was and what was happening to him sunk in again.

"Oh no." Seth said quietly.

"Hi." A woman said. She had very messy red hair and had a deranged look in her red colored eyes. Seth recognized the face of the woman sitting next to him as one of the rogue Phoenixes that he had learned about when he was in Remtaya. Seth was not sure, but the woman looked like the one named Seala. No matter which one she was, Seth knew this was very bad for him.

"I watched you sleep." Seala said with a crazy look.

"That's nice," Seth said nervously, trying to move away from her.

"Leave him alone." The soldier next to Seth said to the rogue Phoenix. Seala hissed at the man and then looked away from Seth, obviously no longer interested in him at the moment.

"Thanks." Seth told the soldier. The soldier had dirty blond scrappy hair that covered up part of his ears. He also had brown facial hair that was very short. Seth noted that his green eyes reminded him of Kitty's eyes.

"So you're the Chosen One." The soldier said with kindness, but also with some resentment.

"Perhaps, but I never wanted to be the Chosen One." Seth explained.

"Wait." The soldier said looking at Seth with surprise. "I thought that the Chosen Ones of Remtaya all volunteered to be the next Chosen One." He said to Seth with shock.

"I did not volunteer. I never even believed in the Chosen Ones." Seth said.

"Then why are you the Chosen One?" The Soldier asked.

"Because of a prophecy that does not make any sense which cryptically mentioned my name." Seth complained. "I was then asked if I wanted to be the Chosen One so that the people of Remtaya could feel good about sending me off to assassinate a King that I don't even know, even though I would probably be killed in the attempt." Seth sighed angrily.

"Well you are definitely not what I expected the Chosen One of Remtaya to be like." The soldier said smiling kindly at Seth.

"I have never met a soldier of Kondoma." Seth said. "It is a pleasure to know that you are just a person like everyone else and not what people say the soldiers of Kondoma are." Seth said happily.

"What do they think we are?" The soldier asked.

"They think that the King of Kondoma used dark magic to control the dead and that is what he uses for his army." Seth explained. The soldier laughed quietly.

"You're joking." He said, still laughing.

"No." Seth said, starting to laugh also. The soldier wiped his eyes as his laughter subsided.

"We have not been properly introduced. My name is Edwin of the White Hills." Edwin said, smiling.

"I'm guessing you know my name?" Seth asked.

"Oh. Yes." Edwin said. "All of Kondoma knows your name now." He explained. Seth first did not recognize Edwin's last name but then it dawned on him.

"Do you know anyone named Kitty?" Seth asked. Edwin thought about the name for a second.

"I have a cousin whose nickname is Kitty." Edwin said.

"Is she a Seer?" Seth asked.

"Yes." Edwin said shocked. "We used to be good friends when I lived in a Seer colony with my mom and dad. When she came of age she went somewhere to practice being a wand maker instead of being a full Seer like the others." Edwin said obviously thinking about the good times they had together.

"So is her full name Glennell Kitty of the White Hills?" Seth asked.

"Yes." Edwin said with amazement. "She hated her full name, her middle name is Kitteara but her father nicknamed her Kitty. How do you know that name?" He asked curiously.

"She is a friend of mine in Remtaya." Seth said.

"Kitty is in Remtaya?" Edwin asked with shock in his voice.

"You did not know?" Seth asked. Edwin shook his head.

"When she left, I only had a year before I came of age and then when I did I went to Kondoma to become a soldier like my brothers and sisters. I just assumed that she went somewhere else besides Remtaya." Edwin said, shrugging. "Tell me, does she still snort when she laughs?" He asked Seth.

"Yes."

"She would always do that when we were kids." Edwin imitated Kitty's laugh.

"That is it!" Seth started to laugh really hard along with Edwin.

"What is going on?" Someone asked. Seth and Edwin looked at the other occupants in the wagon. Seth had almost completely forgotten that he had just been kidnapped by these same people just a few hours ago. The realization of the gravity of his situation suddenly dawned on him once more.

"Are you two actually being civil to each other?" Septa asked, sounding disgusted. She glared at Seth with her red, piercing eyes.

"Stop trying to entangle this weak-willed boy into being your friend." Septa spat at Seth, gesturing to Edwin.

"I am fine with it." Edwin said.

"Shut up." Septa said angrily to Edwin. Seth was going to say something but then the wagon started to shake.

"What is this?" Seapa asked as the wagon shook harder.

Seth looked out the back of the wagon to see that they were going through a river. Some of the water splashed up to the opening of the wagon.

"Hey!" Septa said nervously as more water splashed up to the opening. "Are you trying to kill us?" Septa shouted to where Loral was driving.

"We are almost across." Loral shouted back.

"We better be…." Septa started to say when suddenly the water behind them shot up into the air with a roar. Septa, Seala, and Seapa all screamed with horror as the water from the river was now rising high into the air.

"Get us out of here!" Seapa screamed as some water of the river spread inside the wagon.

Seth saw, as the wagon left the water, what looked like the bottom part of a giant snake that was made of water.

"It's a water snake thing!" One of the other soldiers shouted in terror.

"Septa, Seala, Seapa get out here!" Loral shouted. The three sisters hurried out of the wagon just as some of the water that was still in the river sprung straight toward the wagon, tearing the cover off of the wagon and throwing it into the nearby woods. Seth could now see the enormous snake made of water in full view. On the other side of the river where they had just come from stood Kitty, Evan, Coven, and the rest of the obviously named, Team Seth. Kitty had her wand in the air.

"Let Seth go." She shouted to his captors.

"That's Kitty." Seth said to Edwin who had a look of fear and amazement on his face.

"Never." Loral shouted back. She pulled out her wand and began to spin it in the air. Fire erupted from her wand and started to form another giant snake made of fire. The two enormous monstrous serpents began to fight above them. Kitty moved her wand around to control where the water snake should attack. Meanwhile, Loral was doing the same thing with her fire snake. As the two serpents batted above them, Evan waved his wand and some more water shot toward the wagon. The water turned into a hand and began to grab the soldiers and throw them into the air. The hand then reached toward Edwin. Edwin moved back trying to run from the giant hand. The hand then stopped moving at Edwin and grabbed Seth.

"No!" Loral shouted as Seth was taken by the hand of water. The fire snake bent down and snapped at the hand, breaking the connection. Seth fell to the wagon as Evan lost control of the water. Seth's head suddenly pounded and the water around him formed a barrier under Seth, stopping him from falling. The water then somehow cut Seth loose.

Use me. A voice whispered to Seth. Now that he was free from the ropes, Seth held up his hands and moved to the other side of the river. Not really knowing what he was doing Seth pointed at the other side of the river.

"Move faster please." Seth told the water as the fire snake moved at him. The water from the river shot at Seth, grabbing him, and throwing him across the river. As Seth soared over the river, he saw some water move over to catch him. As he landed on the bed of water he bounced slightly and landed on the dry ground next to his friends.

"We have him." Evan shouted to Kitty. Kitty moved her wand and other hand up in the air. All the water from the river suddenly erupted into the sky and the water snake blended into the wall of water. The rouge Phoenixes screamed in horror as the water fell upon them, extinguishing the fire snake.

"No!" Loral shouted waving her wand. Loral, the three sisters, and the horse all disappeared before the water got to them. The flood of water crashed into the wagon with Edwin almost missing it as he quickly climbed out. Unfortunately, Edwin was caught up in the wave. Kitty moved her wand to form a bubble of water around Edwin. She moved the floating ball of water over to where they were.

"What should we do with him?" Kitty asked as Edwin floated in the water, obviously drowning.

"Let him die," Coven said.

"No," Seth protested.

"Why?" Coven asked looking at Seth. "He helped kidnap you." Coven said pointing at Edwin.

"Kitty, that's Edwin of the White Hills." Seth said.

"What?" Kitty said shocked.

"He's your cousin." Seth explained. Kitty waved her wand, dropping the ball of water and Edwin to the ground. Edwin laid there coughing and gasping.

"Edwin, is that really you?" Kitty asked, walking over to him.

"It's nice... to see... you again Kitty," Edwin said, gasping for air.

"Why were you helping the enemy?" Kitty asked with anger in her voice.

"Enemy?" Edwin asked, getting up, his whole body drenched with water. "I thought that the Seers saw themselves as neutral only loyal to the Kry and the Great One." Edwin accused Kitty without showing anger like she did.

"I never completed my Seer training, so I never learned how to see things with an objective or neutral eye." Kitty said still with anger. "Now why did you kidnap my friend and why are you with the evil King?" Kitty asked, feeling betrayed.

"If I had known that you were in Remtaya I would have not come." Edwin said. "And remember? When we were kids, I told you about how I wanted to go off to Kondoma with the rest of my brothers and sisters... you know, *your cousins.*" Edwin emphasized. "And become soldiers like them." Edwin ended. Kitty held out her wand and Edwin began to lift in the air.

"Edwin, I am sorry, but you are an enemy soldier which means we either kill you or hold you prisoner." Kitty said with sadness.

"You can hold me prisoner." Edwin said while he hung in the air.

"We are not going back to Remtaya yet and we do not have another horse for him to ride." Coven explained. "You have to kill him," he said.

"No," Seth protested getting up from the ground. "You are not going to kill him." He demanded. Seth walked up to Kitty, still soaking wet. "I rarely make friends with people. Evan has been my only friend for many years, but since I moved into the castle I have found another friend in you, and also some treasured acquaintances." Seth said, gesturing to all the people who were in his namesake group. Seth stopped talking suddenly, all the things he was going to say left him.

"Yes?" Kitty asked, waiting for Seth to say something profound and cherishing.

"I lost my train of thought." Seth said trying to remember what he was going to say. Then something hit him. Seth turned and looked at Coven.

"What do you mean we are not going back to Remtaya right now?" Seth asked fearing what Coven would say.

"The Queen and King have decided to have us go to Kondoma now so you can kill the King sooner rather than later."

"What!" Seth shouted, his anger growing. "Are you kidding me?" He asked, still shouting. Seth began to get very angry. "I don't care what the King and Queen want, I have been kidnapped and harassed by a rogue Phoenix and the King and Queen want me to go Kondoma so that I can be killed by Korson just because a stupid prophecy just coincidentally mentions my name!" Seth yelled at Coven and everyone else. Suddenly the wind began to blow and the water that was still all over the other side of the empty riverbed started to slowly move toward them.

"Now just you listen..." Coven began.

"NO!" Seth shot him down. "I will not GO ANYWHERE!" Seth screamed at the top of his lungs. As he did the wind gusted all around them and the water rose into the air and began to spin around Seth. The anger Seth had felt ever since this whole Chosen One thing had entered his life sprung to the surface. The clouds began to gather around him and he felt like he was levitating. Then a thought came into Seth's head.

Kill them. The thought said. *Kill all of them.* It persisted. Suddenly a feeling of sadness filled Seth and the anger faded away. As Seth began to cry the wind died down and the water fell to the ground. Seth then began to cry uncontrollably. Evan patted him on the back.

"Please do not kill him." Seth sobbed to Kitty. "I... I L...Like him a...as a fr...friend." Seth stuttered stilling sobbing.

Kitty sighed and looked at Seth, she then dropped Edwin back to the ground.

"Does this mean I am your prisoner?" Edwin asked with a concerned look on his face.

"No." Kitty answered. "I trust you still know how to trans luminate?" She asked.

"Yes." Edwin stated nodding.

"Can you trans luminate more than one or two people?" Kitty asked, raising an eyebrow.

"No." Edwin responded truthfully.

"Okay then." Kitty stated. "Sorry for this." She apologized.

"Sorry for wh…" Kitty suddenly pulled out her knife and cut Edwin on his right cheek. Edwin naturally recoiled and pulled his sword from its sheath.

"What was that for?" He asked.

"To make it look like you got attacked." Kitty insisted.

"One cut will not be convincing." Coven said angrily.

"I know but I know Edwin can weave a good convincing story if he puts his mind to it." Kitty said, winking at Edwin. Edwin nodded and then held up his hands. A small blue ball formed in between them.

"I hope to see you sometime when you are not trying to kill me." Edwin said honestly, just as the small ball grew and engulfed him. It then shrunk back down and flew into the air where it seemed to explode in all directions.

Seth lay there on the ground still crying, Evan patting him on the back.

"I'm still mad at all of you." Seth cried softly.

CHAPTER SEVENTEEN

A LONG JOURNEY

A very prominent ethiristicist once said that a long journey is like the scientific method. When you start out you are excited for what is to come. You are ready for anything, but as the days go on you start to lose heart. You run into obstacles, you have to make a different path and even double back from where you were. Sometimes you even find out you have been going the wrong way. Days become weeks and weeks suddenly become a year, especially if you are going somewhere no one else has gone before, but through your tiresome journey you come to the end and hold your hands up in victory.

Well Seth did not feel this way. In fact, Seth was feeling just the opposite from being ready for anything. He had gone from a hostage/ kidnapped to being rescued by his friends and being forced to go on a journey where there was a big chance that his head was going to be chopped off at the end of this trip. The other thing was that Seth was riding on a horse. Seth had nothing wrong with horses; he actually liked them. It is just he was very afraid of them. He had never ridden one before and had a fear of falling off and being trampled. The other thing that Seth was mad/worried about was the fact the Biz and Shadow were home all alone. He was told by Kitty that the Queen had said that she would take care of them while he was away, but Seth could not help but worry about them.

Seth waved a wand in the air causing a tent that he was given to rise and construct itself. He looked around the camp that was being built around him. Seth walked to Evan, who was putting a sleeping bag into his tent.

"Evan, before I was captured, I was with the Queen and Orin and I was supposed to go into a safe room, but Orin was not coming so I waited and then he was hit by an energy pulse. Is he okay?" Seth asked. Evan got up and smiled.

"Yes. He just needed to recover from the energy pulse. He is supposed to be here tomorrow actually." Evan said.

"You mean he still is coming?" Seth asked.

"Yep." Evan said, "He and a few others who volunteered when you were kidnapped will trans luminate here tomorrow." He explained to Seth.

"Great, I have more people to die for me." Seth said, throwing up his hands with annoyance.

"Get some sleep, we have a long journey tomorrow." Evan insisted. Seth sighed and walked over to his tent and went inside. He lay on his sleeping bag which had been placed on a cot. There Seth pondered what was going to happen. He was going to Kondoma where his friends would fight off as many people as they could for him, as long as it wasn't the evil King. Seth imagined them watching from a distance as he fought the evil King, his head ultimately removed by the King. Seth moaned and turned on his stomach. Slowly but surely Seth's mind began to wander and he fell asleep.

The next day Seth awoke thinking that these past few hours had been some kind of nightmare but then Seth realized that the nightmare was real. He got up and left his tent to see Kitty; Coven and a few other soldiers were already awake. Kitty saw Seth and waved at him.

"Good morning Seth." Kitty said cheerfully. Seth walked over to her and sat down next to her.

"Is there a place I can get clean?" Seth asked.

"Yes." Kitty said. "Just go down that path and you will find a small river," she said pointing at the nearby forest.

"A river?" Seth asked, feeling like a river wouldn't be any cleaner than he was.

"It is perfectly clean." Kitty said, seeming as if she'd read his mind.

Seth shrugged and got up from his seat. He moved back to his tent and grabbed a towel and some clean clothes that were in a trunk Evan had given him last night, along with some sweet-smelling soap.

He turned away from his tent and looked at the forest that stood at the edge of their camp. The pines that sat at the edge were tall and green. They gave off the feeling of watchers, like keepers making sure that one would treat the woods with respect. Seth liked the woods, the trees held an air of mystery that attracted him. He remembered the time before he was in the city of Remtaya, when he was very young. The woods where he lived were always so fun and exciting to think about. It was on the road to the woods where he met Shadow and Biz for the first time. Seth smiled at the memory that came over him. His eyes moved over the line that separated their camp from the forest. He was walking now, closer to the path that Kitty pointed out. As Seth thought about what secrets the forest held, he suddenly became aware that this was the Forest of Conching, the largest forest on Terina and one of the largest in the whole world. The woodlands that he would see and think about before he moved to the city were the same woods that he was looking at right now, only in a different location. Suddenly, Seth felt like he was moving towards an old and mysterious friend. He followed the path into the forest. He could hear running water close by. He kept walking down the path until he saw the river through some trees. Seth walked around the tree to get a good view. The water slowly ran north to south, Seth walked closer to the edge of a small pond that had formed as the water moved down to wherever it was going. Seth put his hand in the cold liquid and looked at it to see if the water was at least a little clean.

"Are you clean?" Seth asked.

No. A voice whispered. Seth took his hand out of the water.

"I have heard you before." Seth said looking around. "Who are you?" He asked.

I am three to form one. I am as old as the places where all life began. Some thought of me as a God but I am not. I live within and without all things. The voice said cryptically.

"I think I know what you are, but I would like you to say it." Seth said looking at the river.

You are not ready Seth. You will be, but not yet. The voice said calmly.

"Are you water?" Seth asked, fearing how that would sound out loud.

You are not ready. The voice said again. *Do you wish to bathe?* The voice asked.

Seth looked around to see if he could see anyone who might be watching.

"Yes, but are you going to be watching?" Seth asked nervously, still looking around.

I do not see as you do. I see in, not out. I have no concept of your kind of vision. The voice explained as calmly as a whisper.

"That really didn't answer my question." Seth said.

Do not be afraid Seth, nothing will harm you. The place where you wish to bathe is clean now. The voice said. Seth decided that he needed to be clean, so he quickly removed all his clothes and stepped into the water. Seth was shocked when he stepped in the water to find it was warm. He lifted his gloved hands in the air to make a curtain of water that went up past his chest so if anyone were to come down they would not see anything. Seth then moved his hands around the water beneath him so that it would cover all of him except his head. Seth washed all of the dirt and grime from his hair, and cleaned off all of the dirt and sweat that had accumulated. Seth then moved the water that he was submerged in back down to the riverbed and opened the curtain of water so he could get the towel that was hanging on a branch of a tree next to him. He then quickly dried off and put on the clean clothes. As Seth walked away from the river, he could not help but think about what the voice said.

"You are not ready yet." Seth said out loud to himself. "What does that even mean?" He asked out loud. The wind breezed through the trees.

You'll see. A voice said in Seth's ear. Seth stopped and looked around to see if he could tell who said that. He shrugged and began to walk up the trail again. As Seth made his way up to the camp, he could hear a lot of talking and laughing. As he got closer Seth could see Evan and the rest of the camp talking to a man and a woman who were facing away from the forest so Seth could not see their faces. Seth stood at the edge of the forest studying what was going on. Evan and Kitty were talking to the man and Coven was talking to the woman. The other people in the group had obviously said their hellos and were now putting the tents away and back on the horses. Seth studied the man and woman. The man was taller than Coven and had short, black hair. He had on a hooded tunic that was a dark brown in color. The man didn't have the hood up, instead it was down resting on his back. He also had on brown pants. The woman also had black hair that was braided up in a ponytail. She was wearing a dark blue dress and was shorter than Coven. Seth stayed there at the edge of the woods still studying the new visitors. Seth watched as the woman talked to Coven and then watched the man talk to Kitty and Evan when he noticed that Evan was looking at him. Seth waved at Evan and mouthed the word "Hi."

"What are you doing?" Evan mouthed back.

"I was taking a shower." Mouthed Seth.

"Where?" Evan asked with no sound leaving his lips.

"At the river." Seth said mouthing the words. Kitty slapped Evan softly on the arm and looked at Seth.

"Are we disturbing you two?" Kitty shouted very loudly, smiling as she did. Both the man and the woman turned around to see what Kitty was shouting about. Seth could now see their faces and was shocked to see that the two newcomers were Agatha and Orin. Kitty motioned for Seth to join them. Seth sighed, not really wanting to visit with anyone but complied and walked over to where Orin, Evan, and Kitty were standing.

"Hi," Orin said.

"Hello," Seth responded. "I am happy that you are okay," he stated.

Orin nodded with a thankful smile. "That ball of energy packed a punch." He admitted. "I'm just sorry that I wasn't able to help you."

Seth really wanted to say how much he wished Orin could have helped him, but he knew that would be rude to say. "You were unconscious at the time, there was nothing you could do." Seth expressed.

Orin chuckled and nodded again. "I hope that you are doing okay. Being kidnapped by three rogue Phoenixes and a crazy witch would make even the most battle-hardened warrior weak in the knees." Seth again felt the sadness that Orin had for him about how he felt sorry that Seth was in this predicament in the first place. "Sorry about almost hitting you with my body." Orin apologized, putting his hand at the back of his head and rubbing it, an apologetic look on his face.

"Hello Seth." Agatha said walking up to Seth and immediately pulling out her wand to move it around Seth's head and body.

"Hi." Seth said feeling a little overcrowded as Agatha moved her wand slowly around him.

"Sorry for this, but I have to check if you are suffering from any certain mental or physical maladies." Agatha said. "Have you been having any headaches or dizziness lately?" She asked.

"Not really since you checked me last time." Seth said nervously. "What mental conditions are you looking for?" He asked.

"You were kidnapped. There are a lot of things that can happen to a person when they have been forcibly taken. You could have been brainwashed." Agatha explained. The wand turned a light blue and Agatha put it back into her pocket. "Good news, you have nothing wrong with you." She said smiling at Seth.

"That's good." Evan said patting him on the back.

"Are you sure?" Seth asked. "I was in the wagon asleep for a long time." He said, starting to feel stressed out. Seth began to think about horrible things that could have happened to him when he was asleep. If there was one thing Seth hated it was not being in control or aware of his surroundings. So the prospect of being manipulated against his will was very frightening to him.

"You are fine." Agatha said. "However, Coven did tell me that you got very angry last night." She mentioned.

"Could that mean something?" Seth asked nervously.

"No, you were just mad at everything." Agatha said, calming Seth down.

"It's time to go soon." Coven told all of them. Evan looked at Seth and pointed at his horse.

"I put down your tent and put everything in your pack." He expressed to Seth. Seth thanked Evan and walked over to his horse.

"Hello again." Seth said nervously as he walked closer to the horse's saddle.

"Hello." The horse answered back with a low clear voice. Seth grabbed the saddle horn and put his right foot in the right stirrup and pulled himself up. He was not that strong in his arms so trying to pull himself up was sometimes difficult. Luckily, Seth made it onto the saddle without falling off.

"Are you ready to go?" Seth asked the horse.

"Do I have to show you where you're supposed to go?" The horse asked with impatience.

"I am the rider on your back, so I think it is only polite for you to decide where to go." Seth reasoned. The horses shook his mane and neighed with laughter.

"You definitely have never done this before." The horse said, still laughing.

"What am I supposed to do?" He asked.

"You are the rider. So you tell me what to do." The horse explained.

"Okay." Seth said, feeling very nervous. He took the reins and moved them to the left. The horse started to walk toward the road where all the others in the group were going.

"Do you have a name?" Seth asked the horse.

"It's Light Fire." The horse answered.

"Why Light Fire? Your hair color is black. Shouldn't it be Black Fire or Dark fire?" Seth asked. Seth did not know why but the name Dark Fire seemed to really appeal to him.

"My owner liked the name so that is my name." Light Fire said simply. "Why is your name Seth?"

"Good point." Seth decided.

As they traveled down the dusty road Seth began to worry about the sun. It was high in the sky and Seth had no protection from it. He pulled out his wand and looked over to where Kitty was riding just a few feet away from him.

"Kitty is there a spell for keeping one from getting sunburnt?" Seth asked her. Kitty smiled and pulled out her wand and waved it in the air. As she did an orange haze moved up Seth's legs and up to the very top of his head where it then disappeared.

"There you go. The spell should last for around four days." Kitty said.

"What is the spell called?" Seth asked, wanting to know how to use it.

"It is a difficult one to master. I will teach it to you some other time." Kitty explained smiling.

Next to Seth, Evan pulled out his wand and did the same spell that Kitty did. Seth observed the same orange haze engulf Evan and then dissipate. Kitty followed suit along with Agatha.

"What is going on here?" Coven asked looking back at most of the group who were now protected from the sun.

"It's called being safe." Kitty said, looking toward Coven. "Sunburn has been proven to cause very bad problems when people get older." She explained.

"I will never believe that." Coven said, shaking his head.

"Very well," Kitty shrugged.

The hours went on as Team Seth rode down the winding road. The horses were doing all the walking, but Seth still felt tired and thirsty. He reached down and pulled out a canteen that felt empty.

"Water please." Seth said to the canteen. Seth heard the sound of water filling up the canteen, and the leather water holder grew as it magically filled. Seth then opened the lid and tipped the canteen over his mouth. Seth gulped down the cold, refreshing liquid. Feeling hydrated he looked around. Seth hadn't noticed it before, but he and Light Fire appeared to be in the middle of the group. Everyone else was surrounding him.

"When did this happen." Seth asked Light Fire, gesturing to the circle that his friends had formed around him.

"You just noticed that?" Light Fire asked. "They made sure to put you in the middle of the group right when we started." The horse explained. The circle did seem to be formed very carefully. Coven, Orin, and two soldiers were in the front of Seth. To Seth's left was Evan and to his right was Kitty. On the right back side of Seth was Agatha who at the moment was doing something with her hair. To the back left were two other soldiers. Seth counted nine people in all that were traveling along with him and ten if he counted himself.

"Coven how long until we get to the nearest rest point?" Evan asked.

Coven pulled out a map from a brown pack that was attached to his horse.

"We are not yet to the disputed lands and that is where we make camp." He explained to Evan.

"The disputed lands?" Seth asked. "Isn't that where the main battles are taking place?" He asked nervously.

"The Kingdoms of Remtaya and Kondoma made an agreement when the war began that the war would not affect the main roads." Kitty explained to Seth.

"Let's just hope that Kondoma has kept its part of the agreement." Coven said as they kept walking.

Seth sighed. "I almost forgot why I was on this journey." Seth said to Light Fire, depression creeping into his voice.

CHAPTER EIGHTEEN

THE DISPUTED LANDS

They that have the mark of the Kry are to be watched and seen. For they are the ones who hold great power. Look for the mark of the Kry, black as the night falls, and which covers the skin with divine power.

The sunny day was too hot, and Seth felt like they had been walking for hours. The day beat down on him and the others with heat that made his eyes heavy and his head light. He leaned on Light Fire's neck and felt the sweat that had accumulated there. Seth gave a weary sigh. "You doing okay Light Fire?" He asked with concern; he may have felt overheated, but Light Fire was sweating like a steady stream.

The horse gave a whinny of laughter. "I'm fine." He said with little strain in his voice. "I've been through hotter days than this."

"I hate the heat." Seth expressed to him with a frown. "I'd rather be in a place that is cold and has a little moisture in the air."

"I could go for that too." Light Fire admitted with a shake of his mane.

Seth was about to answer back when suddenly he had the sense that they were being watched. Almost instinctively Seth's body grew more rigid as he could feel a powerful set of eyes on him. Slowly he straightened up and looked around. He was still in the middle of the group as everyone else had formed a perimeter around him. As Seth looked around the area, he could feel like the steady gaze was getting stronger. They were walking along the path near the Conching Forest, which lay to the right and west of him. The tall pines and iron wood trees made it difficult for Seth to actually see into the forest itself, but he felt like the gaze he was somehow detecting was coming from there.

"Light Fire," Seth expressed looking down at the horse he was riding. "Do you feel that?" He asked.

"Feel wha…" Light Fire's words faded away as his ears immediately stood straight up. "We're being watched." He said with concern in his voice.

Seth's heart stopped as he heard what Light Fire said. He could feel the gaze of this being almost like it was piercing into his flesh. It was like this gaze was only on him, and no one else. Seth suddenly felt very exposed. Light Fire abruptly stopped and as a consequence everyone else stopped their horses. Many of the other horses whinnied with annoyance as the whole group halted.

"What's going on?" Coven's voice held nothing but irritation, irritation that always made Seth want to hide and cry with shame.

Seth turned to Kitty with the almost overwhelming feeling of being watched. "Something is spying on us." He spoke mostly as a whisper only to her.

Kitty immediately turned her head to where Orin and his horse were standing. Without saying anything Orin gave a worried nod before he started to scan the tree line. Kitty turned back to Seth with concern, her green eyes were afraid yet held great determination on them. "Orin heard you," she told him calmly. "He also feels the gaze. Just stay calm and," Kitty was cut short when Orin shouted look out.

Seth's eyes moved upwards to the top of the trees to see a large, black bird-like beast soaring down right at him. The creature's wings seemed pitch-black and appeared larger than that of any eagle hc had seen in books at the library. His eyes widened as the massive bird swooped upon him, its red shining eyes completely fixed on him. Kitty and Evan, without any hesitation, shot two brightly colored spells at the massive avian. Without faltering the monstrous bird twisted its form and dodged both volleys before swiftly moving upon where Seth was sitting. Seth yelled in fear as the bird was almost on top of him. He held out his hands and closed his eyes while also leaning very far to the left side of his saddle. Gravity took hold and Seth fell over Light Fire and off the saddle completely. There was a whoosh of air as the massive bird missed Seth by mere inches. Seth fell hard on the dirt and gasped as Light Fire neighed with great distress over how close the bird had come to them. The large creature gave out a loud screech and zoomed back up into the air, its wingspan now fully exposed as it appeared to turn around and move back over to them. As it did this, Seth saw, with some amazement, energy come off its immense wingspan and shoot right at the group.

"Take cover!" Coven shouted; his yells now filled with nothing but fear.

Kitty leapt off her horse and landed next to Seth, she held out her wand pointing it to the sky and directly at the daggers of light that were zooming at them. With a song-like tone to her voice Kitty began to enact a spell. The stilettos made of energy were almost upon them when a nearly see-through shield formed above her and Seth. Evan ran over to Seth and knelt by him right as the knives made of light smashed into the mostly transparent shield. Kitty gasped and held both her hands on her wand as the magic of the daggers seemed to be stronger than the shield.

"I can't hold this forever!" Kitty shouted at both him and Seth. "Run, get to safety." She commanded.

The massive bird flew past them and gave out another loud shriek.

Kitty dropped her wand and the shield she made dissipated. "Hurry, into the forest with the others." She said with urgency in her voice as she ushered Seth, Evan, and their horses over to where the others were hiding.

They were almost there when Seth heard the screech again. It felt very close behind them. "It's coming back around!" Evan yelled with panic.

Kitty stopped and turned, as did Evan. The horses ran over to the others, but Seth felt frozen with fear. He turned to see Kitty and Evan sing the shield spell back into being as the monster bird was soaring right at them. Suddenly, Agatha ran past Seth toward Kitty and Evan, pulling her own wand out and using the same spell to help make the shielding stronger. The bird swung down at them before zooming quickly back up. As it did a dark blast of red energy shot toward where Evan, Kitty and Agatha were standing. The energy hit the shield hard, sending all three spell casters sprawling to the ground. Dirt and dust were in the air as Seth's ears were ringing over the loud blast. He was confused by what was going on until a hand grabbed at him and Seth found himself being pulled up on his feet by Agatha. She looked injured, but she also had a determined look on her face. She was looking away from Seth and moving her hands in a come-on motion as Seth saw the rest of his group running over to them. Seth saw that Orin was holding on to Kitty who appeared dazed, she was leaning on him greatly. Seth's heart dropped as he saw Evan's body draped over his horse. Light Fire and the other horses were being pulled by one of the soldiers. Seth heard the loud shriek of the creature attacking them. He couldn't see it due to the dust in the air. Seth's attention returned to what Agatha was doing. She had her hands out in front of her and a small blue light appeared near them. Seth readied himself to be trans luminated away from this danger they were in. He closed his eyes and suddenly felt like he was weightless. That feeling quickly faded as there was a flash of blue light and Seth felt his feet on sturdier ground. The light of the sun was shining hard on them as Seth shielded his eyes from it. Suddenly, Agatha gave a low moan and fell beside him. Seth gasped with fear and stepped away from her just as one of the other soldiers ran over.

"Halt!" someone shouted with determination. "Who goes there?"

Seth turned to see a young man wearing a Remtayan military uniform. He had a wand pointed at them. Behind the man was a small city that had a stone wall around it. Seth could see a spire standing up high, its point looking to the sky.

"Stand down soldier." Coven commanded with concern on his voice. "We need medical help."

"Please," Orin stated while he still let a nearly unconscious Kitty lean on him. "Help us."

Evan lay unconscious on a medical cot, which was in a tent that held around ten similar beds. Seth sat next to him, watching his friend slowly breathe, calm and steady. In all his fourteen years Seth never thought he'd be in a military medical tent worrying about his best friend's life. He never wanted to be in such a situation, a situation that had him at the very middle of all the conflict. Evan, Kitty, and Agatha all were willing to lay down their lives for him, and for what? If they died that would be it, he couldn't bring them back, and at least to him their sacrifice would be in vain.

As Seth sat next to the slumbering Evan, Kitty walked in, moving one of the flaps that was the entrance to the tent. "Any change?" She asked, her voice low as to not startle any of the other sleeping people in the tent. Three other beds were full in the pavilion, all of them were asleep.

Seth shook his head, sadness entering his mind. "No." He answered quietly. "It's been a day, are you sure that he'll be okay?" Seth had nothing but concern in his voice as he asked.

Kitty smiled a little and nodded with cool confidence. "He'll be okay." She reassured Seth. "The reason Evan is still in here and Agatha and I aren't, is because he isn't as skilled at magic as we are. My Seer Stone was also helpful in protecting me and healing me faster. Agatha didn't get the full brunt of the explosion like Evan and I did, so she healed faster as well." Kitty sat next to Seth and looked him in the eyes with her signature confidence. "I don't have to be a mind reader to tell that what happened has bothered you." She said with wisdom in her eyes.

Seth looked down from her gaze in shame. "You guys almost died." He said sadly. "Evan almost died, and I couldn't stop it." He answered, closing his eyes as tears formed under his lids. His throat grew thick as Seth's sadness expanded.

"Seth we were willing to sacrifice our lives, so you could end this war." Kitty answered him gently. "Can't you see such a sacrifice as an incentive to go on, to fight the good fight, to end tyranny and restore peace?"

Seth slowly raised his head and looked at Kitty with a tear-stained face. Kitty stared back at him, her hopeful gaze faltering a little. "Oh," she said, appearing a bit surprised. "You don't." she answered with the same gentleness, only this time it was mixed with disbelief.

"I don't see it that way." Seth expressed shaking his head. "If you and the others died for me, I wouldn't go on, I would run and hide. My fear would overrun any kind of obligation or incentive I might feel. Your death would be in vain, you're fighting for someone who isn't worthy of such obligation." He had nothing but sadness and shame over his face. "I'm a coward."

Kitty sighed and shook her head a little. "I don't think you are." She answered back, narrowing her eyes on him a bit. "Seth you're a thinker, you have a powerful imagination, but most of all you are a kind person. You don't like conflict, and you would rather find a peaceful resolution to this war than a violent one. That's who I see, not a coward."

Tears still were in Seth's eyes as he wiped them and gave a soft sniff. "I can be both you know." He chuckled a little while still holding back his tears.

"I know." Kitty said standing up from her seat. "But I choose to see more than that." She explained to him with a smile. "Now come on, Evan isn't going to be awake for at least a few more hours and Coven wants you to meet with the commander of this place." Kitty said, a bit of playful annoyance in her voice. "I think Coven wants to show you off," she said, her smile growing.

Seth looked back at Evan, concern over what Kitty stated. "I don't want to be shown off." He answered back, reluctantly getting up and walking closer to Kitty.

"Just be yourself." Kitty said, giving him a wink. "It'll make Coven furious, but he wouldn't dare yell at the Chosen One in front of an acting commander. He'd be so embarrassed." She giggled mischievously.

A little smile peeked its way over Seth's face at what Kitty just said. He nodded to her and looked over at Evan with more concern. "Will they tell us when he's awake?" Seth asked looking back at Kitty.

She nodded and walked over to the opening of the tent. "Don't worry, Evan is going to be fine." She explained before walking out. Seth followed and had to cover his eyes due to the brightness of the day outside. The good news was that the day felt much cooler than yesterday. Seth actually felt like this was the perfect temperature for the season and that made him happier about the situation. They were at the edge of the city wall, in a camp that seemed to operate mostly as a medical site. There were around twenty tents surrounding the area, each of various sizes and lengths. When they first came, Kitty, Evan, and Agatha were taken to one of the smaller tents because it was determined that their wounds were not that severe.

Seth could see that there were a fair number of officers and military personnel around the camp. They all were doing different activities that appeared to be important for camp function. Along with the soldiers, there were nurses and doctors that took care of all the wounded in the camp. Seth saw a few but they all seemed very busy.

He and Kitty walked down to the south-east part of the camp where the main tent stood. He could see it standing a little taller than other tents around it. As they got closer, they walked past a bunch of wooden barrels that all were standing straight up but were placed in random areas. Seth focused on the timber-made containers wondering what was inside of them when suddenly Kitty stopped. Seth looked up right in time and stopped right behind her. She was looking straight ahead and seemed to be surprised. Seth looked around her to see that, trotting calmly through the camp and across their path, there was a beautiful white fox. Its whole body was as white as the snow, it was walking with a cute little bounce to its adorable steps. Seth smiled as he saw it shake its fluffy and bushy tail. It was so cute.

"A fox." Kitty said with a sound of concern in her voice.

"Ah," Seth said looking at the cute being as it made its way past them. "So adorable, look how tiny its paws are." He remarked, his smile widening.

"Be careful Seth," Kitty said, still watching the fox closely. "Foxes are dangerous. You can never be sure if they're on your side or not."

Seth watched as the white fox trotted out of sight and around a tent. He looked back at Kitty, feeling confused. "You don't like foxes?" he asked her, a little surprised.

"I don't trust them," Kitty explained as they continued walking. "The Seers and foxes have a strained history. They are shape-shifters and are always working an angle that you'll never see coming until after they've shown it."

"I've only read a little about the fox," Seth explained as they weaved their way through the assortment of barrels and to the other side. "All I know about them is that they are long lived and, as you said, can shift their shape and appearance."

Kitty stopped and turned to Seth with worry. "I know a little bit more thanks to the stories told by my people. Apparently, a group of foxes did something to the Seers of old. Something that we have never forgiven them for."

Seth tilted his head in confusion. "Do you know what they did?" He asked, curiosity coming over him.

"No," Kitty said with a bit of a chuckle in her voice. "But the stories told to me and my siblings always have a fox stealing something important and then tricking the Seer into allowing it to keep whatever it stole."

"Are you sure that these stories aren't some kind of prejudiced myths created by your people?" Seth asked with interest.

Kitty shrugged. "It could be, but I've learned thanks to those stories my parents told me, to give foxes a wide berth." Kitty continued walking with Seth following alongside her. "I'll find out if the commander of this place has any knowledge of that fox, after that, if it doesn't bother me, I won't bother it."

The white tent stood higher than the other tents around it. It had one long spire that appeared to hold it up while four shorter spokes stood at the large shelter's four corners. The thing that was interesting to Seth was that the tent looked more like something people would use for a party, not for a war. The tent had grayish cloth walls around it, they only had a slit for an opening like the medical tent that Seth had just left. As they got closer Seth noticed the Remtayan sign of the tree. The symbol appeared on both sides of the opening. All in all, the tent looked well made, and didn't seem to have a scratch on it. Seth gave Kitty a questioning look.

"How long have these guys been here?"

Kitty looked at him and shrugged. "I'd say a few weeks. Depending on their wounded. Why do you ask?"

Seth looked back at the nice-looking tent. "I don't know how war works, but this tent looks like it was just set up. If it was here for a few weeks, shouldn't it look a little dirty?"

"It could have a kind of protection spell on it." Kitty suggested. "But I see your point."

Seth was able to see Coven, Orin, Agatha, and other soldiers in the tent talking to each other. Some of the soldiers Seth recognized as the ones that were with him and his friends, they were wearing different clothes than the other soldiers he had seen around the camp. Those knights had armor on, white and gray in color with the tree insignia on their breast plate.

They finally made it to the tent and Kitty opened the tent flap so that she and Seth could walk into the sheltered area. As Seth walked in with Kitty, the aroma of grass and nature filled his nose. It looked as large inside as it did outside. A table stood around the center as most of the people in the tent stood about it. Another table was at the eastern side of the tent. It was longer than the one near the middle, and it had an assortment of food and drink on it. A desk with paper, quill, and ink stood at the north end; Seth felt like that was a place where the captain of the camp could sit and jot down their thoughts and feelings about the war. He began to imagine what the captain would write down. Something like, 'Dear diary: War sucks, why didn't I become a carpenter like my parents wanted me to?' or 'To whom it may concern, I'm so bored. Where's the action I was promised? All we do is…' Seth then imagined the commander being immediately attacked by assassins and the commander harshly thinking about how this was too much action.

"Seth," Kitty's voice interrupted his imaginings, and he was brought back into reality. Seth looked at Kitty only to notice that everyone was looking at him. Most of the soldiers had a look of respect on their faces, while others had an expression that Seth guessed was confusion. He was never good at understanding expressions. The thing that alarmed him the most was that everyone was looking at him.

Seth awkwardly smiled. "Hi." He said, trying not to act too odd. He felt like it wasn't working.

A man wearing the armor of the camp soldiers walked up to Seth and smiled at him. He was an older looking man, with gray eyes and a mustache that covered most of his upper lip. "Good to meet you Chosen One." He said with respect in his voice. "I'm sorry about how you and your group came to us. It's a good thing you did though. Athex is not a bird you want to mess with."

"Athex?" Seth said not knowing that word at all. It sounded like a dangerous chemical, but the man who was obviously a commander said it was a bird. So, he must have been talking about the creature that attacked them.

"Athex is the name of that monstrous fowl that attacked your group." The commander confirmed.

"That's what we were talking about before you got here." Agatha told both Seth and Kitty. "This Athex is a Croan, a rather nasty one." She explained to both of them. Seth noticed that Agatha still looked tired which worried him. She got the full brunt of this Athex's full power.

"A Croan!" Kitty stated with surprise in her voice. "They're native to Celesta, why is one of them here?"

"Our intelligence says that this one is loyal to the witch Loral," the commander stated, looking at Kitty. "It seems like he's also an outcast to his own kind."

"The Croan are known to be peaceful birds on Celesta." Orin said looking around at all of them. "I'm surprised one of them could have become so corrupted."

"Whatever his reasons, this one wanted us dead." Coven responded to Orin.

Orin shook his head a little as if he was disagreeing with Coven. "I don't think he wanted us dead." He then turned and looked at Seth with concern in his eyes. "He wanted Seth dead; we were just in his way."

Seth gulped in fear. Why was he in the middle of all of this?

"Well, with you all here now I don't think that wicked bird can do anything to the Chosen One. We can keep him safe." The commander promised.

"That's good for now." Coven said looking at the general. "But eventually we will need to leave, our quest to kill the evil King is paramount." He expressed.

"I understand." The commander responded. "But for now, you are safe." He looked at Seth with a smile. Seth smiled back but had no confidence in what the older man was saying.

"I'm not too sure about that." Kitty answered looking at the commander of the camp. "This Athex wasn't using normal magic. He was using what my people call Kiunshow, a form of dark magic that comes from within the body of the being using it. This kind of magic is more powerful than enchantments from an average spell caster." She explained solemnly. "If he's using Kiunshow then I'm afraid a simple protection spell isn't going to cut it."

"I'm quite aware of this dark magic that Athex has." The commander explained to Kitty with a smile. "But lucky for us, we have an advantage that Athex wasn't counting on."

"How do you mean?" Kitty asked, folding her arms in interest.

"Our guess is that the King of Kondoma ordered Athex over to this area because of how brutal the bird is in his attacks. He strikes fast and hard, using that dark magic you talked about." The commander walked over to the map that most everyone stood around. "The evil King must have thought that Athex could break through our lines and force us from Vennire leaving it open for him to take. But, like I said, we have an advantage. A fox by the name of Kei has offered her assistance."

Kitty's eyes widened slightly, and she nodded slowly. "So, you've been in communication with that fox. Well at least you know of her." Kitty said with more concern on her face. "Commander, it's good that this Kei has been helping you, but foxes are tricky, she may leave you without warning, leaving you almost defenseless against Athex."

"She gave me her word she wouldn't." The commander expressed. "Kei seems like she keeps her promises."

"Let's hope so." Kitty answered back with concern still shadowing her face.

CHAPTER NINETEEN

UP CLOSE AND TERRIFYING

Night had come to the camp by the city of Vennire. Seth was outside Evan's medical tent, looking at the stars in the night sky. It was a moonless night, but the stars and the strands of milky dust seemed to make up for its absence. Seth liked looking up at the stars, it made him wonder about other worlds that might be out there. The white clumps that made a steady path across the sky had always amazed Seth. Stories of how it was the road to the Great One were always prevalent in some of the books he read. He agreed with researchers who believed it to be dust out in space, lit up and shining, thanks to the millions of stars out there.

Seth sighed and looked down from his wondering, his thoughts returning to Evan and the others. They were all willing to die for him, but he couldn't say the same. Yes, he would want the bad things to only happen to him, instead of his friends. But this whole Chosen One thing, Seth knew that if it was someone else, like Evan or Kitty, he wouldn't volunteer to go on this journey with them. This whole quest felt like a horrible plan, killing someone he didn't even know. What kind of a kingdom did he live in where that was an option, and why were his friends so willing to follow him through it? Seth stood there thinking about how all of this could have happened when he heard quiet talking and laughing further down the camp. The talking sounded friendly and nice. Seth narrowed his eyes and walked a little way from the medical tent and over to where he could hear where the voices were coming from. As he walked over to the corner of the next tent, he looked around it to see Orin and the white fox named Kei talking to each other. Orin was bent down with his knees as he held himself in a position that Seth had always had trouble making. It was where only his feet were on the ground, but his knees were bent like he was sitting on his thighs. The white fox was talking happily with Orin and said something that made Orin give a pleasant chuckle. Did Orin know this fox? He didn't say anything about it in the meeting they were in earlier that day. Orin's relaxed and friendly manner made it obvious that he somehow knew the fox. This troubled Seth a little due to what Kitty said about foxes, they were not to be trusted, she would say. However, to Seth there was nothing threatening about the fox he was watching, he still thought the fox was adorable, and Orin appeared to be a good person, why would he affiliate himself with a bad and dangerous figure? If there was one thing Seth didn't like, it was a mystery, yet there was nothing he could do. All Seth could do was stare around the corner, wondering about the fox and why Orin was talking and laughing with it. Seth then made the mistake of moving a little, accidentally stepping on a random twig that caused a good amount of noise. Orin and the fox both turned their heads to look directly at Seth. His eyes widened, and his heart jumped a bit at the idea that he was going to get in trouble with Orin or the fox. Seth timidly turned away and ran over to the tent where Evan was still resting. Little did he know that Orin had given him a kind smile right before he turned away from them.

Seth sat on the chair next to Evan and looked at his sleeping friend for a while. He watched him breathe and hoped that he would just wake up and they could then go home. But no matter how much Seth wished, Evan stayed asleep, and no matter how much he hoped, they weren't going home. Once Evan was up and walking, Coven said that they would take their leave of the camp and continue on with their mission. Seth wanted to scream over that idea, but he just held it in, it would have done nothing anyway.

"It's not polite to eavesdrop." A tiny female voice said out of nowhere. Seth turned his head to the entrance and looked down to see a beautiful white furred fox with an adorable bushy tail looking up at him with its bright blue eyes.

Seth was at first speechless. The fox had found him.

"What's the matter?" The fox asked with a sound of confidence to her voice. "Sand Sarth got your tongue?"

"I'm," Seth cleared his throat and started again. "I'm sorry." He said timidly. "I didn't mean to eavesdrop, I just heard talking and thought it sounded like Orin."

"Yes," The fox said with a tiny chuckle. "Keep a good eye on that one, he's got horrible luck."

"Orin?" Seth asked.

"Yes," The Fox answered again with a kind warmth to her voice. "I'd stay close to him as well, he's one of the good ones."

"The good ones?" Seth asked once more.

"A good person." The fox answered back. "There's good ones, and then there's bad ones. Orin Wolfhart is one of those men you can trust to the end, you're lucky he's with you on your journey."

Seth smiled a little at what the fox was saying to him. He did think Orin was a good person, and it made sense that the fox would say that. The white fox walked further into the tent and looked intently at Seth. Suddenly, light immersed the fox and shone out from its body. Seth covered his eyes as the fox began to change and grow taller. Seth was able to watch as the fox changed into a woman with white flowing hair, a beautiful white dress that fit her new figure perfectly, and a blue jeweled tiara that was draped over the woman's white hair. The woman walked over to where Evan was resting. Her steps were smooth, almost like she was floating as she walked closer to the bed. Seth watched in amazement as she stood over the bed that Evan was laying on.

The white, shining woman waved her hand over Evan before she smiled with a loving grin. "He's dreaming?" She expressed still smiling kindly. She then looked up at Seth with a glad beam over her perfect and very beautiful face. "He has a good heart this one," Her blue eyes twinkled a little as she moved her hand right over Evan's resting chest. "Good, but fragile." She said with a hint of concern.

"What do you mean?" Seth asked, a little mesmerized by the fox's transformation.

"No matter," The shining woman said, moving her hand away from Evan. "Your friend is healed and will awaken soon."

The woman moved away from Evan's resting place and closer to Seth. She then waved her glowing left hand and a silver shining chair appeared next to her and Seth. She gracefully sat on it and looked at Seth with deep contemplation in her blue eyes.

"The chosen one." She said out of nowhere. The way she said the words made Seth think she was saying it as a tease, a joke that he didn't care for.

Seth gave a deep sigh and nodded a little. "That's what they call me." He answered with sad annoyance.

Kei smiled with knowing in her eyes. "But you know there are no more chosen ones." She said with a wink.

Seth shrugged. "I wish that was true, the prophesiers say that, and I always believed it, but a prophecy was made about me."

"You and I both know how those kinds of prophecies work." She said, keeping her smile. "They are never one-hundred percent."

Seth nodded with understanding. "But everyone wants it to be true, they want it to be real."

"Real, is perspective. Perspective is not always real, real is real in the eyes of the perceiver not the perceived." Kei said with a cryptic smile on her face. "That is the path of the Shinsun'i."

"Shinsun'i?" Seth asked with confusion.

"The middle one," Kei said looking at Seth with her blue eyes shining. "You are Shinsun'i."

"I am?" Seth asked with deepening confusion.

"The Seer's word for balance is Shinsun'i." Kei explained with calmness in her kind voice. "Those who seek the truth of who they are shine with the might of the Shinsun'i."

"Am I balanced?" Seth asked with interest. He didn't feel like he was.

"To be balanced is a journey not a destination, to be the middle one is an action that must become second nature." Kei said, her smile growing.

"That would be hard for me." Seth said shyly looking at the shining woman. "I'm not good at change, even changing how I act is hard."

"Allow me to show you something." Kei said as she bent down and started to draw in the dirt. She drew a circle with a line forming an arch, below the end of the line she drew the same symbol only opposite of the first.

"This is the sign of light." She said to him gently. The shining woman drew another symbol between the symbol of light. It was like a curvy line. "This is the sign of night." Kei drew another symbol on top of the other signs. It was a diamond with four lines that extended from the right and left points of the diamond, two on each side. "This is the symbol of willpower." She drew another symbol this time two parallel lines. "This is the symbol of faith." She explained to him. Kei then drew a triangle on top of the other symbols. "This is the sign of space." She then drew two circles that were right next to each other. "And this is the symbol of time. They are all connected by the Shinsun'i." Kei explained drawing a circle around the symbols she had drawn on the dirt. "You are the Shinsun'i."

"But what does that mean?" Seth asked her.

Suddenly, Kei's smile turned to surprise, and she stood up turning to her left facing further into the tent. Seth looked over to see what had startled the fox. His eyes widened when he saw a hooded figure standing around two yards away from them. The being was cloaked in a robe of black feathers. Its face was pale with dark, pitch-black eyes and a beak-like nose. A wicked smile moved over his thin, lipless mouth.

"Pain, my young child. Pain is the only motivation." The hooded figure said in such a way that he was choking out the words. Its voice was clear, but the way it said the words sounded hurried, like this being had little time for what it said.

Kei gave a slight laugh and stood straight, looking at the figure with determination. "Athex, I pity your mind."

Seth's eyes widened more in panic. Athex? That massive bird that almost killed them. This was Athex? He looked terrifying. Suddenly, the hooded being gave a loud high pitched scream and energy seemed to swirl around it as it bent down to the floor. Seth yelled in panic as the scream was too loud for him. He covered his ears as Kei assumed an attack stance. The screaming was so loud that it seemed to shake everything in the tent. As Seth held his hands over his ears, he looked over at Evan to see that his eyes were open, and he had a very bewildered expression on his face.

The energy around Athex changed the hooded figure into a massive black bird with a wingspan that almost matched the width of the tent. With a powerful flap of his wings, Athex zoomed at Seth with lightning perfection. Everything fell into slow motion as Seth hardly had time to see Athex right on him, his large talons reaching out for him just inches away from where he sat. The tent behind Athex was in chaos as the very flap from his wings caused many of the empty cots to be lifted up and thrown about. One thing that was not in chaos was Kei who was right at Seth's side. With a quick step she blocked Athex from grabbing him, causing all three of them to be violently pushed out of the tent. Seth landed hard on the dirt and rolled on the ground, still in a daze. He coughed and sat up to see Athex overhead, his massive wings flapping as to keep him airborne. Kei was just a few feet away from Seth. She was shining more and was kneeling on one knee. She then slowly lifted both her arms until they were aligned with her head. Seth watched in amazement as seven shimmering knives appeared around her. All seven had wispy strands of energy that all connected to the small of Kei's back. It was like she had a tail of knives. Overhead Athex made a scoffing noise as the bird also began to glow. Suddenly, Kei lifted her arms high and all seven knives flew at Athex with incredible force. With little warning the large black bird zoomed at the knives and spun around the daggers of light with lightning-fast speed. Athex sped at Seth with his talons ready to grab him. Kei seemed to be ready for this as her knives materialized around Seth like a shield blocking Athex from getting to him. The massive bird gave a loud screech just as Orin, Kitty, and many Remtayan soldiers came running to see what was happening. Kitty immediately pulled out her wand and started to shoot Athex with spells. Agatha came around a corner and started to sing spells at the bird as well. Athex gave another loud screech followed by a cry: attack! Seth saw as a large group of men wearing Kondoman attire run out of hiding and started to attack the Remtayan soldiers. Seth saw that one of the Kondoman soldiers was running at Orin while another drew their sword on Kitty. This caused Kitty to stop attacking Athex and aim her wand at the enemy soldier that had his sword ready. Orin had his sword on the soldier that was attacking him. Seth watched as he quickly disarmed the young man before the enemy turned and ran the other way. Kitty had also disarmed the enemy soldier with her wand and with one song-like spell she sent the soldier sprawling on the ground. Agatha was also under attack, and the only one who was now fighting Athex was Kei and her barrage of magic at the bird. The swords were still over Seth in a shield-like formation. Athex was dodging the magic that Kei was sending out with her hands. The large bird was swerving so much it was hard to tell if he was getting closer to Seth or not. Seth himself felt helpless as there was nowhere to run, and he couldn't help his friends; there was nothing he could do.

The enemy soldiers were all around them. Orin, Kitty, Agatha, and Coven were all under attack, and Kei was trying her best to fend off Athex. The massive bird was trying to get to where Seth was still laying, but Kei had been mostly successful in keeping him from getting too close to the sword-made shield that was still over Seth. She would send out beams of light from her hands at the large black bird, but Athex was fast and would dodge every one of the light beams. Athex's full form would shine for a short second followed by a blast of energy from the bird at Kei. She would hold up her hands and dissipate the attack, but it seemed to harm her every time she did. Seth looked around in panic. What was he going to do? That's when he saw Evan stumble out of the tent that Seth and Kei had been in. He looked confused as he walked further away from the tent. Seth had to get him out of harm's way. He couldn't let anything else happen to him. "Evan!" Seth yelled before he got up and ran over to where he was.

"Seth no!" Kei shouted, just as Athex sent a blast of energy right to where Seth was. The energy hit the ground next to Seth and sent him flying to the ground.

Seth coughed as the dirt and dust filled his nostrils. He rose from the ground only to be pushed back down by the powerful flap of Athex's wings. The massive bird was right over him. With an unearthly spin the bird turned into the hooded figure with a cloak made of feathers. He landed on the ground and bent down, grabbing at Seth's neck and slowly raising him up in the air. Seth couldn't breathe and gripped at the cold hand of the figure as he held him in the air. A look of triumph over his pale face and dark eyes.

"No!" Kei shouted, shooting a beam of light at Athex. The hooded figure held out his other hand and stopped the blast with ease.

"Seth!" Orin shouted as he disarmed another soldier only for another one to come running at him. "Someone get to Seth!" He yelled. But everyone was fighting for their own lives and couldn't get to him.

"You're coming with me." Athex said to Seth with a deep grin over his lipless face.

Suddenly the swords that had been around Seth raced to his aid. One made contact with Athex, and this caused the bird-like man to drop Seth and back away from him. Seth landed on the ground and coughed some more, after almost being choked by Athex. The other swords of light spun around Athex with great force. Seth then looked at Kei, as he could hear her starting to shout to the sky.

"Oh, by the grace of the Great Ones, and the Great One of Terinta, oh by the power of the Kry we need your help in our hour of need!" She called out before she clapped her hands together and a beam of light shot into the sky. It burst out in all directions, suddenly there was a flash of light and Seth looked up to see a being overhead, glowing with a slight brilliance. Seth saw the gloved hands and knew that this had to be a Kry, only a Kry could float in the air like that. She looked female and had long, flowing red hair.

"Kei'shonejoan," The red haired Kry said, calmly, a tone of slight amusement in her voice. "You've got yourself into some trouble I see." The Kry looked over at Athex who gave a loud shriek as the blades of light still spun around him. "Begone fowl." The Kry said with a wave of her hand. Athex vanished and the knives of light zoomed back to Kei where they connected with her as she glowed slightly. The Kry looked over at the fighting that was going on with the Kondoman soldiers. "You bothering bunch too." She said without even lifting a finger as all the enemy soldiers vanished. "Well, there you have it." The Kry said looking down at Kei with a smile. "Humans and their wars, what is to be done with them?" The Kry said before vanishing herself.

Seth was still looking at the sky where the Kry had come from in wonder. Then he remembered Evan, his eyes grew wide and he surveyed the area around the medical tent. His eyes rested on Evan who was kneeling on the ground, astonishment on his face.

"Seth." Orin ran to Seth with concern. "You alright?" He asked holding out a hand to Seth. He took Orin's hand and stood up with his help.

"Yes," Seth said with a gulp of stress. "But Evan." He said, pointing at him.

Orin ran over to Evan, followed by Seth, Kitty, and the others. "Evan." Orin said kneeling next to Evan while taking hold of his shoulder. "How are you?" Orin asked.

Evan looked at Orin for a second with a hazy expression. "Orin," Evan said, blinking a few times. He then smacked his lips and put both his hands over his face before slowly sliding them down his countenance. "What time is it? I'm hungry." Evan finished with a slight smile.

Seth gave a sigh and Orin chuckled, patting Evan on the shoulder. "You're fine," Orin's eyes crinkled into a smile.

CHAPTER TWENTY

KRY ME A RIVER

It had been three days since the attack on the camp near Vennire. In those three days Seth's emotions ranged from wretchedly sad, aggressively annoyed, miserably depressed, and tyrannically angry. This led to his relationship with the rest of the party becoming rather strained. So strained in fact that Kitty yelled at him, Evan kicked the ground so hard that grass and dirt were flung into the air, and Coven almost hit him. For the most part, Seth felt like he had no control of his life anymore, and so he was venting his frustration unfairly on his friends. From the time he had been abducted by Loral, he was more than just unhappy.

Seth's unhappiness was in the back of his mind however as he and his friends stood around a table with a map on it. The map was of Terinta as it showed Remtaya, Kondoma, and the towns and cities that belonged to both kingdoms. Seth could see a strip of land that was in the middle of the map. It went as far as to the western sea all the way to the east near the Shivl'en mountains.

"This is where we are." Orin said, pointing at a dot on the map that said 'Vennire.' "Close to the disputed lands. We need to move southwest where we will meet up with the main road." Orin followed a line with his finger until the line met up with another and he tapped it a few times showing that's where they needed to go.

"Or we could go home." Seth said under his breath. The only one that seemed to hear Seth was Orin who smiled at him with a deep kindness. Orin seemed to be the only one in the group who wasn't mad or annoyed over how Seth was acting. He always had a level head and nothing but kind smiles to give him. Seth found his kindness and optimism refreshing and he couldn't help but smile bashfully back at Orin.

"My big concern is that bird, Athex." Kitty said with a hit of uneasiness.

"Kei says that Athex is gone from the Kondoman camp." Orin said looking at Kitty. "She also said something about how he left for Kondoma and won't be a bother to us for a while."

"I don't know about that fox." Kitty said looking at Orin. "Where did she get that kind of information?"

Orin cleared his throat and appeared a little worried. "She asked one of the Kondoman soldiers she knows, and she checked for herself."

Kitty threw up her arms in protest. "I knew it."

"I believe her." Orin stated, folding his arms.

"How could you believe her after she does something like that?" Kitty asks. "She's playing both sides."

"No, she's healing both sides." Orin countered.

"Oh, and I'm sure she told you that as well." Kitty argued with a smile on her face.

"How can you doubt her after what she did with summoning the Kry to help protect Seth?" Orin asked Kitty honestly, wanting an answer it seemed.

Coven laughed and looked at Kitty and Orin. "I think she's a big traitor because of the Kry. Only someone who is truly evil inside would call on them for aid."

Kitty gazed at Coven for a second, annoyed, before she turned back to Orin. "I've never trusted that fox, despite what she did to help Seth.

Healing both sides is helping both sides, and only two-faced opportun-ists do that."

Orin sighed and put his hands on his hips. "I trust her."

Kitty looked at Orin before she too sighed and put her hands on her hips. "I don't trust that fox." She said adamantly. "But I do trust you." She expressed looking at Orin with a respectful nod.

"We all trust Orin." Agatha chimed in. "But what really concerns me is if Athex is working with Kondoma, then they broke the treaty. No one is supposed to be attacked on the main roads that connect any of the cities of Terina. We were attacked on the main road to Kondoma. Who's to say it won't happen again?"

"We don't have a choice." Coven said looking at everyone. "Because Evan is healed and ready to leave, we need to get to the road soon."

Seth looked over at Evan who appeared to be perfectly fine now. He was standing with the others around the map. Seth was the only one not standing with the rest of the group. He was closest to Kitty and Orin, but he stood a few inches away from them. He didn't want to be part of the group, not really. But deep down he knew that he was. It was called Team Seth after all.

"Okay," Evan said looking at everyone with a determination on his face. "Not that I'm wanting to get away from the great hospitality that this camp has shown, it's just I feel like we need to keep moving with the mission."

"Agreed," Coven said, looking at Evan with a nod. "We leave today."

The trip away from the camp didn't take too long, in fact Light Fire and the rest of the horses were all ready for them. Orin showed Seth that the way he had been mounting Light Fire was the wrong way, which led to Seth apologizing to Light Fire who just laughed. The day went on without much of a problem. It was cloudy as they got to the main road, the fact that it was cloudy made Seth happy. However, now Seth was feeling overjoyed because of one thing, it was raining, and if there was one thing Seth loved it was the rain. He loved its calmness as it fell gently to the ground, and he showed his joy with a wide shy smile on his face. The clouds above them were gray and just slightly moving to the north. It was not a heavy rain and there was no fear of thunder or lightning. It was just a smooth drizzle accompanied by the clean smell that rainstorms make in the air.

Unlike Seth, his friends sat on their horses wearing hunched shoulders and droopy eyes. They all appeared to move mindlessly with the rhythm of their horses as they trudged up and down over the muddy ground. Evan and Kitty were closest to Seth, and he could see how much they were despising the rain. Evan sported a frown that was supported by a dim almost silent madness that lay barely dormant in his gloomy eyes. He looked like he was either close to shouting out in annoyance or breaking down in tears. Kitty on the other hand seemed to be in the midst of an existential crisis with her head deeply bowed and her hair soaking wet. Seth could hardly see her face behind the veil that was created by her rain saturated locks. What he could see of her face was her green eyes slowly blinking almost with the rhythm of her horse's footsteps. The rest of the company didn't seem to be faring any better. From what Seth could see everyone else was in a miserable state. Seth could sympathize with his comrades. However, while they were hunched over in gloom acting like undead versions of themselves, he was sitting straight basking in a kind of rain-fueled euphoria, this was because he never experienced a rainstorm outside of Remtaya before, and he was loving every minute of it. The pitter patter of the droplets rang peacefully in his ears, and as the rain quickly yet gently passed by his earlobes, he heard it whisper his name softly.

Sssethhh. It whispered. Seth closed his eyes and listened to its calming voice. He tilted his head back and the rain gently landed on his face.

Ssseth. They are here Sethhh. They have come to greet you. The rain whispered as it ran softly down his face.

"What?" Seth asked quietly, opening his eyes and moving his head up straight. "Who has come?" He looked around at his depressed companions. Trying to see if there was anyone there that was not supposed to be with them, Seth looked up at the front of the group where Orin and Coven were. He didn't see anything in front of them that would prove to be out of the ordinary, but as Seth looked a little way beyond them he saw what appeared to be a hooded figure suddenly appear out of nowhere. At first he thought it was just his eyes playing tricks on him, but as they got closer to the figure he realized that it was not his imagination. The entity was in the middle of the path and seemed to have no desire to move even though Seth and his friends were almost on top of it. Coven held out his hand to signal for all of them to stop and Seth looked closer at the hooded figure as it just stood there. The rain seemed to increase slightly, much to the chagrin of the group, Seth simply smiled to himself at how lovely the rain felt.

"Who goes there?" Coven asked forcefully. The hooded personage stood like a stone, silent and unmoving.

"Who goes there?" Coven asked this time with anger in his voice.

"That is not the question you should ask." The hooded figure suddenly responded with a clear and almost cheerful-sounding voice. "The question you should be asking is, 'what's the password?'"

There was silence for a second, it was as if Coven didn't know how to answer the hooded being's response. "What?" He finally asked, perplexed. Seth was a few feet behind Coven and to the right so he couldn't really see the expression on Coven's face, but he guessed he appeared confused over such an odd answer.

"That's not a good question either," answered the hooded figure. "The next question you should have asked is, 'why are we in a bottle?'" Right then the rain falling on everyone stopped, yet the sound of rain falling was still present, only now it sounded like it was hitting something above them. Seth looked up in slight annoyance that the rain was not falling around him, but mostly in curiosity because of the still soft pattering of rain over their heads. Seth could see nothing over them, which only made him more curious about what was happening.

Meanwhile, Orin turned his head toward Coven who was obviously losing his patience with the being. "We aren't in a bottle." Orin answered back looking at the hooded being with confusion surrounding the tones in his voice.

"Um." The voice of Evan sounded out in slight concern. Seth and everyone turned to look at him. He had his left gloved hand stretched out to his port side. Before Evan's hand could stretch out all the way it stopped as if it was being blocked by an invisible surface. "I think we are." He stated, a worried expression obviously showing over his handsome features.

Kitty reached out her hand to her right. "It's here also." She commented. "Are we surrounded?" Kitty asked looking around at the whole group in concern.

Coven looked at the hooded figure. "What kind of dark magic is this?" He asked with great anger. Suddenly, another person just appeared next to the hooded one. This person didn't have a hood on and was wearing a black suit and bowtie.

"Hello." The person said, smiling happily. He had dark brown hair that was long enough to cover most of his ears, and he seemed to have brown eyes. The hooded figure stepped closer to the other person.

"Why are you wearing that?" The figure asked, suddenly changing attire. Now Seth could see what the hooded person looked like. He looked a lot like the other did. Except instead of a suit and tie, he was wearing a black short sleeved shirt with brown pants and shoes. The other thing that Seth noticed was both of them had black gloves on their hands much like his.

"I was at a wedding." The second person said looking at the first.

"What wedding?" Asked the first.

"Do I have to tell you who got married?" The second one asked, rolling his eyes.

"They got married? When did they actually start liking each other?" The first asked shocked. The second person looked at Seth and his friends. He smiled at them kindly.

"Hi, I am Erin and the previously hooded person is my brother Terrin." Erin said, both of the brothers bowing. "Now do not panic, but you are all being confined by a giant bottle." Erin said, knocking on the glass; the resounding chime was low and reverberated over the whole structure.

"Who are you?" Coven asked, still with anger. Erin looked at Coven with a scrutinizing gaze.

"Why are you so mad?" Erin asked, looking very closely at Coven. "It's not because you feel out of control of your environment. If it were that I would understand. You are mad because you think you know what we are and that makes you furious. Why?" Erin asked, his penetrating eyes fixed on Coven with great intent.

"It's because his entire family hunted down and killed many who were expected to be what he thinks we are." Terrin said looking closely at Coven. The two brothers turned their heads to each other and began to whisper. Then Erin turned and looked at Seth and then at Kitty then he turned his attention onto Evan.

"All of you are wondering who we are and so without further ado or letdown I will tell you. We are Kry and we are here to stall you." Erin said, throwing his hands in the air flamboyantly. Terrin looked at Erin with an annoyed gaze.

"We weren't supposed to tell them that." He exclaimed, folding his arms showing a bit of annoyance.

"What. What do you mean we weren't supposed to tell them that? We weren't supposed to tell them what?" Erin asked looking intensely at Terrin.

"We weren't supposed to tell them that we were stalling them." Terrin explained. Erin looked at Team Seth again.

"Oh, My mistake." Erin said. "I was just thinking about how strange Team Seth sounds. So I forgot to not tell them that." He said to Terrin.

"Team Seth don't you think that is just a little obvious?" Erin said looking at Coven. "Why not call it Team Chosen or Team Prophecy or Team Obscure."

"Why would they call themselves Team Obscure?" Terrin asked.

"Well, it's better than basically shouting to the world 'we have Seth the new Chosen One with us come and get him.'" Erin explained.

"Well, calling them Team Obscure I think would not be very obscure at all. It would be just as obvious as calling them Team Seth." Terrin said leaning against the glass of the giant bottle that was still enclosing Seth and his friends.

"Oh, I have it." Terrin shouted standing straight and looking at the whole group. "They can call themselves Team C.H.I.P.S." Erin stood there with wonderment.

"Wonderful, C.H.I.P.S as in Chosen Hiding In Plain Sight!" Erin said jumping up and down with excitement.

"Or they could be called Team S.T.A.C.I as in Secret Transport About Chosen Intervention." Erin said happily. Terrin turned and looked at Coven.

"Well, Coven you are the self-appointed leader of this Team what do you think, C.H.I.P.S or S.T.A.C.I?" Terrin asked. Coven pulled out his sword and pointed it at the two Kry.

"If you are Kry I will kill you where you stand." Coven said with cold rage moving through his voice like a blistering breeze. Terrin and Erin both looked at Coven with disbelief.

"That's just rude." Erin said shaking his head at Coven in disapproval. "You should know better than to try to intimidate a Kry and also not to interrupt one like that. I am very ashamed of you Clover."

Coven's hand that was holding his sword faltered. "How do you know that name?" He asked, his anger increasing exponentially.

"We are Kry, we know all the juicy details of all your lives." Terrin said looking at Coven but talking to everyone. "For example, your full name is Clovis Coven Strong-arm the third and your rather mean older brothers would call you Clover, the fact of which you hated greatly."

"And you." Erin said pointing at Orin. "You have someone you care so much about that they are the last thing you think about when you fall asleep and the first when you wake up."

"Oh that's sweet." Terrin said honestly, batting his eyes.

"Orin isn't your real name either." Erin said, still pointing at Orin. "It's Cilio, Cilio Orin Wolfhart." He said smiling.

"Oh I like that, Wolfhart it's very catchy and also ironic." Terrin said. Coven got off his horse, still pointing his sword at the two brothers.

"I have had enough of your blathering!" Coven shouted at them through the glass container that was holding him and everyone else inside. Erin looked at Coven with an expression of shock and amusement.

"Blather? We do not blather. No Kry has ever blathered." Erin said with assurance.

"Yes, if we were blathering then we would sound more like this." Terrin began to make random noises and facial expressions. Erin gave Terrin a look of disbelief.

"Correction, no Kry has ever blathered until now." Erin said, still looking at Terrin with a questioning gaze.

"I don't care! Let us go or I will kill you!" Coven promised. Erin and Terrin both looked at Coven questioningly.

"Okay, Coven if you could harm us with a piece of sharpened alloy composed of iron and carbon how are you going to get through the unbreakable glass container that all of you are being, well, contained in?" Erin asked while looking at Coven with an expression that could only be described with the word 'duh.' Coven yelled and began to bang his sword against the glass that was dividing him from the Kry.

"You poor thing you're going to hurt yourself." Terrin said as Coven was banging on the glass. Evan walked his horse closer to the Kry.

"I don't know why you are doing this but is your intent to kill us because we are going to run out of air in here eventually." Evan shouted over Coven's banging.

"Well, that will not happen for another three hours and twenty-two minutes, and we are not going to keep you in here for that long." Terrin said reassuringly.

"Then let us out." Kitty said forcefully.

"Say the password and we will." Erin said.

"What's the password?" Orin asked, starting to sound impatient. Coven was still banging on the obviously unbreakable glass.

"You come down a road and see some gold. You go to pick it up but before you do a word comes to you. The word is golden that much is true. All but one word and one is all. One must say it or be like him." Erin said cryptically, he snapped his fingers, right when he did Coven's sword turned into a bouquet of flowers and Coven was back sitting on his horse. Coven looked at the two Kry with anger.

"You have three tries to give us the password." Terrin and Erin said at the same time.

"Where is my sword?" Coven asked with anger.

"No, that is not it. You only have two tries left." Erin exclaimed, giggling.

"We don't have time for this." Evan said, also starting to sound angry.

"Again, not the password. You all are aware that it is password not passwords. We're using the singular here. So it is obviously one word and not a full sentence." Erin said looking around the ever-more inpatient people in the glass container. The only one that seemed to be okay with everything was Seth. He sat there quite amused and intrigued by the two Kry. They were the second Kry he had ever seen, and they behaved nothing like what everyone made the Kry out to be. Seth thought about the very odd riddle that Erin had given them.

You are going down a road and see some gold. Seth thought in his head. *That part seems obvious.* He thought to himself. *You go to pick it up but before you do a word comes to you. The word is golden that much is true. All but one word and one is all.* Seth thought.

"Do you have any ideas?" Seth asked Light Fire.

"I thought it was obvious. They are trying to make it as easy as possible." Light Fire told Seth.

"Well, I think I know what it is but please don't keep your ideas a secret." Seth said to Light Fire. Light Fire laughed with amusement. "You just said it," he said.

"I thought that was what it was." Seth said, smiling. "Do you want to say it or should I?" He asked Light Fire.

"Oh please, you." Light Fire said, chuckling. Seth laughed out loud and then realized that he laughed too loud. Everyone was looking at him; Seth's friends looked with confusion, but Erin and Terrin were looking at Seth with something close to pride.

"Do you want to tell us something?" Erin asked, smiling. Seth looked at Erin and Terrin.

"Please." Seth said simply. Terrin smiled and snapped his fingers. As he did the bouquet Coven was still angrily holding turned back into a sword. There was a popping sound and the massive container they were in turned into a kaleidoscope of butterflies that all moved to where Terrin was standing. The Kry held out his hand and the swarm all began to move around it. Terrin then clapped his hands together and the butterflies vanished.

"Congratulations, you are now free." Erin said as Terrin clapped his hands. "You had me worried there Seth, but you got it." Erin said, winking at Seth. The rain which had been stopped by the glass container started to fall on Seth's and everyone else's heads again.

"Well, we will be going now. It has been a pleasure indeed to be threatened and yelled at by all of you except for Seth who has more sense than most of you combined, by the way." Terrin said looking at Coven but talking to everyone. Coven got down from his horse and walked over to the two Kry his right hand grasped tight around the handle of his blade.

"Can I help you?" Erin asked as Coven stepped very close to him. Coven glared at Erin with disgust. Then he suddenly swung his sword straight through Erin's chest.

"For the countless people you have killed you filth." Coven said, his sword still in Erin's chest. Erin looked at Coven with an unimpressed look on his face.

"Coven what have you done?" Agatha asked in shock.

"Oh, don't worry Agatha I'm fine." Erin said, waving at her. "And what do you mean about all the people I have killed? I have been alive for infinity and can remember every millisecond of my life and I have never outright killed anyone." Erin explained to Coven with his sword still in him. Seth looked in amazement to see that Coven's sword was going through Erin, but it was not in his body. It was like Erin's body was not tangible and anything could go through it.

"How is that possible?" Coven said with fear as he pulled his sword away from Erin's body. "You are not really here," he said. Erin slapped Coven, sending Coven's face in the opposite direction.

"Of course I am really here stupid. My brother and I told you that your sword or anything else for that matter can't harm us. See that is why we said we are Kry. We cannot be killed by anything and we certainly can't be killed by a feebleminded human like you." Erin stated clearly. Terrin snapped his fingers and Coven was back on his horse.

"Now despite the outrageously rude behavior that Coven has shown it has been a pleasure stalling you." Terrin said.

"Now we must be going. Goodbye Team C.H.I.P.S." Erin said.

"I like that one also." Terrin said, smiling. Both Erin and Terrin snapped their fingers as the rain kept drizzling down and vanished. Everyone just sat there on their horses in absolute bewilderment at the current events which had happened, while Seth found it very fascinating.

The rain kept drizzling as Seth and his friends got their tents ready for bed. Seth looked around to see that most of the group were already in their tents. The only people who were not were Kitty, Evan, Orin, and Coven who were all sitting at the slowly dying fire that was being constantly bombarded by the calmly falling rain. Seth walked to Light fire who was close to the fire along with the other horses. As Seth got closer, he could hear Coven talking about their encounter with the Kry.

"I know a Kry when I see one and those two were Kry." Coven said angrily stabbing at the fire with a stick, sending embers up in the air.

"All I'm saying is that they could have been Demi-Kry." Kitty explained looking at Coven. "They are also very powerful."

"You don't really believe in Demi-Kry." Coven said with a laugh. "Demi-Kry aren't real. The Kry made them up to make it look like they had nothing to do with the Kry wars." Coven took the stick out of the fire and looked at the burning red tip. "The Kry are evil incarnate in this world, and it's been the duty of my family for four generations to wipe them from existence." He said stabbing the stick back into the fire sending more embers into the air. Coven looked over at Orin who was sitting quietly looking at the flames obviously thinking about something heavily.

"What about you Orin?" Coven asked. Orin looked up at Coven, having been drawn out of his contemplations.

"About what?" Orin asked, looking very worried about something.

"You're a werewolf, and the Kry have some sort of alliance with your race. What do you think about them?" Coven asked, sounding like he was accusing Orin of something.

"Coven stop it." Kitty said, looking him down.

"The Kry that we saw today did seem to like your last name." Coven said glaring at Kitty but talking to Orin.

"Well why wouldn't they like his last name, it is very catchy and ironic." Evan blurted out, honestly. Coven turned his glare on Evan who quickly looked at the fire in embarrassment.

"I have no opinion of the Kry." Orin said standing up and brushing off some of the soot from the fire that was on his pants. "The two Kry that we saw today were the first I have seen in a long time." Orin said before walking to his tent. Seth watched the conversation from a distance quietly giving Light Fire some sugar he had on his hand. Seth thought that his passive covert listening was going unnoticed until he heard Coven say his name. Seth turned around and saw that everyone that was still around the glowing fire was looking at him.

"What do you think of the Kry, Seth?" Coven asked, looking at Seth with a cold gaze. Seth looked at Kitty and Evan who obviously were just curious about what Seth thought about the Kry. Coven on the other hand seemed to be more interrogative than just curious.

"I think that they were…" Seth stopped and thought about what he could say that didn't sound like he really admired them even though he actually sort of did, but also didn't sound like he hated them.

"I think that they were funny." Seth decided to say. Coven laughed loud.

"You would." He said, still laughing. Seth had a feeling that even though Coven was laughing he was really mocking Seth. Coven got up and walked over to his tent still laughing when he walked inside and disappeared.

"What a jerk." Kitty said getting up also from the wood she and Evan were sitting on next to the fire. Evan got up and walked over to Seth.

"Good night." Evan said to Seth and Kitty. He walked past Seth and sat down on a stump of wood that was next to the forest that their camp was next to.

"Aren't you going to bed also?" Seth asked Evan.

"Not right now. I am on watch for an hour." Evan explained with a yawn.

"Lucky you." Seth said, sarcastically.

"Good night you two." Kitty said as she walked to her tent. Seth and Evan said good night back to her as she strolled into her tent.

"Do you want me to stay up with you?" Seth asked.

"No, you need to get your rest." Evan said smiling. "Do not worry I have done this before." He reassured Seth.

"When?" Seth asked.

"When I was training to be a prophesier, I got to keep watch on one of the guard posts in Remtaya." Evan said.

"How fun." Seth said sarcastically again.

"It was." Even said smiling.

"Well then good night you two." Seth said.

"You two? What do you mean?" Evan asked, looking around nervously.

"Oh I meant you and Light Fire." Seth explained pointing at Light Fire who appeared to be sleeping while he was standing with the other horses. Seth walked to his tent which was surrounded by the other nine tents which formed a half circle in the clearing that they were in. The road was just a few feet away from the camp. Seth's tent was to the right of the campfire that was in the middle of the camp. As he walked to his tent the rain drizzled quietly down from the sky. Seth walked into his tent and grabbed a towel to dry his hair. He then put on his pajamas and got into bed. He laid there wondering why they were taking him to the evil King, who would most likely kill him. Seth sighed and turned on his right side and closed his eyes.

"I hope Biz and Shadow are okay." Seth thought before eventually falling asleep.

Seth awoke to the sound of howling outside his tent. He looked around to find that his tent was still dark. It was still night. He listened some more to the howling and realized that the noises he was hearing were from wolves. Seth sat up and got off the cot he was sleeping on. The night was cold, but he felt comfortable in it. Seth walked to the opening of his tent and looked out into the darkness. The moon was high, casting a pale glow onto the dark world around Seth. He looked straight away from him to see a large wolf walking into the forest that they were close to. For some reason Seth wasn't scared, he felt intrigued. The wolf he had just seen was bigger than he imagined a wolf to be. Was that Orin? He was a werewolf, maybe he changed to see why wolves were out in the forest. Seth stepped out of his tent and quickly moved closer to the woods. There was another howl and Seth stopped. He knew wolves were predators, this could be dangerous. Still Seth felt no fear, instead he felt curious. Seth sighed and walked into the woods. The wind blew through the trees, a voice whispering him forward. Seth walked closer to the sound of howling down a trail that was illuminated by the moon's soft glow. Seth looked out from the trail he was on to see a group of wolves standing around under the trees. One of the wolves was larger than the others. Its fur was a soft brown that covered the wolf's body. Its coat was clean and looked almost well brushed, unlike the other wolves around the big one whose coats looked matted and rundown. The big wolf was talking to one of the other wolves and Seth recognized the voice from the large wolf as Orin. Seth got closer and the other wolves in the pack he was looking at stopped howling and gazed at Seth with their yellow eyes. Some moved away from Seth while others stood their ground but looked like they were ready to run if they needed to. Orin turned and looked at Seth with interest. Seth was surprised to see that Orin's eyes were not yellow like the other wolves. His eyes glowed a sapphire blue the same color of his human eyes, only as a wolf his eyes seemed to shine like they held power.

"Seth?" Orin asked, his mouth moving as he talked. "Did the howling of my friends wake you?"

Seth nodded slowly. He wasn't scared, but he was coming to realize that he was surrounded by wolves. Should he be scared? "Orin," Seth stated looking at his wolf form with amazement. "What are you doing out here?"

Orin sniffed the air and gave a huff. "I heard the wolves start howling and thought I'd come and visit with them."

The wolf that Orin was talking to, turned and looked at Seth. "What brings you here?"

"Seth is a friend of mine." Orin told the wolf calmly. "He's the Chosen One of Remtaya." Orin looked at Seth with a teasing sound to his voice.

Seth looked at Orin with a frown. "You really don't believe I'm the Chosen One, do you?"

Orin chuckled and shook his large head. "No, Serena gave me a very passionate speech about how there are no more Chosen Ones. Admittedly I already knew that, but Serena gave some good points anyways." Orin looked down with his eyes like he was sad about something. Seth could feel the worry Orin had for Serena. He was concerned if she was okay at Remtaya.

Seth looked at the wolves that seemed to be playing with each other in the moonlight. He looked back at Orin gazing at the large wolf in front of him. "You care for Serena a lot, don't you?" Seth said already knowing the answer.

Orin nodded. "The Kry Erin and Terrin were right. She is the first thing I think of as I rise and the last thing I think of before I rest."

Seth smiled a little thinking about how Serena was lucky to have a father like Orin in her life. Then a terrible thought came to Seth. Everyone that was with him were there to protect him so that he could get to Korson and kill him. But what if Orin or any of his other friends were struck down and killed in the process. Seth looked at Orin and gazed at his rather beautiful glowing blue eyes.

"Orin, if the time comes and you have a chance. I want to you run away from whatever battle that happens when we get to Kondoma. Serena needs you; I couldn't handle it if you or anyone would die because of me." Seth said nervously.

Orin looked at the wolf that he had been talking to before Seth got to where they were. "I'm happy to hear your pack is doing good." He told the wolf. "I need to leave now." He said with a snort. The wolf bowed their head to him and walked over to where the other wolves were. Orin turned and walked closer to Seth so that his large body was right next to him. "Let's go back to the camp." Orin said as Seth walked with him. "My watch is almost up."

They walked up the trail as Orin looked at Seth.

"Seth, I'm sorry that this is happening to you." he said wholeheartedly. "I would have tried to fight it for you, but the senate would have stopped me, plus I'm not your care giver or none of this would be happening to you."

"I wish more people thought like you." Seth insisted. "Almost everyone thinks I'm the Chosen One and that makes me expendable it seems like."

Orin looked ahead and sighed. "Not everyone follows Remtaya so blindly like Coven." Orin stated. "Kitty and Evan for example. The promise that Kitty made is a good example that they care for you deeply. That kind of friendship is powerful. I know that deep down they don't think you're the Chosen One, and that they will protect you the best they can."

Seth smiled a little and nodded. "I just hope it doesn't kill them."

"Don't worry about others dying around you. I have hope that there could be a different way this adventure could play out." Orin looked at Seth with is kind glowing eyes.

"Really?" Seth asked, looking at Orin with hope.

"Yes, you're not like the other Chosen Ones. You could find a way to peace without killing Korson." Orin stated with a soft non-threating growl deep in his throat.

Seth thought about what Kei had told him about how Orin was one of the good ones. Orin truly seemed like he cared and was hoping for another way to end the conflict they were all in.

Seth looked at Orin smiling shyly. "Sorry I interrupted the conversation you had with Kei." He apologized to him.

Orin chuckled. "It's fine, Kei and I go way back. I was actually wondering if it was the same fox that I knew. The first time I met them they were a boy." He explained.

Seth tilted his head slightly. "How could it be the same fox if this Kei is a female?"

"Foxes like the Kry, and some other creatures, are gender fluid, they can change their gender as easily as a human can put on a hat." Orin explained. "If Kei hadn't shown it to me, I don't think I would have believed it."

"That's fascinating." Seth stated thinking about how interesting that could be.

They had made it back to the camp and Orin looked over at Seth's tent. "You should rest." He told him kindly. I'm about to wake my replacements and turn in myself."

Seth nodded and smiled at Orin. "Thank you for talking with me." He told him before saying goodnight and walking back to his tent.

CHAPTER TWENTY-ONE

THE KING OF KONDOMA
AND THE CHOSEN ONE

So, you got to see your first few Kry (that you know of). What did you think about them? Did you find them intriguing, or did you hate them like Coven does? Well, whichever way you see them you have to get used to them because more Kry will come into this story and let me say that even though you only have eleven chapters left until this book is over. This story is just beginning.

Seth awoke slowly and looked around his tent. With his eyes still tired he noticed that it was still dark, but Seth could hear the distant chatter of morning birds as they sang their songs. Seth looked to the entrance to his tent and saw a figure standing in the entrance.

"Good morning." Seth said, still mostly asleep.

"Good morning." A woman's voice said. Seth guessed it was Agatha.

"What time is it?" Seth asked, yawning and slowly batting his eyes so he could see Agatha's face closely.

"It's time to go." The woman said calmly.

"Go, go where?" Seth asked as he got up from his bed, still very sleepy.

"It is time to go to your fate." The woman said with a hint of darkness in her voice. Seth's eyes suddenly widened, and he looked at the entrance of his tent.

"Loral," Seth said with dread. Loral smiled darkly at Seth.

"That's right." She said walking into Seth's tent. "This time your friends won't be able to save you." Loral said. She grabbed Seth by the arm and started pulling him out of his tent.

"No!" Seth screamed, pulling away from her. He was able to get free and as he did, he fell to the side of his bed. Seth looked up in horror as Loral pulled out her wand and walked closer to him. Seth grabbed a food box that had the same spell on it that all of Remtaya had.

"Stay back!" Seth yelled at Loral.

"Seth!" Someone yelled from outside of his tent.

"Help!" Seth screamed at the top of his lungs. Loral waved her wand and a portal opened behind Seth. Seth turned and faced the portal in shock. He suddenly felt Loral push him, sending him falling into the portal.

"No!" Seth screamed out as he fell through. He seemed to fall into a blue mist that had different colors spinning around it. As Seth clung to the food box as he fell, a small white ball floated next to him.

"Give me your permission please." The ball twinkled.

"Why, who are you? Please help me." Seth asked the small white ball.

"Give me your permission and you will be out of the rift." The white ball twinkled again. Seth looked as the colors that were spinning around the blue mist became more vibrant.

"I give you my permission!" Seth yelled as the colors began to make a high-pitched screaming sound. The white ball floated to Seth and touched his arm. There was a sudden flash and Seth then found himself on a stone floor with diamond shaped tiles.

"Get up." Loral demanded pulling him up. Seth now stood in a room that was very big and grand. As his eyes adjusted to the light that was coming from the windows that lined the top of the chamber, Seth was able to get a better look at where he was. Stone pillars lined the left and right sides of the room. As Seth looked around more, he saw two giant dark wood doors that were behind him.

"On your knees." Loral said, forcing Seth down on his knees. Seth was now looking at the front of the chamber. The large hall led up to a throne that was black in color and had a man sitting on it. The man's left arm was on the arm rest and his right arm was on his right knee. His right hand was in a fist, resting under his chin. Above the man and at the top of the throne was a triangular spire that went up for about three feet. The man looked at Seth. He had dark hair and was wearing nothing but black. He sat there with dark brown eyes studying Seth. Seth stared back, still wondering where he was. Then Seth really looked at the man.

"Oh no." Seth said under his breath in fear. The man got up and started walking toward Seth. He chuckled and smiled as he got closer.

"So you are Seth." He said walking up and bending down so he could look Seth in the eyes. Seth looked into the man's eyes with fear.

This is it; I am going to die. Seth said in his mind, starting to panic.

"You have been an item of great discussion in my city Seth. A lot of the people in the city want me to kill you like I did the others." Korson said getting up and walking toward a sword that was sheathed on one of the stone pillars. He pulled it out and walked over to where Seth was kneeling. Seth got ready as Korson stood over him.

"Most think that I would just kill the Chosen Ones once I see them." Korson said holding the point of the sword at Seth. "But no one knows what I do before I kill the Chosen Ones." Korson dropped the sword at Seth's knees. Seth looked at the sword confused. He then looked up at Korson.

"I don't understand." Seth said, still with great fear. Korson bent down and looked at Seth.

"Do you want to kill me?" Korson asked, looking seriously at Seth. The room was silent as Seth stared into Korson's brown eyes.

"No." Seth said honestly. Korson looked up at Loral, who had a look of shock and disgust on her face. Korson got up and walked over to his throne.

"Loral, please leave us." Korson said waving his hand at her, gesturing for her to leave. Loral bowed and left the room.

"Get up Seth, you have passed my test. In fact you are the only Chosen One who has." Korson said looking at him. Seth got up and walked past the sword toward Korson. Seth looked around nervously, still thinking that this was some kind of cruel joke.

"Tell me Seth, what did your friends at Remtaya say about me?" Korson asked. "What did they say I was?" he inquired. Seth looked at the King nervously. Korson smiled at Seth kindly. "Seth if we are to trust each other then you must be honest with me. I promise that I will not kill you if you do not try to kill me or maliciously deceive me." He said reassuring Seth.

"They called you a demon or a monster." Seth said. "They call you the evil King."

Korson laughed heartily. "Do I seem like a demon or a monster to you?" He asked Seth, holding out his arms from his sides so Seth could see all of him. Korson looked like a very normal human to Seth. In fact, Seth thought that Korson looked good for a man who he was told was forty.

"No." Seth acknowledged. Korson got up from his chair and walked down the small steps that led up to his throne. He stepped closer to Seth.

"Come with me." Korson said kindly, gently putting his right hand on his back and gesturing for Seth to follow him to one of the doors that led out of the chamber.

Kitty walked frantically through the chaotic camp. She walked over to Agatha who was tending to three wounded soldiers.

"How bad is it?" Kitty asked in a frenzy.

"Loral got them hard. She used a spell that made the soldier who was keeping watch think that everything was okay until it was too late." Agatha sighed shaking her head.

"And the other two?" Kitty asked.

"They were just in the wrong place at the wrong time. One had just come back from the woods to relieve himself and the other was going to be the next one to keep watch. They are all going to have to come back to Remtaya." Agatha explained.

"Okay." Kitty said walking away.

"Wait, please I can still help." One of the soldiers said to Kitty.

"Sorry but you can't." Kitty said simply as she walked away. Orin suddenly appeared out of the forest, shirtless his bare chest moving up and down rhythmically. Kitty walked quickly over to him.

"Anything?" Kitty asked Orin as she got closer to him.

"No." Orin said, still breathing steadily. "I could not smell Seth or Loral anywhere for around five miles." He explained.

"That must mean that they portaled all the way to Kondoma." Kitty said cursing under her breath.

"I did find this." Orin said holding up a piece of red fabric that looked like it was torn off a dress. Orin gave it to Kitty who examined it.

"Could it be a piece from one of those rogue Phoenixes?" Kitty asked Orin.

"I would say so. The smell from the rogue Phoenix is not easy to miss." Orin explained. Kitty looked at the forest.

"Were they here before we were?" She asked Orin.

"The fabric smells at most two days old." Orin said.

"Then they must have been waiting for us here." Kitty said with disbelief.

"I didn't detect them even in my wolf form. Seth and I were out in the forest last night, I should have been more vigilant." Orin rubbed his right arm as he shook his head.

"Are you okay?" Kitty asked, looking Orin's bare chest over.

"When I was in my wolf form a strange little creature almost bit my right front leg." Orin said, checking his arm to see if it made a mark.

"There are more than just a few strange things in the forest of Conching." Kitty explained slapping Orin's arm twice.

"I wish I could help more." Orin said sadly.

"You may have helped enough." Kitty said reassuringly. "What would I do without your sense of smell?" Kitty asked Orin.

Orin shrugged "I better put a shirt on." He stated with a sigh.

"I'm not complaining." Kitty said with a tease. She knew that while Orin took his shirt off often he never did it to show off. It was always for more particle reasons. Orin was not vain, which was one thing that Kitty liked about him. Orin smiled and ran to his tent to put on a shirt. Kitty walked over to her own tent holding the red cloth. Evan hurried over to where Kitty was walking.

"I heard what you and Orin were talking about." Evan said. "I think I have an idea of what happened." He said to her.

"What?" Kitty asked, still walking to her tent.

"The Kry that we met said that they were stalling us." Evan explained. "Maybe they were helping Loral capture Seth." Evan speculated. Kitty got to her tent and walked inside, then came back out with a marble bowl and the glass bottle of the orange liquid that she had used only a few days ago to find Seth.

"The Kry are not like paid thugs. They only interact with other species if they find it amusing or if it is somehow very important." Kitty said sitting cross-legged on the grass.

"Well, why else would the Kry want to stall us?" Evan asked sitting next to Kitty as she placed the marble bowl on the grass in front of her.

"I am not saying that there is not a correlation between the Kry and

Seth's abduction by Loral. I am saying that the motives of the Kry are never understood by anyone else except to the Kry themselves." Kitty explained. Agatha ran up to Kitty as she was about to put down a map that she had also taken out of her tent.

"Kitty one of the soldiers just went into a coma. I am going to have to go with them back to Remtaya." Agatha said hurriedly.

"Okay, tell someone that they will be seeing four of the horses back in Remtaya in a few minutes and the rest of them after we get to Kondoma." Kitty shouted at Agatha as she ran back to where the wounded soldiers were. Kitty placed the red cloth inside of the marble bowl and poured in the orange liquid. She then put down a map of Terina, pulled out her wand, and began chanting. As Kitty chanted Evan looked over to see Agatha and the three wounded soldiers disappear in a small blue ball that flew high into the air and then pulsed in all directions.

"I do not mean to worry you, but wasn't our plan to trans luminate all of us back to Remtaya when Seth killed the evil King?" Evan asked Kitty. Kitty stopped chanting.

"Yes and we are still going to do that." Kitty told Evan.

"But without Agatha, you, Seth, and I are the only ones who can do that, and I can only trans luminate myself and Seth has never even trans luminated before. You're the only one who has ever trans luminated more than two people and you said it was only three people." Evan said, agitated.

"We will manage." Kitty said to Evan.

"What are you doing?" Coven asked, running over to Kitty and Evan.

"The reason why we cannot just transport ourselves to Kondoma is because neither Evan, Agatha, nor myself have ever been there and one can only transport oneself to a place they have already been." Kitty explained.

"Everyone already knows this." Coven said looking down at them.

"But hopefully this piece of dress that Orin gave me can give us a shortcut, much like how we were able to get to Seth the first time he was captured." Kitty said, starting to chant again. Evan looked around the camp as everyone got all the tents down and back on the horses. Suddenly there was a flash of light and a sizzling sound coming from the marble bowl.

"No!" Kitty shouted with anger. Evan saw the red cloth that was floating on the orange liquid burn into ash.

"The last time you did this it was a lucky mistake." Evan said with sadness.

"I don't believe in luck." Kitty said, pouring the liquid out of the bowl and putting all of her stuff on her horse.

"What do we do now?" Evan asked nervously.

"Hopefully Seth is stalling for us to get there." Kitty said with a worried face.

"Hopefully he has killed the King by now." Evan said.

"What is that you are holding?" Korson asked Seth as they walked down a long and narrow corridor.

"It's a food box. It gives you food if you ask for it. It can also give you clothing or medicine." Seth explained to Korson.

"Can it give you weapons?" Korson asked as they kept walking down the hall.

"No." Seth said looking at Korson worriedly. Korson smiled at Seth and then noticed that Seth was looking worried.

"Oh, I just can't seem to get you to fully trust me yet, can I?" Korson said looking at Seth.

"I just met you." Seth explained.

"Well, if we are to be friends then you are going to have to know things about me." Korson said, turning a corner where there was a door. Korson opened the door and looked at Seth. "I know exactly where to begin." He said letting Seth walk in first. Seth looked around the room. It was black mostly, and dank. The only thing that seemed to be in the room was a table with a blue orb sitting in the middle of the small table. The orb sat on a pedestal and shone a dark blue into the rest of the dark room.

"Tell me Seth do you believe in the prophecy that brought you here to me?" Korson asked.

"No." Seth said looking at Korson. Korson looked taken aback.

"What do you mean?" he asked, obviously surprised.

"I have learned that most prophecies are not always going to come true. They have a fifty-fifty chance of actually succeeding. It is more like looking into the *possible* future." Seth explained to Korson. Korson walked to the blue orb and touched it with his hands.

"But prophecies involving Chosen Ones are different, they will always happen." Korson said with a smile.

"That is n…" Before Seth could finish Korson started to talk.

"You see when I heard that the Chosen One had been found I was rather worried about it. So I searched for a solution and with some help with my brother I found it." Korson said looking at the blue orb with a greedy smile. "It is a prophecy orb and it was able to destroy the prophecies of all the Chosen Ones. So when the Chosen Ones came to kill me the prophecy foretelling their victory over me was gone so it was even. I gave them the chance to not fight and join me but all of them made the wrong decision and died." Korson explained to Seth. He took his hands off the orb and walked over to Seth. "You have passed my test Seth. That however does not make you completely safe. I need you to make a commitment to me. I need you to tell me in writing that you will join me." Korson said looking at Seth.

"How do you know that the orb has really worked?" Seth asked Korson shyly.

Korson smiled. "First of all, the other Chosen Ones did not succeed in fulfilling their prophecies. And this orb can change the very essence of a prophecy. In fact, I learned that this orb can change more than just prophecies. I still haven't found out how but it can change the very essence of someone's soul." Korson gazed at the orb greedily. "Think of the power one could have if they fully understood how this orb fully worked." He looked at Seth. "Well Seth, will you join me?"

Seth stood there looking at Korson. *If I don't join him then I will most definitely be killed.* One part of Seth said.

If you do then you will be betraying your friends and country. Another part of Seth said.

Die or be a traitor. Both sides of Seth said at once. *Die or be a traitor.* Seth thought again. *Traitor or die.* He thought one more time. Korson was still looking at Seth.

"Can I think about it?" Seth asked Korson.

"How old are you?" Korson asked randomly.

"Fourteen." Seth said.

The King gazed at Seth for a second. He was scrutinizing Seth closely. "You look much younger then fourteen. But either way. I have never killed a fourteen-year-old and I would hate to start." Korson said. "I will give you a day to decide." He said to Seth as they left the dark room.

CHAPTER TWENTY-TWO

TO DIE A HERO OR TO LIVE A TRAITOR?

A very interesting question. If you die a hero, you would be immortalized in song, but you would also be dead and no one really wants that. If you live a traitor then you will be alive, but you would be bombarded by peer-based mocking for the rest of your life. It is a conundrum and something Seth will have to choose quickly.

Seth sat in his room that Korson had shown him. It wasn't as big as his room in Remtaya but that was not the problem that Seth was dealing with. Korson had pretty much told Seth that if he did not join him then he would be killed. Seth sat on the bed, conflicted. He didn't see the point in dying for nothing, but he also didn't want to seem like a completely selfish person who would save his life by betraying his friends.

It's too late, you had a day and now it's gone. Make up your mind. Seth thought to himself. The doors opened to his room and Korson walked in. "Have you made up your mind?" Korson asked Seth. Seth closed his eyes.

"I will…join with you." Seth decided right then and there. Korson smiled and pulled out a piece of paper putting it onto a small desk that was to the right of Seth. Seth looked at the paper.

"What is that?" Seth asked nervously.

"Loral is a very powerful witch. She has placed a powerful spell on this piece of paper and when you sign it you will have to do what I say, or you will die." Korson told Seth. Seth walked over to the desk and sat on the chair that was in front of the desk.

"It's a contract." Seth said as he observed the paper.

"Yes, I drew up the contract and Loral placed the spell upon it." Korson explained. Seth looked closer at the contract and began to read it to himself:

I, Seth do agree to be the loyal and willing servant to the King of Kondoma and his constituents. I furthermore, relinquish my ties to the Kingdom of Remtaya and will become a full occupant of Kondoma and will follow the rules set down by the ruler of the state. I hereby agree that I will be the Sergeant General for the King and will be in charge of the soldiers of Kondoma so that I may protect and keep the populace of the state safe from invading forces or individuals who would want to do great harm to the city. In full volition and without coercion I do renounce my Chosen One status and join with the King of Kondoma with a sound mind and understanding heart.

Seth's mouth dropped in absolute shock and bewilderment. The King had just given Seth more than just a means to live—he had given Seth the ability to control his armies.

"What is a Sergeant General?" Seth asked.

"It is a new rank I just made for you." Korson explained. "I will admit your age was an issue, but I was able to reassure the courts that not only would you make a perfect Sergeant General, you will also send a very strong message to Remtaya. Showing that even their Chosen One will join with me willingly." Korson said. Seth thought about the gravity of the situation. He did not want to betray his friends or country. Seth sat there thinking about what he was going to do. Then an idea came to him—a marvelous, brilliant, masterful plan. Seth looked at Korson.

"The contract said 'in full volition and without coercion,' but you said that Loral put a spell on it so that I would do whatever you say, which is as if I would not have free will. So wouldn't that be lying?" Seth asked the King, trying to see if he could trap him in his own game.

"In a manner of speaking, you will have signed the contract first with your free will intact and then, afterward, you will have lost your right to choose." Korson explained very skillfully. Seth sat on the chair, his once brilliant plan shot down by the King's skillful word play. Seth realized that it was this or death. Seth picked up the red inked quill that was given to him by Korson and looked at the paper. He moved the quill to the paper still trying to think himself out of this. He put the quill on the paper and formed a S.

Think, think. Seth thought to himself. E

Come on you still have time to change your mind. He screamed in his head. T

No no no no. Seth thought. H. As Seth put the last letter of his name on the paper, giant chains suddenly emerged from the contract. They began to wrap themselves around Seth. The King began to laugh as the chains moved to Seth's head, entangling him.

No! Seth shouted in his head. Suddenly, Seth's head pounded with pain, the chains abruptly stopped moving toward his head and disintegrated all around. Meanwhile, the contract upon the table burst into flames with a strong hissing noise. Seth looked at the now smoldering contract in shock. The King looked just as shocked and confused as Seth did.

"What happened?" Seth asked.

"Get up Seth." Korson said. Seth, thinking that there might be another secondary explosion, got up from the desk and moved away.

Seth looked at Korson who was no longer looking at the ash remains of the contract but was looking at Seth with dark happiness.

"Sit down." Korson said. For a fraction of a second Seth did not understand what the King was so happy about. Then it hit him, the King must think that the spell worked and he was now under the King's influence. Seth quickly formulated a plan and sat down to make it look like the spell had worked, even if Seth was ninety nine percent positive that it had not.

"Wonderful!" The King shouted in excitement. "You will begin your duties tomorrow." The King said to Seth, still smiling with joy. He walked to the door that led out of Seth's room and then turned around and looked at Seth with excitement.

"You will never say anything bad about me at all. You will only say good and kind things about your King." Korson commanded Seth.

"Okay." Seth said, trying to mimic the attitude of someone who had no free will. Korson smiled again and left Seth's room.

"You're annoying, bad, and black don't look good on you." Seth said under his breath trying to test if the spell had actually worked or not. There were no ill side effects that Seth could detect after his character assassination of the King.

Seth awoke the next day feeling depressed and still very tired. It had taken Seth half the night to eventually fall asleep. He was up thinking about the unforeseeable outcome that had led him to this very moment. Seth thought about how if he had just stayed in the orphanage, none of this would be happening to him or his friends. Seth had done more than worry about what the next day would hold for him, he was extremely distraught and sad about the fact that if his friends were to ever find him, they would probably kill him themselves for being a traitor. He laid on his bed for a long time thinking about what was going to happen now. His stomach rumbled with nervousness as he constantly hypothesized scenarios in his head about what the King would do to him or what his friends would do to him. A knock came to the door making Seth recoil in fright.

"Who is it?" Seth asked with nervousness.

"Clothes for Seth." Someone said.

"Um, come in?" Seth said, very confused. A woman walked in holding a bundle of clothing in her arms.

"The King would like it if you could wear this when you come to meet him." The woman said.

"Okay, thank you." Seth said to the woman as she left the room. The clothes she left were bundled up as if they were a package. Seth picked up the bundle and walked over to the bathroom. He walked into a room that had something that resembled a facility and closed the door. A few minutes later Seth emerged from the bathroom wearing a brown tunic with black pants and black knee-high boots. Along with that was a brown belt and a deep red cloak with a gold clasp. Behind his back was a short sword sheathed in a brown leather scabbard. The clothes were okay, but he didn't like the sword. He walked to a full body mirror that was facing his bed. Seth observed the clothing as he moved around. Then Seth twirled around to see how it really looked. He was impressed, even though a part of him was trying not to be. Seth then remembered that the King had told him that today he would start his duties. He turned to the door and took a deep breath then let all of the air out.

"I can do this." Seth said walking to the door. "I just have to do what the King asks me to do until my friends get here and then we all can get out of here." He told himself as he opened the door and walked into the narrow hallway. He walked past many other doors and got lost down some dead ends. Soon Seth concluded that he was lost and tried to backtrack. He found himself at another dead end when a noise got his attention. It was like a slow hissing coming from a door that was at the very end of the hall. Seth walked over to the door and listened by pressing his left ear on the closed door. It was definitely coming from inside. As curiousness bested him, Seth reached out and started to turn the doorknob to open the door.

"What are you doing?" A man shouted at Seth. Seth turned in fright and stared at the man. He looked to be in his early thirties and had black hair, similar to Korson's. Then the face of the man registered: it was Korson's younger brother Orson.

"Did you not hear me boy?" Orson asked looking at Seth with anger. "I said what are you doing?" Orson asked again. Seth snapped out of his thoughts.

"I'm sorry I was looking for the Throne Room and I got lost. Then I heard something come from this door and it sounded like a hissing noise." Seth explained pointing at the door.

"What is your name, child, so that I can report you to the King personally?" Orson demanded.

"Seth." Seth said feeling very stressed. Orson's eyes widened a little bit surprised at what Seth said.

"As in Seth the old Chosen One who is now the first Sergeant General that my brother just appointed?" Orson asked.

"Yes." Seth said, looking at Orson, still very worried.

"I thought that my brother placed a spell on you that would make it impossible for you to disobey him." Orson said to Seth.

"He did." Seth lied to Orson just like he was going to lie to everyone else about the failed spell for the time being.

"Then how did you get lost? I thought that the spell would literally force you to walk the right direction to the Throne Room, and if you were to deviate then you would die." Orson said, obviously confused. Seth thought quickly, trying to think of something that could explain why he had deviated.

"He didn't command me, I just assumed to go to the Throne Room." Seth said quickly walking past Orson. Orson walked up to Seth as he made his way through the labyrinth of halls.

"Would you like me to show you where the Throne Room is?" Orson asked. Seth looked at Orson and nodded shyly. Orson motioned for Seth to follow him. They walked through the halls silently until Orson looked at Seth. Seth looked back at Orson and suddenly heard Orson's internal voice, talking with himself. Seth felt a sudden force push him out of Orson's mind. A powerful pain penetrated Seth's head almost as if a very hot knife was going through his head. Before Seth could even react, the pain left his head as soon as it had come. The two looked away from one another. They continued to walk through the halls in silence. Seth's head swam with thoughts of what had just happened. Seth had never felt anything like that when he heard other people's thoughts. It was a very bizarre and scary experience that Seth did not want to repeat. He only hoped that he would not randomly connect to Orson's mind again. They walked to a door and as Orson opened it, Seth found himself looking at the same room he had been in yesterday when he was transported by Loral. Seth and Orson walked into the Throne Room. As they went to the middle of the room Seth saw Korson sitting on his throne, studying a weapon of some sorts.

"Aw, Seth, Orson, I was hoping you two would eventually meet." Korson said, smiling cleverly. "Seth, I just want to tell you that I got word that your friends are almost halfway through the main road through the disputed lands. They'll be here in around two weeks." Korson told Seth, studying him closely.

"Oh." Seth said simply, not really knowing what else to say for fear that Korson would take any excited actions as an insult.

"I hope you realize that I will have to kill them when they are captured by you." Korson said.

"What, me?" Seth asked in shock.

"Yes, I will find it quite amusing to see the old Chosen One and my new Sergeant General capture his once-friends for the glory of Kondoma." Korson said, smiling darkly. Seth gulped at how hard his little charade just became.

"Is that going to be a problem?" Korson asked Seth obviously testing the spell he supposedly placed upon Seth.

"No sir." Seth lied.

"Good." Korson said. "Now before your friends get here you need to learn all about your new command." Korson began. "You are going to command the soldiers that help guard the city from invaders or intruders. You will be helped by a very formidable soldier, and trustworthy friend of mine and of yours." He explained to Seth, smiling when he said 'of yours.' Korson clapped his hands to signal for the mystery person to reveal themselves. One of the doors opened and Edwin walked out.

"Edwin!" Seth said in shock.

"Edwin told me everything that happened after he found out you were here. I must say Seth I already knew you were not an average Chosen One, but actually helping an enemy soldier not be killed by his treacherous cousin, and after he had helped kidnap you just a few hours before? I admit that was more than I expected." Korson said to Seth as Edwin walked toward them. "Edwin will help you with your duties, technically he is your subordinate, but I would like it if you two would work together to protect the city. Your mission at the moment is to capture Seth's former friends and if absolutely necessary, kill them." Korson said to Seth and Edwin. Seth kept quiet, though it was difficult.

"Do any of you have any questions?" Korson asked.

"No sir." Edwin said, standing at attention and looking at Korson. Korson turned his gaze to Seth.

"I do have one question." Seth said walking nervously closer to Korson. "Is there a chance that I could be reassigned as a scientist? I have no experience with any kind of military life." Seth explained.

Korson laughed. "To be given a military title by me is the greatest honor anyone in my city can be given Seth." He said, still chuckling. "But, if you must know the real reason for my decision to give you a very high command in my military, then I shall reveal it. I just could not resist the irony of a Chosen One who came here to kill me becoming the very one who is going to help me capture and kill his own friends." Korson explained laughing very hard. "Don't you find that hilarious?" He asked Seth, still laughing.

"No." Seth said bluntly. "To force me to capture and kill my very own friends could be possibly the cruelest thing anyone could make someone else do. Where is your humanity?" Seth stated, immediately realizing he should have kept quiet. Orson and Edwin both looked at Seth with shock and awe. Seth looked at Korson with fear but to his surprise Korson was smiling.

"Very good Seth." Korson said, clapping his hands. "I will say that your unwillingness to kill me was the main reason why I spared you. However, I was rather worried that you were a weak-willed spineless coward who could not speak his mind. Now I am again pleasantly surprised. I want us to be friends and a friend should never be afraid to speak his mind to his friends." Korson explained walking down from his chair. "I hope one day that you will be able to feel completely free speaking your mind to me without fear of retribution." Korson said, walking to Seth and patting him on the shoulder.

"Then if you want to be my friend, why did you put a spell on me to make me do whatever you say?" Seth asked nervously.

"I want to be your friend Seth but I am not stupid. Only a few days ago you were with your friends who are bent on killing me. You are most likely still loyal to them. So I had to make it so even if you wanted to help them when they got here you could not." Korson told Seth simply. "Now Seth I need to go and talk to the courts about the ongoing war. It would be wise for you and Edwin to talk about your assignment." Korson said as he and Orson walked out of the Throne Room. Seth and Edwin both stood quietly in the Throne Room for a few minutes. Edwin then broke the silence.

"So was Kitty okay when you were captured by Loral the second time?" Edwin asked.

"I think so." Seth replied. Seth stood there thinking about the things that were going on. He had been called as an unwilling Chosen One and forced to go kill an evil King, then he was captured by a crazy witch who sent him to the King he was supposed to kill and now he was working for the King to help capture and kill his friends. Seth could not help but want to cry.

"Can we go back to my quarters, please?" Seth asked, panicking.

"Are you going to have another panic attack?" Edwin asked Seth, sounding worried.

"I already am." Seth said, starting to breathe hard. Seth's vision became blurry and his body became cold and clammy. Sweat began to exude from Seth's body and his heart started to beat really fast.

"Oh my." Seth said lying on the ground and trembling.

"It is okay." Edwin said to Seth sitting on the ground with him.

"Okay, this… is anything but okay." Seth gasped as he started to breathe very hard. Seth began to weep on the floor of the Throne Room.

"Would it help you to know that I had panic attacks when I was younger also?" Edwin asked Seth.

"R-r-rel-really?" Seth asked trembling as the intense fear and sadness lessened a tiny bit.

"Oh yes, I used to get them all the time." Edwin began to explain. "I would just get them randomly even if everything was just fine around me. I would suddenly get this overwhelming fear come over me." Edwin told Seth.

"W-wha-what d-did y-y-you do t-to s-st-stop th-em?" Seth asked trying to focus all of his energy on listening to Edwin and not listening to the voices in his head that were telling him different scenarios of the deaths his friend could suffer if they were captured by Korson.

"Well I could do nothing. When the attack hit me, I could not think properly or anything, but my mom would come to my rescue every time. She would place her hand on my head and tell me to see my own world, the world that we all have in our minds. She would tell me to go to it and find the most beautiful place in that world. Then she would tell me to compress that world into my hands. As I did, she told me that as long as I have my world in my hand I would never be truly alone and nothing could really ever harm me." Edwin explained softly to Seth as they both sat on the floor of the large Throne Room.

"Di-d it h-h-elp you?" Seth asked, calming down a little bit.

"Yes." Edwin said smiling at Seth. "It helped me every time," he said. Seth closed his eyes and concentrated on his world that he had in his head. As he concentrated more, a world began to form in his mind. It was a land with mountains surrounding all sides, green hills and small forests blanketed the inner landscape. Clouds that had rain, drizzled all around the valley. It was the perfect place for Seth. He began to relax and his heartbeat slowed. The imaginary rain fell upon his face and whispered kind calming things to him. Seth breathed in and out slowly and calmly. He was sitting in a place that was near a great waterfall that flowed down to the valley below. Seth was soon completely relaxed when there was a sudden gust of wind that pushed him to the waterfall. He looked at the waterfall and noticed that it was being obstructed by a dam. The wind began to blow Seth closer to the dam and his breathing became rapid again. His pulse began to speed up. The water that was being blocked by the dam roared with anger and tried to break free. As it did Seth's head began to pound really hard. Seth opened his eyes and screamed as the pain in his head grew stronger.

"Seth!" Edwin yelled over his scream, grabbing hold of Seth's arm as Seth began to rise into the air. As Edwin made contact with Seth the pain left, and Seth fell to the ground. Seth lay on the ground looking up at Edwin's worried face.

"What happened?" Seth sat up and asked Edwin, not really remembering what had just occurred.

"You don't remember?" Edwin asked Seth still with a worried look on his face.

"I remember I was somewhere in my imagination." Seth said getting up from the floor. "I remember I was having a panic attack and then I went to my imagination to calm down. Then there was wind and pain and that is all I remember."

"My mom said that I should not always live in my world or I would want to be there all the time and that would mean leaving the real world and going to the imagination." Edwin explained.

"I will have to have more evidence to believe that the imagination is actually more than something in one's mind." Seth said looking around the Throne Room. "Can we go to my room?" Seth asked Edwin.

"Sure." Edwin said walking with Seth out of the Throne Room. They walked down the halls to where Seth hoped his room was. Seth opened the door and established that this was indeed his room that Korson had given him. Edwin walked in and sat on Seth's bed.

"So, we should talk about what the King wants us to do." Edwin said as Seth came to sit beside him.

"Are you completely loyal to the King?" Seth asked him.

"I try to be. I have sworn an oath to serve the King." Edwin said.

"Do you have any spells on you that make you have to obey the King no matter what?" Seth asked.

"No." Edwin said looking perplexed.

"When I got here the King made me sign a contract that had a spell on it that would make me do whatever the King asked no matter what, but." Seth stopped and looked at Edwin. "Do you tell the King everything that people tell you?" He asked.

"No, as long as it is not treasonous." Edwin said.

"The spell did not work. I don't want Korson or anyone else to know yet." Seth said to Edwin. "Can you keep this a secret?" Seth asked.

"As long as it has nothing to do with treason then I do not have to tell anyone." Edwin told Seth. They sat on the edge of the bed in silence for a while. Seth was thinking about the plan he still had. All he had to do was do what the King told him, then when Evan and Kitty and the rest got here, they could leave this place behind.

CHAPTER TWENTY-THREE

A TOWN FORGOTTEN

T he horses galloped across the long and dusty road. As the sky grew dark from overhead clouds, Team C.H.I.P.S kept going trying to get to the city of Kondoma as fast as they could. Evan looked up to the sky as the clouds grew denser.

"How long until we get to Kondoma." Kitty shouted to Coven as they kept riding.

"We are more than halfway there; I will say we will get there in around four days." Coven shouted back. Evan hoped that somehow Seth was still alive. He had heard Kitty and Orin discuss that if Seth had been killed, then they would try to kill the evil King. Orin told Kitty that he didn't want to kill the evil King, but he would do it if Seth had been killed. Evan had a strong feeling that Seth was still alive, and he was waiting for them to get there. Evan also knew that if Seth was dead then he would stop at nothing to punish the evil King and anyone else who had helped with his best friend's demise. The clouds began to rain hard on their heads as they rode to what looked like a small town.

"Should we stop or keep going?" Orin shouted over the pouring rain.

"We keep going." Coven shouted. Right as he said that the sky was lit up by a bright flash and was almost immediately followed by a loud bang.

"Never mind." Coven said as the storm started to erupt with bright flashes of lightning and loud booms of thunder. As they got closer to the town Evan noticed that it looked abandoned. Many of the buildings that were in the center of the town still had their doors opened but there appeared to be no one inside. They all stopped and took their horses into a close by enclosure to keep them safe from the ongoing storm outside. Evan looked around the enclosure they were in. It looked in very good shape, as if it had been made only a few days ago. Kitty walked past him and looked outside at the storm that was raging. She held up her wand and incanted a spell. A small light came from her wand and left the enclosure. It then returned and winked out of existence.

"Is anyone else here?" Evan asked.

"No, but I did the same spell at the camping place where Seth was recaptured by Loral and there is evidence that she could have been there watching us, so do not trust it too much." Kitty said walking over to a door that led into another room.

"We should see if we can find some more weapons here." Coven said walking over to the door Kitty was looking at. "Evan, Kitty, and Orin you go to part of the town and try to find any weaponry we can use. The rest of us will check the rest of the town." Coven said to everyone. Evan walked over to the door that Kitty and Orin were already at. As they walked in Evan observed that it looked like a store. There appeared to still be food and other goods on the shelves that lined the store. Evan walked over to carrots and lettuce sitting on one of the shelves. As he got closer Evan expected the food to be bad but as he looked closer at the food on the shelves it all looked edible.

"Kitty, if there is no one here then why does all of the food in the store look like it was just placed here recently?" Evan asked Kitty nervously. Kitty walked over to where Evan was and looked at the food.

"We are technically still in the boundaries of Remtaya so the spell that is on Remtaya is also here." Kitty explained to Evan.

"These are the disputed lands, I thought no one owned it yet." Evan said.

"Before the Kry wars, Remtaya took these lands as its own and that was before the spell was placed on the city. Then all of the territories that Remtaya had was given the same spell." Kitty told Evan, looking around for weapons with Orin.

"Then why did the people leave?" Evan asked as they kept looking. "This place could have fed them and everything," he said.

"This town has been abandoned for years." Orin said solemnly.

"The buildings look almost new." Evan said looking at the structural stability of the building they were in.

"The same spell that gives food and clothing also keeps the building or food that was already here from decaying." Kitty said.

"Then how do you know that the people of the town left so long ago?" Evan asked Orin sincerely.

"Because I was here when they left." Orin said, sounding very sad.

"Why?" Evan asked. Orin bowed his head and sighed then he walked over to a closet.

"Keep looking for weapons." He said changing the subject. Evan walked over to where Kitty was.

"What was that about?" Evan whispered to Kitty.

"The people of this town were forced out because of the Kry wars and Orin fought in the Kry wars." Kitty explained.

"I didn't know that." Evan whispered back to Kitty.

"It is something he really doesn't like to talk about." Kitty explained to Evan whispering as she continued to look for any weapons. They looked thoroughly through the room but found no weapons anywhere. Evan, Orin, and Kitty left the abandoned store and continued looking for any weapons in the other vacant buildings nearby. As the night fell the storm continued to rage outside. The group made camp in one of the larger abandoned buildings. Evan, Kitty, and the rest of the team did not put up their tents and all slept around the smoldering fireplace that was in the building. Evan was laying there in his sleeping bag thinking about what could be happening to Seth right now. He could be in the King's dungeon or somewhere being tortured.

Or he could be dead. Evan thought to himself. He tried to think of more positive scenarios that could be happening to Seth.

Perhaps the King is dead and Seth is setting up a new democracy in Kondoma right now. Then when we get there we will be welcomed by Seth. Evan imagined a parade being held by Seth to welcome Evan and the rest to the newly reformed kingdom.

"What are you thinking about?" Kitty asked Evan. Evan was only a few inches away from Kitty's sleeping bag.

"I am just worried about Seth." Evan whispered back to Kitty.

"He will be fine." Kitty said quietly.

"I hope so." Evan quietly responded. "I was wondering. Why did Orin fight in the Kry wars?" Evan asked, whispering to Kitty. "I thought that he was doing hero stuff, before he went looking for Serena." He said, still whispering. Kitty looked to where Orin was snoring soundly a little ways from them.

"He would not tell me everything, it's a very dark part of his history. All I know is he was forced by a necromancer to fight in the Kry wars." Kitty quietly explained.

"What? A necromancer!" Evan exclaimed very silently. He had only heard stories, but the books that he had read explained that if a wizard or witch became a necromancer then they had become pure evil. The power to control the souls of the living and dead is the darkest of arts.

"The dark wizard used a blood stone to make Orin and other werewolves fight in the wars. They were forced to do terrible things for him." Kitty explained to Evan quietly.

"That's awful." Evan said without making too much noise.

As the night went on the rain continued to pour down on the roof of the building that Evan and the rest of the group were sleeping in. Evan tried to sleep but his mind could not relax. However, as the rain continued to pour on the roof Evan was soothed to sleep. Soon he found himself waking up to the sound of birds singing outside. He got up and noticed that everyone else was already up and getting ready to go. Evan quickly got up from his sleeping bag and went to where the horses were being kept.

"Did I oversleep?" Evan asked Kitty as he walked over to where she was putting some supplies on the holder that was on her horse.

"No." Kitty said giggling happily. "I just thought you could get some more sleep. You have been so worried about Seth that you have not been getting enough sleep." She said walking over to him and punching him on the arm. Kitty's arm punches hurt a bit, but Evan always liked it when she would give him a kind punch in the arm. Orin walked up to them with a chuckle.

"You two are like a loving brother and sister." Orin said, smiling.

"More like I am the mean older sister who takes great pleasure in making my younger brother squirm." Kitty said laughing as she ruffled up Evan's hair. Evan definitely didn't see Kitty as a sister.

Evan walked back to his sleeping bag and began to roll it up. He then put the sleeping bag into a sack and put it on the holder on his horse. The sun was just above the mountains and white clouds moved across the blue morning sky as Evan and the rest of the group all left the small, long lost town.

Three days later.

"Only one more day until we get to Kondoma." Coven whispered to the group as they waited in the trees for a patrol of Kondoma guards to pass by. They had left the disputed lands and entered the territory of Kondoma around two days ago where Evan and his friends had to quickly avoid an unexpected patrol. Since then, the team had to evade four other random patrols that were getting more frequent as they moved farther into Kondoma territory. Evan was getting tired of the constant hiding and running that they'd had to do for the last two days. The idea that they would be in Kondoma in just one more day did not make Evan feel any better either. They would most likely have to hide even more frequently inside the city. Plus, they would have to find a way to help Seth if he were in trouble as soon as possible. Evan looked out of the dense overgrowth where they were all hiding and noticed that the patrol was moving off.

"Okay, quietly let's move on." Coven said, whispering as they made their way through the overgrown forest and past the guards. They soon were clear to get back on their horses and make their way to the city.

"Kitty, you keep look out, ride ahead and make sure no one is coming." Coven said strategically.

"I know, you don't have to keep telling me the same thing over and over again." Kitty said impatiently, galloping off ahead of the group. Evan kicked his horse so it would start to run along with the others. The countryside around Evan became nothing but a blur as they moved fast across the road. The minutes turned into hours and Evan was starting to get more and more nervous as the sun climbed the sky and then began to set. Evan began to think about what was going to happen when they got to the city of Kondoma and what might have become of Seth. The evil King had around two weeks to do anything to Seth. It became more and more likely to Evan that Seth was dead and the evil King was planning to capture them and kill them too. As Evan continued to think about this very precarious mission, Kitty came riding up.

"There is another patrol coming." Kitty said quickly. Evan stopped his horse and followed the rest to a grove of trees nearby.

"This will not be enough to hide us from the patrol." Coven said looking around for another spot to hide them and the horses.

"We can try to walk past the patrol." Kitty said.

"We would need Kondoman passes and we don't have them." Coven said to Kitty. Kitty picked up five leaves and took her wand out from her pocket. She closed her eyes and waved the wand around the five leaves. As she did the air around the leaves began to fluctuate and warp like there was heat coming off of them. Soon the leaves completely changed appearance. They looked like five passes that had the name Kondoma on them, along with the symbol for the city. Which was a Phoenix rising from a fire and holding a scroll, with a tree branch in its beak.

"I was planning to do this when we entered the city, but we'll have to do it now," Kitty said, handing out the fake passes to everyone.

"Why did you not do it sooner?" Coven asked.

"The spell only works for one hour and it is a very tricky spell to do. I'm not very good at glamour spells." Kitty explained putting her wand back in her right pocket. Evan and the others got back on their horses and began to walk to where the patrol was. As they got closer Coven quietly told them to not panic and act natural. The guards got closer and signaled them to stop.

"Passport please." One of the guards said to Coven and Orin who were in the front of the group. Coven and Orin both gave the guard the counterfeit passports. The guard looked at the passes for what seemed like an eternity. Evan began to start breathing hard when the guard asked the other guard to come and look at the passes that Orin and Coven had given them.

It's not working. Evan thought to himself.

"Both of your passports are very close to expiring." The first guard told Coven and Orin. "I would suggest renewing them when you get to the city." The first guard explained to them, giving Orin and Coven back the passes and asking Evan and Kitty for theirs. Evan gave the guard his passport and waited for him to give it back. The other guard was looking at Kitty's pass very closely.

"How long have you been away from the city?" The second guard asked Coven.

"We have been gone for around three years." Coven lied to the two guards. "It will be a pleasure to come back home." He said smiling at the guards.

"That will explain these passes." The first guard said, giving Evan's his back. They walked over to the soldier that was still with them. Soon after thoroughly checking his passports the guards let them all go on their way. As the guards fell out of view Kitty instructed them all to throw away the passes on the main road, the passes began to burn away as they caught fire. Evan threw his fake pass away as he caught a glimpse of the city that was not very far away from them.

"Is that Kondoma?" Evan asked.

"Yes." Coven said with a sound of disgust. Evan had heard so many stories about the city of Kondoma. How it was dark and damp and festered with darkness, but from where Evan was looking, the city looked quite beautiful. The city was still too far away to really make out an individual house. Evan could see four, grand spires that looked to be in the center of the city. They were white and seemed to have some sort of pure magnificence to them.

"Is that the castle?" Evan asked Kitty.

"Yes. If Seth is still alive, he will most likely be in the dungeon somewhere in the castle." Kitty explained.

As they got closer Evan could see giant gates blocking the way and a wall surrounding the city. Coven turned his horse so that it left the path and moved to a small area with green grass. Evan and the others all turned their horses to follow him to where he was going. Coven got to the small green meadow and got off his horse. Evan and the others followed and got off their horses.

"Kitty, I think it is time to return the horses back to Remtaya." Coven said to Kitty.

"Very well." Kitty said, taking and gathering all the horses. She took her wand out of her pocket and waved it around her and the horses. She then stopped and looked at Evan.

"I will need your help." Kitty told Evan.

"I can't trans luminate five horses." Evan told Kitty.

"Maybe not alone but I will help you." Kitty said. "Just picture the Remtaya stables in your head." Kitty told him. Evan closed his eyes and began to picture what Kitty wanted. He and Kitty then both moved their hands upward. Evan felt the power that he needed flow through his gloved hands and into the world. A small ball formed in the center where Evan and Kitty were concentrating on.

"Good, now just think trans luminate." Kitty told Evan. Evan thought the word and suddenly felt like he was floating. As he opened his eyes he could only see the color of blue and a light shade of green all around him. Evan shut his eyes because it soon became very disorienting. Soon he felt like he was on the ground again and opened his eyes. They were standing in the stalls that were at Remtaya.

"We do not have time to wait for someone to notice the horses are here." Kitty said walking up to Evan and saying the word trans luminate. Evan suddenly felt the feeling of weightlessness again as the scenery around him turned blue and green once more. As the colors flowed around him, they soon began to make shapes of trees and then shapes of people. Soon Evan was standing back where he had just been before they sent the horses home. Despite the disorientation, trans luminating seemed very easy and painless.

"We just have to get into the kingdom and find Seth and then kill the evil King." Coven told everyone as they moved to the city.

CHAPTER TWENTY-FOUR

THE MIRROR OF NIGHT

Loyalty is a very important thing when it comes to friends. If a friend lacks loyalty, then most likely they are not your friend. Seth knew this and feared that because of what he did he has betrayed his friends. Seth had a plan though. He knew that his friends were coming, and the King still thinks that Seth is unable to refuse him. All Seth has to do is keep making everyone think that the spell that the King placed on him had worked even though Seth was one hundred percent sure that it had not.

Seth watched from a shaded part of the inner castle courtyard as Edwin and the soldiers that he and Seth commanded were practicing fighting styles. As Seth watched he realized why the war between Remtaya and Kondoma was lasting so long. Remtaya was very rich and powerful; they could afford the best weapons and could supply their armies with food and medicine as much as needed. Kondoma placed special emphasis on being a soldier or a warrior of some type, and the soldiers of Kondoma were obviously better at fighting than soldiers of Remtaya. So even though Remtaya had better supplies and could supply its troops almost infinitely, Kondoma was better at warfare. In which case, Seth concluded that it would make sense for both sides to be at a stalemate. Seth watched as Edwin had twin sabers and was flipping around in an intricate pattern of battling that looked extremely complex and hard. Right when Edwin was done the soldiers around him began to mimic his movements with their own wooden twin sabers.

"Enjoying the view?" Korson asked Seth as he walked up behind him. Seth looked at the King and nodded complacently.

"What do you think about your division?" Korson asked Seth, smiling at the training session they were both watching.

"They appear to be very efficient." Seth said trying to give a compliment to something that Seth personally thought was unnecessary.

"I am happy you approve of your men." Korson said to Seth. "I do have something I want you to do Seth." The King began to explain. "In the castle basements there is a brown box which is holding weapons supplies that I believe your division would like to have. Would you please go retrieve it for them?" The King commanded.

"Okay." Seth said, pretending that he had no choice.

"Oh and Seth I should warn you." Korson said before Seth left the courtyard to go back into the castle. "The basement is a place that has been acquiring unwanted or unknown things for years. I would suggest not to look around, you might find something that is unappealing or dangerous. I would hate to have you die down there." Korson said nonchalantly but meant it honestly.

"Okay." Seth said nervously as he went into the castle. A little way into the castle Seth pulled out a paper from his left pocket. Seth had no idea where the many things were in the castle and Korson was still under the impression that the spell he thought he had put on Seth would tell him where to go. Luckily, Edwin, who was keeping Seth's secrets, had made him a map so that Seth could find his way easily through the castle. He looked at the map and found a room that said "basement" on it. Seth tracked where he was in relation to where the basement was and found the shortest route to get there. Seth walked down the halls keeping to the visual markers at the map on it so to make sure he was still going the right way. Seth was almost there when he heard something behind him. Seth turned to find that there was no one there. The halls he was walking in had servants here and there, but Seth hadn't seen any for a while. He kept walking when he heard the same noise again. The noise sounded something akin to feverish giggling. Then Seth had a feeling who it was. He looked around frantically trying to find where the rogue Phoenix that Seth believed was making the noise was hiding.

"Seala is that you?" Seth asked nervously to the empty hall. The giggling seemed to be right behind him. Seth turned to find Seala standing next to him holding what looked to be a knife.

"Hello." Seala said with a hiss. "What is a Chosen One like you doing in a place like this?" Seala asked pouting.

"The King needs me to do something for him." Seth explained nervously as Seala drew her knife closer to him. "He is expecting me." Seth said.

"I was expecting you to be dead by now." Seala spat at Seth. "The King has denied me so much but I really wanted you to die." Seala pouted to Seth. "So I will do it myself." She said as she pressed the knife against Seth's throat.

"Seala! What are you doing?" Orson yelled at her as he turned a corner. He pulled out a small vial of water from his jacket.

"I was just playing." Seala pleaded as Orson uncorked the vile and moved closer to Seala.

"Play with your sisters." Orson said, splashing the small amount of water at Seala. She screeched with fright and ran down the halls as fast as she could.

"Thank you." Seth said to Orson. Seth touched his throat to make sure that Seala hadn't done any permanent damage.

"My brother has kept those vile things ever since he became King. I have learned to keep a security net just in case one of them gets out of line." Orson said, putting the small bottle of water back in his jacket.

"I may have to start doing that also." Seth said. "What is the problem with Seala? She seems more unstable than her two other sisters." Seth asked Orson.

"There are some rumors that say when Seala was born her mother found out that Seala could be used as a force for great good. So she tried to drown her multiple times, but just couldn't go through with it. Other rumors say that her despicable mother took the infant Seala and had a powerful witch put a blood curse on her to make her simpleminded and erratic so that Seala would never live up to her good potential." Orson explained.

"That is horrible." Seth said.

"It is just a story, for all we know Seala was just born that way. It really doesn't matter. All that does matter is that she and her sisters would kill anyone if it suited them." Orson said as he started to walk down the hall past Seth. "I would suggest watching your back or getting a small bottle of water like me to protect yourself from Seala." Orson told Seth before disappearing behind a corner.

Seth sighed and walked on to the basement. Seth looked at the map and noticed that he had been to where the door that led down to the basement was before. Around five days ago when Seth found out that Edwin would be helping him with commanding his division and when he had a panic attack in the Throne Room. Seth walked past two halls before seeing the familiar dead-end hall that had the door that had made the very mysterious hissing sound the first time. Seth walked to the door and listened to see if he could hear the sound again. He could hear nothing coming from the basement behind the door. Seth looked at the handle and reached out to turn it. As the door opened a cold breeze left the basement and began to mingle with the warmer air above. A damp smell accompanied the breeze as it escaped from the basement below.

Seth beware. A voice so quiet that Seth could barely hear it whispered to him as the breeze diminished. Seth looked around to see if anyone was there but then he concluded that it was just his imagination. Seth looked down the stairs that led down to the dark basement below. It was so dark that Seth could not see anything past the first few stairs. Seth pulled out the wand that Korson had actually given him. He pointed it at the darkness.

"Light." Seth said. As he did a light erupted from his wand and lit up the darkness that was surrounding the basement. Now that Seth could see, he began to walk down the creaking wooden stairs. He soon reached the bottom and looked around at all the objects that were down in the surprisingly massive basement. Seth turned and saw a brown box with a weapon in it and walked over to pick it up.

Seth. A voice hissed in the darkness. Seth turned to where the voice had come from.

"Who said that?" Seth asked, feeling frightened.

Come so I can see you, Seth. The raspy sounding voice asked. Seth walked over to where the darkness was not being affected by his light. Seth pointed his wand at the darkness and incanted the light spell once more. As the new light illuminated the dark area, Seth could see a large dark mirror that was reclined against the basement wall.

"Where are you?" Seth asked nervously around the barely illuminated section of the basement.

I am here. A pair of bright red eyes suddenly appeared inside the mirror. Seth stepped back in fear.

"What are you?" Seth asked, very fearful of the bright red eyes that stared back at him through the mirror.

I will not harm you, Seth. I cannot harm you in fact. I am only a mirror after all. The raspy voice said.

"How do you know my name?" Seth asked.

I know all the names of the people who talk with me. You are Seth the Chosen One sent to kill the evil King of Kondoma. Why have you not? The dark raspy voice asked Seth.

"I don't want to kill the King." Seth said. "I never wanted to kill any-one." He told the mirror. The voice inside of the mirror laughed darkly.

You do not know who the King of Kondoma really is do you? The voice asked Seth.

"He is the King of Kondoma that is all." Seth said, confused.

His family and your family are connected. His very uncle killed your mother, and your father was killed by his father in the great Kry wars. The dark voice told Seth. *You have no family because of his family.* The voice laughed evilly.

"What?" Seth said in shock. "You are lying." Seth accused the mirror.

Am I? The mirror suddenly fluctuated, and an image appeared. The image began to move. It was of a man running in what looked to be a war. He held a sword he one hand and a wand in the other. As Seth watched in horror another man came into the image holding a sword and knocking the wand out of the first man's hands.

This was your father when he was killed by Korson's father. The voice told Seth right as the first man was stabbed in the chest by the second.

"No." Seth said looking away from the image. "I don't believe you." Seth said to the mirror. "You are some kind of magic mirror that no one wants and I will not empower you." Seth said walking away from it.

Haven't you wanted to know how your mother died and how you were born? The mirror asked Seth. He stopped and looked at the brown box that had the weapons in it.

"My mom died in a cave somewhere in the Conching forest after a very mentally insane man ambushed her and her friends when she was about to have me. The woman who found me told me before I went to Remtaya that they had gone to the cave because they knew that some-one wanted her dead. I was told everything and I will never look back in a part of my past that I do not even remember and is irrelevant to my current life." Seth told the mirror.

Not even when the man who killed her was Korson's own uncle? The raspy voice asked darkly. Seth turned and looked at the mirror defiantly.

"I do not care if he is the reincarnation of his uncle. I will not kill someone just because one of their relatives may or may not have killed my mom when she had given birth to me. I was told that she was a kind, compassionate, and very smart person and that is what I want to be. I was told that my dad was also that way, and killing people seems to be a step in the wrong direction." Seth told the mirror, turning and grabbing the brown box full of weapons and walking up the stairs as quickly as he could. As Seth shut the door he could hear the mirror laugh and start to hiss. He stood there, stressed and rattled.

"I hope that mirror breaks." Seth said angrily as he walked away from the basement.

Seth walked down the hallway holding the brown box that Korson wanted while he thought about what the horrible mirror had said to him. If Korson's uncle did kill his mom what did that mean for him? Seth soon concluded that he could not listen to a mirror who really knew nothing about him. The fact that it knew his name was just mind reading or something, Seth determined. As Seth tried to think about something else, he could hear some commotion up ahead and walked quicker to see what was going on. As he got closer, he saw some of the soldiers that Edwin had been training run past him. Seth put the box down and walked into the courtyard to see that the training had obviously ended, but something else was happening because Edwin was talking frantically to one of the soldiers. Seth ran up to him as the soldier he was talking to ran past him and into the castle.

"What's going on?" Seth asked Edwin.

"We have just got multiple reports of people matching the description of your friends entering the city." Edwin explained to Seth.

"What!" Seth exclaimed. "They have come to rescue me!" Seth first said with excitement but then when the reality of what was going on and where he was dawned on him, the excitement turned to nervousness. "Edwin they are going to be killed if we don't stop the King, or just stop them from being captured." Seth said looking pleadingly at Edwin.

"Seth I am sorry, but the King has given me orders that I must follow." Edwin said walking away.

"You do not have to follow them. You do not have a spell placed on you to make you do things you don't want to do." Seth said frantically to Edwin as they walked closer to the end of the courtyard.

"I swore an oath to the King of Kondoma that I will follow him to the end and obey all his orders to the best of my abilities." Edwin told Seth as they walked into the castle.

"Kitty is your cousin, would you capture her and let her die?" Seth asked Edwin.

"I will do what I have to. You are a part of the search you need to get into your sergeant general's clothes." Edwin said to Seth coldly. Seth scoffed, angrily stamping his foot as he walked to his room. As he made his way there, Seth saw multiple soldiers running through the halls. Seth worried that the entire army that protected the city would be part of the search for Evan, Kitty, and the rest of his friends. Seth soon got to his room and quickly took off the clothes he was wearing and put on his uniform the King had given him. Seth attached the bright red cape to his person and sat on his bed.

"All I have to do is keep to the plan." Seth said to himself. "They will not like it at first but it will save their lives. I just need to keep Edwin and the rest of the soldiers away from them until the spell works." Seth said. He got up and walked out of his room.

CHAPTER TWENTY-FIVE

TRUTH

Have you ever wondered why Korson is the way he is? Could it be because he is just a bad guy? Could it be because he did not grow up in a loving environment as a child? Korson's attitude is a very complex thing much like the rest of humanity. Think of it this way, if you were told that someone was going to harm you just because they believe that you are evil what would you do? Would you try to protect yourself? Would you try to keep away from the individual who might harm you? And if it actually came down to a life-threatening situation, would you not put your life ahead of your adversaries? Nature has made the need to survive so strong that it would be perfectly natural for you to protect your life as much as possible. Korson's desire to live is strong. So, he has resorted to killing individuals who have come to kill him. Does that make him a bad guy? Think about it.

Seth walked across the streets that were in the center of Kondoma. Shops and homes lined the street as Seth and Edwin walked across the very empty city.

"Where is everyone?" Seth asked Edwin. The only people who appeared to be around were Edwin and the hundreds of soldiers that were walking along with them.

"When the reports came out that the others in your group were seen, every civilian was ordered to go to their houses so that the only people who would be out would be the group we are looking for." Edwin explained to Seth. "Divisions four, five, and eight you take the west side of the city." Edwin commanded around thirty soldiers. "Divisions one, three, and ten take the southern side of the city. Divisions two, six, and seven you take the eastern side. I, Seth, and division nine will take the north side of the city." Edwin explained. "Remember the King wants them alive." He told all of them before the divisions left to their assigned areas. Seth walked with Edwin and division nine as they moved through the city.

"Seth all the residents of the city were told to hide in their homes and to lock their doors. If you see any doors that are opened, you need to check it out." Edwin said.

"Okay." Seth said nervously. As they looked around the city Seth was thinking about how his plan was going to work if they did not find them. Then suddenly Seth could hear Evan thinking. Seth stopped and tried to focus on Evan. He closed his eyes and tried to determine where Evan was. He focused more until Seth could hear Orin and Coven as well.

"Seth what is it?" Edwin asked. Seth did not answer, trying to find where they were before anyone else. It gave Seth great joy hearing his friends again even if they were thinking about how they were going to evade patrols that were hunting them. He focused more and then felt Kitty's mind. Seth realized where they were and opened his eyes to find that Edwin and the rest of the soldiers were looking at him in question.

"Seth what are you doing?" Edwin asked.

"I'm-" Seth hurried and thought of a lie. "I'm meditating." Seth lied with reassurance. Edwin and the others shrugged and moved on. Seth quickly moved away from the group and walked over to an alleyway. As he walked inside, he noticed what looked like an abandoned house awkwardly reclining on the alley wall. The wood of the house looked rotten, like flimsy bread. The window seemed to have been shattered long ago leaving empty hollows that slightly creaked in the still air. The abandoned house was dark, but he could hear all of his friends' thoughts now. One of the thoughts that Seth could hear came from Coven. He was saying he'd kill anyone if they came to close. Seth stopped realizing that this was not a good place for his plan to work. He knew what he had to do next was going to be hard, but he had to do it. He walked over to the doorway of the dark old house causing the broken wood under him to creak. He cringed and looked around nervously at the state of the house, it looked like it was going to fall in at any moment. He looked over to where he knew everyone was hiding and swallowed nervously.

"Evan, it is me, Seth." He said walking slightly closer.

Evan suddenly stood up from the darkness with shock on his face. "Seth?" He said his eyes wide. "You're still alive?" He asked.

"Yes, I'm still alive." Seth said simply. Kitty and everyone else stood up and gazed at him with dumbfounded looks on their faces.

Evan moved out of their hiding place and walked closer to him, his eyes still wide. Coven told him to stop but he didn't heed him. He touched Seth with his pointer finger slightly pushing him on the shoulder.

"Ouch," Seth said quietly.

Evan suddenly smiled, grabbing him with a thankful embrace. "What are you doing here?" He asked happily.

Seth stood there with mixed feelings as his best friend hugged him. He looked over at the others who all seemed glad to see him if not a little confused. Seth smiled slightly and patted Evan on the back trying not to notice how dirty he looked and smelt. "Ya, that's the problem." He told Evan and the others the moment Evan let go of him.

"What are you talking about?" Evan asked, still smiling.

Seth grinned awkwardly. "I'm kind of working for the King now." He said bluntly. He decided to approach telling his friends the truth like ripping off something sticky. Evan's and Kitty's mouths dropped while Orin's eyes widened.

Coven's expression changed from fascination to anger. "You what?" He asked walking up to him with anger strewn all over his face. The wood underneath his heavy feet cracked a little too loudly and Seth flinched in nervousness.

"I am working for the King of Kondoma." He said again, this time his heart was pounding as he looked into Coven's angry eyes.

"Why, you little traitor!" Coven shouted at him, taking a knife out and pointing it at his throat.

The others suddenly rushed on Coven blocking his way as Orin grabbed the knife from him. The sounds of soldiers reached their ears as Coven's outburst echoed over the quiet city.

"You idiot," Kitty said to Coven anger in her voice.

"What do we do?" Evan asked frantically. Seth walked out of the house and looked down the alley.

"Run further down the alley and I will hold them off." Seth said.

"You?" Evan asked, looking at him with confusion.

Seth shrugged. "I'll try," he admitted.

"We can't trust him." Coven said anger still in his eyes.

"You've done enough," Orin said quickly walking over to the alley Seth was pointing at. He looked down at him with an inquisitive gaze before looking at the others. "We have no choice but to trust him." He told the others.

"I know I do." Evan said moving quickly over to where Orin was standing. He and everyone else ran down the alley as Seth watched for Edwin and the others to come around the corner. He turned to see

Kitty run out of view while Coven stood close next to Seth. Suddenly he quickly turned around and pushed Seth hard on the shoulders. Seth fell to the ground with a gasp.

"Traitor," Coven spat again before hurrying down the alley out of sight.

"Seth," Edwin's voice came behind him. Seth looked over at him and grimaced as he stood himself up. "What was that, Seth?" Edwin asked.

"It was a goat." Seth said, trying to think of something clever while he wiped himself off.

"A goat?" Edwin asked Seth obviously not believing it. "A goat made that noise and then knocked you down?"

"Yes, I heard something and when I checked it out it was a goat—that was yelling." Seth said, trying to twist the story into something more realistic.

"Goats don't yell." Edwin explained.

"Yes they do." Seth insisted. "Especially if you startle them and they kick you over," he stated, rubbing his arm.

"How would you know? Have you ever seen a goat?" Edwin asked, still not believing his story.

"Not until today." Seth admitted. "I have read books about them, and let me tell you, they are mean and really loud." Seth explained. Edwin and the rest of the soldiers passed him and walked to the now empty house.

"Where is it now?" Edwin asked, looking around, seeing no goat.

"It ran away." Seth said. Edwin shook his head just as a shout came from the western side of the city.

"Come on." Edwin shouted, running past Seth to where the yelling was coming from. Seth ran to another alleyway. It seemed to be like a very long game of cat and mouse. Seth would be running across alley after alley trying to find the perfect place where he could enact his plan. The yells of the different divisions shouting that they had found them kept going on for what seemed like forever. Seth was running in what seemed like circles. The sweat ran down his face and he was breathing really hard. Seth walked over to a wall and sat down trying to catch his breath, thinking about how he could find his friends when someone yelled close by the words "they're over here." Seth got up and ran; as he turned a corner he almost ran in to Edwin.

"Did you find them?" Edwin asked.

"No—but I found the goat again." Seth gasped trying to sound as carefree as he could given the things he would have to do to his friends once they were in the right spot.

"Try to be serious Seth." Edwin accused as they moved on to another alleyway. Seth turned and looked around the roofs of the buildings realizing he needed a better view. Seth called to Edwin who came over reluctantly.

"What." He asked, sounding angry.

"Can you send me to the top of that building?" Seth asked. Edwin looked up and nodded.

"Then do it." Seth said nervously.

"Are you sure?" Edwin asked.

"Yes." Seth said, not really wanting to do it. Edwin pointed his wand at Seth and spoke aloud a spell. Seth braced himself for what the spell would do. Nothing happened. Seth looked at Edwin who was just as confused as Seth was.

"Why isn't it working?" Seth asked.

"Just give me a second." Edwin said looking at his wand. As Edwin inspected his wand Seth began to try to pump himself up to be so high.

"I can do this." Seth told himself jumping up and down. "I will do this." He said trying to stretch. "I want to do this." Seth said to himself rubbing his hands together.

"Okay, let's try this again." Edwin said pointing the wand at Seth. He spoke the spell and Seth found himself floating off the ground. He gradually rose higher until he was above the roof of the building. Seth then moved toward the buildings until he gradually was set down on top of them. Seth looked down at Edwin and the rest of division nine.

"Thank you." Seth said nervously. He then ran off across the roof of the buildings to see if he could find his friends again. He ran toward the yelling of another division shouting that they had found them. As he got closer, he looked down the edge to find that Evan, Kitty, and the rest of the team were running down the alley. Seth looked back to see that Edwin and most of the other divisions were chasing them down across alley ways.

"Perfect." Seth said to himself. Seth ran farther across the roofs to where everyone was heading. He looked down and determined that is where he should go down. Seth concentrated on the spell he heard Edwin use and then said it aloud. Seth was suddenly flung into the air. Seth yelled in terror as he almost hit the end of one of the buildings as he fell down the alleyway that everyone was heading down. Seth noticed that he was actually falling right to where his friends were running. As Evan and the rest of Team Seth looked up in shock Seth realized his velocity was too fast as he fell. Seth held out his wand and shouted the levitation spell that he had just heard from Edwin again, and stopped just a few inches above his friends.

"Hi." Seth said just as the spell failed and Seth fell to the ground, mostly unscathed. Seth lay on his back looking up at his friends who was looking down at him in absolute awe.

"I'm sorry for this." Seth said, holding up his wand. "Sleep." He spoke. A gray smoke emerged from his wand and surrounded his friends. Orin, Coven, and the soldier that was still with them fell immediately when the smoke touched them. Evan and Kitty tried to stop it by using their own wands but it was too late. Seth got up and checked to make sure they were all asleep. He then turned around right as Edwin and the soldiers arrived.

"You did it." Edwin said in shock. "You captured them."

CHAPTER TWENTY-SIX

BETRAYED

Seth stood in the Throne Room as he and Edwin waited for the King. Edwin looked at Seth with a questioning gaze.

"Why did you capture them?" he asked Seth.

"I have devised a masterful and cunning plan that will help me solve everything," Seth explained, quietly.

"So, capturing your friends is part of this plan of yours?" Edwin asked, sounding uncertain.

"Precisely." Seth said, with confidence. The truth was, his plan was anything but masterful. It was sloppy and riddled with inconsistencies. He tried to appear confident in his plan, but he feared it could lead to multiple deaths.

The King walked in and clapped his hands.

"Seth, you have surprised me once again," he said, walking up and patting him on the back gleefully. "You have proven, once and for all, that I can trust you completely."

The King's remarks were shocking to Seth, as gaining the complete trust of the King was a major point in his plan.

"All we have to do is plan their execution," the King said, as he walked to his throne.

"What?" Seth asked in shock. The King turned and smiled at Seth.

"You knew we were going to execute them, didn't you?" Korson asked. "I do remember telling you that."

"But I thought you would interrogate them first," Seth said, in an attempt to convince the King.

"Oh, we will. They will be fully interrogated by Loral and the three sisters before their execution, but that will not take long," Korson explained to Seth and Edwin, smiling darkly. "Loral really knows how to make people talk."

Seth tried to remain calm as he watched his plan fall to pieces. Edwin approached the King and bowed.

"My King, may I please visit the prisoners?" Edwin asked.

"Of course. You may both visit with them," Korson said to Edwin and Seth. Edwin bowed and left the room.

Seth remained motionless, pondering what to do with this new complication. As he continued to mull it over, he could tell the King was speaking, but Seth was not listening. In his mind, he was devising a plan to free his friends and rescue them from the castle before anyone was aware. Seth imagined setting fire to the castle and rescuing his friends while everyone was busy trying to extinguish it, but he concluded that would be too extreme. Seth then began to think about dressing in a black cloak, getting a staff and a pet raven. He would wait until Korson had a baby girl, and then place a spell on her, so that on her 18th birthday she would eat an apple and fall into a deep, dark sleep. The only way for her to wake would be if Korson would apologize to Seth for being a horrible person. Then Seth imagined learning to create genetically modified shrimp that could be his minions and would kill anyone who got in his way. Seth could simply release his friends without anyone being able to stop him, but after further reflection, Seth decided the death toll would be too catastrophic. He also conceded that his ideas were just impossible and illogical.

"Seth!" Korson said, snapping Seth out of his imagination. "Are you listening to me?" he asked.

"No, sorry," Seth said honestly. "Can I go?" he asked.

"Fine." Korson said, waving Seth off. Seth bowed and left the Throne Room.

A few minutes later, Seth was in his room, lying on his bed and trying to think of what to do next. The ideas that Seth was thinking about were all too strange and impractical to have any true validity. He began to start thinking about what his friends would do when he tried to help them.

"They all think I'm a traitor now," Seth said to himself.

"Well, what do you want to do, just let them die?" he heard himself respond.

"Don't say that! I know I can think of something," Seth argued back.

"You can't even make a good plan," Seth taunted himself. He began to walk around in circles, panicking over what to do.

"Shut up! I can do this," Seth retorted, still talking to himself.

"You are going mad already, Seth. You are talking to yourself." Seth turned to look at his reflection in the mirror.

"Well then, we will go mad together," Seth told his reflection. The reflection stared back at him.

"Yes, I am going insane," Seth said, sitting on his bed again.

Evan awoke yawning. He got up from the floor and stretched. As he looked around, he saw Kitty and the rest of the group standing on the other side of the dungeon.

"Kitty, you would not believe the strange dream I had! We were running from some Kondoman guards and then Seth fell out of the sky and put a sleeping spell on us," Evan said, as he walked over to Kitty and the others. He noticed that Kitty appeared to be confused.

"Evan, that actually happened! If you didn't notice, we are in a cage," Kitty said, gesturing around them at the dungeon that they were enclosed within. Evan looked around, still drowsy, and then realized what was really going on.

"Oh, my Great One!" Evan uttered in shock, "We were captured by Seth!"

"No really, what gave it away?" Kitty said sarcastically, gesturing to the cell again.

"Why would he capture us?" Evan asked Kitty.

"Isn't it obvious?" Coven asked, as he stood and spit on the floor, "Seth is a dirty little traitor."

"There could be many reasons why Seth captured us," Orin said, looking at Coven. "I can't imagine he would turn his back on his friends."

"You barely know him," Coven accused Orin.

"He may not, but I know Seth very well, and he would not do something like this unless he had a plan," Evan said assuredly.

"Is Seth good at planning?" Kitty asked Evan hopefully.

"At one time, Seth planned to invent a device that could manipulate time," Evan explained to the others. "However, it did not turn out very well." Evan looked at the guards that were standing at the entrance of the cell.

"We are doomed," Evan said to Kitty.

"Maybe not." Orin said standing up. "I might be strong enough to break open the cell doors."

"Let's keep that option in reserve," Kitty told Orin. "I think if we give Seth a chance, he could come through for us."

"I think this is a foolish venture, entrusting our fate to someone who is most likely a traitor," Coven said. "I have no hope of getting out of here, so let's hope that Seth has a plan."

CHAPTER
TWENTY-SEVEN

PLANNING AN ESCAPE

The world of Terinta is a very strange place. It obeys the laws of ethiristics, although there are magical loopholes to these laws. For example, on the continent of Celesta, there is a pit known as the Infinite Chasm. The chasm is called infinite due to some interesting experiments that were performed there. During one such experiment, a scientist threw a flash rock down the pit. The thought was that the rock would hit the bottom and send a bright burst of photons to the top of the chasm. However, once the rock was thrown, no light was detected from the pit. Scientists stayed at the pit for many months, performing experiments and spells that could detect even the most minute particle of light, but none was discovered. Therefore, two theories were devised: one, that the rock malfunctioned, which was considered impossible, and two, the infinite theory, which suggests that the rock never hit the ground and has continued moving infinitely through space all this time. Other experiments have suggested that this infinite theory is correct, thus, by the scientific method, the chasm was named the Infinite Chasm and it remains one of the most fascinating mysteries of Terinta to date. Seth knew of the Infinite Chasm. He believed if the chasm really was infinite, that it could change all scientific knowledge. Seth, in fact, had a very amazing experiment that could change everything. Unfortunately, he was too preoccupied with saving his friends from their upcoming execution, so his brain, in an attempt to free up space for his new plans, effectively deleted the idea from Seth's mind, sending Terinta back decades from discovering the truth of the chasm. Seth, on the other hand, was completely unaware of this loss of data and kept on planning what he was going to do. That is why the human mind, even though it can comprehend the universe, is still trying to sabotage your ideas.

S eth paced about his room, thinking about what he was going to do. He soon decided that the best thing to do was go down to the dungeons and determine the best place and time to release his friends from the prison. After removing his Sergeant General uniform, he put on his everyday tunic and brown pants. He then walked out of his room and shut the door behind him. Seth looked at the map that Edwin had given him a few weeks ago. He studied it until he found where the dungeons were located in the castle. As he walked down the halls, Seth thought about what his friends were going to do when they saw him. Coven had already called him a traitor, what would the others say? Would the rest of them consider him a traitor, too? As he continued down the halls, Seth envisioned the many reactions his friends might have once he reached them. How would Evan behave? Would Kitty even talk to him? How would Orin act? Seth didn't even know the name of the soldier that was with his friends. He kept walking, hoping that when this entire ordeal was over, his friends would forgive him for what he had to do. He closed his eyes and tried to soothe his mind. He trudged past many halls and corridors, until he reached the dungeons. As Seth looked at the dungeon's door, he realized that rescuing his friends in the conventional sense would be all but impossible. The two soldiers guarding the door looked at Seth questioningly.

"Can we help you?" the soldier on the right asked. Seth mustered up enough courage to go down the dungeons to meet his friends.

"Yes...um...may I go down and talk with the prisoners?" Seth asked nervously. Both soldiers looked at each other and then nodded to Seth. They opened the large door and let him in. Seth descended the stone steps, as torch light flickered on both sides. He walked to the last step and stopped at a metal gate. The soldiers standing guard looked at Seth and asked the same question as the soldiers at the top of the staircase. Seth asked the same question, and after nodding to each other, the soldiers let him in. Seth walked past the guards feeling completely overwhelmed at the amount of security in the prison. He continued past many empty cells until he came to one that was occupied. Seth looked into the cell to see Evan, Kitty, Orin, and Coven sitting on the cell floor, with their heads bowed with sadness.

"Hello," Seth said quietly. Evan, Kitty, and Orin all raised their heads to see who was talking.

"Seth!" Evan said, getting up and running to the cell bars with excitement. "You came to save us."

"What?" Seth asked. "You're not angry?"

"No, I know you captured us because you had a brilliant plan of escape," Evan said with happiness. Seth looked toward the guards who were monitoring the conversation. Seth motioned with his eyes to Evan that their conversation was being watched.

"I have not come to help you—you scum," Seth said dramatically, trying to convince the soldiers that he was on their side. "Your mother was part fish and your father was a sea monster, so therefore, when you were born, the reaction was obviously aggressive," Seth told Evan with fake anger. The soldiers and Coven, who was now looking at Seth, appeared completely confused. Evan, Kitty and Orin looked shocked at this sudden, rather unfair, characterization of Evan's birth. Seth looked at the soldiers.

"That's right you heard me." Seth said even more dramatic. Kitty got up and walked to the cell bars, where Evan was looking at Seth, with a very amused face.

"That is a little harsh," Kitty told Seth quietly.

"My birth was very calm," Evan whispered.

"As insults go that one wasn't bad" Orin said, laughing quietly. The two soldiers looked away from Seth. He felt that his secret was safe with them.

"I am only here to see what I can do. This dungeon is heavily fortified; I don't think we can just walk out of here. I will have to get creative," Seth told them quietly.

"Can you get creative like this?" Evan asked.

"I did think of a very bizarre way of capturing you," Seth said.

"That was obviously not part of your original plan," Kitty said to Seth, whispering. Seth bowed his head and nodded with sadness. He looked around the dungeon, trying to find something that could be used as a good escape plan. He then saw the cell keys hanging on a nail at the end of the dungeon.

"Did they take your wands?" Seth asked.

"Yes," Kitty said, with a hit of anger. "Loral took them."

Seth's eyes grew wide with fright. "Loral has each of your wands?" he asked, fear in his voice.

Kitty nodded. "She took them after we were put in the cell. She came and gloated about it when she took Tomas."

"Who is Tomas?" Seth asked quietly.

"He is the other fellow that was with us," Kitty explained. "You didn't really talk to the soldiers that were in our group, did you?" Kitty asked accusingly.

"I know, I feel bad about that," Seth said, still trying to be quiet.

"What is Loral going to do to him?" Coven asked, walking over to the cell bars. He glared at Seth as he got closer.

"Loral is—" Seth stopped and glanced at the soldiers who did not seem to be listening. "Loral is a very dangerous person, and she is most likely torturing Tomas. The only thing I can really say, is that she is loyal to the King," Seth explained to all of them.

"Like you are," Coven said to Seth, still glaring at him.

"I am very loyal to the King," Seth said so that the soldiers could hear him. "The King and I are so close; we are like bread and butter." Seth said.

"You need to stop making analogies," Kitty informed Seth matter-of-factly.

"Sorry," Seth apologized.

"Seth, when are you going to put your plan into motion?" Kitty asked very quietly. Seth sighed and looked at the soldiers who were now talking to each other.

"I need to retrieve your wands, then I will come and release you somehow," Seth assured his friends. "I need to go now," he told them, looking at the two soldiers.

"Goodbye, my former friends!" Seth exclaimed with dramatic flair. "I shall be happy to see you die in whatever gruesome and horrifying manner the King has planned for you." He gave an evil laugh, winked at Evan and Kitty, then walked toward the soldiers.

As Seth walked away from the entrance to the dungeon, he began to devise a plan to get Kitty's and Evan's wands back from Loral. He needed to discover where she had put the wands and then determine the best time to get them when no one was around. As he walked to his room, Seth realized he would have to find a way to befriend Loral, or find another way to get close to her somehow.

As the night turned to day, Seth realized he had not slept at all. He was too busy trying to wrest Kitty's and Evan's wands from Loral. Seth looked at the map that Edwin had given him and tried to pinpoint the place where Loral would torture people. He noticed that one of the rooms in the castle was named the Torture Room. Glossing over the name coincidence, Seth tried to plan a route without looking too suspicious, when bird calls reached his ears from the nearby window. He looked over to the window and yawned. Seth knew he was tired, but he had no time to sleep. The King had told Seth that prior to the execution, Loral would try to torture his friends for information. Tomas was already at the Torture Room and was probably being brutalized by Loral. Seth had determined that the only way to find Kitty's and Evan's wands was to go down there personally and discover where Loral had put them. Seth hoped that Loral had not killed Tomas. As he got up from sitting on his bed all night, Seth tried to invigorate himself, but to no avail. As he left his room, Seth yawned once more. Studying the map, he followed the hallways until he came to the Torture Room. Seth closed his eyes and took a deep breath. He could hear yelling from inside the chamber. He exhaled, opened his eyes and entered the room.

CHAPTER TWENTY-EIGHT

LORAL'S STORY

Seth watched with interest and surprise as Loral and a man who must have been Tomas were fighting. Tomas had a wooden staff and was swinging it at Loral trying to knock her down. Loral was dodging every swing like a very agile cat with a dark smile on her face. Tomas screamed with anger as he swung the staff at Loral who dodged it and knocked him down with ease. He went flying to the other side of the room slamming hard on the wall. Loral walked over and picked up the staff he had dropped and then lifted her right hand up in the air. As she did, Tomas lifted up into the air, his arms stretched out to the sides as if an invisible cross was holding him up. His head was bowed in fatigue as he moaned in pain.

"Oh, did I harm you too much, my dear?" Loral asked darkly. "I will stop if you tell me what I want to know." She said walking over and placing the back of her hand on Tomas's cheek to caress it softly. Seth could tell that Tomas wanted nothing more than to get away from her.

"I will—not—tell you—an—ything," Tomas said with pain. Loral slapped Tomas on the face.

"I can do this the easy way. I can give you to the rogue Phoenixes. All they have to do is infect you with Phoenix flame and you will tell them anything they want to know. You will do anything they want als

o." Loral turned and walked away from the soldier. "You can't fight Phoenix flame even if you wanted to. It will make you a mindless servant with a need for killing." She told Tomas, turning and looking at him with an evil smile. "Of course I like a strong-willed man, it makes it harder to break them I will admit, but when I do I like to watch them fall to their knees and know that they are now mine and there is nothing they can do about it. Then they will tell me anything I want." Loral said walking over to Tomas and smiling darkly at him.

"I—will—never be – yours." Tomas said trying to hold back the pain he was feeling.

Loral shrugged and moved closer to him. "If you will not break then you will have to die and I will move on to the werewolf." She said with a dark giggle. "Werewolves are so loyal to whomever or whatever they believe in or love, all you have to do he attack the people they love, and they can be easily manipulated. It should be fun to see what will happen with… Orin… I believe his name is." Loral said while patting Tomas's hair. "Then there is Coven. He will most likely be more like you. I will enjoy breaking him just as I will you. The only ones that worry me are miss-goody-two-shoes the Seer and the boy wonder the prophesier. The Seer named Kitty, a ridiculous name, is a woman, making her better at resisting me, and the one named Evan is no doubt protected by spells so he cannot be manipulated so easily. No matter though, I will have enough answers from you weak men that I will not need them." Loral said dropping the man on the ground. Tomas struggled to get up. Seth pulled out his wand and incanted a quick healing spell. Tomas got up and looked over at Seth with a questioning gaze. Seth put away his wand and looked over at Loral who had her back turned to him and apparently did not notice him. Seth cleared his throat to inform her that he was there. Loral turned and smiled.

"Seth what an honor for you to come and visit me, did the King send you?" She asked walking over to Seth.

"No, I just thought that since you were the most skilled magic user in all of Kondoma, I would come and see if I could learn something." Seth lied to her.

"Well, if it is teaching you want, I can give you some pointers." Loral said to Seth, motioning for him to walk with her. She held up the wooden staff, throwing Tomas back in the air. As he floated there, Loral looked at Seth and smiled.

"Seth, I like to use threatening techniques on my victims to make them more compliant." Loral started to hit Tomas over the head and on the chest with her staff.

Seth flinched as she began to hit Tomas harder. "That is nice but I do not want to torture people." He told Loral.

Loral whacked Tomas hard on the face and then looked at Seth. "My dear boy that's what magic is, it is for the strong to become stronger and to make the weak weaker." She sang.

If Seth didn't know any better it seemed like she was about to do a musical. She began to hit Tomas again.

"I just think that magic can be used to do great good, and can you please stop hitting him." Seth insisted to Loral. She stopped and looked at Seth.

"I will if you can answer a question for me." She told Seth.

"What question?" Seth asked.

"The Queen of Remtaya, is she as formidable a warrior as people say?" She asked Seth.

"I never saw her fight." Seth said honestly.

"Then tell me Seth what is her name?" Loral asked.

"Her name? Why do you want to know her name?" Seth asked, confused. Loral pushed something on her staff and a metal blade protruded from the bottom of the staff. She pointed it at Tomas's face.

"Tell me her name or your friend dies here and now." Loral said, smiling.

"Why?" Seth asked, panicking.

"No one knows her name outside of Remtaya." Loral explained.

"Do—not tell—her." Tomas said, with great pain.

"Shut up." Loral said, hitting Tomas in the head, knocking him out.

"Her name is Jan." Seth lied.

Loral looked at Seth with an inquisitive face. "Her name is Jan?" She asked.

"Yes, Queen Jan of Remtaya." Seth told Loral.

"What is the King's name?" Loral asked.

Seth tried to figure out if she knew the King's name or not, then decided that she did and this was a test. "Leo, his name is King Leo." Seth said.

Loral smiled darkly at Seth. "I didn't know the Queen's name, but I did know the King's name. You seem to have really become part of Kondoma, Seth I'm quite surprised." Loral said to Seth.

"Come, walk with me." She said, dropping the unconscious Tomas to the floor. She walked over to the door that led out of the torture room and opened the door. She then motioned for some guards that were standing outside to come and take Tomas back to the cell with the others. As the guards came in to take Tomas away Loral walked toward Seth and motioned for him to follow her. Seth looked at the unconscious Tomas with worry and then walked over to Loral. Loral was still holding her staff and was looking at Seth with interest.

"You seem to have the potential for great power Seth. I sense it could be used for good or evil." Loral told Seth as they walked to the end of the room.

"How can you tell?" Seth asked. He was intrigued with this, but he was really trying to get onto Loral's good side, if even she had a good side.

"I'm a witch. I can feel magic flowing through the universe itself. You give off much power Seth, yet I feel as if it is trapped and can't get out." Loral said looking at Seth. "You have met my despicable sister, haven't you?" Loral asked Seth with a dark smile.

"I think so. Is your sister Agatha?" Seth asked knowing full well that it was, but Seth wanted Loral to think that she was smarter than him.

"Yes, she didn't tell you about the power that you have inside?" Loral asked.

Seth thought about it; he remembered that Agatha did tell him he had great power, but she didn't seem to think it was special.

"Not in so many words." Seth told Loral.

Loral laughed with amusement. "Agatha was always dull when it came to predicting other people's potential." She said, still laughing. Loral opened a door that they had reached on the other side of the torture chamber. As she opened it Seth saw that it was like a bedroom and a work area. Various things were strewn across the floor and papers that were worn and tattered lay on Loral's bed.

At least, messiness is a universal trait. Seth thought to himself. Thinking that this place looked a lot like Kitty's room/work area.

The room was big enough to fit at least five people comfortably inside, but with so many things before and piled high on what appeared to be a desk, Seth found that there was little room to move. Loral sat on a bench on the far side of her room and motioned for Seth to come sit next to her. Wary, Seth walked over to the bench and sat by Loral.

"Tell me Seth. Did my sister accompany you on the first leg of your journey, and then did something unfortunate happened to her?" Loral asked Seth.

"I do not know, before you kidnapped me, she was there with us but when I captured my—I mean the enemy she was not there." Seth said, catching himself before he said friends.

"She most likely didn't want to face me again." Loral told herself to Seth. She held up the staff and rubbed it with her right hand as if she were trying to polish it.

"Why didn't you use that staff when you were fighting the enemy?" Seth asked getting better at not referring to his friends as his friends.

"I did." Loral said. "Staffs and wands are all the same thing. You can think of a staff as an oversized wand and a wand as a very small staff." Loral said. She twirled the staff around in her hands and it suddenly shrunk to the size of the original wand that Seth had seen her use before.

"Do you want to know something about my wand?" She asked Seth. Seth nodded, knowing that this was the right direction he wanted their conversation to go.

"This wand is my mother's. She was a doctor like my sister is and the rest of the women in my family were." Loral scoffed at this showing that she did not appreciate her family. "I was the oldest of my family. Agatha was the youngest. When I was eight, I found my mother's wand as if it had called to me. I remember picking it up and feeling the power in it. That was when I almost burnt down my home. My parents chastised me and I was told by my mother that I could not have the wand unless I learned control. Being a child, I could not fight back at that time, but as I got older my mother knew I was not interested in becoming a healer like her. I wanted to leave and become something more than a doctor, so I did." Loral stopped talking and Seth could tell that Loral acutely felt sad about leaving her family. "I remember the look on Agatha's face when I left. She thought she would never see me and that gave her so much grief." Loral said. Seth could tell that most of Loral wanted to keep a very small part of her hidden away like she was ashamed of it. She was ashamed of how she used to feel toward her sister.

Loral then smiled evilly. "I would not go back for years. I traveled throughout all of Terinta itself and learned much. The thing that always seemed to bring my mind back to my old home was the wand. When I would sleep in the cool nights, the wand that I had held called to me. It called to me in my dreams and as I would listen to the cold winds of night. I soon came back and found that my father was on his deathbed and my mother was grieved, knowing that she could not stop his death." Loral now sounded almost deranged as she spoke. "I did not grieve with her. I took my wand and burned my old house to the ground with my parents, inside. I will never forget their screams as they blazed with the house." Loral said darkly. Seth gulped in fear and shock. He would admit that most likely Loral was once a good person, but now she was all but evil in his opinion.

Loral looked at Seth. "Do I frighten you?" She asked Seth.

Seth felt like this was no time for lying. "Yes." Seth said honestly.

"Good." Loral said with a dark laugh. "I want all the people of Terina and the entire planet of Terinta to fear me." She told Seth.

"If that is what you want to do, keep aspiring do to that." Seth said trying to keep on Loral's okay side even though he personally thought Loral should be prevented from doing anything that she wants to do this very instant.

"I will. Tell me Seth have you been to the basement yet?" She asked him.

"Yes." Seth said not really wanting to remember what happened down there. "There was some crazy talking mirror that scared me down there." Seth told Loral.

Loral laughed. "Do not let it scare you off. It is just a mirror, nothing more nothing less," she said. Seth could tell that Loral had more to say about this mirror but he needed to get her on the topic of wands again.

"I have heard that all wands need a name. What do you call yours?" Seth asked.

"It is said that when a wand is made it will take the name of the first important name its creator says." Loral looked at her wand. "It is said that my wand's creator said Shiv Anti, which in the ancient language means giver of life or give some life. I did not like that name so I found a spell that could change its name." Loral said, still looking at her wand.

"Why do you need a spell? Can't you just name it something else?" Seth asked, confused.

"When a wand gets a name, it will embody the meaning of that name, it will become the name. It was believed that one could not change the name of one's own wand, but I had learned in my travels of a very powerful wizard or powerful entity of some sorts that used a spell to change their true name. I followed rumor and myth until eventually I found the exact cave. The spell was cast long ago, but it left a trace inside the cave itself. I was able to learn the spell. I admit it took many failures and even some life-threatening costs to change the name of my wand. I almost destroyed the wand and almost killed myself with many attempts, but soon I did it. Now my wand is not Shiv Anti it is Shiv Kontic which means 'Gives Death.'" Loral said, holding up her wand. Seth was amazed that Loral had been willing to tell him her entire life story. He concluded that he just is very easy to talk to.

Seth had one time a long time ago, considered becoming a psychiatrist because people always seemed to tell him things about their lives. Loral waved her wand and two wands floated from the top of what looked to be a wand rack that had many wands upon it.

"These are your old friends' wands." Loral said with a dark chuckle, "they will be perfect for my collection."

"You collect wands?" Seth asked, trying to keep the conversation going. Loral had just shown Seth his friend's wands without any prodding from him. Now all he had to do was determine how to get them when she would not be in her room.

"Yes, Kitty's wand is powerful and so is Evan's, but they are not as powerful as mine." Loral said, smiling, waving her wand and placing the wands back upon the wand rack.

"Is there any wand that is more powerful than yours?" Seth asked, trying to sound interested, but really thinking about how he was going to get Kitty's and Evan's wands back to them in time before their execution.

"There is said to be a wand that is all powerful. It is called the Kry wand, but there is no true evidence that it even exists." Loral said.

"Well thank you for having me over." Seth said, trying to sound sincere. "The King wants me to come and talk to him at noon today and I think it is that time." He said getting up and walking over to the door that led out of Loral's work area/bedroom.

"I look forward to teaching you more magic." Loral told Seth with a villainess laugh.

"So do I." Seth lied. He quickly walked across the torture chamber and walked through the door that he had come in when he first came to see Loral. Seth sighed as he walked through the door.

I know where Evan's and Kitty's wands are now. I just need to think of a way to get them out of Loral's clutches. Seth thought to himself as he walked down the hall back to his room.

CHAPTER TWENTY-NINE

KORSON TALKS WITH SETH

S eth pointed his wand at Edwin. Edwin then aimed his wand at Seth. They both stared at each other as the seconds ticked. Seth wondered how he could get the wands from Loral's room with Edwin in the way. He had to try and reason with him to convince him to help save his friends.

"Gimtoragmeum!" Edwin shouted at Seth. A giant blue image of Edwin suddenly appeared.

Seth held up his wand with his right hand. "Invisible," he said, and both wand and hand vanished. Seth walked slowly toward Edwin and his giant blue image.

"You can't hide like this forever," Edwin told Seth, as his doppelgänger looked around for him. Seth pointed his wand at Edwin and smiled.

"Ignitetus," Seth said, his eyes turning red as fire erupted from his wand and flew at Edwin. Edwin barely had time to deflect the spell, which sent him sprawling on the ground, as the fire dissipated mere inches from him. Seth ran over to see if Edwin was alright.

"Are you okay?" Seth asked, holding out his hand.

"Where are you?" Edwin asked Seth.

Seth realized that he was still invisible. "Oh, sorry," he apologized, incanting a spell to make himself visible again. Seth then helped Edwin to his feet.

"I am fine. You're getting better at training, Seth, especially the magic part," Edwin said, patting Seth on the back.

"Thank you," Seth said, bashfully. Edwin suddenly stood straight and said "sir."

Seth laughed. "That's funny, but I told you not to do that," he reminded Edwin, who was looking away. Seth turned around to see Korson approaching him.

"Hello Edwin, Seth. How's training?" he asked kindly.

"Training is fine, sir," Edwin said to the King. Seth could not help but wonder why people in the military acted like that around their superiors. It seemed very uncomfortable and unnecessary to him.

"At ease, Edwin," Korson said calmly. Edwin relaxed and put his hands to his back.

"Edwin, if you could excuse us, I need to talk to Seth," Korson expressed.

"Of course, my King," Edwin said, walking away. Korson gestured for Seth to follow him out of the courtyard and back into the castle.

"I wanted to tell you, Seth, that the courts have made a decision. Your friends will be executed this Tuesday," Korson informed Seth as they walked through the castle.

"What?" Seth asked, in shock. "What about Loral? They can't die until Loral has tortured all of them."

Korson laughed as they continued walking down the hall. "The longer your old friends are in the dungeons, the more likely they are to escape," Korson told Seth. Seth did not dare complain to Korson, even though he only had four days to try to free his friends. Korson and Seth moved down the hall in silence. Seth was busily trying to think of a way to get into Loral's room so he could retrieve Kitty's and Evan's wands. He also was strategizing how he could get them out of the castle. As they walked through the castle to the Throne Room, Seth began to wonder about what might happen when the King discovered that Seth had betrayed him. Seth hoped that he would be far away from Kondoma by then. Seth and the King walked around the corner to find Orson approaching them. He had a frantic look on his face and appeared to be very nervous.

"Orson!" Korson said, with happiness. "Where are you off to?"

"Oh, I am just going to the basement for a moment," Orson told Korson. Korson looked at Orson with disappointment.

"What you do with your time is none of my business," Korson said with annoyance.

"Good day, brother," Orson said, nodding to Seth as he walked past. Korson sighed with sadness as he continued walking.

"What's the matter?" Seth asked. Seth found it interesting that Korson was worried about his brother.

"Seth, when I sent you down to the basement before your old friends were captured, did you see anything that looked like a mirror?" Korson asked.

"Yes," Seth said, wanting to forget the encounter.

"Orson has become very attached to it. He has spent hours down there almost every day," Korson explained to Seth.

"Where did it come from?" Seth asked, with interest.

"The mirror belonged to my uncle. He was a very eccentric man with strange beliefs," Korson told Seth. "He allegedly killed a woman and her child and then committed suicide. He was my father's younger brother, with no family of his own, so all of his possessions were left to my father. The mirror was one of my uncle's most-prized possessions," Korson said. "I remember the last time I saw my uncle. He was arguing with my father about how the mirror could help our kingdom." Korson shook his head. "When my uncle died, my father did the smart thing and put all of his effects in the basement where they belong, except for my uncle's knife that I received from my father. The mirror has stayed there ever since," Korson told Seth.

"A knife?" Seth asked.

"Yes. It's a rather curious knife, I must admit. Its blade is made of silver, with strange cryptic markings all over it," Korson explained. "Despite the fact that silver is a very malleable metal, the knife itself is very strong and sharp."

Seth was not very interested in the weapon, but he was interested in the markings. "What do the markings mean?" he asked Korson as they got closer to the Throne Room.

"I have had the markings analyzed by many scientists, wizards, and sorcerers, but none of them have been able to decipher the markings," Korson said to Seth.

"Intriguing," Seth said as Korson opened the door to the Throne Room. Seth looked around the chamber. It was spacious and grand; it also was the perfect place to go if one needed to escape the castle as quickly as possible. As Korson approached a group of people standing near the throne, Seth realized that if he were going to rescue his friends from the castle, he would have to take them through the Throne Room. Seth walked over to Korson, who was still talking to the group.

"Did you want me to stay?" Seth asked Korson.

"Oh no. You may go if you wish. I have conveyed the message I intended while we were walking," Korson told Seth, smiling. Seth bowed slightly and then walked up the Throne Room.

All I have to do is get my friends' wands out of Loral's room. Then we will escape, Seth told himself.

CHAPTER THIRTY

To Be Invisible

Well, we're nearly finished. There are only three chapters until book one of the Kry Chronicles concludes. I will not be speaking to you again until the second book. I will talk to you before the end of this book, but not in the way you would expect. Don't worry! This saga and the story of Seth have only just begun.

I t was dark as Seth made his way quietly through the halls of the castle. He had waited for the night so that he could sneak about discreetly. Seth planned to go to Loral's quarters to retrieve Evan's and Kitty's wands and then release them. He was fleeing Kondoma and never looking back. Seth crept through the hallways, making his way toward the torture chamber and Loral's quarters. Seth raised his wand and recited the invisibility spell. Unable to see his gloved hands, Seth edged through the halls. He made his way past some soldiers that were patrolling the halls. He continued west through the castle until he found his way blocked by three figures. As Seth moved closer, recognition swept over him, and he stopped and stared with fear. Septa, Seala and Seapa, the rogue Phoenixes, stood idly in the hall peering around. Septa and Seala appeared to be bored, but Seapa's face was dark with anger. Seth began to walk toward them, the stone floor muffling his steps as he tried to formulate an escape plan. Seth backed up against the right-hand wall and slowly inched his way along, trying to remain inconspicuous.

"I am so tired of waiting!" he heard Septa sigh as he began to move to pass Seala who was mere inches from him.

Seala moaned with boredom. "Why are we still here?" she rasped.

"He said to remain here and keep watch," Seapa snapped at Seala with a hiss of anger.

Seth was nearly out of reach of the sisters when one of them uttered his name.

"What?" Septa asked Seala.

"I can smell Seth!" Seala said with excitement. Seth quickly, but quietly, distanced himself from the awful rogue Phoenixes. When he could no longer hear them, Seth sighed with relief and continued walking. After what seemed like an eternity, Seth found himself at the door of the torture chamber.

"Unlock," Seth commanded, holding his wand to the door. The lock made a clicking noise and Seth turned the knob, opening the door. Seth glanced around in the darkness, trying to make certain that he was alone. He then proceeded across the room toward Loral's quarters, shuddering at what looked like strange torture devices lurking in the shadows. Seth tried to remain as silent as possible as he walked across the chamber's creaky wooden floors.

Seth eventually reached Loral's door and using his wand as before, recited a spell to open the lock which made the same clicking noise. Seth pressed his ear to the door, listening. A low snore drifted from behind the door, confirming that Loral was inside. Seth sighed; he had secretly hoped that he would find the room empty. Nevertheless, he slowly opened the door, trying to remain as silent as possible. Seth entered the room and saw a figure sleeping soundly on the bed. Loral snorted suddenly as Seth approached. Although hard to see, Seth could make out the shape of the wand rack. He drew near the rack and studied his friends' wands. Very slowly, Seth reached out and grasped Kitty's wand. As he did so, the wand immediately disappeared as Seth's hand made contact with it. The same thing happened to Evan's wand as Seth removed it from the rack. Seth quickly placed the wands in his pockets and turned to leave Loral's room undetected. Suddenly, Seth realized that Loral's snoring had stopped. He wheeled around, hoping that she had just shifted her position, but let out a silent gasp as he found Loral standing face-to-face with him.

"I can hear you," Loral said, looking straight through Seth. She could not see him, which was to his advantage. Seth slid toward the door, trying to avoid making any noise whatsoever.

"Where are you?" Loral suddenly shouted, running straight at Seth with her staff raised high in the air. Loral swung her staff violently in Seth's general vicinity, barely missing him. Seth let out a gasp.

"I can hear you breathe. I can sense your terror. I can smell your fear," Loral said darkly to the seemingly empty room. Seth knew that if he opened the door, she would know exactly where he was. He frantically pointed his wand at random in the darkness of Loral's room. Using a moving spell, Seth caused some objects at the other side of the room to shift slightly. Loral instinctively swirled around and pointed her staff in the direction of the noise. Seth quickly grabbed a nearby vase and threw it toward Loral's head. Before she could react, the vase slammed into the back of Loral's head, causing her to collapse into unconsciousness. Seth threw open the door and ran out of Loral's room as fast as he could. He quickly exited the torture chamber and raced down the hall, trying to put as much distance as possible between himself and the still comatose Loral. Breathing hard, Seth reached the dungeons where he stopped to catch his breath. Unfortunately, in his exhaustion, Seth was oblivious to the two soldiers standing guard by the dungeon doors.

"Who's there?" one of the soldiers asked, unsheathing his sword and pointing it into the empty corridor.

"Sorry, I just have to catch my breath," Seth said nonchalantly. A look of confusion crossed the other soldier's face as he joined his companion, sword drawn.

"I am not where you think I am," Seth said, still breathing hard. He held up his wand and pointed it at the closest soldier.

"Then, where are you?" the first soldier asked. Seth moved away from the wall and walked past both soldiers toward the dungeon door.

"Just sleep," Seth said softly. A thick, green smoke emanated from his wand which caused both soldiers to collapse in a daze. Seth opened the giant doors and proceeded down the stone steps. As he reached the bottom of the stairs, he quickly put the two guards to sleep. Seth used the Open Spell and the gates that blocked his way swung open before him. He walked to the cell where his friends were being held, pulling out Kitty's and Evan's wands as he approached. When he peered into the cell, Seth noticed that Kitty, Coven, and Orin were all awake, while Evan and Tomas were asleep.

"Kitty!" Seth whispered through the cell bars. Kitty looked in his direction.

"Did you hear that?" Kitty asked Coven and Orin. Orin nodded his head and rose, looking toward Seth.

"It sounded like Seth," Orin said.

"That's because I am standing right here," Seth said. "Now wake up Evan and Tomas and come and get your wands!" he urged, holding out Kitty's wand.

"Seth where are you?" Kitty asked. Seth suddenly realized that he was still invisible.

"Oh, sorry," Seth said, reciting the spell to make himself visible again. Kitty walked over to Seth, taking the wands in her hand. Meanwhile, Coven woke Evan and Tomas from their slumber.

"Seth, what are you doing here?" Evan asked with excitement.

"The King is planning to execute each of you within the next four days. We are getting out of here tonight," Seth said. He pointed his wand at the cell door that confined his friends and commanded it to open. The door slowly swung open, and each prisoner quietly filed out into the corridor. Coven gave Seth an accusing look.

"Why are you helping us now?" he interrogated.

"I want to return to Remtaya and I don't want to see you die," Seth responded as they quickly walked up the stone stairs that led out of the dungeon and emerged into the hallway.

"Where are we going?" Kitty asked.

"The throne room," Seth responded. "It's the fastest way out of the castle." The fugitives began running down the sparsely inhabited halls. Within a few minutes, Seth and his friends found themselves in the Throne Room.

"Come on!" Seth said, walking to the giant door that led out of the Throne Room, the castle, and into the city streets.

"Wait! You do have a plan, don't you?" Evan asked Seth as everyone looked at him.

"What?" Seth asked.

"Seth, did you kill the King before you released us?" Kitty asked with a hopeful look.

"No," Seth told them, "I will not kill the King."

"So you went through the trouble of getting our wands and freeing us, but you didn't kill the evil King?" Evan asked incredulously.

"I will not kill the King!" Seth repeated angrily. "Now let's get out of here before someone catches us!" he said frantically.

"I'm with Seth." Orin said quietly, looking at the others. "It's foolish to try and kill Korson. Especially when you are making a child do it for you."

Coven growled and gazed at Seth and Orin. "Your both traitors." Cover said a little too loudly. Coven moved at Seth with anger on his face and pushed him slightly. Seth stumbled backward from the push.

Orin immediately stood in front of Seth with anger in his eyes. Coven scowled at Seth who stood behind Orin. "I knew we shouldn't have trusted you." He angerly said.

"Don't touch him." Orin said to Coven with warning in his voice.

Kitty rolled her eyes. "Where are the King's chamber?" Kitty asked Seth.

"Why?" Seth asked in exasperation.

"Because the prophecy said you would kill the King and we're not going to disregard it!" Kitty said to Seth with determination. "Now, he's most likely a—"

"No!" Seth erupted, silencing Kitty. "I am not going to fight the King! I am not going to kill the King! I will not do anything to harm him unless I have no choice!"

"Seth, you need to do your part to end the war," Evan pleaded.

"No, I don't!" Seth retorted. "I will not be some puppet made to kill just because the Remtayans are stupid enough to believe in the Chosen Ones! I will not fight a meaningless war!" he hissed.

"This war is not meaningless," Coven told Seth resolutely.

"Yes, it *is*! This is a stupid, pointless war caused by a land dispute no one really even remembers. People are dying over land!" Seth shouted. "If Remtaya would just acknowledge Kondoma's right to the land then this war and this Chosen One thing wouldn't be happening at all! I could be learning how to be a very good ethiristicist by now!" Seth was furious. "If you think killing Korson will solve your problems, you've got another thing coming! Orson is as passionate as his brother, and he'll probably keep the war going out of pure spite!"

"Seth, I see what you are saying, but if we leave without even trying then we will all be seen as traitors to Remtaya." Kitty moved past Orin who was still standing in between Coven and Seth. She pointed her wand at Seth with a concerned gaze.

"What are you doing?" Seth asked in shock.

"Seth, I'm sorry but either you kill the King, or take responsibility for his death. I'll do the dirty work. You just need to hold the blade afterwards. However, I think you'd just slow us down if you were awake." Kitty insisted.

"Kitty don't." Orin said in a gentler tone. He took her wrist softly and shook his head.

"Unless the only time you want to see Serena is when you're in a jail cell, then this is the only choice." Kitty told Orin with sadness mixed with determination. Orin gazed and Kitty and then at Seth his sapphire blue eyes gleamed with sadness and understanding. He let Kitty's wrist go and bowed his head. Kitty took a deep breath and recited the spell. "Sleep," she said.

Seth braced himself for a sudden urge to sleep, but none came. He looked at Kitty who looked at her wand with confusion.

"Sleep!" Kitty said again, pointing the wand at Seth. Nothing happened. Kitty held her wand up and a light shot from her wand and dissipated.

"It's working perfectly." Kitty said, sounding puzzled. She looked at Seth with narrowed eyes.

"I am not killing the King!" Seth shouted again, seeing the malfunctioning wand as providence.

"Right you are," someone said, emerging from the shadows. Seth looked in horror as Korson stepped into the light, holding a sword in his right hand.

CHAPTER THIRTY-ONE

FIGHTING THE KING OF KONDOMA

K orson emerged into the Throne Room with Loral and the three sisters. Soldiers marched in from each of the chamber doors, forming a large circle around Seth and his friends. Korson, along with Loral and the sisters, stood in the center of the room, looking at Seth with disappointment.

Korson stepped toward Seth; his sword clutched in his right hand. He made a clicking noise with his tongue as he neared Seth and his friends. "I am very disappointed in you, Seth. I thought we were friends. I thought we could trust each other," Korson said to Seth shaking his head. His gaze fell on the scabbard that held the sword that Seth had on him.

"Well Seth, this is how it's going to be. Either you take out your sword and face me, or your friends die. He pointed his sword at Evan while Loral had her wand pointed at Kitty. The three sisters looked villainously at Orin. Kitty and Evan held up their wands and looked defiantly at the opposing group.

"We are more than capable of defending ourselves," Kitty said to Korson boldly.

"I am sure you are, but I know you can't withstand my entire force," Korson said, gesturing at the soldiers that filled the chamber.

"I don't want to fight you. Can't you make this stop?" Seth pleaded with the King.

"I'm sorry Seth, but you have betrayed me," Korson responded. "There is nothing left to do, either you die, or I die. Now pick up your sword and fight like a man."

"No!" Seth shouted with anger. Suddenly his head pounded with excruciating pain as Korson, Loral, and the three rogue Phoenixes hurtled across the room, leaving everyone else but Seth sprawling across the floor. Standing not too far from where Orin had fallen to the ground Erin and Terrin appeared with interested looks over their flawless faces.

"Well, look at this." Erin said to his brother. "Seth called us to see a battle."

"Well, if it's a battle they want then let's have some fun." Terrin said with a wide grin.

Korson stood and called for the large group of soldiers to fight. Suddenly Seth heard a screech and saw a massive black bird come swooping in through the rafters of the Throne Room. Erin vanished and reappeared with Kei standing by him.

"Someone is aching for a rematch." Terrin told Kei as he helped Orin off the ground. "There you go Orin," Terrin stated. "By the away Serena is fine at Remtaya, she really misses you though," he told him with a smile patting him on the shoulder.

Seth turned from where Erin and Terrin were when he heard the whole chamber explode with yells. Korson ran at Seth with his sword raised.

The soldiers ran at Kitty and the others seemingly giving their King a wide berth so that he could be the one to kill Seth. Kitty looked at Evan and the others. Erin and Terrin were not too far away as the soldiers ran at them. Kitty pointed her wand at one of the knights when Erin suddenly jumped into the air and landed next to the closest soldier. He snapped his fingers and the knight collapsed to the ground. A pillow and blanket appeared under and on the soldier. The other soldiers stopped and looked at their comrade with shocked looks on their faces.

"He's just asleep." Erin said to the shocked knights.

Terrin appeared by Erin and clapped his hands together causing five of the soldiers that had stopped to fall. "Good night." Terrin said with a grin.

"What are you people doing!" Loral shouted to the knights. She walked to the front holding her wand held as she looked at the two Kry. With little warning she pointed her wand at Erin. Nothing happened. Erin sighed and looked over at Kitty who was watching what was happening with surprise. Orin, Evan, Coven, and Tomas were fighting off knights that hadn't stopped the best they could. Evan and Orin seemed to be the ones that were holding off the most.

"She's all yours Kitty." Erin said to her, causing her to turn and look back at Loral and the soldiers that had stopped.

Terrin snapped his fingers and swords appeared in the hands of Orin, Coven, and Tomas. "There none killing versions." Terrin said with a wide grin. The two Kry jumped around putting soldier after soldier to sleep as Loral turned and looked at Kitty.

"A Seer and her precious Kry." Loral mocked.

Kitty scowled at Loral and held up her wand. She shouted a spell, but Loral deflected it back at Kitty who blocked her own spell with a shield of blue light.

"Loral shouted a powerful spell holding her wand in the air. The fire from the torches streamed toward Loral's wand. She pointed her wand at the ground causing the flames to form a giant lion. In response, Kitty used a similar spell to form a firebird. Kitty looked quickly over at Seth as he tried to keep away from the evil King. She turned her attention to Evan who was pulling water from the air and turning it into a whip to keep the three sisters at bay. Kitty heard Loral chant a spell and quickly blocked it as her firebird and the lion collided with each other. Kitty looked at Kei to see she was sending shards of energy at Athex who was holding her off with his own energy coming. Kitty shot a spell that passed through her firebird and struck Loral's fire lion. The lion dissipated and transformed into a wall under Kitty's control. The firebird merged with the wall of fire. Kitty made a pushing motion and the inferno crept toward Loral. Loral shouted a spell at the wall, and it shrank into a small crystal. Loral retrieved the stone and then threw it at Kitty with her wand. The gem turned red and began to make a loud humming sound as it zoomed closer to Kitty. She held up her wand and made the same blue shield again. As the gem hit the light shield it exploded, sending Kitty flying in the other direction.

Evan used his water whip to halt the advance of the three sisters. Realizing that they were fooling with him, Evan began to spin the water into a ball around him. He pushed his arms outward, sending the water flying at the rogue Phoenixes who scurried from the room. After the sisters disappeared, Evan used the water to place a barrier in the doorway. A soldier ran at Evan and held his sword up at him. Evan didn't have time to do anything when Orin came rushing over. He moved in front of Evan and held his sword up, blocking the knight's weapon. Evan watched as Orin pushed his sword up causing the soldier to yell as he tried in vain to keep his weapon down. Orin's werewolf strength was too much for the soldier and he backed away from Orin and Evan.

"Thanks," Evan said to Orin as the soldier looked at them with an angry scowl.

Suddenly, more soldiers came rushing into the chamber, some holding bows and arrows. Orin looked at Evan with concern as the soldiers stood at the ready.

'Orin look out." Evan said pointing at the knight Orin had stopped from harming him. Evan shot a spell at the solider causing the man to fall to the ground.

"Thanks." Orin said back to Evan. The knights with the bows and arrows pointed their weapons at Evan, Orin, Tomas, and Coven. "Get down!" Orin shouted at Evan. The soldiers let go of the arrows sending them speeding at Orin and Evan. Kei, who had seemed to have knocked Athex out, ran over to them and stretched out her arms. Her tails grew in length, and she formed a shield around anyone that would be affected by the arrows. The darts hit the shield and fell harmlessly to the ground. Kei hurried back over to see if Athex was still unconscious. Soldiers ran at Evan and Orin as they prepared themselves for more fighting.

Seth continued to evade Korson as he pursued him throughout the chamber. Suddenly, Seth slipped and spun around before falling flat on his back. He hefted his sword just as Korson swung his weapon. As both swords connected, Seth's head pounded, and his blade clanged as it pushed Korson and his sword backward.

"You are stronger than you look, Seth," Korson said as Seth held his sword aloft, trying to keep Korson at bay. Korson deftly freed his blade and thrust it toward Seth. Seth dodged the strike and scrambled to his feet. He turned to face Korson, who was directly behind him. Korson swung his sword and successfully disarmed Seth, who stood staring at the King.

"Retrieve your weapon! I will not kill an unarmed boy," Korson commanded. Seth gazed at his sword and picked it up.

"Very well," Seth said, waving the sword around him with ease. The King and Seth began to spar. For every move the King made, Seth cleverly countered the advance, showing his advanced training. Everyone else stopped to watch Seth and the King fight to the death.

"How did you learn how to fight like this?" Korson asked Seth in amazement, their blades ringing with each connection. Seth stopped and stared at the King.

"I don't know. I really shouldn't know how to fight at all," Seth answered Korson with curiosity and confusion.

"Then how are you fighting?" Korson asked, as their swords were still colliding above them.

"I don't know," Seth said.

"Perhaps you could use the scientific method and form a hypothesis," Korson suggested.

"But I don't have anything in mind," Seth said.

"Perhaps you are daydreaming, pinch yourself."

Seth reached with his left hand and pinched his heavily engaged right arm.

"Nothing happened. Perhaps this will work." Seth replied, taking his sword and stabbing it into Korson's chest. Korson fell to the ground with a gasp.

"Seth...Seth...Seth." Korson panted weakly.

"Yes, what is it?" Seth asked Korson.

"Seth!" Seth snapped back to reality to find Korson looking at him with a confused expression. Seth could have sworn he heard a quiet voice whisper do not kill as he emerged from his daydream.

"Seth, I would appreciate it if you wouldn't zone out when I'm trying to kill you, it is very rude," Korson said flatly.

"Sorry," Seth replied. Suddenly, Korson swung his sword at Seth and let out a yell. Seth held up his sword blocking the Kings. His attention grew to his friends who were fighting the soldiers in the chamber.

Kitty pointed her wand at Loral and a bright yellow ball of energy shot from her wand, heading straight for Loral's face. Loral dodged the spell and shot one at Kitty who dissipated it. Seth pushed as hard as he could against Korson's blade. He swirled around and ran hiding behind one of the pillars that stood at the side of the Throne Room. Seth looked over at Kitty just as he heard Loral say something.

"You can't beat me!" Loral told Kitty with giddy rage.

"I can and I will," Kitty said, shooting another spell at Loral.

Seth looked behind him to see Korson moving closer to him with a dark grin on his face. Seth turned and looked over to see Evan and Orin fighting together. Erin and Terrin were jumping around still putting people to sleep near them.

"Orin, we could use your wolf form right now," Seth heard Evan call to Orin just as he knocked out three soldiers at once.

"I agree!" Orin shouted over the din, "cover for me." Seth watched as Evan used his wand to make a temporary barrier around himself and Orin. Orin removed his shirt and loosened his belt. He then growled like a wolf. His muscles tensed and he fell to his knees. His body trans-formed into a brown colored wolf about the size of a full-grown man. Orin snarled at the soldiers behind the barrier who looked on with shock. Evan dropped the barrier and let Orin finish them off. Seth noticed that Orin didn't kill them, he had just taken hold of them with his mouth and throw them across the chamber. Seth looked at Evan to see him hurry toward Coven and Tomas who were still fighting another band of soldiers. Using his wand, Evan froze most of the men in ice.

"Why didn't you do that before?" Seth heard Coven ask Evan.

"I was too busy," Evan said simply as more soldiers, with Edwin in the lead, advanced to attack them. Edwin pointed his wand at Evan with a shaky hand. Seth turned to see Korson was almost on him. He ran over to another pillar. His sword ready to use. Seth looked over at Evan and Edwin as they started to fight. Just then Erin appeared behind Edwin and tapped him on the shoulder. Edwin's eyes rolled to the back of his head, and he fell to the ground a pillow appearing under his head. Erin then disappeared and reappeared next to Orin. He touched his fur and Seth saw energy start to leave Erin's hand and enter into Orin. Seth was interested in what was going on. Orin seemed to be filled with more vigor as he growled with intimidation at soldiers that were about to face him and the others. The knights looked frightened.

"Don't mess with our dear Orin here." Seth heard Erin say to the soldiers.

Seth turned and saw Korson was right on him. Seth dodged the King's sword as he tried to evade him. He held his wand up at Korson and uttered a deflecting spell. Korson's sword left his hands and flew into the air. Korson quickly grabbed his wand and used it to deflect Seth's wand. Seth and the King both scrambled after their instruments. Seth grabbed his wand and retrieved his sword just as a fireball emerged from Korson's wand and hurtled toward him. Seth narrowly missed the fireball. He staggered up from the floor, panting hard.

When would this be over? he thought.

"Oh, Seth! I trusted you and then you turned and stabbed me in the back. Why did you lie to me and attack Loral?" Korson asked.

"I didn't want to fight you, but you were going to kill my friends. All I ever wanted was to be a scientist and learn new things," Seth replied.

"You will never return to Remtaya alive and realize your dreams," Korson said, running at Seth again. Seth fled from Korson, trying to stay as far away from him as possible.

As he ran Seth looked over at Kitty who was still facing Loral. Both of them had lost their wands and they hurried to retrieve them. Suddenly, Loral ran straight at Kitty, hitting her squarely in the face. Kitty returned the assault, grabbing Loral's hair and pulling it tightly to prevent her from reaching her wand. Seth's head suddenly pounded as he ran and he heard Kitty ask in her mind why there was a red lump on the back of Loral's head. Seth looked over to see Kitty hit the lump forcefully, causing Loral to scream in pain and collapse on the floor. Kitty lunged for her wand. As she retrieved it, she pointed its tip at Loral, just before Loral recovered her own wand. Loral looked at Kitty with pure anger.

"This is not over," Loral said. Seth barely heard her as he tried to evade Korson, Seth saw her reach for an object in her pocket and threw it on the floor. The object made contact with the ground and exploded with acrid smoke, causing Kitty to cover her eyes and nose. She walked over to where Loral was and found that she had vanished.

Seth turned to see that his friends had somehow fended off the majority of the soldiers. Most of the soldiers were asleep thanks to Erin and Terrin. Loral and the three sisters were nowhere to be seen. Athex was on the ground with Kei over him her energy shards ready for anything. Korson ran up behind Seth and swung his blade. Seth tried to dodge it, but it struck him squarely on his left cheek. The force of the attack sent Seth to the ground. He gazed up in pain as Korson loomed over him. Seth's sword lay on the floor, just out of reach. He held up his wand, but Korson quickly snatched it and snapped it in two. Seth gaped in horror as Korson raised his sword above his head.

"And Seth the Chosen One died," Korson crowed with a dark, triumphant smile.

CHAPTER THIRTY-TWO

DEATH OF THE KING

K itty used her wand to throw two soldiers against the wall and causing other soldiers to fall unconscious. Evan fought along with the wolf form of Orin. Coven and Tomas were fighting four remaining soldiers. Kitty looked around the chamber and noticed that Erin and Terrin had put to sleep most of the knights.

"Kitty, Seth's in trouble!" Evan yelled, while trying to fight off two other soldiers. Kitty looked toward Seth, who was lying on the floor at the King's feet.

Korson held his sword high in the air. Seth's left cheek was bleeding from a deep cut stretched across his face. He looked on in horror as the King smiled devilishly and readied his sword for impact. Seth closed his eyes, preparing to face horrible pain and death. A low thud and a whooshing noise reached Seth's ears. He opened his eyes in shock. Korson had a look of confusion on his face. The sword he had raised high above him dropped behind him. Korson turned around clumsily, as he did Seth could see his back. Seth held up his right hand and pressed the back of it to his mouth in horror as he saw an arrow protruding from Korson's back. Korson looked in the direction from which the arrow had come. Kitty held her bow up right and had already strung another arrow aiming it at Korson's chest. Seth watched as Kitty let the arrow fly where it hit its target. Korson gave a dull gasp and then fell on his back next to Seth. The arrow that was in his back broke as Korson fell on it. Seth looked at Korson as he laid on the ground now just a few inches away from the fallen King.

"I'm sorry." Seth said to Korson who still had a dumbfounded look on his face. Kitty ran over to Seth, pulling him up and taking the arrow that was in Korson's chest out and putting it back in her quiver.

"Let's go." Kitty said to Seth who was still shocked at what had just happened.

"You killed him." Seth said to Kitty as they ran toward the Throne Room doors. Erin and Terrin looked at what had just happened with slight frowns.

"Time to go." Erin said snapping his gloved fingers making Kei vanish. Orin, who was in his human form seemed to be magically clothed. As Seth and the others ran, Orson appeared through the door and gasped in horror as he saw his brother on the ground.

"Korson!" Orson shouted with grief, running over to him as Orin and Coven pushed the giant doors open. Seth looked back at Orson who was holding his brother's dying body. Orson looked at Seth with tears streaming down his face.

"Guards GET THEM!" Orson shouted with rage. Kitty dragged Seth past the opened doors. More soldiers ran at them as they made their way to the main street, which was empty as most of the residents of Kondoma were still sleeping. Orin, Coven, and Tomas formed a circle around Kitty, Evan, and Seth.

Kitty looked at Seth. "We need to transport back to Remtaya." Kitty told Seth, holding her hands straight in front of her. Evan did the same thing.

"What, I can't do that. I have never trans luminated before." Seth said with panic.

"We will help you, just picture Remtaya in your mind." Evan told Seth.

"They're coming!" Coven shouted as the soldiers of Kondoma began to surround them. Kitty quickly took her wand and waved it. As she did a giant bubble formed around them. Archers that were on the castle surrounding them drew their arrows and fired. The arrows hit the bubble and bounced off.

"We have to hurry. The bubble will not hold for long." Kitty said to Evan and Seth. Evan and Kitty closed their eyes and began to concentrate. Seth closed his eyes and concentrated on Remtaya. The city became a picture in his mind.

"I want to go there." Seth said, hopefully. A small blue ball of light formed in the middle of Evan's, Kitty's, and Seth's outstretched hands. Suddenly, Loral appeared and began bombarding the bubble that surrounded Seth and his friends with spells. The bubble began to collapse. The small blue ball began to grow and expanded around Seth and his friends. Seth opened his eyes just to see an archer shoot an arrow straight at him. The giant blue ball collapsed into a small ball again, right when the arrow hit the blue barrier. The small blue ball zoomed to the sky and burst in all directions. Seth kept his eyes closed as he felt himself float in what seemed like nothingness.

At the edge of the city of Remtaya a shock wave seemed to implode. A small blue ball fell from the sky and as it fell to the ground, it expanded revealing Seth and his friends inside and then dissipated. Safely on the ground, Seth felt Orin grab him, pulling Seth out of the way from the arrow that had made the journey with them.

"Thank you." Seth said to Orin, still feeling overwhelmed at what just occurred. Seth looked over at the Castle Wall of Remtaya.

"We're back." Seth said with relief. "It's over." He said, collapsing to the ground, having fainted.

Korson was dying. He had been shot by Kitty in the back and chest. Believe me when I say that the shock of being impaled by an arrow hurts more than the actual pain. Korson always knew that everyone died, but he had always thought that he could somehow escape the inevitable. It was very odd to him that he hadn't. However, that was not the interesting part, Korson had expected that dying would be a very painful event, but Korson felt no pain at all. In fact, Korson felt more alive than he had before. The other very strange but fascinating thing was that he could see the face of a woman that was surrounded by light. She smiled at him kindly and Korson could not help but smile back at the very kind looking woman.

Orson's face suddenly appeared in Korson's view. Korson was somewhat annoyed because he was blocking the face of the kind woman with flowing dark hair.

"Korson can you hear me?" Orson asked him frantically.

Hear you of course I can hear you. Korson said. *Now I have a sudden feeling that I need to release something.* He told Orson. *It feels very curious.* Korson said calmly.

"Korson, tell me who did this to you." Orson said sobbing.

I am having a very amazing experience and all you care about is who killed me? Korson asked with impatience. *I think I am having a spiritual experience. The first one for me I assure you.* Korson said as the feeling to release something became more urgent.

The woman's face beckoned Korson closer. Korson tried to go to her and felt that something wonderful was about to be released from him, something that had always secretly hoped to be released.

"Korson, please do not leave me." Orson pleaded, sobbing.

Are you kidding me I'm going, I have never felt so alive. Korson said with excitement. *Sort of ironic that I think about it,* he said with a laugh.

"Brother, please tell me who did this, who did this to you? Was it Seth?" Orson asked his dying brother.

Seth no it was not Seth. He would not kill me. It was his girlfriend. I think her name was Kitty. Yes that's right. Seth did not know it was Kitty. Korson said with calming assuredness. Just then a feeling of releasing something almost overwhelmed Korson, he sighed with happiness and closed his eyes. As he did everything went white, Korson felt at peace.

Unfortunately, Orson was not sharing in Korson's amazing experience and was instead feeling great anger. When Orson had asked his brother who had killed him, Korson told the truth but he was so amazed at what was happening that he was not speaking everything out loud, so all Orson heard from his dying brother was Seth did. Then Korson died.

As Orson held his brother's body he screamed with rage.

"I will take my revenge upon you, Seth!" Orson vowed.

Seth awoke and looked up to find that he was looking at a ceiling that was a grayish color. He turned his head to see that Evan was sitting next to him in a chair. Evan was, at the moment, reading a book and was not aware of Seth's awakening. Seth was about to talk to Evan when suddenly the events of the past few months came to him. He was about to say something else when he realized he was shirtless. He confirmed his suspicion and got a little uncomfortable.

"Evan, where is my shirt?" Seth said looking at Evan.

"Seth, you're awake." Evan said with excitement.

"Yes, I am now, where is my shirt? You know I hate it when I am shirtless." Seth said, feeling very self-aware.

"Oh sorry," Evan said, giving Seth a shirt from under his bed. Seth quickly took the gray shirt and put it on. He smiled at Evan, feeling better.

"Why am I in the hospital?" Seth asked, looking around as he sat at the edge of the bed he was resting on.

"When we got back, you fainted and you had a rather bad cut on your face. Lucky Agatha healed it." Evan told Seth.

"I'm home." Seth said with happiness. "The madness of the past months is finally over." Seth said, feeling very relaxed.

"Well, you still are the Chosen One." Evan said to Seth.

"No, I'm not. Kitty was the one wh—" Evan stopped Seth from talking by quietly telling him to shush.

"What?" Seth asked. Evan called to Kitty, who was talking to Agatha.

"You should probably tell him." Evan told Kitty as she approached.

"Tell me what?" Seth asked.

Kitty smiled kindly at Seth and sat next to him. "Seth, while you were unconscious Evan, Coven, Orin and I went to the King and Queen and the Council. We told them most of what happened but when we said that the evil King was dead, they thought it was you who did it." Kitty explained to Seth.

"What?" Seth asked with a hint of anger. "I didn't do it though, you did." Seth said pointing to Kitty.

"Seth, you know how I told you that you needed to take responsibility for killing the King even if you didn't really do it?" Kitty asked Seth.

"When you tried to put me to sleep." Seth said to Kitty, still feeling a little betrayed after that.

"Yes, sorry by the way, I meant what I said. The people of Remtaya want a Chosen One to win the battles they think they can't win on their own." Kitty explained. "I did not tell them that you killed the King, they just assumed and that's all they needed to do. Chosen One or not, you give hope to the people." Kitty told Seth.

"That sounds great, but it is something I never wanted." Seth said, feeling sad.

"What do you mean?" Evan asked.

"I wanted to be known as Seth the scientist who helped contribute much to the further knowledge of mankind itself. Especially in ethiristics, I don't want to be known as Seth the Chosen One who killed a King that was supposedly evil." Seth told Evan and Kitty.

"You have given the people of Remtaya hope though. There is talk that the war could end soon." Evan said, trying to cheer Seth up.

"What about you Kitty? I might go down in history for killing Korson but you were the one who shot the arrow." Seth stated to her.

Kitty nodded and placed her hand on Seth's right shoulder. "Korson was not the first person I had to kill Seth. You never fully forget killing someone, however all the times I have killed someone I did it because I had no choice. I killed Korson because I made a promise to you that I would not let you die and killing Korson fulfilled that promise." Kitty said, smiling at Seth. The hospital doors opened, and Seth saw Shadow run over to him, his tail wagging excitedly. The Queen had Biz in her arms as she walked over to him. Biz had his ears back with his curly tail wagging excitedly.

"Shadow, Biz!" Seth said with happiness. Shadow jumped on the bed and started to lick Seth on the face. Queen Julia placed Biz on the bed and Biz excitedly walked over to Seth and started licking his hand.

"I missed you two so much." Seth said happily.

"We missed you too." Shadow told Seth.

"The Queen was very nice to us and I was wondering if you could go on another adventure so she could keep taking care of us." Biz squeaked.

"Ha ha." Seth said, sarcastically.

"It is good that you are safe Seth." Queen Julia said to him with happiness.

"It is very good to be home." Seth said, petting Biz and Shadow. "Very good indeed."

Kitty stood by a window looking out at the city. She had her arms folded with her right hand under her chin. Orin walked next to her looking out at the city with her.

"The prophecy was wrong." Orin said to her with a calm sound to his voice. "I for one didn't think Seth was the Chosen One but weren't those kinds of prophecies supposed to come true no matter what?" He asked her simply.

Kitty nodded. "For the time being everyone needs to know Seth is the Chosen One, even now, when it appears he really is not."

"Where did that prophecy come from then if Seth isn't the Chosen One?" Orin asked looking at Kitty.

"I asked Evan the same question and he stated he doesn't know where such a powerful prophecy came from." Kitty answered back.

Orin and Kitty looked out at the city thinking about these strange events. Orin suddenly straightened and smiled turning. Kitty turned with him to see Serena walking over to them with a smile on her face. Orin laughed and held out his arms to her. Serena laughed and ran at Orin as he picked her up and twirled her around with ease.

"I missed you." Serena said hugging Orin.

"Not as much as I missed you." Orin hugged his daughter back. Both had tears coming from their eyes.

Kitty smiled and watched as father and daughter were reunited.

"I'm home." Orin told Serena tenderly as he hugged her gently.

END OF BOOK ONE

EPILOGUE

Orson paced back and forth. "My brother is dead because of Seth. You promised that if I did what you said, my brother would be safe," he fumed, looking at the mirror in anger.

"*I said no such thing,*" the mirror replied sharply, in a cold, raspy voice. "*I told you that if you did as I said then Kondoma would be safe. Your brother was a fool and he is better off dead.*" The dark mirror told Orson.

"He was my brother!" Orson shouted at the mirror. "Seth will rue the day that he met me and my brother. I will not stop the war, it will go on until Seth is killed by the people of Remtaya themselves and they send me his corpse. Then and only then will the war end." Orson said with rage.

"*No,*" The raspy voice said forcefully. Orson cringed in pain as the voice spoke in his head and aloud. "*You must call off the soldiers; make Remtaya think that they have won. Let them sit in their solitude believing that they are safe. When the time comes they will feel your rage.*" The mirror told Orson.

"What about Seth?" Orson asked with great anger in his voice.

"*Seth will fall more than you can imagine. He may not know it but his refusal to kill will be his greatest challenge.*" The mirror said with a raspy laugh.

"What do I have to do?" Orson asked the mirror angrily.

"*Did you bring it?*" The mirror asked.

Orson pulled out a knife from a satchel. He looked at the silver blade with wonder. The markings on the blade began to glow blue. "My brother wanted to know what this weapon was. He thought it held more than one mystery." Orson said entranced by the blade.

"*Everything is falling into place.*" The mirror said laughing.

To Be Continued...

THE KRY CHRONICLES: THE SILVER BLADE

The shadow moved across the long streets. The streets were quiet, and the night was just beginning. The Shadow moved past the homes where the living were snuggled in their beds, dreaming of so many different things that the mind could not keep them straight. It skulked past all the buildings until it came to a giant gate, a golden gate, watched by two guards. The dark form moved along with the shadows formed by the torch light that shone high above the Castle, illuminating everything below. It moved into one of the guards' shadows and waited. As the guard moved toward the gate, the shadow quickly flew to the monolithic form and straight under the crack beneath the gate. The Shadow found itself within the Castle; it smiled darkly as it moved from one corridor to another. The candles cast light and shadows on the floor, so the entity moved freely without detection. As it moved across the long halls it stopped at a door and looked at it for a while.

He doesn't even know who he is, foolishness, the entity thought to itself. It then moved past the door and continued down the halls. It began to move faster until it turned a corner. It looked down the hallway, which ended in a door with two guards standing on each side. The shadow zoomed toward the end of the hallway. It then stopped right in front of the two guards. The right guard lifted his spear and pointed it at the ground where the shadow was resting.

"Who goes there?" The guard inquired strongly.

"No one," The Shadow said with a laugh. The other guard lifted his spear and pointed it at the Shadow on the floor. The Shadow slowly moved into the air, shifting into a physical form. The physical being smiled at the guards with a look of pure amusement.

"Who are you?" One guard asked with horror.

"I am your doom." The being said simply. Suddenly the being stretched out both its hands and began to raise them gently upward. As the entity did so the two guards rose. The former Shadow gently pulled its arms to its chest. The guards began to moan as light began to flow out of their bodies. The energy moved out of the guards and twisted and turned all around the entity. The dark form then moved its arms above its head. The energy swirled around its body and moved up to its arms, flowing upward until it reached the hands. There, the light lingered like two small orbs. The guards hung there as their energy was slowly being drawn out. Then with one last moan they both went limp. The entity sighed and grinned darkly at the two unconscious guards.

"I should thank you," The being said to them. "But I won't," the entity laughed as the two guards fell to the ground with a thud. The entity looked at the door before changing into a shadow again. It moved passed the unconscious guards and under the door. Then the entity moved across the floor until it reached a bed. Without making a sound the being became a snake and moved up the bed. It slithered under the covers past the forms of the two people who were sleeping, happily una-ware of what was going to happen. It reached the top of the bed where the man and woman were still sleeping soundly. The snake moved to the man and opened its mouth, showing its fangs. Suddenly, there was a loud scream as the woman awoke to see a snake over her husband. The snake turned to the woman and hissed loudly. She grabbed a knife and swung it. The snake dodged the knife and transformed back into a human form as it leapt off the bed with a movement that would make a cat jealous. The door behind the figure crashed open as people with wands and swords rushed into the room. A prophesier held a wand to the imposter's neck.

"Who are you?" The prophesier asked with anger. The entity smiled and changed back into a shadow. It flew up into the air and passed the people. As the Shadow zoomed from one hallway to another the sound of pursuit followed behind. It stopped and looked up at the ceiling and grinned with impish delight. It shot straight upward into the ceiling. There was a crash as the entity broke through the ceiling and shot up into the sky. It looked down at the Castle wall to see the people it had tried to kill running frantically by the giant hole it had made in the ceiling. The prophesier, the one who had pointed his wand at it, stopped and looked up through the hole at the entity. There was fear on his face.

Good, the entity thought as it smiled back down upon the prophesier. Then, with one last laugh, the entity flew into the sky and vanished.